CORRUPTED

THE TRUTH SHALL
BE THE NAIL IN
YOUR COFFIN

Next Generation IBA,

    Thank you for the opportunity to share my work with you. Hope you enjoy reading this book,

                          Yours Truly,
                          Jared Dixon

JARED DIXON

FULL CIRCLE PRESS
700 E. Redlands Blvd, Suite U #293
Redlands, CA 92373

Cataloging-in-Publication data for this book is available from the Library of Congress

ISBN 978-1-7334494-1-0   10152019

Copies of this book are available at special discounts for bulk purchases in the U.S. by schools, non-profit organizations, and other government and private agencies. For more information, please contact the Special Markets Department, Full Circle Press at 700 E. Redlands Blvd, Ste U #293, Redlands CA 92373 or at www.fullcirclepress.org.

Cover design and layout by Laura Marie

CORRUPTED

THE TRUTH SHALL BE THE NAIL IN YOUR COFFIN

"OUR LIVES BEGIN TO END THE DAY WE BECOME SILENT ABOUT THINGS THAT MATTER."

- REV. DR. MARTIN LUTHER KING, JR.

DEDICATION

TO FATHER EDWARD "SKIP" KORITZER
(OCTOBER 3, 1948 - NOVEMBER 5, 2015).

THANK YOU FOR REMINDING ME THAT I WAS WORTHY
OF GOD'S LOVE. YOU'RE MY GUARDIAN ANGEL.
LOVE YOU ALWAYS AND FOREVER.

CONTENTS

PART ONE: MAY – JULY 2014

CHAPTER 1: WHO SAYS YOU CAN'T GO HOME 13

CHAPTER 2: DISTANT MEMORIES 19

CHAPTER 3: BACK TO REALITY 25

CHAPTER 4: EPIPHANY 33

CHAPTER 5: THE MESS HE MADE 41

CHAPTER 6: CHEERS TO MY MISERABLE LIFE 45

CHAPTER 7: BEAUTIFUL MESS 59

CHAPTER 8: SPEAK TO MY HEART 67

CHAPTER 9: ALL IN 81

CHAPTER 10: WHO KNEW? 101

CHAPTER 11: THE DRAGON THAT NEEDS SLAYING 111

CHAPTER 12: IT'S NEVER BLACK AND WHITE 125

CHAPTER 13: SAFE SPACE 131

PART TWO: SEPTEMBER 2014

CHAPTER 14: WELCOME HOME 139

CHAPTER 15: THE HEART OF THE MATTER 145

CHAPTER 16: PEOPLE LIKE US 151

CHAPTER 17: QUEERS DON'T QUIT 157

CHAPTER 18: GUNPOWDER AND LEAD 169

CHAPTER 19: LIES UPON LIES 177

CHAPTER 20: THE LORD WORKS IN MYSTERIOUS WAYS 189

CHAPTER 21: TURNING TABLES 199

PART THREE: JANUARY – MARCH 2015

   CHAPTER 22: THERE'S A STORM OUT ON THE OCEAN 217

   CHAPTER 23: NO LONGER SILENT 229

   CHAPTER 24: DIRTY LAUNDRY 241

   CHAPTER 25: STILL WITH YOU... 253

   CHAPTER 26: NO TURNING BACK 257

   CHAPTER 27: MAN DOWN 263

EPILOGUE 269

GRATITUDE.. 273

ABOUT THE AUTHOR.. 275

ABOUT FULL CIRCLE PRESS 277

PART 1

MAY - JULY 2014

1

WHO SAYS YOU CAN'T GO HOME?

Jerry looked down at his phone for the tenth time in as many minutes, hoping that the 81°F forecast staring up at him from his weather app had somehow magically changed. Maryland's oppressive humidity, even in May, was one of the many reasons Jerry hated coming home.

"Grosvenor Station. Doors opening on the right." The conductor's monotone voice dragged on as Jerry gathered the only two items he brought with him: his black suitcase and laptop bag. The doors swung open, the humidity immediately engulfing Jerry as he stepped onto the platform. He stood there for a moment, trance-like, as he watched passengers scurry past him.

"Red line to Shady Grove. Doors closing." The train screeched away, and the crowd dissipated as Jerry surveyed the dusky May sky, its dark orange hue blanketing downtown Bethesda. Jerry exhaled sharply and headed down the escalator to the station's entrance, where he was greeted by a pale-skinned man playing his guitar and crooning away. The tune, one Jerry had heard many times on the radio, pierced him like a knife: *There's only one place left I wanna go. Who says you can't go home?*

Jerry took out his fare card as the guitarist strummed his way to the bridge. Once the orange gates opened and he stepped through them, he knew there was no going back. For a moment, he stood there unable to move – arms stiff by his side, thumb clutching his fare card, eyes fixated on the motion sensor. *I'm not supposed to be here,* Jerry thought to himself. *I wasn't supposed to come home.*

His heart raced as he replayed the last 24 hours in his mind. So much had changed so quickly it was hard for him to get his bearings. And yet Jerry knew deep down that coming home wasn't a choice. He had no other option. With a deep sigh, he swiped his fare card and moved through the gates, noting their swishing sound to be louder than he ever remembered.

• • •

"Evicted? Are you kidding?" Jerry stood inside the rental office of his apartment. The damp, mildew smell permeated the air, and the rust-colored, stained carpet accentuated the office's discomfort.

Ethel, the leasing agent, crossed her arms over her considerable bosom and looked up at Jerry from the T.V. with a furrowed brow. "Look at my face. Does it look like I'm kidding?"

"The notice says I failed to pay my rent three months in a row. I just don't understand. My roommate, Rick, and I have always paid our rent. On time."

"Well, your roommate's checks bounded. We sent you notices. It ain't my fault you didn't read them. You have twenty-four hours to vacate your unit."

"No...no...no. Ms. Ethel. I really had no idea. I can pay Rick's outstanding balance. I'll ask my mom for money. Please. I really wanna be here. I literally have nowhere to go, and things are just starting to turn around for me. I re-submitted my portfolio to NYU. I need to be in New York. I need this. I need this."

• • •

A car honked its horn, startling Jerry from his thoughts and alerting him to the fact that he was standing in the middle of the street. A blue Mercedes stood inches away from him, the disgruntled man behind the wheel yelling obscenities in his direction. Jerry put up his hand and quickly crossed the street. As the car sped off, he forced himself to come back to reality, to be present and aware of where he was. He wasn't in New York City anymore, sharing a cramped one-bedroom apartment with Rick, a stoner he had met on Craig's List. He wasn't a waiter/pianist at the jazz lounge in SoHo who played Dean Martin for tips. That life, although painstakingly wonderful and challenging, was over.

The familiar sound of crickets greeted Jerry as he trekked the remaining three blocks to his childhood home. He turned a corner, his eyes resting on the 7-Eleven he had once frequented. Before he left for MIT, when things at home had been awful, he had sought solace in each box of powdered doughnuts, found peace with every bite of a Snicker's bar, and relaxed with every ice cream sandwich. But this tranquility was always fleeting. That was how eating disorders worked. Food provided him with a brief high similar to the one he imagined that addicts were forever chasing. Once Jerry came down from that high, the temporary security and serenity he felt were replaced with an overwhelming shame. He felt this ugliness coursing through his body, with images of his waistline expanding or his face fattening etched into his mind. And he knew he had to pay for the endless processed sugar, saturated fat, and empty calories in which he selfishly indulged. For him, that penance always came in the form of locking the bathroom door, turning on the faucet, and shoving his finger down his throat until he became dizzy and disoriented to the point of nearly fainting.

• • •

"Dude, I'm sorry. I kinda forgot to tell you." Jerry remembered Rick standing in their cramped kitchen, his girlfriend Ginger prancing around topless in nothing but her pink laced underwear. Jerry had regretted telling Ginger that he was gay.

"Well, thanks to you and your absentmindedness, we're now homeless."

"Oh my God, Rick! You and Jerry can totally come live with me. I have a one-bedroom that can fit three people, though I will say that my friend Sparkle has been sleeping on my couch since her married boyfriend decided to be faithful to his wife."

Jerry made a mental note to never use Craig's List to find a roommate again. "I don't know. I just don't know," was all he could muster in response to Ginger's overly enthusiastic invitation. As his mind drifted back to that moment, the memory of the strong stench of marijuana caused him nearly to choke. As Ginger had rattled on about how Jerry would need to pay $450 for his first month's rent, his phone rang. Jerry had picked it up and listened as the SoHo Lounge manager, Michelle, rambled on about how the restaurant needed to make budget cuts. She danced around the point of the phone call for nearly three minutes until finally informing Jerry that he was being let go.

He took the words in as he surveyed his tiny apartment, the walls decorated with graffiti, the off-white radiator that always malfunctioned during the dead of winter, the air mattress he slept on in the living room. He knew in an instant that he had to leave. He had to go home. He was broke, and between the pending eviction and job loss, he felt like he had no other options. *I guess this is what I get for dropping out of MIT and moving to New York City on a whim,* he thought. *How stupid was I to believe that I'd actually be able to make it here?!*

• • •

As Jerry opened the doors of the 7-Eleven, his sweat-stained back welcomed the cold rush of the air conditioner. He lugged his suitcase down the narrow aisles and scanned the contents of the shelves: Doritos, large bags of Utz sourdough pretzels, cinnamon buns, Oreos. He froze as he examined the dark blue container with the expanded cookie dipped in milk. Oreos were the first thing he had binged on, and their presence brought him back to an almost ritualistic moment of comfort. Without another thought, he grabbed two containers of Oreos, six cinnamon buns, and three bags of Doritos.

The clerk's eyebrows raised as he started ringing up Jerry's order. "Having a party?" The man's thick, accented voice resonated throughout the store. Several people turned to stare at Jerry as he fumbled for his wallet. People always stared at him when he was preparing for a food binge. He surmised they knew what he was up to, their judgment made visible with each eye slant, distant stare, and whispered conversation.

"No. Just hungry," Jerry grumbled as he handed the clerk a wrinkled $20 bill. He thought about ditching the food and just booking it the few remaining blocks home or calling his best friend Mel in a last-minute SOS, but he didn't do either of those things. Instead, he just took the bag wordlessly as the clerk handed it to him. As he turned to exit the store, he noticed a janitor humming to the Bryan Adams song, Heaven, that blared from the speakers as he mopped up spilled coffee.

Leaving the store with his loot, Jerry recognized that he was about to throw away the last three months when he hadn't even once had the urge to binge and purge. A light breeze greeted Jerry as he walked the final two blocks home.

• • •

Memories continued to flood his brain, memories he had tried so hard to purge each time he hovered over a toilet, the acidity of vomit fresh in his mouth. "Jerry, dude. You gotta promise me something." Rick held onto Jerry's arm as he angrily slammed his laptop into his bag. He glanced at the paint peeling off the living room walls, the tan bedspread strewn hastily over the air mattress. This had been his home for the past six months. This small, sad, smelly apartment had been a place where he could be himself, a place not clouded with secrets or sadness or shame.

"Promise you what Rick?" Jerry remembered not being in a sentimental mood. Despite that, Rick's request assuaged the blinding rage he felt toward him, toward his blatant irresponsibility.

"Promise me you'll be okay. Whatever happens, don't hurt yourself. You scared me."

"I promise."

• • •

Jerry stood in the driveway of his parents' house, the red brick exterior staring back at him hauntingly. He tried to rehearse what he'd say to his parents when he walked inside the house. He pondered telling them the truth, but he wasn't even sure what that was anymore. He had been miserable at MIT, had dropped out last December, and had moved to New York – all unbeknownst to his parents. He had used the money his mom sent him to pay part of his rent and had worked as a lounge pianist at a restaurant in SoHo to make ends meet. He had thought that dropping out of school and moving to NYC was the right thing, but now he wasn't so sure. Given the recent events that had transpired, he wasn't sure he believed these truths anymore. He had been naïve to think that moving to New York would work out in his favor, naïve to think that he would ever be free of his demons. As he approached the front of the house, the lawn perfectly manicured, peonies blooming vibrantly by the front porch, he silently apologized to Rick. Once he opened the front door, he knew he would break that promise.

2

DISTANT MEMORIES

Heather begrudgingly adjusted her ponytail, dismayed that Percy had insisted on working late. Who was Heather kidding? They weren't working. They were fucking and had been for over three years now. She had lost count of how many "late nights" she spent at Opto-Electronics Inc., legs sprawled across the conference room table where Percy had just led his weekly staff meeting a couple hours prior. Last week, they had snuck into the office of Percy's boss, Greg Hammond, at Percy's insistence. Heather despised performing fellatio on Percy, but found a perverse satisfaction in watching Percy ejaculate on the very chair Greg sat in daily.

"God, do I love working overtime," Heather purred as she mechanically unbuttoned her white blouse and revealed her sky blue laced bra. Percy hurried toward her, kissing her neck and lips with an urgency that Heather couldn't even pretend to match. He unzipped her pants, two of his fingers traversing between her legs before they entered her. The prickly sensation Heather felt as his large hands brushed against her thighs made her regret not keeping that waxing appointment earlier in the week.

"Oh, yeah," Heather moaned almost mechanically during what she knew would be no more than three or so painful minutes of intercourse. Percy was never one to last long. As he spread her legs across his desk, she focused on a scratch at the edge of the mahogany surface before fixating on the dust particles scattered mere inches away from where she lay. She wondered how his office managed to get so dirty even though the maintenance crew cleaned it daily. *Was Percy this messy at home? Was that why he complained about his wife, Harriet, so much? Did she also find him insufferable?*

"I'm close. I'm really close," Percy's face contorted as his breath quickened. His legs shook violently against the desk, sweat trickling down his bronze skin. One thing Heather had to admit was that Percy's skin was beautiful. He had very few wrinkles for a middle-aged man, and aside from his potbelly, nothing sagged.

Before pulling out, Percy placed his hand behind Heather's neck, bringing her in for a kiss. Their lips intertwined as Heather tasted the stale coffee on his breath. As soon as she felt she could, she wriggled herself from underneath him and collected her clothing that had been strewn across the office. She hurriedly pulled up her pants and caught Percy grinning as she struggled to hook her bra.

"Here. Let me."

Reluctantly, Heather turned around while Percy maneuvered the hooks. His knuckles dug into her, and she winced.

"Got it!"

Heather turned around and forced a smile as Percy brushed a strand of Heather's brown hair away from her face. "What should I charge this time to?" She made sure her tone wasn't too sardonic so that Percy's first response wouldn't be uproarious laughter. His brow furrowed and a light chuckle emerged from his large body.

"Just hit Greg's overhead. You've already worked forty hours this week, haven't you?" Heather's eyes narrowed in Percy's direction. She never worked a minute over forty hours. Percy knew that. However, it was going on 8, which meant she had been at the office for over 11 hours. She did take a two-hour lunch break, but she had no intention of reminding Percy of that.

"You know what? I did."

Percy's smile widened. "Great! So this time we spent together can be considered overtime. Greg hates it when salaried employees charge overtime. Go ahead and do it. It'll piss him off." Percy snickered menacingly as he dressed. He noticed a sizeable crimson lipstick stain on the collar of his dress shirt. "Shit." Percy fervently started picking at the stain, practically licking his hand as he rubbed his spit filled thumb over it to no avail.

"Here," said Heather impatiently. "Give it to me." Percy's eyes widened as he quickly unbuttoned his shirt and tossed it to Heather. Without thinking, he pecked her on the cheek as if *she* was his wife, not the woman he used to keep his mind off of his wife who he knew at this hour would be wondering why he hadn't made it home for dinner.

"You're a lifesaver. I have another shirt in my car. God, can you imagine if Harriet would have seen that lipstick stain?"

"Do you think she knows? About us?"

Percy shrugged ambivalently. "Don't know. Don't care. We've been married for 25 years, and she has made it very clear that she finds the mere thought of my body against hers repulsive. And I have made it very clear that making love to her is like making love to a brick."

Heather had no response to Percy's revelation about his sexless marriage. She regretted asking the question. Percy and Heather had an understanding that they would discuss neither their personal lives nor their feelings. Discussions like this one were bordering on taboo.

Heather had sought out Percy at the insistence of Greg Hammond, Percy's boss and the vice president and general manager of Opto-Electronics, Inc. (OEI). Greg lived and breathed OEI and prided himself on his managerial skills, which were nothing short of oppressive. Percy was one of his direct subordinates, and Heather recalled many occasions during which Greg referred to Percy with disdain. Inept, idiotic, and clueless were words Greg used to describe Percy.

• • •

"A rusty nail is more useful than that sad sack of shit," Greg had ranted one day about Percy's lack of business acumen. According to Greg, Percy had used poor judgment when he hastily accepted a two-month contractual delivery date on a job that required a year to complete. Greg had wanted to fire Percy but feared Percy would sue for discrimination. As Heather had sat there and listened to Greg go on and on about Percy, she saw a rare opportunity to fulfill Greg's most sinister desire and fund her side business.

• • •

Percy's grating voice jolted Heather back to the present. "Well, I gotta get home. My son, Leo, is graduating from high school tomorrow. The kid was at the bottom of his class. You know, I told Harriet to take him out of that fancy private school and stick him in public school, but she insisted on sending him to a school that would adequately prepare him for college. She paid the 20-grand tuition, not me."

Heather nodded while Percy continued talking, her eyes wandering to the photos on a shelf by Percy's window. She never paid much attention to these kinds of details – his kids, his wife. Her eyes rested on a photo of Percy with his arms around Harriet and an adorable little girl. *Did Percy have another child?* she asked herself. He never talked about her, only mentioning his sons Jerry and Leo. Heather wondered what had happened to her. Heather also wondered why she cared.

"Heather? Heather?" Percy snapped his fingers as Heather directed her gaze toward Percy. "Can you make sure my office door is locked before you leave?"

Heather nodded. "No problem. Have a good night." She sighed deeply as Percy walked out and closed the door behind him. She was thankful Percy didn't kiss her again, thankful she didn't have to smell that stale coffee on his breath or feel his fat fingers caress her thighs.

The elevator dinged faintly as Heather gathered her things. She let her mind wander for a bit, pretending for a minute that she was someone other than herself.

She'd like to be Jacquelyn Metz, she thought, the fearless dancer who had graduated from Julliard and toured the world with the best of the best: Janet Jackson, Madonna, Usher. Heather brought herself back to reality with the realization that her life didn't even remotely resemble Jacquelyn's. Jacquelyn had a great life, one free from responsibilities, one free from taking care of two kids that weren't her own.

Heather's reflection stared back at her from the plasma TV screen on Percy's wall. She toyed with her ponytail as she made a mental note to get new hair extensions. She hated the pink acrylic nails she wore every day. Everything about Heather had been carefully fabricated, from the hair she had sewn in, to the breasts she had augmented, to the size two figure she starved herself to maintain. Who was she kidding? Her life looked nothing like Jacquelyn's. She was no longer that dauntless, hard-working dancer whose gifts were praised by both professors and peers. Her identity now could be described as nothing more than a white-collar criminal whose lofty dreams of being a famous dancer and traveling the world had been reduced to ones of merely making enough money to quit this dismal desk job and, quite possibly, stop fucking her repulsive boss.

• • •

When she had approached Greg about her escorting business, he hadn't been taken aback at all. In fact, he had been supportive and eager to collude with Heather in misappropriating OEI's resources to resurrect Heather's flailing business. The two of them had devised a plan. Heather's business partner, Devin, would create a shell company, Mid-IR Solutions, that manufactured mid-infrared lasers. Once Devin created it, Greg and Heather would present this fictitious vendor to Percy, a vendor that promised to deliver a laser Percy desperately needed for several of his active contracts. Devin added enticing verbiage about a 30-day delivery for all customers who paid an additional ten percent. As Heather and Greg had predicted, Percy immediately put in a request for two lasers, with a price of $22K.

"Percy doesn't know the meaning of due diligence. You'll be seeing an invoice so fast your head will spin," Heather smiled satisfactorily as she reflected on the day Devin texted her with the confirmation of Percy's payment.

• • •

Closing Percy's office door behind her, she sauntered through the empty cubicles. The software engineers were notorious for leaving unopened bags of food on their desks. Heather almost felt compelled to discard several half-eaten bags of potato chips and Skittles as she headed toward the elevator. The silhouette of the janitor, a short Belizean man with a hunched back, crept toward her. She never remembered his name, although he remembered hers.

"Late night again, Ms. Heather?" he asked cheerfully.

"Yeah. It's the month-end. Late nights are pretty much expected."

"Don't work too hard. Family time is important."

"Tell that to upper management. Goodnight." As the metallic elevator doors closed, she saw her distorted reflection staring back at her. She hated her reflection in the best of mirrors, but there was something about this distortion that she always found especially repulsive.

3

BACK TO REALITY

Heather's white Ford Fusion was waiting for her in the parking garage, street lamps illuminating its glossy paint and silver edges. As she fumbled in her purse for her keys, her phone rang. It was Devin. Reluctantly, she answered.

"Devin, what do you want?" Heather and Devin were beyond exchanging pleasantries when they spoke. He knew she cared about him and that he cared about her. After all, she did raise him and his brother for the past eleven years. Heather Carter became who she was because of the fact that she had been thrown into the role of raising her best friend's sons. Even though Heather didn't have a motherly instinct in her body, neither had Jacquelyn, her identity in a former life. In this one way, maybe she *had* held on to a piece of who she was before she decided that she had no choice but to shed the life she had known before becoming Heather.

"I just got off the phone with Earl Wilson, that sadistic Methodist bishop who requested adult diapers for every single one of his perverted fantasies."

Heather groaned as she finally located her keys at the bottom of her purse and unlocked her car door. As the engine and Bluetooth started simultaneously, she recalled the many unusual requests that Earl, one of her escort business' high-profile clients, had made of late. Even thinking about his requests made her stomach squirm.

"So what *exactly* does he want this time?" Heather's disgust was palpable in her tone. How this man had beguiled his way into being a sought after conservative author, pundit, religious leader, and the epitome of traditional family values was something Heather would never understand. Of course, she speculated that no one had ever caught Earl Wilson wearing an adult diaper while being sodomized by a strap-on dildo one of her prostitutes wore.

"He is anxious to know when our office location will be up and running. He hates having to spring for hotel rooms every time he has a rendezvous." Heather turned on the radio, making sure to turn the volume down enough so that she could still hear Devin. It was a beautiful evening. The stars sparkled in the night sky. She noticed these little things to distract herself. A shrink she once saw called it "active gratitude." Heather just saw it as a way to forget about the disgusting feeling of Percy's skin against her own and the repulsive look on his face as he had entered her.

"We'll be up and running once the brownstone in Capitol Hill is finished being painted. And if the bishop hates springing for hotel rooms, he should watch porn because my escorts are high-class, and they don't get paid to have sex in cars or in back alleys."

Devin sighed on the other end of the phone. Heather knew that sigh. Devin was stressing out about this client, and about something else.

Heather stopped at a red light, the radio playing cheesy love songs of the Target soundtrack variety. Not in the mood to hear Celine Dion belt out one of her tired ballads about unconditional love, she turned the radio off. As the light turned green, she decided to ask Devin how the dissolution of Mid-IR Solutions was coming. She sensed that was the source of his stressful sigh. "Devin, I assume we're on track for dissolving Mid-IR Solutions. Any updates you'd like to share?"

"I've already closed the website, deactivated our Salesforce customer portal, and closed all user accounts. I will be sending emails to Percy, notifying him that we've gone bankrupt and have dissolved our corporation."

"The money has been transferred?"

"It's been transferred and is ready to use. And we should really discuss how we're going to pay this back to OEI."

Heather approached her house, a modest two-story home she rented in a quaint, family-friendly suburb of Fairfax, noting how she wished her landlord would agree to paint the house. The tan, brick exterior and pale white siding struck her as so *blah*. But she was just renting and had no control over much of anything when it came to her home's aesthetics. God, she hated not being in control. Remembering that Devin was still talking, she turned her attention back to their conversation. He was going on and on about a topic that they'd already covered more times than she could count.

"Heather, I need to get out. You know that any reputable Department of Defense contractor isn't gonna hire a former pimp with a computer engineering degree. You've seen the news. These security clearances uncover every little thing about you. They can find out what you had for breakfast in May 2008."

"Devin, you're melodramatic. Toughen up. If you're hard-pressed for a job, I can get you one. We have Greg Hammond eating out of our hands. "

"And the program director eating you out."

Heather grabbed her purse and slammed her car door. A light breeze blew in her direction as she walked up the driveway. She just didn't have the energy to do this with Devin right now.

"Does it bother you that he's married?"

Heather groaned. She couldn't believe he was asking her this question. Again. He knew that her interactions with Percy were necessary for expanding the business. Why he felt the need to perpetually remind her of her ignominious behavior was beyond her.

She unlocked her door, punching in the security code to disable the alarm. As she turned on the lights to the foyer, the brightness causing her to strain, she took another deep sigh and resolved to wrap up this useless conversation with Devin as quickly as possible.

"Devin, it bothers me that you feel the need to throw Percy in my face every time we talk. I did not pursue him. He pursued me relentlessly for weeks. Some would call it sexual harassment, but I saw an opportunity to get the funding we needed to expand our business. I found Percy's weakness and formed a crucial alliance with his boss. None of what I'm doing is bringing me satisfaction. It has to be done."

"It doesn't. We can walk away, Heather. This isn't 2003 anymore. Trey and I aren't kids. We can take care of ourselves."

Heather was at a loss for words. She knew Devin was right – she didn't have to run this underground escorting business. She wasn't strapped for cash. She had paid off her 16 maxed-out credit cards and had a secure job despite its mundanity. She had the option of walking away.

The hardwood floors glistened against the light as Heather sauntered into the kitchen to pour herself a glass of wine. "We can't, and we're not. There is a need for the service I'm providing. I have the chance to be my own boss and do not have to answer to anyone. For years, I've sacrificed so much for so many people, and I fucking deserve a break. This is my break."

She yanked her top cabinet open and grabbed a 2012 Cabernet, smiling at the comforting sound as she uncorked the bottle and the sweet, familiar smell as she poured it into one of the overpriced wine glasses she had just ordered online the week before. Heather took conservative sips, savoring the bitterness that hit her taste buds. She could hear through the phone that Devin had begun playing one of his video games. She took this as a sign that their conversation was over. There was nothing else to say. Devin had again begged her to walk away from the business she had been building for five years, and she had firmly rejected his pleas.

She hung up the phone and leaned against her kitchen counter, looking around at all the outdated appliances. She wanted to remodel the entire kitchen, update the appliances, have an island countertop constructed in the middle. Better yet, she wanted to renovate the whole house. The backyard, an empty wooded space occupied with dandelions and weeds, could have an expanded deck with a dance floor for parties. She began envisioning the lavish décor, the plush leather couches with matching throw pillows and the lively crowd of friends who would dance the night away to Gloria Estefan tunes while sipping champagne. Heather became delirious with these thoughts, but then remembered she had no close friends. Jacquelyn's friends had loved her, adored her. But Jacquelyn didn't exist anymore. Plus, the house wasn't hers to renovate anyway.

•••

Today is a good day. You are alive and healthy. You are a strong, confident woman. You are unique, talented, tenacious, This pain you are feeling is only fleeting. It will pass with time. As these same words crossed her mind for the tenth time in as many minutes, Harriet made a conscious decision to throw away those affirmation CDs her therapist, Dr. Rowan, had talked her into ordering. She couldn't affirm her way out of grief, no matter how long she silently meditated or journaled. And God, she hated journaling anyway. All it did was make her right hand go numb. Dr. Rowan had told Harriet that writing her feelings would help her understand her grief's origins. What a moron. An hour a day was not going to result in any sort of breakthrough and was not going to take away her pain. For the past five years, she had woken up every single day feeling like shit. Ella's death had changed everything for her, and she wasn't going to let anyone tell her that something as painful and tragic as the death of a child was going to be "fixed" by some affirmation CDs and journaling.

"Harriet, are you hungry? You haven't even touched your hummus." Harriet looked up and realized she had been so absorbed in her own dreary reflections that she had forgotten she was at her monthly book club. Harriet was supposed to be normal tonight, not sad or bitter. So what if her husband of almost 25 years was cold and heartless? Nobody, not even any of your friends, wants to be around someone who just belabors the same issue over and over again. So Harriet didn't. She pretended she was content. To the outside world, Harriet Thompson-Nelson was a happy suburban wife and mother who enjoyed cooking, gardening, reading, and knitting. No one cared to be reminded of the miserable, grief-stricken, 47-year-old who felt unappreciated by her husband and so deeply saddened over the death of her daughter that sometimes made her wonder how she could even breathe.

Amy and Louisa were the only two friends who had stuck by her side after Ella's death. At Ella's funeral, her other friends had promised the same thing, but their actions had cemented a harsh truth that Harriet had come to realize about people in general – they supported you as long as it was convenient for them. It wasn't personal. It was merely the way of the world.

"I'm fine. I had a late lunch." Harriet dipped the triangular edge of a pita chip into the hummus resting neatly in the middle of the vegetable platter, the creamy texture surprisingly spicy. Amy must have purchased the tray from Whole Foods. Throughout their 28-year friendship, Harriet had witnessed Amy's countless disastrous attempts to cook the simplest of dishes. Louisa, on the other hand, was a natural in the kitchen, her cross-shaped fruit platter with its intricate placements of pineapples and strawberries superiorly situated next to Amy's store-bought hummus.

The book they were discussing was "A Thousand Splendid Suns," which had been Amy's selection. Initially, she had recommended "Fifty Shades of Grey," but Louisa strongly objected to reading literature that she deemed pornographic. Louisa also went on to talk about how Jesus' presence needed to be felt in everything she did. Apparently, this extended to reading.

"Mariam's character represents Christ in so many ways. Think about it."

Harriet silently groaned as Louisa compared Mariam's sacrificing her life for Laila to the one Christ had made when he died on the cross. Bored with Louisa's unsurprising attempt to use even the most mundane of events to preach the Gospel, Harriet scanned Amy's living room, stifling uproarious laughter as she observed how Louisa was sitting directly across from Amy's statue of Rati Devi, her voluptuous breasts and erect nipples pointing like darts toward Louisa's head. Harriet found sinister humor behind watching Louisa elucidate Jesus' transformative power in a room full of half-naked, intersex deities.

"What were your thoughts, Harriet?"

Amy's eyes widened, a signal Harriet and Amy devised to cut Louisa off. Harriet, who had only read the first fifty pages, offered her feeble opinion. She wasn't really much of a reader these days, although she used to love reading before Ella's death.

"I found Mariam to be quite tragic."

"Tragic?" Louisa's forehead narrowed, her frown lines quite noticeable.

"Yes, tragic," Harriet explained how Mariam's life had been a series of hapless events: being born to an unwed, bitter mother who perpetually reminded Mariam that her life was inferior because she was a bastard, realizing her father had always been ashamed of her because of how she was conceived, marrying an emotionally and physically abusive man who blamed her for the miscarriages she had.

"But that's not entirely who she is. She has the heart of a servant, which is exactly how Christ is," Harriet cut Louisa off.

"You can't compare everyone to Jesus, Louisa. Did Mariam tell people she was God in the flesh?" Harriet assumed Mariam did not profess to be Christ based on the tiny portion of the book she did read.

Amy broke the awkward silence between the two women with an announcement, rambling as she fumbled around the hall closet for the first prototype of a new product she and her husband, Michael, were selling. What came out of the closet reddened Louisa's cheeks.

"Ta-da!" A long dildo emerged out of a silver embroidered box, the title Treasure of Pleasure written in black cursive ink along the embroidery. Amy demonstrated its functionality by taking out a remote control, fervently pressing buttons that made the dildo vibrate both horizontally and vertically.

"Why do you have that in your hall closet?" asked Louisa, her voice trembling. Harriet knew why. She had provided Amy with the initial investment to start a sex toy line. The vibrating dildo was one of many innovative products Amy and Michael were planning to sell.

"Thanks to Harriet's initial investment, Michael and I can start a sex toy line. This line is going to transform the way we as women achieve orgasm. We have gels that will stimulate the nipples, butt plugs for those of us curious about anal, and vibrators that can stimulate the clitoris in ways our competitors can't."

"I think it's a fantastic idea," Harriet replied. "I am so proud of you." Harriet smiled as Amy beamed with excitement. Harriet's financial adviser had suggested she diversify her portfolio, something everyone with a trust fund of $25 million was supposed to do. Why not invest in a product Harriet believed in? She hadn't had a proper orgasm since 2005. Percy's exponential weight gain did not invigorate Harriet's already diminished sex drive.

Louisa sat there, speechless. Harriet sometimes wished Louisa hadn't rededicated her life to Christ back in college. She and Amy missed the Louisa they knew before that fateful rededication, the girl who could burp the entire alphabet when she was drunk, who openly talked about her hot summer fling with her art instructor in Paris, leaving nothing to the imagination. What had happened to that girl?

Harriet had noticed little changes in Louisa over time – the way she'd refrain from using profanity, or say grace before every meal, or wake up early for church. These minute changes had been the start of Louisa's journey back into the folds of her childhood faith and had precipitated evenings plagued with awkward silences. Harriet wondered if she and Louisa were really still friends, or had become mere acquaintances too polite to admit their friendship had run its course. The two women were on very different paths, Harriet struggling to find meaning after tragedy and Louisa inundating everyone with her spiritual acuity. Was Harriet a terrible person for wanting a friendship that didn't involve one friend praying for the other friend's deliverance?

"I don't think Carl's graduation party is an appropriate venue to advertise your new business, Amy," Louisa was trying to hide her mortification when Amy had casually suggested she bring business cards to Carl's graduation party. The mere thought of her friends and family being asked if they've ever used anal beads while enjoying hot dogs made Louisa sick.

"Really? I pass out business cards all the time for my divorce practice."

"That's different, Amy. Carl's party is gonna have a diverse group of people, many of whom attend our church."

As Amy began opening her mouth to rebuff Louisa's polite rejection, her daughter,

Mel, came rushing down the stairs, her dark curly hair pulled back with an orange rubber band. She appeared flustered.

"Mel, honey? What's wrong?" Amy asked.

"Two things. I got the summer internship at Justice For All."

Harriet beamed with excitement over Mel's news. She rushed over to hug her, with Amy and Louisa following.

"What's the other thing?"

Mel stared at Harriet, her eyes darting toward Harriet's purse.

"Did Jerry tell you he's home?"

Harriet rushed over to the couch and snatched her purse. She whipped out her phone, frustrated that she had to type in her password to access the main screen. Her text messages had revealed five new texts from Jerry. She also had two missed calls.

"He's home," Harriet managed. "He decided to come home." For some odd reason, the pain she felt dissipated at that moment. Jerry had decided to come home to be with his family.

4

EPIPHANY

Carl sincerely regretted drinking all those tequila shots at Leo's impromptu graduation party last night. Tiny clear shot glasses arranged vertically along Deanne's stomach, the shimmer from her navel ring making Carl dizzier as he bit into the lime. The burning sensation still lingered in his throat as he sat at the kitchen table. He watched as his mother made pancakes, mesmerized as she poured the batter onto the sizzling skillet. Already fully dressed for the day in an ethereal floral print white dress, Louisa bustled around the kitchen cheerily. Carl wanted to help, but he was afraid of knocking over dishes. One of the many drawbacks of being hungover.

"I can help," he said. Louisa eyed him playfully as she set the table, a large plate of bacon appearing in front of him. *Where did that come from?* he wondered. He hadn't even smelled the bacon before the moment that it was literally placed right under his nose.

"It's your graduation. You don't lift a finger mister. Did you and Leo have fun last night? What movie did you end up seeing again?"

"The new Spiderman one. It was pretty good." Carl's phone vibrated, a shirtless picture of Leo appearing on his screen. Carl vaguely remembered Leo losing a game of strip poker, his hazy memory confirmed as Leo texted Carl another photo of him in his boxer shorts, a crude drawing of breasts with obscenely large areolas plastered across his bare chest. Carl found Leo's sporadic chest hair insanely sexy. He became semi-aroused as he replied to the text Leo had sent. *Still fucked up.* That's what the text read. Carl sent the laughing hilariously emoticon as Louisa placed a piping hot plate of pancakes next to the bacon.

"Your father's fast ended this morning."

Carl nodded absentmindedly in his mother's direction, his eyes remaining fixed on his phone as he scanned his texts about the party the night before, derivative in their progression: a mass text message sent by Leo the day before with explicit instructions to bring your own booze, replies from random attendees offering to bring chips or brownies or buckets of fried chicken from KFC, and a final text message from Leo with the start and end time of the party. Everyone had understood that covering up the remnants of an unauthorized party with alcohol involved cleaning up an hour and a half before the party ended. All of the attendees had known that at least five people needed to be reasonably sober to spearhead the meticulous cleaning required: the rearranging of furniture, the mopping up of vomit, the disposal of condoms, and – last night – the delicate retrieval and disposition of fecal matter on the bathroom floor. Carl chuckled to himself as he landed on a picture of him kissing Deanne on the mouth. A girl with whom Carl had Spanish class was in the background, obscuring a large family photo in the living room. Her long frizzy hair covered Harriet's face.

"Are you gonna be glued to your phone all morning?"

Carl immediately shoved it in his pocket as his father, Mark, came downstairs. Louisa smiled. There was a family rule: no electronic devices at the table. His father, already dressed in his crisp navy blue suit, took a seat across from Carl, grinning widely.

"Hey, why aren't you wearing your cap and gown?"

"I'll put it on after I eat."

Mark nodded as he licked his lips at the sight of the pancakes and bacon placed in front of him. Louisa hurried over with a carton of orange juice and sat down. "Let's bless the food and eat!"

Carl automatically bowed his head and closed his eyes. His father's voice made his ears ring. *How hungover was he?*

"Most gracious and loving God, we thank you for this day. We praise you for all of your many blessings. Thank you for revealing your truth to me this morning and for allowing us to celebrate Carl's accomplishments. We ask you to bless this food for the nourishment of our bodies. Bless the hands that lovingly prepared them. In Jesus' name, we pray. Amen."

"Amen." Carl dug in, dousing his pancakes in syrup, curious about this revelation his father mentioned.

"Carl, what do you think about expanding our ministry in the church?" Carl shrugged as he stuffed his mouth full of pancakes, the sweetness of the maple syrup clearing up the fogginess of his hangover. Louisa elaborated, her petite frame nearly bouncing as she discussed Mark's plan. Carl turned his head toward his father, his mouth full of food as he crammed a slice of bacon into his mouth. A 40 day fast was torture. Carl had only endured single-day fasts when the church held their annual back to school prayer and fast extravaganza. Carl remembered it being advertised as a "cleansing of the heart and mind so that God's soldiers can excel academically." Carl thought that was utter bullshit, but whatever. He had gone along with it. Kind of.

"Your father awoke this morning with a scripture God placed on his heart. You know, God often speaks to us when we don't *want* to listen. Anyway, through this scripture, God revealed that our church should preach change for homosexuals." A loud thumping noise resonated in Carl's right ear. Why did his father have to have an epiphany about the evils of *homosexuality*, of all things? Really?!

Carl recalled many solitary evenings he spent in his room, listening to Phyllis Hyman or Amy Winehouse on his iPod, the hopelessness and heartbreak apparent in the voices of these departed souls. He identified with the lyrics, mainly because being gay was equated with unimaginable rejection. In his church, he knew that homosexuality had been looked upon with disdain, even though it was rarely discussed explicitly.

Carl recounted the church deacon, Hubert, standing outside of the main sanctuary just a few weeks before, commenting in a hushed, but harsh tone: "Why does the praise team always have to sing songs by that faggot, Donnie McClurkin?" This wasn't the first comment like this he had heard come out of Hubert's mouth – Hubert was always quick to express disapproval toward some public figure who had just come out or endorsed marriage equality. And now, Carl's own *father* was about to preach something Carl knew deep down was impossible?

Mark's booming voice brought Carl back to the breakfast table: "So many homosexuals think they're born that way. What if that's not true? I mean, Earl said homosexuality and transgenderism are linked to these unhealed wounds from childhood: molestation, bullying, rejection from a parent. And so many homosexuals think God doesn't love them, because they believe there's no hope. They believe they're doomed to rot in hell. God told me this morning that it's not that simple."

"Carl, you okay?" his mother's soothing voice reverberating over the ringing in his ears.

Carl nodded, barely mustering a mumbled *mmmhmmm* in his parents' direction as he pondered a part of his life that he refused to fully acknowledge to himself, let alone articulate aloud to his parents of all people. For one, Carl was attracted to men and had been attracted to boys since he was 12 years old. He had heard horror stories of conversion therapy on news specials and knew enough to know that being gay was not sunshine and rainbows and freedom. "Will and Grace" and "Glee" might have given visibility to gay people, but he knew that the world in which he lived was a far cry from these fabricated utopias.

Carl glanced over at his mother and managed a smile. She smiled back, light pink lipstick marks framing the ring of the coffee mug she held tightly in her delicate hands. Carl focused on the strange yet fascinating way in which the crimson lipstick marks contrasted with the bright white of the coffee mug. He had to focus on this, instead of on all he would be losing if he ever came out to his parents: the clothes and generous allowance, the car he received on his sixteenth birthday, the promises of college tuition paid in full – all of that could be gone in a minute. He had to will his mind to not ask questions he perpetually asked himself: *Could he give it all up to be himself? Was he strong enough to do that?* The answer was, as it had been for the past six years, a resounding "no." Resigned, Carl finished his breakfast in silence.

• • •

Mark looked over at his son, worrying that *something* was wrong, but too exhausted to try to figure out what exactly was ailing his son at this particular moment in time. Mark chalked it up to his son's impending graduation, gave both Carl and his wife the obligatory kisses on the head, and excused himself from the breakfast table to head to the office.

A few short hours later, the sun etched its way through the blinds in Mark's home office, a thin reflection projecting onto a plaque he had received from his old job at Lewis & Houghton. "Outstanding Service in Corporate Law" was the award. Mark faintly recalled the aristocratic evening: the black tuxedo that made his skin itch, Louisa's long-sleeved navy blue dress and the confused stares of the other wives in attendance, many of whom decided to exploit their breast augmentations and tummy tucks and thin waistlines with the most revealing evening gowns. He remembered the sound of his forced chuckles when Bernard Houghton made a joke and the dry piece of steak accompanied by undercooked string beans and cold mashed potatoes. The joys of working for a soul-sucking, amoral, for-profit law firm that demanded all staff attorneys work a minimum of 60 hours a week. Oh, how he didn't miss that life.

Mark rested his head against the plush black headrest of his office chair, meditating on a scripture God had placed on his heart in the middle of the night. God often did this at the most inconvenient times. When he first entered into ministry, he would be awakened in the middle of the night by the thought of a Bible verse that he had been avoiding for one reason or another. Today was one of those days. Mark had awakened at 2 o'clock in the morning, hours before he had planned to wake up to begin his usual hour of morning prayer of Thanksgiving. God laid a scripture on his heart, one he had actively avoided due to its divisive nature in the church.

Mark picked his Bible up off of his desk and found the scripture in question: *For this reason, God gave them up to degrading passions. Their women exchanged natural intercourse for unnatural, and in the same way also the men, giving up natural intercourse with women, were consumed with passion for one another.* He continued reading, his brow furrowing at the final scripture: *Men committed shameless acts with men and received in their own persons the due penalty for their error. And since they did not see fit to acknowledge God, God gave them up to a debased mind and to things that should not be done.* The words in his Bible blurred together as Mark placed his hand over his temple. Maybe his pounding headache was just the result of him coming off of his 40-day fast. His body wasn't used to any solid food, let alone the pancakes, bacon, coffee, and orange juice he had inhaled at breakfast.

• • •

Mark felt his headache spreading as he remembered a recent church leadership meeting that had derailed into a heated debate. The debate was centered on the issues of homosexuality and transgenderism. As his memory took him back into the stuffy conference room at Holy Boldness United Methodist Church, he now knew why God had placed this scripture on his heart.

Deacon Hubert Adams, whom Mark genuinely liked and admired for his devotion to Christ, had brought up the issue. A quintessential "old-timer," Hubert knew the Bible inside and out, and had strong views about what church was and was not. Unfortunately, he lacked the temperament to be a pastor. Mark had watched as Hubert squandered countless opportunities to further his education in theology.

"That's the problem with these so-called Bible colleges," Hubert had ranted one recent afternoon. "They spend too much time tripping you up on all the cultural contexts that the atheists use to discredit the Bible. Ya can't trust 'em. And the issue of homosexuality is becoming something that churches celebrate."

If Mark were honest with himself, he had dismissed Hubert's remarks as being steeped in ignorance. His mentor, Bishop Earl Wilson, had cautioned him regarding seeking counsel from well-meaning, but uninformed church members. Hubert was one of those members.

"Hubert, I think our church should focus on serving the poor," Sandy, one of the church board members, had chimed in. "We need to talk about how to expand our meal delivery ministry. Save the theological debates for after the meeting." Sandy's brisk tone, which had a particular punch when her long, veiny neck arched as she spoke, indicated Mark needed to intervene quickly. As usual, Mark's comments had been neutral, not wanting to stir that familiar, proverbial pot of controversy.

• • •

And yet today, he couldn't stop thinking about how the scripture that had come to him in the night, Romans 1:26-28, was instructing Mark to stop responding to homosexuality with neutrality. The ending, though, confounded him to no avail. Resting his head against the chair, he glanced at his phone sitting at the edge of his desk: 1:19. His daughter, Natalie, was flying home for Carl's graduation and would land at Reagan at 3, which meant that with traffic and the fact that it was Memorial Day weekend, they would be hard-pressed to even arrive at the graduation on time. He groaned.

As he got up from his desk and headed to the master bedroom to retrieve the suit

Louisa had laid out for him, his mind wandered to the end of that passage in the book of Romans. Hubert had made a valid point, despite the superiority with which he delivered it. The Methodist church was embroiled in a culture war. One side decried the teachings regarding homosexuality in the Book of Discipline; the other side revered those same teachings.

As Mark headed into the master bedroom, he reflected on something Earl had told him when he first entered the seminary: "God is counting on you to discern what is moral and what is immoral. An evil influence might be obvious to us. It might be clearly stated in the Bible. However, our approach to addressing this evil influence has to come from a place of love, compassion, and respect. It's the only way to save souls."

Mark stopped in the hallway, instantly realizing why God placed that scripture on his heart. The faint rumble of the air conditioner hummed in the background as Mark opened his bedroom door and walked toward the bathroom. Louisa was standing there in a towel, the steam from the shower she had just stepped out of enveloping her. She looked so angelic standing there it almost took his breath away.

She smiled when she saw the way he looked at her. "Your suit's hanging behind the door in the bathroom. It's the navy blue one you like. Oh, and Natalie texted me before she left. She'll take a cab to graduation, so you don't have to worry about doing the airport pick-up."

Mark wasn't really listening as he walked toward the bathroom. His mind was elsewhere.

"So, I want to talk a little bit more about that Bible verse that's been tugging at my spirit since last night."

"Yes?" Louisa's voice carried into the bathroom where Mark had begun brushing his teeth.

"So Romans 1:26-28. I first thought God wanted me to stop being neutral toward homosexuality. Educate myself, you know? Then, the last part of that verse threw me for a loop. What if God is telling me to show our church how to minister to homosexuals without approving their lifestyle?"

Louisa appeared at the bathroom door, leaning against the frame of the wall as Mark spat his mouthful of toothpaste into the sink. "I'm listening," she said with curiosity. Mark grabbed the mouthwash and began gargling, spitting into the sink and wiping his mouth with his washcloth.

"Earl mentioned organizations that reorient homosexuals. These programs don't use electroshock therapy or any of those archaic practices from the sixties and seventies. They address the emotional and psychological issues that cause homosexuality. What if our church partnered with them? What if we explicitly preached this?" Louisa smiled as she walked toward Mark, hugging him tightly.

"We preach God's word with compassion and love."

"Exactly. I should ask Earl the best way to approach this. He's written about homosexuality, and how many members give up on Christ because they've been told they can't change." Louisa kissed him gingerly on the forehead as he washed his face.

"I knew God was speaking to you this morning. Let's talk with Earl tomorrow about this. I think it's wise to get his input." Mark smiled as Louisa's eyes glimmered with a joy he only saw when she felt the Holy Spirit.

"I love you." He brought her in for a kiss as he silently prayed a prayer of thanksgiving. God had immeasurably blessed him with so much. He thanked God for giving him the willpower to see his fast through because in those moments of extreme hunger, of utter physical emptiness, God had revealed his truth to Mark in the most profound of ways.

5

THE MESS HE MADE

Jerry's old bedroom was a lot smaller than he had remembered. His bed, neatly made with the old, faded Pokémon covers of his childhood, appeared shrunken, diminished. He scanned the room, wondering when the desk had been moved to the other side. And by whom. He recalled the reassuring conversation he had had with Mel the night before, her terse tone pressing him for an explanation as to why he had been avoiding her for over six months. When he had told her about dropping out of MIT and secretly moving to New York City, her reproachfulness quickly turned to compassion.

"Why didn't you tell me? I haven't heard from you in six months! What the hell?" Her voice had quivered as Jerry tried to formulate a plausible explanation, one that didn't involve revealing the painful memories and paralyzing secrets he was trying to escape. Their friendship had been built on unequivocal transparency; Jerry had been the first person Mel had turned to when an inebriated Deanne had slurred her confessions of secretly hooking up with Mel's boyfriend at the time, Leo, vomiting on Mel's dress in front of everyone at Jerry's graduation party. Jerry had patiently provided Mel with a fresh set of clothes and a shoulder to cry on as she cursed herself for dating Jerry's brother; Mel had been the first person Jerry had come out to, the first person who discovered his bulimia one fateful Saturday evening as he vomited the candy and Cheetos they had eaten while watching eighties films.

Despite their closeness, Jerry had kept the memory of his brief, but indelible stint in conversion therapy to himself, his mind traversing the halls of his therapist's office while listening to Mel excitedly discuss her internship with the non-profit law firm, Justice For All. He had responded with the appropriate *oohs* and *ahhs*, and had profusely congratulated her, but he had still felt detached from his environment; he had felt disconnected from the place he once called home.

• • •

He stared at himself in the mirror, strands of his curly hair falling in front of his face as he buttoned his shirt. A classic white dress shirt with khaki pants was what he decided to wear to Leo's graduation. Now all he had to do was wash his face and brush his teeth. As he started walking toward the hall bathroom, his mother stopped him. Jerry had pretended to be asleep when Harriet came home from her book club last night. He feared having to explain why he would be back for a few months. He dreaded the questions she was going to ask him.

Harriet was already dressed in a sleek red dress, her long red hair pulled back into a ponytail. Harriet was quite slim, the shiny bracelet she wore nearly falling off her tiny wrists. A cream-colored sweater covered her shoulders.

"Hey, mom. You look good."

Harriet smiled as she pulled Jerry in for a hug. She exhaled sharply as if she had been holding her breath for a long time. She brushed Jerry's hair back as he breathed in the sweet scent of her perfume. "You need a haircut mister. When was the last time you cut your hair?"

He shrugged. "A month before finals," he lied. Jerry had become adept at lying on the spot, pretending issues didn't exist, covering up dirty secrets. Even he was amazed by how well he had gotten at keeping track of his lies.

"Well, try to get it cut within the next week before your internship starts. Oh, and let me know where you're staying in case I need to send you some mail."

"Okay. It's in my email. I can get it for you now if you'd like." Jerry hoped his mother didn't probe him any further. There was no internship at MIT, of course, and Jerry had requested that all mail from the school be sent to a P.O. Box in Silver Spring, Maryland the day he withdrew from the university.

"No. Go and get ready." Harriet kissed him on the cheek as she hurried back into the master bedroom, turning around swiftly to ask another question. "Last question. Have you seen my bottle of Don Perignon? It's missing from my cabinet." Jerry shrugged, shaking his head, though he knew exactly what had happened to it.

• • •

As Jerry headed into the bathroom, turning on the faucet as he grabbed a washcloth from the towel rack, he recalled the disaster that had descended upon him when he opened the front door last night. Beer bottles were everywhere; Carl was frantically wiping up a puddle of vomit next to the speakers. Three more of Leo's classmates had scurried from the kitchen with large, black trash bags, putrid odors emanating from them as they dashed toward the dumpster.

"Five minutes, everyone. Jerry?! What's up, man! What are you doing here?" Jerry, unfortunately, recollected Leo's drunken embrace, followed by his subsequent vomiting on Jerry's clothes. He hurried upstairs to change, seething with rage when he realized that Leo's vomit had gotten on the bag of food he just bought. Jerry had dashed into the bathroom to grab a spare plastic bag, the stench of Leo's vomit burning his nostrils as he dumped the food into the plastic bag. Another one of Leo's unsupervised parties. He began washing his face, the minty smell of the body wash waking him up as he combed his curly, messy hair.

"Jerry?" Leo's hoarse voice echoed through the hollow bathroom walls.

Jerry opened the door to find Leo's face appearing in all its hungover glory: the bloodshot eyes, the disheveled hair. He wasn't even dressed. Leo sauntered in and pulled down his pants, urinating without even asking Jerry to leave. Jerry merely shook his head and continued to brush his teeth. Leo coughed loudly, not even looking over at the sink after he flushed the toilet.

"Do you think mom knows about the party?"

Leo's whispering infuriated Jerry. "I think she does!" Jerry nearly screamed into Leo's ear as he walked out of the bathroom. He finished washing up as his eyes darted toward the toilet. Jerry spent countless days and nights hovered over that toilet, the shower running in the background to stifle the sounds of his retching. His purge always left that acidic aftertaste, a reminder of the ugliness within him that had to be expelled in the most volatile of ways. As he finished brushing his hair, heading to the bedroom to get dressed, the silhouette of a large man appeared behind him.

"You're home." Percy, his father, was standing three feet behind him.

Jerry didn't even bother responding. He opened his bedroom door, slammed it, and immediately got down on his knees. Jerry crawled toward the dark, hollow space underneath his bed, pulling out the loose floorboard. The food he bought was safely stowed away. He touched it gently, his heart racing. Percy's presence conjured up many emotions, presenting him with the stark reminder of the mess he had made of his life. Back here, back home, there was only one way to escape for Jerry, and it was neatly tied in a plastic 7-Eleven bag.

6

CHEERS TO MY MISERABLE LIFE

Heather's desk chair needed replacing. The lever on it didn't work, and whenever she tried to adjust it, the whole seat of the chair lurched her forward, nearly catapulting her out of it. She looked ridiculous, sitting at her desk with her posture mirroring that of Quasimodo from "The Hunchback of Notre-Dame." Heather got up from her chair and forced it backward. Some of the engineers working nearby craned their necks to see what Heather was doing, her grunts becoming louder and laced with the most obscene, unprofessional language.

"You. Motherfucking. Piece. Of Shit." Her chair's backside eventually detached, the rest of the contraption toppling over into the middle of the aisle. Greg walked by, dressed in his crudest casual outfit to date – sky blue jeans paired with a tan polo shirt. The ridiculous, red suspenders were an affront to fashion. His eyebrows raised as he examined Heather's fallen chair obfuscating his path.

"Looks like you need a new chair, Heather."

She smiled while brushing back a strand of hair that had made its way into her mouth. Greg motioned for Heather to follow him into his office. Hastily kicking the contents of her broken chair into her cubicle, she followed Greg toward his office. He exchanged pleasantries with people passing by, names Heather never knew. *Why bother learning names of people she'd most likely never see outside of work? Why bother forming relationships with individuals who were quite dull?*

Heather reflected on her first job after graduating from Juilliard: Madonna's "The Girlie Show World Tour." She remembered the exhilaration and fatigue, the wonder and awe of seeing Paris for the first time, Madonna's demand for precision in every dance move executed. That euphoric exhaustion, the kind you experienced when you were living and breathing your passion, was a feeling Heather would never experience. She sauntered behind Greg as he picked up the pace down the hall containing his office. Greg didn't even bother acknowledging Nikki, his underwhelming secretary who consistently had her music turned to the loudest setting. Today, it was a Miley Cyrus song reverberating through her headphones. Heather liked Nikki, finding the pink highlights in her hair spunky, albeit wishing she had better taste in music.

A rustic yet flowery aroma emanated from Greg's office. It must have been that potpourri his wife had made for him. Heather found it surprisingly pleasant. His office appeared to have been accentuated with more accolades from OEI: "2013 General Manager of The Year," "The James Fujimoto Award for Innovation in Optics." The shiny plaques hung on Greg's shelf, perfectly situated so that every person walking into his office couldn't help but see them. Smug bastard.

"Mint?" Greg extended a black circular jar of Lifesavers wrapped in clear plastic. Heather took one and sat down. Greg reclined backward, his eyes glimmering with optimism that indicated only one thing.

"Eve Parsons, the VP of finance, came barging into my office today. She wanted to know how and why Percy bypassed every single procurement regulation to buy two mid-infrared lasers."

Heather smirked as she popped the mint into her mouth. The sweetness alerted Heather to the sugar of which she typically deprived herself.

"Good work Ms. Carter."

Heather stood up to take a bow, Greg clapping modestly.

"When will Percy be terminated? I'm getting tired of dismissing his not-so-subtle advances. You get my drift?" Heather thought it best to omit the details of these advances. Greg didn't need to know that Percy ate her out on the same conference room table at which board members ate their corporate lunches, or that Percy's cum had doused the very chair in which Greg was now comfortably reclining. Those details were immaterial to the matter at hand.

"Well, I told Eve to get one of her minions to run the financials for that contract. In the meantime, forward me that email saying Mid-IR Solutions went bankrupt. I'll need it as justification to walk Percy out."

Heather smirked as she adjusted her purple blouse. She caught Greg's eyes drifting toward her chest as she sat back in the chair. A strange yet satisfactory silence lingered between them. They secretly disliked each other but had bonded over their mutual disdain for Percy. Heather had an inkling that Greg was interested in utilizing some of Heather's services. As she got up to leave, her inkling was confirmed.

Greg cleared his throat, coughing sporadically as he nearly sputtered his question. "You said you have girls who perform various services?"

Heather nodded.

"Sexual in nature?"

She nodded again. "We'll have a location next week. I'll send you the details."

Heather turned to leave Greg's office, her phone vibrating as she walked out the door. A cryptic text from Devin about another one of Earl Wilson's absurd requests. She decided to examine it later as Greg's voice called her name. She hadn't even made it back to her desk. *What did he want now?*

"Heather, I'll have someone from facilities provide you with a more durable chair right away. If you take lunch now, they'll have a new chair for you by the time you come back."

"Thank you, Greg." She turned, a tiny grin spreading across her face. The exhilaration she once felt on stage, her torso's effortless movements in lockstep with the percussive sounds of "Deeper and Deeper," might never be reclaimed, but it was being replaced with an indescribable feeling: one that evoked euphoria, a high from which she didn't want to come down. Maybe this was what power felt like.

•••

Carl disliked celebrations of any kind. The fanfare and unnecessary pomp and circumstance served no purpose. He survived 13 years of school. Big deal. Why did all of these people have to show up at his house to wish him well? In the grand scheme of things, graduating from high school was not an accomplishment. Having a high-school graduation party was akin to having a party for getting your driver's license. It was annoyingly absurd.

Louisa had begun taking the food out of the refrigerator: a large basin of homemade potato salad, fruit salad in an elaborate punch bowl, ribs that were soon to be grilled and marinated in her homemade spicy barbecue sauce. The kitchen emanated a sweet aroma, which Carl instantly recognized as his mother's signature pound cake. Louisa set the bright yellow contraption onto the marbled counter, her brow furrowed as she placed her hands on her hips. The denim overalls she donned were speckled with flour.

Carl, seeing his mother becoming flustered, offered his help. "Let me get the potato salad."

Louisa beamed, kissing him on the forehead as she opened the freezer to take out the ribs. "Thank you, sweetie," she said as she placed the container of ribs onto the counter. Carl dutifully carried the potato salad outside. Mark was operating the grill, his formerly-snug tan apron now hanging off him. His father appeared to have lost close to thirty pounds while on his fast, his slender frame accentuated as he leaned forward to place coal underneath the grill. Carl set the bowl of potato salad onto the table.

"You got some music, Carl?" Mark looked up from the grill as Carl started to head back inside. "Ready to see your old man bust a move?"

Carl chuckled as Mark did an amateurish interpretation of the shuffle, turning back around without response as he headed back inside to find his mother putting the finishing touches on her famous fruit punch. As he watched her measure the perfect amount of orange, watermelon, and pineapple juice into the large yellow bowl, his mouth watered at the thought of the buzz he'd get once the sweetness of the punch matched the potency of the rum that Leo had already planned to sneak into the party. That was one of the few things he had to look forward to today. He smiled in spite of his attempt not to.

Carl headed upstairs to grab his iPod and speakers and returned to the back yard. The warm breeze had dissipated and left just the sun ferociously glaring onto the deck. Carl began setting up the music station, plugging his iPod into the cassette tape converter he purchased at one of the local electronic stores two years ago and selecting the graduation party playlist he had created – Earth, Wind, & Fire, Stevie Wonder, The Beatles. He wondered if some of the music he added would fare well with the melting pot of church members, school friends, and family. What harm was there in playing some Matchbox Twenty, John Mayer, or Imagine Dragons? He started the playlist, putting it on shuffle mode as Stevie Wonder's "Higher Ground" blared through the speakers. Mark began swaying to the beat while he placed burgers on the grill.

"Nice moves, dad," Carl smirked as he walked toward his dad. If Carl were honest, he found himself building walls between himself and his father at every turn. He loved his father, but Mark's announcement earlier of his revelation had stirred something in Carl, a surge of uneasiness that made his stomach clench. *How was Carl to argue with Mark's directive from God to promote sexual reorientation therapy? How was anyone able to challenge a directive from God? Did God really talk to people?* In all of the years Carl had spent in church, he had never heard God's voice directly. He had never felt the transformative power of the Holy Spirit. He believed God existed, but he never felt His presence in the way he heard other people describe.

"Hey, Carl. I'm proud of you. You're growing into a fine young man, a strong Christian man."

Carl managed a feeble smile as he watched Mark flip a burger over. He leaned onto his father's shoulder and his father, in turn, embraced him and kissed him on the forehead.

"Whatever you decide to do, I'll support you."

There was an irony to Mark's proclamation. He *said* he'd support Carl no matter what, but Carl knew that this promise had many conditions attached to it, one of them being that Carl was not to live a homosexual lifestyle. Carl walked into the house as the front door opened, and his sister, Natalie, walked through, struggling to balance a much-too-large bag of snacks. Carl hurried over to help.

"Thank you, little brother."

Natalie's face had gotten a little plump, her once bony features resembling that of one of those fleeting starlets on the covers of the magazines you saw at the grocery store. Her brown hair swung as she yanked the door shut.

"Did mom send you to get *more* food?" Carl asked as he tried to pull the bag out of Natalie's hands without everything toppling to the floor. Their mother always wanted to be over-prepared for parties, and this one was no exception.

"I should have pretended to be studying this morning. Why didn't I do that? I left my damn bar exam books on my kitchen counter." Natalie made sure to lower her voice. Profanity was akin to blasphemy in the Perkins' house. Carl examined his sister's worn features: the frown lines, the tiny bit of fat around her arms, her overall weary demeanor. Whatever Carl did with his future, he decided at that moment that he was *definitely* not going to law school.

"Go rest. I'll take care of this."

Natalie placed the bags of food on the kitchen counter, sliding over an elaborate platter of vegetables. Their mother believed in eating the "rainbow," a slogan employed by many health experts who made frequent appearances on daytime talk shows. The circular pattern of the carrots, broccoli, tomatoes, celery, and squash had been neatly chopped and meticulously arranged. Carl wondered how long it took his mother to prepare that platter.

"Carl, you're not supposed to lift a finger. Today is your day. I just wish there was booze."

Carl coyly tapped his sister's shoulder, pointing to his bedroom. "Leo is gonna take care of our problem."

A menacing grin appeared across Natalie's face as the graduation party commenced, guests arriving in large drones: church members who sang with him in the choir, deacons, trustees, elders who had known Carl since infancy. He made a concerted effort to include the catchphrases expected from a pastor's kid – "Praise the Lord." "God is good." "All glory belongs to Him." As the living room filled with church members, Carl sighed in relief when he saw Jerry, Leo, and Mel come through the door. Percy and Harriet followed, Harriet muttering something to Percy through gritted teeth as they all congratulated Carl. Mel's parents, Amy and Michael, began talking animatedly to some of Carl's guests. Carl noticed Amy passing out index cards. One of the trustees, who was wearing a purple W.W.J.D. polo shirt, nearly doubled over when she read the card.

"My parents are passing out business cards for their sex toy line," Mel stood behind Carl as he turned around, snickering as she adjusted her ponytail. Leo and Jerry walked over, Carl wrapping his arms around them.

"Jerry, you're home. How's MIT?" Carl greeted them.

Jerry glanced down, his eyes focusing on his tan sandals. Carl knew that Jerry had been hiding something. For the past year, he had been evasive. One word responses to Carl's texts, Jerry's sudden deletion of all his social media accounts. What was going on with him?

"We'll talk about this over punch." That was code for rum. Leo tapped his side pocket, a faint tin sound coming from it. Natalie rushed over toward Carl, impatiently excusing herself as she grabbed his shoulder. Carl forgot how strong she was. Natalie began giving Carl the details about a brewing argument between their grandparents. Unbeknownst to Mark, Louisa had invited Big Jim, Carl's grandfather, to the party. He and his son, Mark, did not get along. To further complicate matters, Louisa's parents, Barry and Jeanine, found Big Jim's personality brash. It was a recipe for disaster all the way around.

"Gramps made an off-color comment about the portrait of Jesus in the living room, and grandma heard it."

Carl groaned as he followed Natalie outside. The playlist he made had landed on "Radioactive," the Imagine Dragons song he had thrown in there at the last minute. Mark and Louisa were speaking to each other at the edge of the deck away from guests. Louisa had changed out of her denim overalls and into a yellow t-shirt with the Holy Boldness logo embroidered in a large purple font. Mark pointed to Carl's grandparents, who were arguing in the middle of the deck. Barry violently shook his head as Big Jim spoke about the obsolescence of organized religion.

"Carl's gonna sing a song," Natalie blurted out, causing Mark and Louisa to look up from their intense conversation. Carl's eyes widened and then narrowed toward Natalie. Although he was the worship leader at church, he was not keen on singing at his own graduation party. What was he going to sing?

Louisa beamed as her parents, and Big Jim continued their impassioned discussion. "Jerry can play the piano. Good idea, Natalie."

Carl hung his head, realizing he had no choice in the matter. Why didn't he protest when his mother started planning this graduation party way back in January?

Carl and Jerry agreed on the classic jazz standard, "Smile." It had no religious undertones to it, yet its message was positive. At the announcement of the impending "concert," the party guests began to cram into the house, people overflowing into the kitchen as Jerry played the introduction on the wooden piano in the living room. Carl sang the first verse as his mom smiled, her hands clasped. Big Jim listened intently, his arms relaxed at his side. Barry and Jeanine stood beside him, their agitation gone. Carl meandered through the chorus and ended the song. Everyone clapped. The promise of spiked fruit punch loomed ahead.

"Finally, some peace and quiet." Carl sat on his bed, exhausted from making idle conversation with people who barely knew him. They attended the same church, but they didn't know Carl. None of them did. Mel drank from her glass while examining the contents of Carl's room. They drank in silence for a while, Carl allowing the temporary euphoria of alcohol to course through his body.

Jerry broke the silence. "I dropped out of MIT in December."

Leo laughed, his curly hair bouncing back and forth. Mel frowned. Even though Jerry had broken the news the night before, she was still getting over the fact that he had held onto this secret from her for so long. Carl felt for Jerry. He knew all too well the pain that came with holding on to such a monstrous secret.

"So what in the hell have you been doing for the past six months?" Carl was curious.

"Moved to New York. Resubmitted my writing portfolio to NYU. Got a shitty job to try to make ends meet. Until I got fired and evicted."

Carl remembered how disappointed Jerry had been when his rejection letter had first come from NYU. He hoped Jerry hadn't coped with this recent setback in his usual way. Carl's chest began to tighten in a way that he'd become all too familiar with. He'd been having these sporadic episodes where he felt as if he couldn't breathe. The episodes would come over him suddenly and last for ten to fifteen minutes at a time. Today, they seemed relentless. With each "Praise the Lord" and "God is good," he felt this stricture. It was as if somebody was choking him.

"I'm gay," he blurted out. Mel, Jerry, and Leo all looked at him for a moment, before bursting out laughing.

"We know," they said in unison.

Carl's brow furrowed as someone faintly tapped against his door.

"How did you know?" Carl got up from his bed and opened the door. Natalie and Big Jim barged inside, their desperate expressions indicating their insatiable desire for rum.

"Know what?" asked Natalie. She sat in Carl's desk chair and began spinning around. Leo handed her the flask of rum. She took a generous sip and passed it to Big Jim. For eighty years old, Carl's grandfather was quite spry. His flirtatious manner was even more aggressive after Carl's grandmother had died.

Carl headed back to his bed and plopped his head against his pillow, staring at the ceiling. *Was this what coming out felt like?* His breathing was no longer shallow. He felt light, unencumbered.

"Sometimes I don't recognize my son," Big Jim poured the rest of the rum into his drink as Carl sat up.

"Who in their right mind thinks that gay people can change?"

Everyone grew silent. Carl stared at his grandfather and sister. Jerry began shifting uncomfortably as Big Jim started ranting about Mark's plan to minister to the hurting homosexual community.

"Gramps, it's not your fault," Natalie interjected. "It's Earl Wilson's. He corrupted dad and almost corrupted Carl and me. Carl, are you okay?"

Carl nodded as he sat up in his bed, smoothing out the black comforter. "Yeah, I'm gay, Nat."

She giggled, clicking her punch glass with Big Jim. "I owe you twenty bucks, Gramps."

Carl tugged on a strand of cotton on his comforter. The room began spinning. Did everyone gossip about his sexuality behind his back?

"How long have you all been making bets on my sexuality?" The euphoria of being accepted by his closest friends and family members wore off once he realized he was the butt of many inside jokes.

"Carl, buddy. It's not that big a deal. You like dick. So what?" Big Jim's long neck shook, his neck bones prominent as he took a swig of his drink. Tiny chunks of pineapple appeared at the bottom of his cup, their yellow particles swimming around in the punch.

Carl turned to Jerry, who had come out just last year. He noticed that Jerry had remained quiet, a faraway expression on his face, throughout the whole conversation. Jerry drank his spiked punch, appearing to be both deep in thought and a bit on edge.

"Jim, it's never that simple," Jerry said bitterly. "Look at who Carl's parents are. Look at how he was raised." The edge in Jerry's voice pierced through Carl. Something had happened to Jerry. Something to do with his coming out. He said his parents were okay with it, although he and his dad didn't discuss it. "Just be careful, Carl." Jerry turned to Carl, their eyes locking.

Carl sat against his bed, the high he had felt moments ago replaced with dread and suspicion.

"Your dad's preaching conversion to heterosexuality. Stay away from any person or group that tells you that change is possible because it's not."

Carl nodded while Jerry brushed a strand of hair away from his face. Carl had no idea who he could trust outside his bedroom walls. Natalie gave him countless assurances that he'll be fine, as did his grandpa, Mel, and Leo. However, he focused on what Jerry said. *Be careful.* Was there a deeper meaning to Jerry's warning?

"Come on. Let's toast." Leo stood up, holding his cup of spiked punch. "To Carl, who graduated with a much higher GPA than me. Cheers."

Cheers. Cheers to my miserable life, Carl's inner voice managing to eviscerate any optimism coming out imbued. Only obstacles lay ahead for him. Of this, he was sure. He instantly felt like he needed a nap.

• • •

Mark and Earl finally had a moment to talk privately. His father's surprise appearance at Carl's graduation party had unsettled his spirit, and Mark knew that a conversation with Earl would help ground him. Big Jim's hedonistic outlook coupled with his agnostic beliefs pained Mark, mainly because his father's worldview reminded him of the person he once was. In college, Mark had enjoyed worldly things: beer, premarital sex, profanity, marijuana. He used to believe organized religion was a cult, a guise utilized by ignorant, power-hungry men who only wanted to fatten their wallets by selling the masses lies. Then, he had met Earl. Earl had disproved all of his preconceived notions surrounding God. He had shown Mark that Christianity was the antithesis of religion because it was a relationship with God through His Son,

Jesus Christ. And how Earl had revealed the transformative power of Christ through his actions won Mark over in a big way.

The two men sat in Mark's study, enjoying Louisa's homemade punch with a slice of her pound cake. Mark had his Bible open to the scripture God had placed on his heart yesterday morning. Earl took a bite of cake and read the highlighted scripture, sitting back and gazing upward. Mark was desperate for his mentor's counsel.

"I remember the first time I preached on this exact scripture," Earl reminisced as he washed down his piece of cake with a large swig of fruit punch. Mark leaned in, studying Earl's surprisingly thinning features. Earl sat back in his chair, placing his hand over his stomach, the loose fabric of his white polo shirt moving with the circular direction of his hand.

"Earl, what do I do? I don't even know how to start." Earl nodded. He was familiar with Mark's dilemma. How was Mark supposed to minister without condemning? How was he supposed to address an entire population of hurting people and their families without passing judgment?

"I'm gonna recommend that you talk to Lester Dawson. He's a psychotherapist at this organization I work with called Global Healing from Homosexuality. Lester's a good friend who lived a gay lifestyle for many years. When you meet him, don't be alarmed by his transparency."

Mark sat back in his chair, hesitant about Earl's recommendation. *Why did Mark have to meet this Lester guy and listen to his story? Why couldn't Earl just give him advice like he always did?*

"I guess I can talk to him. How did you as a pastor deal with this issue?"

Earl nodded, sighing heavily. "I emphasized compassion. There were members in my congregation who were living that lifestyle. I never told them they were evil. I welcomed them, just like I did everyone else. However, I preached the word of God. Global Healing came and led seminars on how to effectively cope with family members who were living a gay lifestyle."

Mark listened as Earl gave a brief history of its origins, mentioning how its founder, Robert Cannon, had developed a sound, scientific method of sexual reorientation, one steeped in both personal experience and psychotherapeutic practices substantiated by several psychological governing bodies.

"Is this organization a Christian organization?" asked Mark.

A grimace appeared across Earl's face. "They're not." Earl seemed unfazed by something that made Mark naturally suspicious of Global Healing. Christ was the motivation for many of these sexual reorientation programs. How did Global Healing espouse change without professing Christ?

"Do they encourage participants to accept Christ?"

"They encourage their patients to believe in a higher power." Earl saw Mark's disapproval and quickly tried to placate his reservations. "Lester is a Christian. Robert

Cannon, the founder, is also a Christian. The majority of the people that come to them are Christians, but as you and I know, Orthodox Judaism, Islam, and many other religions also believe homosexuality is a sin. Global Healing wants to minister to those people as well."

Mark nodded, unconvinced. Earl went on to discuss how preaching a message of conversion was difficult but imperative to salvation.

Mark wrestled with another issue, Lester's supposed transparency. To speak about deliverance from sin was one thing. To go into graphic detail of that sin was a whole other thing. Was Mark able to quell his discomfort toward homosexual behavior to receive Lester's testimony? These were challenges he had to take to God. Mark peered out his office window. Louisa's parents were talking to her, smiling and seeming to enjoy themselves. Mark reflected back to a few hours ago when his father had ushered in the spirit of discord with his distasteful joke. At times, Mark wanted his father to open his heart to God. He wanted to talk to him about his faith and how Christ had changed him. He was beginning to relinquish these hopes for that kind of relationship. In many ways, Mark found that paternal bond with Earl, and he praised God for that every day.

"Mark, remind me where your bathroom is," Earl belched loudly as he got up.

Mark opened his office door and directed him down the hall. As Earl headed to the bathroom, Mark began to tidy up, understanding why Earl had to use the bathroom as he collected his emptied cup of punch. As Mark picked up a napkin that had fallen onto the floor, a phone vibrated from underneath the seat Earl in which Earl had been sitting. He picked up Earl's phone, deciding to let it go to voicemail. However, the phone rang moments later, the same name, *Heather*, flashing across Earl's screen.

"Hello?" Mark was greeted by a woman's sharp, impatient tone.

"Earl, you owe me money! We had a deal you sick fuck!"

"Who is this?" Mark asked.

"It's Heather. Stop playing dumb, and the next time I call, answer your phone!" The line disconnected as Earl walked back into Mark's office. Mark was stunned. *Why was a woman named Heather calling Earl? Why did he owe her money?*

"Earl, you dropped your phone when you got up to use the bathroom." He handed Earl's phone to him, the questions he had still dancing around in his mind. Earl voluntarily started answering Mark's question as he glanced at the missed call that had appeared on his screen. "Heather. She's this woman Agnes and I are helping through the Ruth and Naomi Project."

Mark grunted as he stood up. Earl chuckled nervously. Something seemed awry. *Why would this woman call Earl personally and demand money?* The Ruth and Naomi Project provided women who were survivors of domestic abuse with resources to help acquire independence. Something did not make sense.

"I did answer the phone, Earl." Earl's face reddened at Mark's revelation.
He did not want to accuse Earl of lying, although his story about Heather being a survivor
of domestic abuse seemed implausible. "What made you wanna help her personally?"
Earl sighed. "Guilt. For some reason, I saw something in her. There was this hurt,
this brokenness, and I knew I had to help her beyond what the center does."

"I feel bad for you, Earl because she was quite hostile when I answered. I pray she
learns how to show gratitude."

"Me too."

Mark listened as Earl rambled on about the disparities many of the women faced.
Earl's demeanor became oddly animated, a nervous energy exuding from his body.
Mark recognized that disposition. He had seen it countless times from his clients
during his tenure as a corporate lawyer. Whenever a CEO was trying to cover up
something or subvert their unsavory behaviors, they rattled off in the same manner.
What was Earl attempting to hide? Was it an affair? Was he being blackmailed?

"If this woman gives me a hard time, you'd help me out legally. Right?"

Mark suspended his cleaning and stared at Earl. Over the years, Mark had provided
legal counsel at a reduced rate to Earl, reviewing and negotiating many of Earl's
book contracts. His expertise in corporate law afforded him many opportunities
to represent some of the businessmen and women within the church. As his tongue
picked at a piece of pineapple lodged between his molars, he wondered if the scenarios
Mark had pictured correlated to Earl's request.

"Sure. Just, please don't do anything to jeopardize your church and all the work
you've done. Help this woman to the best of your ability. Don't put yourself or your
family in danger." Earl nodded as the two of them headed back to the party. Mark made
a mental note to reach out to Agnes and confirm Earl's story. Before heading outside,
Mark stopped in the kitchen and added Heather's number as a contact in his phone.

• • •

Jerry sat in a curled up position on his bedroom floor, the dark outlines of the
wooden floorboards fuzzy as he clutched his stomach. Two weeks and three days.
That was how long Jerry had lasted without binging and purging. He tried to stave
off this temptation by running, playing music, journaling, meditating. However, no
amount of sweat induced jogs or deep breathing or Bach inventions managed to keep
the painful memories he had buried at bay.

An empty bag of Doritos lay on the floor next to him. Jerry could still taste the
artificial cheddar cheese on his tongue, the myriad of processed ingredients lingering
in his system and making him sluggish. His insides hurt. His head spun. He thought
back to Carl's party, to the announcement of Mark's revelation to preach conversion
therapy to his church. He thought about Carl sitting on his bed, simultaneous feelings
of terror and tranquility apparent on his face. That was what coming out felt like,

euphoria coupled with angst. You were actualizing a part of yourself to the world while inviting rejection and condemnation. The profundity of these contradictory emotions was what made coming out so difficult. Jerry feared for Carl. He feared for Carl's ability to cope with the harsh realization that his parents would ultimately reject that part of him. Jerry understood what that rejection felt like and recalled the painful memory as if it were yesterday.

• • •

"Jerry, can we talk to you?" Jerry had come home one Saturday evening after catching a movie with Mel. He had remembered that the caramel taste from the ice cream he and Mel ordered after the movie still lingered on his tongue. Jerry had entered the living room, the gravelly voice of Billie Holiday saying good morning to heartache belting from the speakers of his dad's stereo. He had walked in on a familiar scene – his parents sitting in the living room, generally ignoring each other. He glanced over at his mom going through old photographs, a rare smile on her face. Percy sat on the other side of the room, laptop on his lap, muttering to himself as he typed what Jerry assumed was a work email. Even with the familiarity of the scene, Jerry had immediately sensed something was wrong.

"What's going on?" Jerry had watched his parents individually cease their respective activities, concerned expressions on both of their faces. *Did his parents know? Did they sneak into his room and read his texts? Did they know he was gay?*

"Eve Parsons called your father today, which was odd seeing as how she only calls him when there's an emergency at work." Harriet's explanation of Jerry's summons had been cut off by Percy's terse tone, Jerry watching his father's chin bouncing back and forth while he spoke.

"She saw you leaving from Our Lady of Good Counsel last week." Percy's eyes had narrowed toward Jerry as Jerry slowly realized one of his secrets was unraveling. He had taken the SAT for Leo last weekend at Our Lady of Good Counsel High School. Since it was on the other side of town, he had thought nobody would recognize him. Clearly, he had been wrong. Jerry had concealed his regret, a stone-cold expression appearing across his face. He had grown tired of Leo's constant pleas for assistance along with the promises of lifetime supplies of bourbon and marijuana. Harriet's insistence that Leo apply to at least five colleges had become a command once she threatened to kick him out of the house. And Jerry, who couldn't care less if Leo attended college or not, had enabled his brother's laziness by taking his SATs for him. Jerry had failed to realize he committed academic fraud until that deafening moment of silence in his parents' living room.

"And?" Jerry had challenged.

Percy's disposition had morphed into one of deep frustration and consternation. He had crossed his arms over his University of Maryland sweatshirt.

"Leo was taking the SATs last week at the same school. Your brother told us he didn't register in time to take the exam at your school, but we both know that was a lie." Harriet's soft tone was immediately rebuffed by Percy's brisk tone. "Harriet, Leo told us. Do you have to pussyfoot around this?" Percy had glared at Jerry, demanding a confession of his crimes.

"Leo doesn't even want to go to college. He wants to move to L.A. and do stand-up comedy, but both of you have been hell-bent on him applying to college. What school's gonna accept an applicant with a 1.7 GPA?" Jerry had countered his parents' accusations somewhat incredulously.

Percy had adjusted his posture to face Harriet, his wife glaring back at him ready to refute any criticism thrown her way. "So you decided to commit academic fraud and take your brother's SATs? Jerry, if NYU found out, your acceptance could be rescinded."

"I didn't get in."

Harriet's face had sunk as Percy's eyes widened, a tiny grin appearing across his face. "Found out last week."

"Well, MIT it is."

Jerry had turned toward his father in frustration. Although Percy had made it clear that being a writer was a one-way ticket to unemployment, he hoped he'd show an ounce of compassion when Jerry broke the news of his rejection.

"Percy, he could reapply." Harriet offered.

Percy's head had reclined backward as he groaned loudly. "Jerry, I'm sorry Leo pressured you into taking his SATs. I'm still having trouble understanding why you did it."

• • •

Jerry's mind jolted back to the present, the sound of water flowing from the bathroom faucet down the sink and traversing through the pipes drowning out the ringing in his ears. He shoved his pointer finger and middle finger down his throat, large chunks of orange-colored vomit plopping into the toilet. The acidity of each iteration of purging grew stronger. Jerry wondered if his teeth had already begun decaying as remnants of his vomit sank between his gums. He struggled to breathe as his throat burned.

The bathroom started spinning. Jerry grabbed both sides of the toilet, its circular exterior becoming hazy as stars appeared in front of his eyes. He steadied himself as he got up from the bathroom floor, turning the faucet off. Still feeling dizzy, Jerry collapsed onto the bathroom floor.

He woke up to find Leo standing over him. His throat still burned, the acidic taste lingering on his tongue. Leo grabbed Jerry's arms and pulled him up.

"Hey, man. Are you okay? What did you do?" Leo placed his hands across Jerry's face, their warmth making Jerry squirm.

"What do you think?" Jerry slurred, still groggy. "What the fuck do you think?"

Leo helped Jerry back into his bedroom and slowly placed his feet into his bed. The evidence of his bulimia was scattered across his floor: empty bags of chips and pretzels. Jerry hadn't eaten his entire stash. The rest of the food was stowed away underneath the loose floorboard. Leo's silhouette scurried around Jerry's room. For once, Leo was cleaning up Jerry's mess.

• • •

As Jerry sat there watching Leo pick up the evidence of his most recent binge and purge, he thought about what had triggered this latest purge. It had been a memory of a conversation that had happened with his parents almost a year prior.

"What is going on, Jerry? You've been so secretive. Every time I come into your room, you close your laptop or tuck away your phone. Are you binging and purging? Do you need to adjust your antidepressants?" his mother had implored.

Jerry couldn't believe she had dared to inquire about his mental health while she walked around the house in a fog for most of the day.

"No. It's not that."

"Then what is it?" Percy had chimed in, obviously growing increasingly irritated.

"I'm gay." The admission was met with a brief, but ominous silence.

"Are you sure?" was all Percy could muster.

Harriet had nodded affirmatively as she walked over to hug her son, "I've known, honey. I've known. It's okay."

Percy had remained stoic and transfixed as he sat in his black recliner. "The hell it is."

"Percy, he's our son. This is who he is. It's who he's always been!"

"I don't believe that!"

Harriet had laughed as she marched over to Percy, who hadn't even been able to look at Jerry. His gaze had minimized to his laptop screen, which he hid behind.

"He has a poster of "Sex and the City" in his bedroom, a poster he asked for when he was twelve."

"So that automatically makes him gay?! Harriet, look at Jerry."

Harriet had turned to face her son. Percy had finally sat up, meeting Jerry's frightened gaze. There had been disappointment in Percy's eyes. Jerry had vanquished Percy's dreams, universal dreams every father secretly has for his son. Jerry had also seen Percy's desperate attempt to cling to them. "When the world sees him, they see a black man. The odds are already against him, and now you add this? Harriet, your white privilege is not gonna bail him out for the rest of his life."

"Percy, do you hear yourself? You sound like a lunatic."

"I did not choose this! I did not choose to wake up every morning with a raging hard-on for Justin Timberlake! Being gay is not a choice."

"But accepting it is. And I don't accept this. I don't."

7

BEAUTIFUL MESS

Harriet awoke from the recurring dream she had had for the past five years. The dream started in the same fashion: Ella was getting ready for school, brushing her hair in front of her bedroom mirror, sunlight hitting her face as she buttoned her maroon blazer. She always posed in a glamorous fashion before grabbing her backpack, puckering her lips, and arching her back. Harriet always walked by her room, urging her to get downstairs and eat her breakfast. Ella looked so ethereal in these dreams. She was happy and carefree and fourteen, the epitome of poise. She was also a manifestation of Harriet's grief.

In her four years of therapy, Harriet had never disclosed the details surrounding Ella's death. Dr. Rowan had probably googled Ella's name, reading through the countless articles describing the accident that took Ella's life. Harriet had read them all, and if she were honest, she did everything she could to push these details out of her mind, unable to actualize the fateful circumstances, unable to accept that her daughter had died in such a horrific manner.

Harriet sauntered into the bathroom, examining her frazzled red hair in desperate need of combing. The edges were frayed, specks of gray appearing by her temples. She scrutinized the bathroom sink, tiny drops of toothpaste and dried up mouthwash affixed at the bottom of the marble washbasin. Camilla, the housekeeper, wasn't scheduled to come until Thursday. She'd have to endure the unsightly strands of hair scattered around the sink and toothpaste stains for another two days.

Before Ella died, Harriet had prided herself on being a self-sufficient socialite. She had had a rewarding career as the vice principal of Shady Grove Elementary. She had cooked her own meals. But those days of running from board meetings to piano lessons to soccer practice in rush hour traffic had become distant memories. She had been unable to return to those busy days of ordinary bliss.

The creak of the front door startled Harriet as she brushed her teeth. Afraid that someone might be breaking into her home, she quickly rinsed her mouth and grabbed her robe at the foot of the bed. Percy's voice reverberated through the house, up to the top of the stairs where Harriet stood. He was talking to someone in a terse tone, growing more agitated with each question he answered.

"No, mom. I didn't piss anyone off." Percy stood in the foyer, his white dress shirt untucked as he adjusted his cellphone. He walked into the living room and sat down. "What do you mean, I rub people the wrong way? I was fired because my job performance was supposedly subpar."

Harriet tied her bathrobe while holding onto the banister. A stark realization hit her – the two of them were going to be alone all day. A chill went down her spine.

"Greg came into my office and said he needed to talk. The next thing I know, the HR rep, Cody, comes sauntering in with a huge binder and a smug look on his face."

Harriet heard the hollow sound of glass being slammed into her favorite coffee table, which had been a wedding present from her father, who Percy abhorred. Maybe that's why this particular piece of furniture often seemed to be the victim of Percy's anger. She made a mental note that she'd have to have Camilla polish it when she came to clean. Harriet slowly descended the stairs, each one creaking louder than the last as she overheard a litany of sighs and grunts. Percy's mother, Krystal, had the unique gift of being able to probe you during the most vulnerable moments in your life.

Percy glanced up from his phone and saw Harriet standing at the foot of the stairs. "Mom, I'll call you back." He hung up the phone, his dark brown eyes both intense and impaired. Harriet took a seat in Percy's black recliner, a deafening silence ensuing between them. Percy turned on the television and started flipping through channels, settling on a news program on CNN, and unbuttoning his shirt. Harriet suffered through several sighs and grunts before mustering the courage to have a conversation with her husband, something she rarely seemed to have the energy for these days.

"Percy, can you please turn off the TV?"

Percy forcefully pressed the *mute* button on the remote before turning to face his wife. "You're up before noon. That's a first."

Percy's confrontational disposition made Harriet want to walk away and leave Percy to wallow in his own self-pity. Maybe he wallowed like this often. Harriet couldn't be sure because they barely talked at all these days, let alone about their feelings. She had long ago stopped explaining her grief to Percy because, at some point, he had stopped listening. They merely coexisted in hollow spaces and awkward silences.

"Did they give you a severance package?"

Percy nodded.

"How much?"

"What does it matter, Harriet? My income's insignificant."

Harriet had no intention of picking a fight with Percy. Shaking her head, she stared at the mahogany grandfather clock. 11:30 was the time. Harriet was not going to make her noon appointment with Dr. Rowan. She grabbed the house phone next to the recliner and dialed his number. Percy turned the volume up on the TV as the reporter's animated tone provided a welcome reprieve from the silent gulf between husband and wife. Expecting to hear her therapist's voicemail message on the other end, Harriet was surprised when Dr. Rowan answered.

"Hello? Dr. Rowan speaking."

Harriet cleared her throat. "Hi, it's Harriet. Sorry for the late notice, but I can't come in. Family emergency."

"I'm sorry. Everything okay?"

"Yes." Harriet feigned a cheerful tone. "We can talk about it next week."

"Okay. Talk to you then."

The line disconnected as Harriet surveyed the living room. Percy's languid figure lounging there made the room seem a lot smaller than it actually was. She rested her eyes on a family photo above Percy. Harriet, Percy, Jerry, Leo, and Ella were smiling broadly, with Mickey Mouse situated right in the middle of the happy family. The vacation to Disney World was one Harriet had spent a year planning. A sharp tinge in Harriet's chest grew more intense the longer Harriet stared at the photo and became almost unmanageable as she rested on her daughter's wide-eyed smile, her two front teeth missing.

"Remember Disney World?"

Percy glanced up and briefly stared at Harriet.

He didn't respond.

"Ella begged us to get a picture with Mickey Mouse. She woke us up at five in the morning, jumping up and down on our bed. She always had so much energy. It..."

Percy finally spoke. "She's dead Harriet. Been dead for five years." With that, he turned his attention back to CNN.

Harriet was trying to get Percy to engage with her, but clearly, he had no intention of doing that. "I know," was all she could muster in reply. Harriet felt like she was about to snap. She shouldn't have been surprised by Percy's response, but something about his words today broke something in her. Percy had avoided talking about their daughter for as long as she could remember. He had wanted to donate her toys a week after the funeral, much to Harriet's objection. Now, only Camilla set foot in Ella's room when she cleaned it. Maybe Harriet needed to discuss this with her therapist next week.

"There are other jobs, Percy. OEI demanded too much of you," she attempted a change in the conversation.

Percy shook his head ruefully, intent on spending the remainder of the day on the couch, ignoring Harriet as much as possible. Harriet gave up. As she began to head upstairs, she overheard Leo shouting in his bedroom. A putrid odor greeted her as she knocked on the ajar door. In situations such as this one, Harriet was eternally grateful for Camilla. She was thankful that Camilla picked up Leo's dirty underwear, dusted his filthy shelves, and discarded the various marijuana paraphernalia scattered on his floor. Leo remained transfixed on his game as a loud explosion erupted from the screen. Harriet peered over Leo's shoulder and caught a glimpse of a convenient store catching fire. Leo's avatar, a man in a black t-shirt, ran from the store and pulled out a gun from his jeans' back pocket. He began shooting at a female assailant who started throwing explosive devices in the man's direction. Harriet found this game unnecessarily violent.

"Hey, mom. What's up?" Leo's fingers dashed from his controller, swearing loudly as his avatar shot his female nemesis in the chest. Blood came spewing from her body as she collapsed onto the pavement.

"So I know you're taking a year off, but I hope you're not planning on spending it playing video games all day."

Leo grunted a response to Harriet's observation. "I was thinking of going out to L.A. for a while, maybe get a few stand-up comedy gigs. Deanne and her folks are heading out there in a month. Thought I'd tag along."

Harriet forced herself to examine Leo's room, the haphazard manner in which clothes were thrown on the floor, half-eaten bags of potato chips and Jolly Ranchers sitting on the window pane. *How did she fail Leo as a mother? How did twelve years of private school translate into Leo's aimless meandering through life?*

"Leo, look at me." Still getting no response, she marched over and turned off Leo's monitor.

"What the fuck?!"

"Language! You need a real job where you have to show up and contribute something. Stand-up comedy is not gonna cut it. I am not paying for you to go to L.A. Jerry is starting an internship at MIT next week. I just wish you'd show half the initiative he shows." Leo snorted loudly.

"Jerry's not interning at MIT."

"What?"

"Nothing. I...nothing." Leo quickly got up from his unmade bed, the blue comforter littered with food stains. He dashed into the bathroom, the door slamming in the distance.

Why did Leo blurt that out? What was Jerry hiding? Harriet was confused. *Did she even understand anyone in her family anymore?*

Feeling at a loss, Harriet decided to investigate Jerry's behavior in the old fashioned way: snooping. She cracked open his door and slowly entered into her son's bedroom. Exhaling sharply, she caught whiffs of cologne and forest scented shampoo. His bedroom was tidy, almost too neat. He had rearranged his old textbooks from high school atop his desk. Perched neatly in the middle of his desk was his laptop. Harriet opened it. It was, of course, locked with a password she didn't know.

Harriet's behavior made her unrecognizable even to herself. She had never been the kind of parent who read her children's emails or texts. She had taken pride in not getting a Facebook account like many of the other mothers she knew who only wanted to monitor their children's social media activity. But things felt different now. Her family felt so out of control. And she knew Jerry was hiding something. She needed to find out what it was.

Harriet listened as Leo resumed playing his video game in his bedroom. Typing frantically, Harriet groaned when Jerry's computer screen notified her that her password attempts were incorrect. Deciding to follow her intuition that maybe Jerry's secret wasn't hidden on his computer at all, but rather right in his bedroom, she closed his laptop and began almost frantically rustling through his things. Harriet started in his closet. She wiped away dust as she dug out the large suitcase that he had taken to college and threw it on Jerry's bed. She started going through the outside pockets. Nothing. She moved onto the inside compartments, her hands grazing a crumpled piece of yellow paper. Harriet reached down into the bottom of the suitcase and pulled it out.

"Eviction Notice – 410 West 56th Street, Unit 1." As she continued to read the eviction notice, she tried to make sense of what she was reading. *New York City? MIT wasn't even IN New York.* Harriet sat on the bed, a tear trickling down her cheek.

Examining the notice, its bold black font grating on the eyes, Harriet rested her head on Jerry's pillow. She began to sob more heavily, tears flowing down her cheek as she let the eviction notice slip onto the floor. Jerry had made a life-altering decision and told no one. *What in the hell was happening to her family? How could Harriet have allowed this to happen?* Drying her eyes, Harriet dug herself up off the bed and restored Jerry's room to the condition in which she found it, adjusting the angle of the laptop and putting Jerry's suitcase back into his closet. She decided not to confront Jerry about his sudden move to New York. She wanted Jerry to feel safe at home. Harriet was disappointed in her son's decision to drop out of college, but she was more disappointed that he chose not to confide in her.

Both of Harriet's sons needed different things from her. She opened Leo's door as his focus remained on the game he was playing. "I'm giving you a week to find a job." Leo looked up from his video game, a horrified expression on his face. Harriet smirked. "You don't wanna know what'll happen if you're still unemployed after next week." Harriet turned and walked away. She did not raise her voice. She did not justify her demand. Leo needed a reality check, and Harriet had to give it to him. Jerry needed a safety net, a place where he could work toward his passion without fear of reproach.

Harriet intended to provide that to him as well. For the first time in as long as she could remember, she felt empowered.

• • •

The consequences of passing out on the bathroom floor manifested themselves in a gnawing stiffness around his neck. Jerry massaged it, rotating his head around in a slow circular fashion while ignoring the sharp abdominal pains that pierced through him. It had been six months since he binged and purged before this latest streak he was on, and so it was only natural that his body's tolerance for the pain was reasonably low. The acidic taste in his mouth lingered, despite having brushed his teeth and gargling with mouthwash three times in a row. Jerry sat across the street from Justice For All, his eyes widening as he saw the rainbow-colored logo of Rainbow Warriors next to Justice For All. His pain lessened as he shifted his focus to the thought that he and Mel could possibly be working next door to each other.

Jerry had submitted an application for a field reporter at Rainbow Warriors a week ago, the requested writing sample a journal entry in which he described an experience he never shared with anyone. He wondered if he would ever be able to talk about what happened to him a year ago. There was so much shame, so much confusion. Thinking about it made the acidic aftertaste in Jerry's mouth even more potent.

Mel texted Jerry her order – a cobb salad with bleu cheese dressing on the side – followed by two subsequent texts in rapid succession: one thanking him in advance for ordering her food, and the other assuring him she would be there in five minutes.

"Ready to order?" A young man wearing a distasteful lime green polo shirt approached his table. His name, Troy, was embroidered onto the right-hand side of the shirt.

"Sir?" Troy had his notepad and blue ink pen ready to take Jerry's order.

Jerry snapped out of his daze. "Two cobb salads. One with Italian dressing and the other with bleu cheese dressing."

Troy wrote down the order.

"And can you bring out two waters with lime?"

Troy nodded as he walked away. Mel hurried across the street, her purple blouse neatly tucked into her black dress pants. She waved as she instructed the hostess that she was with Jerry.

"Sorry, I'm late." Jerry got up and hugged her, strands of her hair lightly tickling Jerry's face.

"Not a problem. I just ordered."

Mel examined Jerry's appearance as she took her seat. Her features hardened. Jerry chastised himself for not wearing sunglasses as he saw the reflection of his bloodshot eyes staring back at him on his phone's screen.

"Your eyes are red."

"Allergies," he lied. "Have you seen the weather? The pollen count is through the roof." Mel took out her phone and typed in her passcode to unlock it, not responding to his observation. Throughout their years of friendship, Mel avoided the frivolity of idle conversation when an issue surfaced. It was what made her a good friend.

"I applied to Rainbow Warriors as a field reporter." Mel scrutinized Jerry, his avoidance transparent. "I binged and purged. I got dizzy and passed out on the bathroom floor. Leo found me."

Mel brushed a strand of hair away from her face and extended her hand onto the table. Jerry took it as Troy brought out their salads and water. Jerry's eyes fixated on the composition of the salad in front of him – the avocados, chicken, tomatoes, and hard-boiled eggs were lined up neatly down the middle of the bowl, the rainbow-colored display making him feel like he was looking at more of an art sculpture than a meal. Mel took conservative bites of her salad, pouring bleu cheese dressing over it while mixing everything together. Jerry was in no mood to discuss what had triggered him to binge and purge. He was never in the mood to explain what had triggered him.

"What happened?" Mel's bites became larger as Jerry sat across from Mel in silence.

What had happened? So many things had happened. He honestly didn't know where to begin.

"What do you mean?" Jerry knew what she meant, shrugging as he took small bites of his salad. His throat was still sore and demanded several gulps of water to quell its pain. As Jerry picked at his salad, the avocados piqued his interest. It was as if he had seen them before in a painting, in the same half-moon configuration in which they were sliced. He remembered a photograph in a waiting room a year ago. Below it read a caption: *Mind. Body. Spirit.* There were four photos: a strange vegetable medley juxtaposed with the silhouette of two bowed heads and clasped hands, a man and a woman exercising, and a woman meditating on a pink yoga mat. *Mind. Body. Spirit.* Its bold letters glared back at him as he had entered into the waiting room of Global Healing from Homosexuality. Jerry immediately started stabbing the avocados, each piece becoming tinier as he applied the same ferocity to the chicken and the tomatoes and the hardboiled eggs.

"Whose bright...idea...was...it?" Jerry forcefully pushed the salad away from him as Mel stared at him in horror. Jerry had inadvertently spilled some of his water on the table and had knocked his phone onto the ground. He bent over and picked it up, the pain in his abdomen searing.

"Jerry?"

He was shaking as Mel rushed over to him, placing her arms around him and bringing him in for an embrace. "It's okay. It's gonna be okay." Jerry wanted to believe Mel, but all he could think about was the uneaten food buried underneath the floorboard in his bedroom. A few patrons had turned their eyes toward the two of them. Jerry paid them no mind. They didn't understand what he was going through.

He didn't even understand what he was going through. Mel released her embrace and sat back down in her seat.

"So, tell me more about the position you applied for at Rainbow Warriors."

Jerry started talking, slowing forming sentences, gradually returning to his present state. A notification appeared on his phone. It was an email from Rainbow Warriors. The editor-in-chief, Brandon Weaver, wanted to meet Jerry over drinks next week.

To change the subject, Mel brought up the recent case she had been assigned at Justice For All. It was about a medical student whose DACA status was in jeopardy due to a prior misdemeanor offense of prostitution. The three-year-old case had been connected to a larger federal case against a hedge fund mogul, Silas Greene and his business partner, Jacquelyn Metz, both of whom had orchestrated an elite, underground sex trafficking business. The prosecutor had offered Alma the misdemeanor charge in exchange for her testimony against Silas and Jacquelyn. Mel explained in great detail how the case had unfolded. Apparently, Jacquelyn had mysteriously vanished the day before the warrant was issued for her arrest.

Jerry absorbed Mel's excitement about her new internship, trying to conjure up that same excitement about his potential job with Rainbow Warriors. They both wanted to affect positive change in the world. Fat paychecks didn't entice them. Amid all the chaos in Jerry's life, he was grateful to have a best friend who got him. He relished each laugh and wistful recollection of their old high-school days as they struggled not to choke on their food while bringing up those humorous moments of their adolescence. Jerry wished he could turn back the clock to those days, but knew that these wishes were futile. He was in the present, in all its ugliness and uncomfortable realities. Through it all, he was lucky to have Mel by his side.

8

SPEAK TO MY HEART

Wednesday night choir rehearsal immediately followed Bible study. The sanctuary quickly emptied after Bible study ended, many attendees gathering their purses and bright red Bible cases.

"Carl?" Kevin had begun playing the introduction to "Speak to My Heart" on the keyboard, a new song the choir had decided to sing. Carl stood in front of the microphone, the seven choir members behind him harmonizing over Kevin's introduction. Grabbing the top of the microphone, he shakily sang the first verse. The detachment in his voice was apparent. Donnie McClurkin had sung it with strong conviction. He believed every word, yearned for the Holy Spirit to send His message of love to encourage him. Carl wasn't sure he believed that. Regardless, he muddled through the rest of the song, adding superficial runs toward the bridge, lifting his hands in an expected display of praise to God. Kevin played the ending, the sanctuary silent, the brown pews empty, Carl empty.

"What's next?" Carl asked, his voice hoarse.

Candace, one of the members, handed him the list of slated songs. He had to suffer through four more songs, none of which he had a solo. He thankfully took his place among the two tenors. Niles, one of the newest choir members, seemed on the verge of tears while the choir sang "Total Praise," his obscenely large sweat stains under his armpits unsettling to Carl. *Did he have to extend his hands during every song? What toothpaste did he use?* Carl refrained from holding out notes when Niles' breath spewed in his direction.

Carl gathered his Bible, relieved that choir rehearsal had ended. He traced the golden embroidered letters on its cover, scrutinizing the pages he had marked, the verses he didn't quite understand, the questions he never asked. Candace approached Carl as he checked his pockets for his keys, relieved when he heard them jangling in the pocket by his knee. Candace cleared her throat, brushing her blond hair back as she stood before Carl.

"Hey," Candace's eyes roamed to Carl's torso. He glanced down at his white polo shirt, wondering if he had unknowingly spilled food on it. Candace's eyes traveled to his legs and back up to his face.

"Hey. Sounded good." The two stood there silently.

"You sounded great," she sputtered. "I've never heard "Speak to My Heart" sung with such conviction."

Was Candace playing some cruel joke? Carl tried to detect any condescension in her tone but found nothing of the sort. Instead of trying to figure it out, he proceeded to head toward the double doors. "See you on Sunday," he tried to sound as breezy as possible.

"Would you like to hang out? Maybe outside of church? Do you like bowling? We can do that?"

Carl turned around, his bemusement apparent. He forced a smile as his heart started racing. "I've got a lot on my plate, and with me starting school in the fall. Uh." His voice trailed off while Candace nodded her head earnestly, her disappointment apparent.

"Yeah. You're right. I didn't even consider that. Sorry to waste your time."

Not knowing what to say, he just smiled, turned, and headed out the door toward his father's office. Carl wasn't surprised to find that his father wasn't alone. Don, the assistant pastor, was seated in a chair across from his dad's desk, looking a little bit too at home in the head pastor's space.

"Hey, Carl." Mark's excited expression made Carl flinch, his eyes roaming to a pamphlet on Mark's desk, Global Healing from Homosexuality. The pamphlet's sky blue background with a Caucasian man and an African American woman embracing one another appeared inexplicably contrived with their eerily white teeth and plastered smiles.

"Your dad and I were just talking about this organization." Don grabbed the pamphlet from Mark's desk, adjusting his black-rimmed glasses to read the overview of the organization. "Restoring the innate heterosexuality in all men and women by addressing the true physical, mental, emotional, and spiritual causes of homosexuality." Don cleared his throat, nodding his approval toward Mark as Mark sat back in his chair. Carl remained silent.

"This was part of your revelation?" Mark nodded in response to Carl's question.

"These people are trained in approaching homosexuality with the compassion it deserves. I'm gonna talk about this on Sunday. Don agrees that we as a church should start explicitly welcoming LGBT people. And slowly, we can show them there's hope for change."

Carl stood in front of his father, his arms at his side. He was exhausted. Being raised in church made him accustomed to the insatiable need for spiritual acuity. However, this issue ushered in unfathomable uncertainty, fear, and pain. These were things God had not given His people. He gave His people power through His love, power through His joy, power through hope of everlasting life. Now, he was implicitly being told that homosexuality was antithetical to the assurances God had given. The pamphlet, with its serene blue background, promised freedom from those desires. But Carl had this sickening feeling about that freedom. While it might have been dressed up in photoshopped smiles and happy babies, its definition was untenable, its price deadly.

"Guys, I'm exhausted. I don't know about you, but I'm heading home. Don, can you lock up?"

"Of course, Mark."

Mark yawned loudly while getting up from his desk. He retrieved the pamphlet as he headed toward the door. As Mark's footsteps echoed down the hall, Carl prepared to leave. Don stopped him.

"Hey. Something going on?" Don had gently grabbed Carl's hand. He turned around, shrugging. A lot of things were going on, things he had no intention of sharing with Don.

"No. Everything's fine."

"You can talk to me if something's not." Carl shook his head, grabbing his keys out of his pocket and heading for the parking lot.

"Mark sprung this on me," Don blurted out. "I'm worried, and I can see you're worried too."

"You have nothing to worry about Don. You're a straight, married man with a son." His phone vibrated in his pocket. It was Leo. "See you Sunday."

Carl answered the phone as he walked down the empty hallway, passing the statue of the outstretched arms of Jesus on his way out. Jesus' blue and white robe strangely projected itself onto people who passed by it. Maybe Carl was seeing things.

"Dude, I can so use a drink right now. Where are you?"

"At church." The weak signal on Carl's phone kept distorting Leo's voice on the other end of the receiver. Standing underneath the canopy, he listened as Leo complained about having to get a summer job, a complaint that apparently warranted getting drunk on a Wednesday.

"Can you swing by and get me? I'm at the liquor store on Hampden."

When Carl arrived at the corner of the liquor store, Leo animatedly waved at him and nearly trampled over a homeless man as he swung open the car door and got in. Carl needed a distraction. What better one than rum and coke? Leo unveiled the bottle of Don Q Cristal from the brown paper bag, digging around the contents of a second plastic bag and unearthing two bottles of Coca-Cola. Carl slowly drove down the street, finding a parking lot with a Shoppers grocery store. Carl's eyes landed on a husband and wife carrying their shopping cart to their Subaru SUV, chatting animatedly with one another. Carl peered out of his rearview mirror and caught a final glimpse of the wife leaning into her husband, her blond hair bouncing as she laughed. A lump materialized in Carl's throat as he pulled into an isolated parking spot at the back of the lot. For the first time, Carl paid attention to Leo's business casual attire: a blue dress shirt and black slacks, the rolled-up sleeves revealing his well-defined biceps Carl found enticing. Leo sighed heavily as he untucked his shirt, his torso briefly appearing as he straightened out the edges. A tightness around Carl's crotch began to form.

Leo stealthily opened a bottle of coke, its contents rising to the top. Carl grabbed the bottle from Leo and quickly slurped the spilled liquid. Leo chuckled.

"Drink a quarter of it, then I'll pour some rum in." Carl took large swigs as he caught one final glance of the couple driving away in their Subaru SUV toward Norman Rockwell bliss. Carl passed the bottle to Leo and watched as Leo carefully poured in the rum.

"Not too much. I still have to drive home."

Leo stopped pouring and handed Carl back his bottle. Carl savored the burning sensation of the rum, the heaviness he was feeling slowing melting away. Leo took the other bottle of coke and fixed himself a drink. His curly hair fell over his face as he coughed in between swigs.

"Do you believe in heaven?" It was a question Carl never asked anyone, not even himself.

Leo chuckled as he wiped his mouth with his shirt sleeve. His grin faded when he saw Carl's stone-cold face, "You're asking the wrong person."

Carl turned off the engine and reclined his seat. The blue pamphlet was still etched in his mind, their smiling faces all part of the façade. *Heal the emotional wounds in which your same-sex attractions are rooted, and you too can have everlasting life.* Carl took another sip of his rum and coke.

"I hope heaven doesn't exist," Carl mused. *But do I want to believe that?* he wondered.

He had been raised to believe that the life you had on Earth prepared you for the life you were going to have in heaven. The only prerequisite for entering heaven was that you had to profess Christ. You had to commit to living a life that was pleasing to Christ. When Carl was a child, this sounded simple. When he entered adulthood, it seemed absurd. "I just hope we find some kind of peace after this life. No heaven. No hell."

"I can drink to that." As Leo took another swig of his rum and coke, Carl closed his eyes. He envisioned a life in which he was at peace as a gay man. He dreamt of the fabulous gay wedding his mother would plan enthusiastically and his father would officiate, the "Love is Love" logo strategically included in every party gift and decoration. He mentally constructed a rustic brick house in an idyllic suburban neighborhood with a spacious backyard. He pictured his husband, a humble man with dark brown hair who had many siblings with whom Carl pretended to like because they were all opinionated and loud and quirky. Maybe he was a project manager or an accountant. He wasn't pursuing music as a career. Maybe his husband was a teacher. Perhaps he needed to open his eyes.

"Dude, your parents will come around. All parents do."

The statement divorced Carl from his utopian fantasy. Leo was already drunk. "I mean my dad's still weird about Jerry being gay, but my mom's cool with it."

"Leo, my situation is different." From what Carl knew about Jerry's coming out, there was a brief period of tension, but eventually, his parents were accepting.

"Jerry binged and purged last night. I found him passed out on the bathroom floor." Carl sat up as Leo turned to face him. Jerry's bulimia wasn't a subject he and Carl discussed. However, Carl wanted to know what had triggered the relapse.

"He was doing it before he left for college."

Carl examined Leo's forlorn glance. His carefree disposition was gone, his brown eyes registering a sorrow Carl had not seen before. Carl misspoke. Something had occurred after Jerry came out. A tear trickled down Carl's cheek. Another tear followed. Before he knew it, Carl was crying. Leo examined Carl, clumsily placing an arm around his shoulder.

"Hey, man. Don't cry. Jerry will get past this. He always does. And you'll be fine too." Carl cried for Jerry, for himself, for that quintessential suburban life he'd never have.

"And if your parents kick you out, you can always crash at my house." Leo wrapped his arm around Carl, strands of his curly hair tickling his face. Carl felt Leo's bicep dig into his neck. At that moment, he felt a rush of euphoria, a combination of arousal and kinship. Carl leaned into Leo and placed his hands around his warm face, kissing him softly on the lips. And then, the euphoria vanished. Carl had kissed his straight best friend. He sobbed into Leo's chest.

"It's okay. It's okay."

Carl wanted to believe it was okay, that being gay was acceptable, that God did not view it as a sin, that there was nothing wrong with him. He continued to sob into Leo's chest, tasting the salt in his tears.

• • •

When God placed a sermon on your heart, Satan often put obstacles in your path to preclude you from delivering it. This week, Big Jim was Mark's obstacle, who showed up at his door at 1 AM, drunk and incoherent. During a raucous night of bottomless tequila shots in Rehoboth Beach, Big Jim explained through slurred, barely decipherable sentences that he had misplaced his wallet and cellphone. Mark didn't care about the details, and couldn't help but be irritated as he sat his father down at the kitchen table and poured him a glass of water. Mark said they needed to cancel all of Jim's credit cards immediately, but of course, Big Jim couldn't even remember his social security number, let alone the banks that held his credit cards. Not knowing what else to do, Mark drove Big Jim home and spent the next hour combing through his files to find his father's social security card. It took another two hours after that to make all the phone calls needed to cancel his seven credit cards while reminding him of the perils of irresponsible alcohol consumption.

Big Jim had countered these reminders with a memorable evening in Mark's youth. "You mighta found Jesus, but I remember when your friends threw your drunk ass onto our front yard 30-some years ago. Don't remember waking up on the front lawn covered in puke, do ya?"

Mark cut the conversation short with his non-response, craving sleep over another pointless argument with his drunk father. By the time he got home, the sun was already starting to peek above the treetops. *Ugh*, he thought, as he flopped back into bed. *So much for a good night's sleep!*

It was now nine in the morning, two hours before the service was to begin. Mark meditated on Romans 1:26-28, and the corresponding message God had given him to preach. He prayed that his intentions were pure and that they did not condemn nor alienate anyone struggling with homosexuality. As he tried to quiet his spirit, Satan attacked. The woman on the other end of Earl's phone came into his mind, her brash tone permeating the very depths of his soul. Taking out his phone, he dialed her number. The call went straight to voicemail, and Mark left a detailed message offering his assistance. If Heather were truly destitute, she would accept his help. He finished up the message just as he heard the gentle knock on his door.

He looked up to see his wife standing there with a man Mark had never seen. Dressed in a dark violet shirt and black necktie, the man's bald head shimmered against the fluorescent light, and his thick eyebrows raised noticeably as he roamed Mark's office with his large brown eyes.

"Honey, this Lester Dawson. He wanted to visit us."

Mark rose, extending his hand toward Lester. Lester shook it firmly as Earl appeared in the doorway.

"Thank you, Louisa. Why don't you stay and join us?" Mark needed his wife's calming presence in the face of this potentially awkward meeting.

She placed her hand over her heart, apologetically. "Unfortunately, I'm teaching Sunday School today. But if you need me, just text."

She made her way out into the hallway as Earl began explaining to Mark the reason for Lester's visit. Already gowned in his green bishop's robe, Earl stealthily lowered himself into Mark's chair. Mark was shocked and somewhat displeased by Earl's disregard for ecclesiastical protocol. Earl was aware that pastors were expected to spend an hour in prayer before church started. No interruptions or unannounced visitors were allowed unless it was a real emergency. Earl had instilled this practice into

Mark; the transformative power of the Holy Spirit often delivered an entirely different sermon during that hour of prayer. Whatever the purpose of Lester's visit, Mark didn't think it classified as an emergency.

Mark noticed Lester's frequent shifting of his posture, crossing and uncrossing his ankles. *Did he think crossed ankles classified as effeminate behavior?* Mark couldn't help but wonder.

"Mark, please forgive me in advance. I begged Earl to let me speak with you this morning."

Mark sat back in his chair, asking God to forgive him for not spending time in prayer before church. Lester continued his explanation, his voice rising in pitch as he talked, modulating with each sentence about the life-changing work Global Healing was doing.

"Earl told me the work you've done, and I'm impressed by what I've heard," Mark remembered reading a particular statistic on Global Healing's website. The program had boasted an 87% success rate. Mark found that hard to fathom and had to admit that he was a little intrigued, but even so, he didn't think a sales pitch on Global Healing warranted an interruption of morning prayers.

"Global Healing has seen its support decline over the past three years."

Mark was genuinely bemused by Lester's revelation, "You have an eighty-seven percent success rate. Why the decline in support?"

"The mainstream media has vilified good people like Lester," Earl jumped in. "This man is doing God's work, and the world is out to get him."

Mark could understand that. When God called you to serve Him, Satan used the world as a weapon to attack you.

"Our current patients are experiencing change, and as a result, beginning the transition into healthy, heterosexual marriages. Our main problem is that we can't attract new patients," Lester continued.

Mark sat back, the encompassing presence of the Holy Spirit pouring over him. Mark knew what had to be done. Lester needed to give his testimony during today's service. "Lester, no pressure, but how would you feel about to giving your testimony during the sermon?"

Earl and Mark turned their attention to Lester, his composure oddly relaxing as he humbly accepted Mark's call, knowing it was from the Holy Spirit. Mark led the men in prayer, its effusive nature causing tears to stream down his face as he praised God for revealing Himself again in the least expected way.

The choir's final song ushered in the Holy Spirit, as Mark proudly watched as his son surrendered to the spirit during the bridge of "Speak to My Heart." Many members were in tears, their hands lifted in exaltation as Carl belted out the end of the song. He had never seen his son so immersed in worship before. Mark fought back tears as he took the podium, resting his hands on both sides and adjusting the microphone before addressing the congregation.

"Speak to my heart. We, as the body of Christ, need the Holy Spirit to speak to us." The congregation responded with a resounding *Amen*. Mark opened his Bible to Romans 1:26-28, instructing his congregation to turn to those two scriptures. He read the passages slowly, pausing at every comma and stopping at every period. The Holy Spirit spoke during those pauses. "Let us pray. God in heaven, we thank you for the word you are about to deliver. Let us be a vessel through which you are glorified. Purify our hearts so that we may receive you. In the name of Jesus, we pray. *Amen*." The congregation responded with that same resounding Amen as Mark slowly began his sermon.

"When this scripture was placed on my heart, it challenged me. These verses clearly condemn homosexual behavior, but I felt as if God didn't want me to preach condemnation. He wanted me to preach hope, compassion, and understanding." Mark proceeded to discuss how divisive homosexuality was in the church. He postulated that the side who celebrated homosexuality through same-sex marriages and the ordination of openly gay and lesbian ministers blindly accepted homosexuality without understanding it. Conversely, Mark proposed that the side that outright condemned homosexuality through hateful speeches willfully ignored it, which in turn affected an entire population of wounded people.

"I am no expert on this. However, we have a visitor who is. He lived a gay lifestyle for years, and through Christ, he was given the tools to change his sexual orientation. Ladies and gentlemen, I'd like to welcome Lester Dawson, a man I just met today, but a man I now consider a brother in Christ."

Lester approached the pulpit, hands quivering slightly. Mark noticed how Lester's quiver diminished as he spoke with a conviction indicative of a close walk with Christ, his once high-pitched tone lowering several octaves, evocative of someone who was an expert in this complex issue. Lester began with a harrowing description of his sexual abuse at the hands of his childhood next-door neighbor. As Lester's voice broke, Mark tasted his tears.

"My next-door neighbor was like a second dad to me, and I trusted him. So when he started massaging my genitals...I thought it was normal. He was showing me he loved me."

Mark sat in his chair on the pulpit, his gaze meeting Earl's as he watched his mentor dry his eyes with tissues. As Lester recounted seven years of dangerous sex with men, substance abuse, and three suicide attempts, Mark gazed in wonder at Lester, the embodiment of Christ's transformation. He had spoken with people who found Christ and were delivered from many afflictions. However, Lester's deliverance had a veracity that Mark had never before encountered.

"I met my mentor, Robert Cannon, a former homosexual himself who had discovered the path to healing. He told me you couldn't pray away the gay. You couldn't fast or read your Bible and expect your homosexual desires to vanish. You had to heal, and he showed me how to do just that." Lester then began to walk the congregation through Global Healing's mission, elucidating the shortcomings of many other conversion therapy organizations, and assuring the congregation of how Global Healing addressed those shortcomings. The congregation remained silent, many members taking notes and soaking up Lester's knowledge. Mark did the same, grateful that his hour of silent prayer had been disrupted because the Holy Spirit had clearly intended for Lester to speak today. As Lester finished his testimony, Mark got up, commencing the call to discipleship. He placed his arm around Lester as his other arm extended toward the congregation. A few people walked down the aisle, ready to give their lives to Christ, ready to experience the transformative power Lester had experienced. Mark's doubts were assuaged. Change to heterosexuality was possible. If you approached LGBT people with love, if you didn't judge them, they too could experience change.

• • •

Heather surveyed the renovated brownstone that was now Capitol Boutique. The living room had been converted into a small shopping area, vintage designer dresses occupying the space typically reserved for a couch, a rack of designer shoes resting comfortably in the former living room. A rack of men's suits was situated nicely beside the part of the dining room that led to the kitchen. She was satisfied with the guise that would facilitate her expanding escorting business.

Heather's client list had grown exponentially during the past month. When new clients called or visited, the ones interested in the sexual services asked for "the special." Once a client had uttered those two words, Heather would hand them a piece of paper detailing the price for each sexual service, and the combination of clothing that equated to the service. As Heather sat in the dining room she had converted into a makeshift office, she irritably stared at her phone. Devin was late for the job interview Heather had scheduled.

The application process to Capitol Boutique had been purposefully unassuming. Heather posted a job description for a retail clerk on a popular fashion blog called "Fashionably Fabulous." The description did not outline any of the unsavory qualifications Heather truly needed, such as having excellent gag reflexes while performing fellatio or a dauntlessness toward being handcuffed to a bed. She revealed those qualifications after offering a generous signing bonus of one thousand dollars in cash.

A knock at the front door startled Heather. Devin had a key, so she knew it couldn't be him. She went to open the door and found a young woman standing in front of her, donning a yellow print sundress that looked more appropriate for an 8-year-old than a young woman of her age, but who was Heather to judge? Deanne

Blake, the applicant who desired to gain experience in the fashion industry through a sales clerk position, stood before Heather in a blissful ignorance magnified by the loud yellow fabric of a cheap dress. She was quite a bit early. Heather tried to not let her irritation at this fact show.

"Hi, Deanne. Please, come in."

Deanne shook Heather's outstretched hand while she walked inside the boutique, gaping non-discreetly at the heavenly display of vintage couture. Heather silently appraised Deanne's unimpressive figure – the untoned arms and soft shoulders, the torso that unkindly revealed hints of a muffin top. Heather was already finding clever ways to recommend Deanne's incorporation of daily exercise into her schedule.

"I should not be doing this. I'm so sorry." Deanne quickly met Heather's gaze, a mixture of apprehension and excitement in her soft blue eyes. Heather ushered the young woman into her makeshift office. Deanne took a seat on the beige couch, unearthed a manila folder from her sizeable red purse, and pulled out a resume. Heather took it, smiling as warmly as she could muster as she scanned its contents.

"I start classes at Marymount in the fall. I wanna major in fashion, so I thought this job was perfect."

Heather saw a familiar naiveté in Deanne; it was an innocence Heather had once possessed herself when she was Jacquelyn. Her former mentor, Silas Greene, had taken away her innocence, her idealistic worldview, and had replaced it with a ruthless pragmatism required to survive in the business. Heather crossed her legs as she took out a folder that outlined Deanne's accurate job description, the qualifications she hoped would be palatable to Deanne with the enticement of the signing bonus.

"Fashion is such an exciting field to go into," Heather began. "It's also a major that has a very high unemployment rate."

Deanne's face sunk as she clutched her abdomen. Heather sensed something was on her mind. Deanne's eyes glimmered, tears falling down her plump cheeks. Some of her mascara had started to run.

"Here, take some tissues." Heather gingerly placed a box of Kleenex in Deanne's hands. She took several tissues and dried her tears, revealing a much paler skin complexion as patches of her mascara appeared on the tissues.

"Deanne, may I ask what's wrong?"

Deanne sniffled as she rested her back against the couch, her breathing becoming steadier. "My dad lost his job a few weeks ago. And it's been hard." Deanne, through intermittent sobs, explained how her dad had secretly struggled with a gambling addiction. She talked to Heather about how her mom had confronted her dad when she found out Deanne's college fund had been emptied, her mom's shrieks of panic ricocheting throughout the house at midnight.

Heather had never met a potential employee who was so forthcoming. She knew it made convincing Deanne to become an escort a lot easier. Heather handed Deanne that folder, Deanne taking it perplexingly.

"Before you read it, I want to start by saying I have a solution that can help you stay out of debt. You'd be able to afford your tuition and living expenses, and will even be able to start saving for your future."

Deanne opened the file, her eyes widening as she read the job description, its expected qualifications, hourly compensation, and generous signing bonus. Deanne closed the folder, speechless. "You're asking me to become a prostitute?!"

Heather shook her head at Deanne's statement, the creak of the front door catching their attention. Devin's heavy footsteps became more prominent as he tapped on the wall outside the dining room, his unprofessional attire infuriating Heather. *Was it too much to ask that he not wear jeans with a hole in the knees and shoes other than tan flip-flops?*

"Deanne, this is my assistant Devin. He goes over the contractual aspects of the work and answers any questions you might have. I assume you'll have some questions. Most people do." Heather watched as Deanne shook Devin's hand timidly.

"Found out what you're really gonna do here?" Deanne nodded as Devin sat down next to her, taking her hand in his. Deanne had begun twitching.

"I'm gonna make sure you're treated with the respect you deserve."

"How?" Deanne's question prompted Devin to take out his phone and open the app he had created. Heather often tuned the portion of this sales pitch out because this was an issue on which she and Devin disagreed. Devin found it necessary to appease his conscience through the creation of an app that detected "safe words." When an escort uttered a safe word, a video recorder Devin had placed in the bedroom was activated.

Deanne listened, her gaze returning to Heather, who smiled demurely.

"Don't think of this job as prostitution," Heather jumped back in. "Think of it as an opportunity to make up to $200 a session. We have over 30 clients. I have two girls. You'd each get 15 clients who pay at least $500 a session. I give you ten percent in cash upfront."

Deanne sat back, her jawline hardening, not convinced by Heather's enticements. "I don't know."

Deanne's mortification was apparent, imploring Heather to calmly direct Deanne to the envelope of cash at the very back of the folder. Devin gently placed his hand on her shoulder. "This is a lot, and you can say *no.*"

Heather wanted to drag Devin by his bleach blond hair and kick him several times in the gut. How dare he encourage Deanne to decline this opportunity?! Heather pursed her lips and bit her tongue as Deanne counted the money silently.

"A grand upfront? To be a prostitute?"

"Deanne," Heather said calmly, trying to disguise her irritation with cheerfulness. "You're not seeing the big picture. Powerful, wealthy men come to me when they want their fantasies fulfilled. They're looking for a girl who can provide them with companionship. Is sex involved? Yes, of course. But *prostitutes* stand on the street corner and give blow jobs in back alleys. That's not you."

Deanne sat there silently, her red hair falling to her sides as she bowed her head. At that moment, Heather tried a deal-making strategy she had learned from Greg Hammond. He often presented future customers with a demonstration of a new product, allowing them to procure a fully-functioning prototype free of charge. "If you say no, the $1,000 is yours, and your job will just be a sales clerk. You'll be on the payroll, and your salary will be $11.50 per hour. All we ask is that you don't say anything about this exclusive service when talking with your friends and family."

Deanne examined the living room, her eyes twinkling as she read over the job description Heather had provided her. "Can I try one client and see how I like it?" Deanne's face had turned pink. That sparkle in her eyes was replaced with something that looked more like dull and hollow desperation than anything else. Before Heather stood a frightened and timid young woman. Heather grabbed Deanne's hands and placed them in hers.

"Of course. You can quit whenever you want." Heather placed her hand on Deanne's face, brushing a strand of hair away from it. Deanne nodded as a tear trickled down her right cheek.

"Devin, go over Deanne's contract with her. I'll work on assigning Deanne her first client."

Devin ushered Deanne into the kitchen, and calmly presented Deanne with her contract. Heather opened the client files, unsure of whom she should assign Deanne. Greg Hammond, her boss, expressed a desire to work with a woman who had no inhibitions. She wasn't sure if *that* was going to be a good fit here. As she ruminated on her choice, her phone vibrated. A link from Earl Wilson pointed her to a church service at Holy Boldness. *Ugh, Earl.* He never shied away from promulgating his beliefs to Heather. She was not a religious person. She did not believe in the power of prayer and certainly did not believe that a man died on the cross to save humanity from damnation.

Heather put on her headphones and clicked on the link Earl had sent. She fast-forwarded to a song she heard sung on the local urban radio stations. The singer, a young man with slicked-back brown hair, sang the first phrase: "Speak to my heart, Holy Spirit. Give me the words that will bring new life." His demeanor appeared contrived, every high note and raised hand feeling rehearsed. The singer Heather was watching had a faraway glance as if his mind were on something else. Heather was just about to turn off the video when she heard a voice she vaguely recognized coming from the pulpit. She immediately paused the sermon and rummaged through old voicemails on her phone.

"If you have any questions, call Heather or me. Okay?" Devin walked Deanne out, the front door creaking shut as he came back inside the dining room.

Heather found the voicemail she was looking for, in which a man named Mark Perkins introduced himself. It was the same voice from the sermon Earl had sent her. "Hi. I'm Reverend Mark Perkins, and I am calling to see if I can provide you with any assistance. Bishop Earl Wilson told me he was helping you financially. Give me a call if you're interested. No pressure. God bless." Heather looked up from her phone to see that Devin had plopped himself lazily on the couch directly across from her.

"We have a potential problem, Devin."

Devin was oblivious to Heather's proclamations, groaning while he took out his phone from his back pocket and sunk deeper into the couch.

"Devin, I need you to look into someone."

"Who?" He sat up, his eyes darting from his phone to Heather.

"Mark Perkins. He's a friend of Earl's. I've got a feeling."

"A feeling?"

"Yes, a feeling. This man left a voicemail thinking I'm some battered woman in need of money. Find out who Mark Perkins is. And why the hell he would have been calling my phone."

Devin shrugged and got up. Heather put her phone aside, not at all interested in revisiting the sermon Earl had sent her until she had some idea of why this Mark guy had contacted her. She turned her attention toward the stack of invoices on her desk for clothing she had purchased recently. She added them up in disgust. *$8,279?!* How the hell had she spent over eight grand on knock-off purses, dresses, and suits?! Her brow furrowed, as Devin gently placed his arms around Heather's neck. They never hugged.

"That was a nice thing you did for Deanne. Offering her a grand upfront without having her commit to anything."

Heather placed her hands across Devin's face, his stubble prickly against her hands. How endearing. *Was it possible that she could be changing?* Devin thought. It seemed like her heart was maybe beginning to soften a bit, but he couldn't be sure. Deciding not to counter his claim with a chagrined remark, she squeezed Devin's hand. He reflexively pulled away. He was becoming his own man who no longer sought Heather's approval. It was a shift that made her uncomfortable, but she knew she couldn't hold on to Devin forever. The day was coming when he'd no longer need her. In the meantime, she wanted to be mindful of not pushing him away too soon.

"Mark Perkins. Find me what you can. Earl's been talking."

As Devin proceeded to leave, Heather grabbed his hand one more time. She couldn't help herself. "Have dinner with me tonight? I wanna hear about your grad school application."

Devin's disbelief registered as he bit his upper lip, an action that immediately reminded Heather of Faith, Devin's mother. "All right. But *please* don't cook. I don't want food poisoning again."

Heather chuckled as she walked Devin to the front door, "Takeout it is."

She watched as Devin's silhouette bounced along the sidewalk, his figure immersing into the crowd of never-ending tourists, their bewildered glances and insatiable desires to photograph themselves commonplace in downtown D.C. Their carefree dispositions no longer made Heather jealous. She was beginning to no longer yearn to go back to her days as Jacquelyn and was seeing now how mourning her was futile. Heather allowed herself to be present, to be accepting of her new life, to be optimistic that she could enjoy walking through the world as Heather. She closed the door and headed back inside the dining room. At her desk, she texted Deanne the name of her first client, Earl. She prayed that a man who enjoyed wearing an adult diaper while being penetrated with a dildo was a sexual fetish that Deanne could find palatable.

9

ALL IN

Carl had succumbed to utilizing "Veggie Tales" to stifle the restlessness of the young children in his care. This was his fourth year teaching Vacation Bible School, and he was irritated that the only job he'd ever held still didn't seem to be getting any easier or more enjoyable with time. When Carl had turned sixteen, he had begged his parents to permit him to audition for "American Idol." They had agreed but insisted that he continue with the VBS teaching. He ransacked his brain as he tried to remember what song he had planned to sing for the "Idol" audition that never came to pass, but found himself incessantly distracted by the images of talking cucumbers and tomatoes dancing on the television screen.

"Red and yellow, black and white," the children sang. "They are precious in his sight. Jesus loves the little children of the world."

Carl interrupted the singalong, the honkey-tonk cadence grating to his ears. "Watch the movie silently, kids. No singing."

Some of the little faces looked up at him pleadingly, but Carl didn't budge. He longed to go back to two summers ago, to the evenings he spent belting out a pop song out in the empty sanctuary, pretending he was on the stage at the Kodak Theater in Los Angeles. As the credits rolled on the "Veggie Tales" film, he surreptitiously stepped out into the hallway as that grating honky-tonk cadence started playing.

God, I hate that fucking song. Carl rarely spoke to himself in church because his thoughts were always laced with profanity, something wholly ungodly in the Lord's house. As Carl closed his eyes, he started humming fragmented phrases of the song he had planned to sing on national television. Rob Thomas' hit, "Ever The Same." It was an ostensible love song that Carl had interpreted as God's answer to his prayers. Two years ago, he had wanted God to change his sexuality. He had been asking God to be everything he needed. He had fallen on his knees and begged God to change him, and he reasoned that if he sang this song enough, he'd be straight. When his audition date loomed, he had panicked, obsessing over his pitch and interpretation of the song. Two nights before his audition, he had stayed up practicing, watching endless YouTube videos of Rob Thomas singing the song live and tweaking his embellishments. One particular video had aroused Carl to the point of frustration, Rob's forlorn glance growing Carl's erection. He had masturbated for the first time in three months, and in that painful clarity realized he was still gay. Forcing those thoughts out of his mind had not made him straight, only chaste. Carl had told his parents "American Idol" wasn't for him, and that he didn't want to audition anymore. They had seemed relieved, Mark even commenting on how professed Christians singing pop music have trouble tolerating the evils of secular music.

Parents had begun picking up their children. Carl made sure every parent signed their child out, watching silently as they scribbled their signature next to their child's name. One mother commented on the sermon about homosexuality and how she had been moved to tears by Lester's testimony. "Just goes to show you how God can work in all of our lives."

Carl grunted as the mother ogled over a picture her daughter had drawn, beaming with pride at the stick figure her daughter proudly displayed, its crude green lines at the bottom of the paper vaguely representative of grass or weeds. Or something to that effect. As the conference room emptied, Carl started arranging the chairs. *The children needed to learn how to clean up after themselves. Was there a Bible story for that? If so, Carl needed to make sure to teach it to them next week.* Carl ransacked his brain for one as he unearthed crayons and scavenged for the tops to magic markers.

"Still here?" Carl had bent over to retrieve a missing cap to a red magic marker when he heard Don's voice. He crawled out from underneath the tiny table and saw Don standing in front of him, his white dress shirt untucked and black dress pants slightly wrinkled. Carl exhaled sharply as he matched the red cap with its magic marker.

"Kids are so messy. You wouldn't believe how many wads of gum I find underneath that table. Chewing gum's against the rules, but those sneaky little brats don't seem to care."

Don chuckled at Carl's irritation as he took a seat at the conference room table, "Wait till you have one of your own."

Carl's eyes narrowed at Don.

"You're at least ten years away from that."

Don and Carl stood in a palpable silence. Lately, Carl viewed Don as a passive participant in his father's crusade to cure the gays. Whatever Mark wanted, Don complied.

"Ummm, you know how last week you said I was a straight, married man with a son who had nothing to worry about?!" Don hesitatingly began, his eyes traveling across the room and landing on Carl, who seemed preoccupied with finding the perfect sharpened pencil from the supply closet, which Don presumed Carl was going to use to remove the wads of gum from underneath the table.

"What about it? It's true."

Don's silence contradicted Carl's pronouncement. Carl pulled himself up from the floor, dusting tiny particles of dirt off his kneecaps. Don was silent, his face pale and his jaw clenched.

"I've known for years," Don continued hoarsely. "I assumed getting married would straighten me out. It didn't."

Carl's ears started ringing as everything in the room except Don's voice faded into the background. Carl no longer saw the tan folding chairs against the wall, the large whiteboard with the day's scripture still scrawled messily across it, or the kids' artwork strewn haphazardly against the table in the corner. All he saw was a white room with Don sitting in the center. Was Don coming out to him? Was he saying that he was gay?

"I'm sorry I snapped at you." Carl swallowed a massive lump in his throat. "I just feel so alone."

Don nodded. He understood Carl's pain in ways that his friends didn't. Carl imagined the decades of suppression Don endured. Carl's prayers were probably Don's prayers too.

"Maybe you don't have to be. Maybe we can support each other." Without even realizing he was doing it, Carl walked over to where Don was sitting. Don stood up, his lips only inches from Carl's mouth. Don's blue eyes stared back at Carl as their lips drew closer. Carl's hands felt the contours of Don's chest, his fingers unbuttoning his shirt, traversing the contours of his ribcage.

Don reciprocated Carl's desire, his hands lifting up Carl's shirt and unzipping his shorts. With trepidation, Carl unbuckled Don's pants and felt Don's erect penis. With each layer of clothing removed, the two men explored each other further. Carl eventually got down on his knees and took Don in his mouth, Don's hairy hips thrusting against his face as Carl pleasured him. Don then lifted Carl onto the table, its metal surface cold against his bare bottom, Don's mouth warm as it enveloped Carl's penis. They did this for what seemed like hours, orally pleasuring each other to the brink of orgasm. Carl's legs quivered as he came inside Don's mouth, Don returning the favor seconds later. Carl brought Don in for a kiss, their mouths full, their bodies touching. Spent, the two lay awkwardly on the tabletop. Carl rested his head against Don's chest, and slowly, the room around them came back into focus. As the objects returned to their original state, Carl realized the magnitude of what he and Don had just done. Carl had been intimate with a married man. He wondered if he would ever be forgiven for committing such an abomination. He wondered if this act was even an abomination at all.

• • •

Harriet always felt that the ambiance in Dr. Rowan's office was contrived. The zen garden on his coffee table, for instance, appeared to be strategically situated so that clients could draw lines in the sand whenever they felt stressed. *Why did people think that a miniature sandbox could quell anxiety? Did people also believe that abstract paintings resembling droplets of blood eased the mind?* Harriet found the décor insufferable. Dr. Rowan sat in his sleek white chair, his notepad ready to transcribe Harriet's ramblings for the week. He inhaled and exhaled loudly, a soft grin appearing across his wrinkled face as he scratched his thinning black hair.

"How are things at home? You mentioned a family emergency last week. Care to elaborate?" Harriet did not care to elaborate on the details surrounding Percy's termination, nor did she care to elucidate her feelings of alienation in her marriage. However, she had been coming to these sessions long enough to know that Dr. Rowan's probing questions would continue in perpetuity if she provided only one-word answers.

"Percy lost his job last week, and, of course, refused to talk about it with me." Dr. Rowan wrote copiously as if this information gave him tremendous insight into Harriet's personality. "I tried to be there for him, but he didn't want me around." Dr. Rowan wrote more notes, his pen moving faster across the page. "Oh, and I found out Jerry dropped out of MIT and moved to New York City without telling anyone."

Dr. Rowan stopped writing, his gaze fixed on Harriet. His dark, thick eyebrows raised in genuine interest.

"Why do you think Percy shut you out?" Dr. Rowan always asked questions whose answers he already knew. Harriet sat in silence, reflecting on the disintegration of her marriage, its catalyst ostensible.

• • •

She remembered the moment as if it were yesterday, no matter how hard she tried to block it out of her mind. It was 4:29 PM on the afternoon of July 9th when her phone had rung. Harriet had been at a teacher's conference in Sterling, Virginia, and had distinctly remembered stepping out into the lobby of the Marriot to take the call, embarrassed that her phone had rung during a seminar on anti-bullying tactics. Harriet had hesitated before answering the phone when she saw the unfamiliar number flash across the screen, but something told her to take the call. She had sensed something tragic had happened upon hearing the calm, detached tone of a woman who introduced herself as an ER doctor at Holy Cross Hospital.

"Are you Ella Nelson's mother?" As soon as Harriet answered in the affirmative, the doctor went on to explain that there had been an accident and that she needed to get to the hospital immediately. The moments that followed were a complete blur to Harriet – rushing into the conference room, grabbing her purse from the back of her seat, sprinting out into the parking lot. Harriet had made a concerted effort to focus on driving, her mind confirming her worst nightmare. She had called Percy but got no answer.

• • •

"Because I blame him."

Dr. Rowan's posture shifted at Harriet's response as she came back to the present, "For what exactly?"

Harriet was irritated by the question. She didn't want to discuss the details of Ella's death, especially today. She had no interest in articulating the stench of isopropyl alcohol that permeated the hospital corridors; nor did she desire to relive the Hello Kitty shirt soaked in her daughter's blood; she did not care to relay the seventeen hours spent in the waiting room with Jerry, Leo, and Percy, the stoic expression on the surgeon's face as she told them – *We did everything we could to save your daughter.* No. Harriet did not want to travel back to that day, the day in which the contents in her daughter's pockets were handed to her in a plastic evidence bag: a package of crumbled Oreo cookies, iPod shuffle.

"I assume you know how my daughter died," Harriet finally said.

Dr. Rowan nodded as he sat back in his chair. "'Hit and run accident kills eight-year-old girl roller skating home.' I'm paraphrasing the headline. Why do you blame Percy?"

Harriet chuckled, the barrage of questions inescapable. "Because I told him not to let her go roller skating unsupervised."

"And that day he did?" Dr. Rowan bowed his head as if praying for the right words to respond to Harriet's revelation. It had taken her a year to tell Dr. Rowan this simple yet devastating fact. "You've been reliving that day for five years. It's been playing in your mind so much that you were unable to tell me about it until today."

Harriet's eyes welled up to the point where Dr. Rowan's face blurred. She inched forward on the black couch, grabbed the tiny blue rake, and started shakily drawing lines in the sand.

"You have two sons," Dr. Rowan's voice was quiet, almost a whisper. Harriet nodded as she yanked two tissues from an open box on the coffee table, dabbing at her eyes. Dr. Rowan's face was still fuzzy, the tears clouding her vision. "Despite all the pain you've endured, you're still here. Your sons are still here. Your husband is still here."

"What does that mean? We're here. We're alive."

Dr. Rowan answered Harriet with a question, "What does it mean to you?"

Only she could answer that question. Harriet sighed deeply, then spoke extemporaneously about being hurt that Jerry chose not to confide in her about dropping out of college.

Dr. Rowan listened with detached empathy as she rambled on, taking notes, grunting and sighing periodically. "Harriet, as we wrap up for today, I want to ask if you're open to going on antidepressants for a while."

Harriet had considered going on antidepressants before but feared their side-effects. She also worried that they would slowly liberate her from her grief, and Harriet wasn't sure who she would even *be* without her pain. That being said, she also knew if she ever wanted to be happy and present in her life again, she'd probably need some help. She nodded affirmatively in Dr. Rowan's direction.

Without another word, he took out his prescription pad and wrote a prescription for 300 milligrams of Wellbutrin. She stared at the white piece of paper, Dr. Rowan's barely legible handwriting staring right back at her. He recommended that she start taking the medication as soon as possible and document any side effects. She nodded again, and without so much as another word, stood up, smiled meekly in the doctor's direction, and walked out of the office.

The predictable June humidity that blasted her face as she stepped out onto the sidewalk made her flinch. Walking to her car, she spotted a lone chrysanthemum blooming against the brick wall that lined the parking lot. Its bright purple almost precisely matched her blouse. *How lovely*, she thought, as she smiled what may have been the first genuine smile to cross her face in a pretty long time.

• • •

Jerry decided to come clean to Mel about his stint in conversion therapy. He knew she deserved an explanation after his recent behavior at lunch a few days prior. It had terrified Jerry to see the one person who always stood by him hurting, confused, and unable to say the right things or understand why he acted out the way he did. *This is going to be the day,* he thought, as he sat across from Mel in Sally's Diner, watching her push around the stale apple pie on her plate with a pensiveness on her face that matched his own.

"Tell me something awful, so I can work up the strength to tell you why I assaulted those poor avocados in my salad the other day."

Jerry searched Mel's face as she followed a strand of her curly hair that had made its way onto her shoulder. Jerry knew something was on Mel's mind because she never picked at her apple pie, regardless of how terrible it was.

"This client I'm working with? The one whose DACA status might be rescinded? She was raped," Mel shoved her apple pie away in disgust, visibly clutching her abdomen as she explained the circumstances in which her client had been sexually assaulted. The assailant had been a prominent bishop who had insisted Mel's client participate in anal sex. When the young woman had refused, the bishop forcibly grabbed her hair and pinned her down onto the bed, sodomizing her while covering her face as she screamed. Jerry tried to catch his breath as Mel recounted her client's violent assault. He wondered if the heaviness of this subject matter would divert Mel's attention away from Jerry's promise to share with her what had been on *his* mind the other day. It did not.

"Your turn," Mel gasped.

Jerry sighed interminably, taking a large bite out of his apple pie and washing it down with a swig of coffee. "I went to conversion therapy last year. At lunch the other day, the avocados in my salad reminded me of a photo in the waiting room of that awful place. And, well, I don't know. I guess it just triggered something in me." Jerry knew that Mel would need more details than *this*. He went on to proffer some superficial reasons for pursuing the therapy, but Mel wasn't buying it.

She leaned in firmly and narrowed her eyes, her bullshit detector firing off.

"After coming out to my dad, he made it clear that there was no way he was going to have a gay son. He all but demanded that I attend some crazy program that he had heard about from one of his friends who had sent his son there. When I refused, he threatened me with notifying the college board about my academic fraud. I honestly felt as if I didn't have a choice." Jerry watched as Mel's nostrils flared.

"That is fucked up."

Jerry nodded agreeably to Mel's sentiment. They sat in silence for a few moments, both reflecting on the unscrupulousness of humanity.

Mel broke the silence with a disturbingly comical anecdote, "So, that bishop who raped my client apparently enjoyed dressing up like a baby and being penetrated with a strap-on dildo. He would turn his adult diaper into an assless chap."

The two friends laughed for several minutes, their eyes wet with tears as they clutched their stomachs. Their laughter was interrupted by Mel's phone, which vibrated on the table as she snorted loudly. When she finally composed herself, she looked down at her phone, eyes widening.

"What's wrong?" Jerry asked.

Mel placed her phone in front of Jerry, where a picture of an incredibly attractive blond-haired man with piercing blue eyes appeared across her screen. Jerry recalled that Mel had mentioned her recent foray into online dating. If men like that appeared on Jerry's screen, *he* might sign up for TheOne.

"I should meet Devin for a drink, right?" Mel scanned Jerry's face for the approval she so desperately sought, even after all this time.

His eyes narrowed toward Mel, "Girl, bye. You know you need to swipe right." Jerry purposely tuned out Mel's concerns about him being a possible serial killer or rapist, countering them with the fact that he was not going to rape and murder her in a crowded bar.

Groaning her agreement with Jerry's assessment, she got up from the booth and headed out. Jerry sat back and finished his apple pie, the guilt of keeping a secret from his best friend no longer permeating his body and mind.

•••

Since Percy's departure from the company, Greg had voluntarily assumed the role of acting program director. As such, Heather and Nikki had become Greg's administrative assistants, an arrangement that would be remedied once he could hire a permanent program director. Heather sat in the irritably drafty conference room, the same one in which her legs had been spread across the dark oak table less than two months ago, Percy's forehead shining with sweat as he approached orgasm. She hoped the maintenance crew had cleaned this table well, she thought, as she doodled aimlessly in her notebook, bracing herself for another one of Greg's boring staff meetings.

"Next week is our annual family and friends cookout at Rock Creek Park," Greg announced proudly. "Bring your kids. Bring your spouses. It's gonna be fun."

Heather tried to remember the last time she had attended a corporate cookout. It had been in 2002. She was still Jacquelyn Metz and had just started working at the hedge fund as a receptionist. Silas Greene had practically begged her to come to a barbecue he was having at his house. It was a time in her life where her general weariness had become cumbersome. Faith had taken off again, this time permanently succumbing to the peripatetic life familiar to an addict. Heather grimly reflected on that hot July day – her wrinkled Madonna t-shirt lathered in sweat as she balanced carrying an aluminum tray of poorly sliced watermelons with chastising Devin and Trey. They had started another fight with each other over the three-headed monsters on their Gameboys.

"Heather, any pet peeves you'd like to voice?"

Heather was jerked back to reality by the perturbed stares of the program managers, "None at the moment."

Satisfied with her response, Greg proceeded to discuss the second quarter projections when the large wooden door of the conference room opened. A tiny figure whose short haircut made her instantly discernible inched her way inside. Eve Parsons, the VP of finance, stood behind Greg, her lips pursed. Heather disapproved of her navy blue pants suit, the garish gold earrings and matching gold crucifix around her neck reminding her of an anorexic version of pundit Christine O'Donnell.

"Greg, we need to speak with you now. It's about Percy Nelson." Greg adjusted his three-piece gray suit and hurriedly followed Eve out of the conference room. As whispers among the program managers ensued, Heather received a cryptic text from Percy – *Meet me at our spot.* She grabbed her purse and exited the conference room, trying to not let her face give away her deep concern as her mind flashed back to the origins of their affair.

Their affair had begun in the most uneventful way. Months of Percy's innocuous compliments on Heather's appearance coupled with casual invitations to have dinner while working late had culminated in a sloppy kiss in the parking lot of Chick-fil-A.

Percy's saliva had dripped from his mouth like a leaky bathroom faucet, his hand groping Heather's thigh as he awkwardly pulled down her pink laced underwear. They had performed oral sex on each other in Percy's BMW, the seats reclined as Heather recalled arching her neck in a way that left her with searing neck pains for a week.

As she reached the parking garage, the sleek silver edges of her Ford Fusion glimmering from the tiny sun rays that illuminated the dark garage, she thought of the perfunctory moan she would utter during her many clandestine meetings with Percy. Just as she put the key in the ignition, her phone rang. It was Devin.

"Mark Perkins isn't just a pastor. He's a licensed attorney who was on the fast track to making partner at Lewis & Houghton when he abruptly resigned to become a full-time Methodist preacher. Graduated from Boston University and clerked for some conservative judge who thinks legalized abortion is akin to slavery. Anyway, he now provides legal representation for Christian-owned businesses and nonprofits. But here's where it gets interesting."

"How so?" Heather turned into the shopping center housing Chick-fil-A as she was greeted with the mouthwatering smell of fresh waffle fries. She parked next to the green garbage dump, its discreet location conducive for secret sexual encounters.

"Earl and Mark are best friends. Mark met him when he was a freshman at the University of Maryland. Earl was a senior majoring in philosophy at the time. Earl baptized Mark, ordained him, was best man at his wedding, and it looks like Mark has been Earl's personal lawyer for all of his book deals and endorsements."

Heather grew concerned. Best friends shared everything with each other. What if Earl had confided in Mark about his unorthodox proclivities? "Thanks, Devin."

"What do you want me to do with this info?"

"Let's just keep an eye on Mark and Earl for a bit." Heather saw Percy's BMW pull into the parking lot. "I gotta go."

The oppressive June heat hit her face as she opened the door. She knew from past experience that Percy expected her to join him in his car. So she did and instantly regretted it when she sat down to see his already disheveled appearance magnified by a large orange stain on his University of Maryland t-shirt.

"You've been too busy to return my calls?" He immediately massaged Heather's thigh, his fingers migrating upward. Heather grabbed Percy's wrist and placed it at his side.

"Percy, why did you wanna meet? I left a work meeting for this, and I don't have a lot of time."

He frowned as he scratched a mosquito bite on his forehead. "I'm suing Greg for wrongful termination. He's been gunning for me since I got that job."

Heather's mind crafted images of Greg pounding his tiny fist on his desk as legal apprised him of this lawsuit.

"Can I count on your support?"

"What are you asking, Percy?"

"I need you to testify to the times you overheard us arguing. Mention the names you heard him call me."

Heather grimly reflected on the colorful amalgam of words Greg utilized to encapsulate Percy's ineptitude. She then pondered the future of her business. Greg's enthusiasm to procure the most exclusive sexual services would probably diminish if this lawsuit came to fruition. Heather had no intention of supporting Percy. In fact, she decided that she was actually going to do everything within her power to derail him.

To placate his request, she unzipped Percy's pants and craned her neck in that familiar strained position. Taking him in her mouth, she listened as Percy began panting, beads of sweat wetting her cheek as his knees shook violently. He came in her mouth, moaning loudly as Heather grabbed a tissue from his glove compartment. She spat out Percy's cum as if it were a rotten piece of fruit.

"Can I see you again? I know Greg's working you hard. I'm sorry you're in the middle of this." Percy drew her in for a kiss, brushing a strand of hair away from her face. "I worry about you."

Heather's stomach churned as Percy's soft, brown eyes gazed at her, expressing something she feared may be love. Heather had no interest in or time for such feelings. She fabricated a story about an emergency meeting back at the office, Percy nodding his head understandably as she opened the passenger door. Heather made false promises to call Percy, to allow him to take her to dinner, to discuss the prospect of going on a weekend trip. She and Percy drove off the parking lot and back to their respective lives. Heather's phone rang again as she drove into the parking garage of OEI. Her Bluetooth displayed Unknown on her car's panel.

"Hello?"

"Heather, it's Annette Greene, Silas' wife."

In that instant, she was pulled back into her last days as Jacquelyn Metz and the damp studio apartment in Arlington where she met Silas' handler, Uriah. It was in this clandestine location that she had been given her new identity – Heather Carter's driver's license, passport, social security card, and birth certificate all packaged together in a manila envelope for a standard fee of five thousand dollars in cash. She had shortly thereafter gone to Dr. Sturgis' office in Sterling, leveraging her subsequent cosmetic surgeries for a year of free sexual services: the facelift, nose reduction, and breast augmentation. She had remembered waking up to numbness, groggy from the anesthesia but grateful she couldn't smell the rubbing alcohol whose scent stayed with her until she had been knocked out. All of these memories flooded Heather's mind.

"Heather, are you there?"

"Yes, sorry. What's the matter?"

"A non-profit, Justice For All, is looking into the story of Alma Velasquez. She was one of the girls charged when the cops raided our home. I don't need to tell you what'll happen if they keep digging."

Heather's thoughts were of Devin and how he would not be protected if this organization kept digging into Alma's story. She wondered how she would handle prison, envisioning herself ripe with odor due to her allowance of one shower per day, her orange jumpsuit sticky against her sweaty skin. She wasn't sure if she would survive, but she could say with 100 percent confidence that Devin definitely wouldn't make it through a prison stint.

Heather killed the engine, her fear mixing with anger: "Who told you this?"

"Doesn't matter. Silas gave me a message to pass on to you – Fix this." Annette's tone was venomous. And dead serious.

"Got it. Thanks," was all Heather could muster in response as she slammed her car door shut and headed back into the office.

Greg summoned Heather to his office via a poorly handwritten Post-It note. She walked down the hall to Greg's office, the annoying text alarm on Nikki's phone sounding off every few seconds. Heather was greeted with the rustic smell of potpourri and calming Vivaldi concertos as she took a seat in one of Greg's chairs.

"Percy Nelson has filed a lawsuit against us."

"Oh?" Heather made a concerted effort to appear bemused as Greg disclosed this information.

"He wants to say I created a hostile work environment for him. Bullshit. It's not my fault he's a sad, incompetent sack of shit. Anyway, legal's proposing we give him *another* two hundred thousand dollar severance package in exchange for him signing an NDA. Can you believe this?"

Heather scanned the photos on Greg's wall, her eyes landing on one in which he was shaking hands with district attorney Brendan Alexander. They smiled widely behind a lush green golf course. And that's when Heather found her solution to her problem. Brendan was a regular customer who derived pleasure from ingesting various bodily fluids. He also happened to be a friend of Greg's.

"Heather, I need dirt on Percy."

She met Greg's frown as he stared at his laptop, furtively typing a response to an email. "Countersue for gross sexual misconduct." Heather described in vivid detail the comments Percy had made toward her, deliberately omitting their frequent sexual encounters around the office.

Greg smirked, clasping his hands while Heather created a version of their relationship that portrayed Percy as a predatory boss who abused his power.

"I have an idea." Greg adjusted his glasses while he finished typing his email, astutely detecting the information Heather had omitted, and its definitive repercussions if brought to light. Heather decided not to confirm nor deny Greg's observations, sitting quietly with her arms folded across her lap while Greg elucidated his diabolical plan to assign Heather's narrative to Nikki.

"People like Nikki," Greg explained gently, popping a Lifesaver into his mouth as he reminded Heather of how her antagonistic attitude often alienated her from her peers. If she were to accuse Percy of sexual harassment, very few people would jump to her defense.

Heather shrugged in her usual perfunctory manner, unfazed by the fact that Greg had just called her a bitch in the most eloquent way. Her eyes darted back to that picture of Greg and Brendan shaking hands, listening passively as Greg assigned Heather the arduous task of grooming Nikki into a believable victim of Percy's unwanted sexual advances.

At this moment, Heather saw an opportunity to exploit Greg's friendship with Brendan, "I had no idea you knew Brendan Alexander."

Greg looked up from his email to the picture Heather was eyeing, "We go way back to my days at Northwestern. He was the one who told me about your services."

"Really? I need to meet with him. Can you get me a reservation at your golf course?"

Greg removed his glasses, the creases in his face prominent. He glanced back at his monitor, which had projected the email he was typing. "Since you're about to save the company a million dollars, I'll set something up."

Heather smirked satisfactorily; her problem would soon be solved over a game she had no idea how to play.

• • •

Camp Wabana's colonial aura facilitated healing through nature, which was the purpose of the weekend excursion led by Lester Dawson. Mark and Earl had been invited by Lester to observe how to approach homosexuality with pastoral care. According to Lester, many gay men and lesbians were trapped in the vicious cycle of the homosexual lifestyle and often turned to pastors and deacons for help. Unfortunately, these same pastors and deacons were rarely equipped with the tools to counsel a gay man or lesbian out of homosexuality.

Over breakfast that morning, Lester had elucidated the church's condemning rhetoric when dealing with homosexuality: "Pastors rush to judgment because their mind jumps to sex, and they can't get past that. My goal is to lead seminars for them on this issue so they can begin the healing process with their flock."

In a remote field on the campground, Mark observed Lester pass around pieces of construction paper and packs of crayons. Mark and Earl watched as a group of young men sat silently, their gazes fixed on Lester as his loose-fitting athletic t-shirt swayed with the gentle breeze. He stood in the middle of the circle, patiently waiting for everyone to get settled.

"Good afternoon, all," he said, his voice authoritative.

"Good afternoon," the men replied in unison. Mark's eyes traveled the circumference of the circle, watching as the men sat attentively with legs crossed. He had met several of the participants at the prayer breakfast earlier that morning.

Donnell, a young African American college student, had elected to work with Lester after several failed attempts to change his sexual orientation. He drifted from church to church, encountering hostility from each pastor for voicing his struggle with homosexuality. "My parents and I found Lester through a deacon at the church we attend now. His nephew went through this program and married a woman last year," Donnell had shared. Mark had been amazed by Donnell's tenacity, yet saddened by the lack of compassion he had received from past churches. Donnell clutched three crayons as he awaited Lester's instructions.

"Today is all about connecting with your inner child. This is often the part of you that experienced trauma so deep that it manifested itself in the form of same-sex attractions. We have to heal that inner child if our natural opposite-sex attractions are to emerge."

Mark was genuinely astonished by Lester's ability to guide a group of men through their traumatic childhoods. Many mainstream therapists were unable to accomplish this on an individual basis.

Lester's instructions for the guided exercise were simple. Each man was supposed to draw themselves as a child, and around their picture, draw situations in which their masculinity was not affirmed. "It could be a small thing like not being picked for kickball at recess or being ridiculed for liking music or dance. If you were abused, draw the incident from the perspective of your age at the time of the abuse. It doesn't have to be pretty or neat."

• • •

Mark watched as one of the participants, Ian, glanced up at the clouds. His distant demeanor resembled that of Carl's; the pensive furrow of his brow brought Mark back to the conversation they had had over dinner last night, where Mark had broken the news to Carl that their scheduled golf outing had to be postponed.

"This weekend only happens once every summer, Carl," Mark had tried to explain to his son. "Earl says it'll be good for me to go."

"So you're bailing to observe a healing seminar for men who don't wanna be gay?" Carl had stared blankly ahead at the dinner table. Mark understood his frustration but had hoped that Carl would also see that an entire population of people was hurting and in need of salvation.

"Honey, I'm sure your father can reschedule," Louisa's optimistic tone had been countered with Mark's grim headshake.

"The next open slot's in September," Mark had watched as Carl stared at his food, his disappointment evident as he mindlessly picked at his asparagus. "Carl, I'm sorry."

His son's response had been a faraway glance as he took a large gulp of his water. "Not really hungry anymore," Carl had retorted as he stood up from the table, pushed his chair in, and marched upstairs, the echo of his footsteps punctuated by the slamming of his bedroom door.

Louisa had reached over and squeezed Mark's hand and exchanged a forlorn glance with her husband. Lately, Carl had slowly been distancing himself from both of them, his once cheerful and acquiescent disposition replaced with an inexplicable sullenness.

"Honey, he's just upset that you two aren't spending as much time together, but trust that God will sort out whatever issues he's dealing with." Louisa's words had sounded hollow to her even as she uttered them.

"Right. He's probably anxious over starting college," Mark had replied, eager to dismiss this outburst as something typical of a kid Carl's age.

But now, as he watched Lester walk around the circle and as he caught glimpses of the pictures many of the men drew, he wondered if he shouldn't have been so quick to dismiss his own son's recent shifts in behavior. The awkward stick figures and disproportionate limbs had similar scenarios depicted: a father carrying a suitcase while walking away from a boy, an older male friend enticing a boy with candy, a group of boys ridiculing a boy with a Barbie doll in his hand. *Was Mark behaving like an absent father? Was Carl experiencing similar issues of the men in the semicircle?*

• • •

"Okay. Who wants to share?" The sounds of birds chirping were the only response to Lester's request. Ian and Donnell exchanged nervous glances with another young man in the circle, whose large black-rimmed glasses looked like they could swallow up his face entirely at any moment.

Lester, patiently waiting for a volunteer, gently tapped Ian on the shoulder, "Ian, your picture looks very impressive. I think you should start so the rest of us can quickly get over how bad our drawings are."

Lester gently chuckled to lighten the mood, as Ian stood, his piece of construction paper shaking. "Um..this is a picture of me in the fifth grade." Ian held up the elaborate drawing of himself, pointing to the clarinet he clutched in his right hand and the doll he clutched in his left. He described how his love of music had made him the source of much ridicule, and how bringing his cousin's Barbie doll to school only sought to intensify those ridicules. "They would call me names," he continued. "Relentlessly."

"What names would they call you?" Lester prodded.

Ian broke down as his brown hair covered his eyes and the hollow sound of tears dropped onto his construction paper. He took a deep breath and continued through sobs, "Faggot. Queer. Homo."

Mark looked around the circle to see that Ian wasn't the only one crying. Lester placed his arms around Ian, holding him like a father might hold an inconsolable child. "Guys, I want you to place an arm around Ian and say things that affirm his masculinity." The sound of shoes stomping on the grass intensified as the circle closed in around Ian. Mark and Earl both placed an arm on Ian's back. Mark silently prayed for peace in Ian's life. He prayed that this exercise would heal the ten-year-old boy who still lived inside of Ian and that, in so doing, Ian would find the peace he was seeking.

"You're tough; a real man; one of the guys."

As the exercise continued in this fashion, Mark's admiration of Lester and his skills as a therapist continued to grow. Lester was able to use a simple activity like this one to identify the root causes of same-sex attractions. Mark had no idea how the psyche's internalization of emotional, physical, and sexual abuses manifested itself as homosexual desires. But with each man who obtained the courage to speak about their father abandoning them or about their older cousin molesting them, Lester facilitated healing from those abuses. It wasn't long before Ian confessed that his desire to sleep with men was dissipating, which only solidified Mark's confidence in the effectiveness of this conversion therapy. *If a person is healed,* he told himself, *then change to heterosexuality was possible.*

On his lunch break, Mark tried to call Carl, still chewing his tuna fish sandwich as he stepped outside the dining hall. He wanted to share with his son his excitement about the transformation he had just witnessed; he also wanted to apologize for having to cancel their father-son golf date. Carl's voicemail message came through, Mark leaving a message as his eyes roamed to two recognizable silhouettes: Lester and Earl spoke, their heads huddled together as if afraid someone would overhear their conversation. Mark's mind went to Heather, that unsettledness in his spirit resurfacing. *What was Earl hiding? And why did he seem to be confiding in Lester instead of him?*

Mark took the brief time he had left on his lunch break to make one more phone call. "Praise the Lord." Earl's wife, Agnes, answered the phone on the first ring with her usual cheerful greeting.

"Agnes, it's Mark. How are you doing?"

"Blessed. How's the retreat going?"

"Great. Very inspirational. Hey, I was wondering if Earl ever mentioned to you a woman he was helping from The Ruth and Naomi Project. Her name's Heather."

Mark's question was greeted with an uncomfortable silence on the other end of the line. After what seemed like an eternity, Agnes replied: "No, not that I can recall. But I'm actually at the church now. Let me look through the records to see if the name, Heather, comes up." For three painful minutes, Mark allowed himself to process what he was feeling; joy from knowing God had placed him into Lester's life, yet a profound sorrow in watching his best friend push him away.

"Mark, no one by that name has come through the center. And even if Earl is providing any kind of help outside of Ruth and Naomi, I would have done an initial intake form for this Heather girl."

"Agnes, this woman called Earl's phone and demanded that he give her money."

"When was this?" the concern in Agnes' voice audible.

Mark sighed, knowing he should have apprised Agnes the day of the phone call.

"Around the time of Carl's graduation. Not long after, Earl asked me if I would help him out legally if anything were to happen."

Agnes did not immediately respond to Mark's revelation. When she finally spoke, Mark felt that her weariness was familiar. It was as if she had experienced this betrayal before. "All we can do is pray," she finally managed. Mark looked up at the sky as clouds descended onto the open field. The grass expanse that had looked so lush just hours before now took on a hue that could only be described as dreary. Not knowing what else to say, Mark thanked Agnes for her time, told her to have a blessed day, and hung up the phone.

• • •

Jerry sat up, naked, in Brandon Weaver's bed. The musky scent of Brandon's cologne lingered in the air, as did the smell of sweat mingled with cum. Jerry hoped Brandon planned on changing his sheets tonight after he left. Jerry felt Brandon sit up next to him, his lips softly kissing Jerry's shoulder as their eyes locked and their lips intertwined yet again.

"He's cute," Mel had practically shouted over the latest remix to a popular Adele song a few hours earlier as she had pushed a nervous Jerry over to the bar. "Is that really Brandon Weaver?" Jerry had nodded as he studied the narrow jawline, the naturally curly hair slicked back, the chest hair glimmering against the dim disco lights.

"Guys, I can't do this." Jerry had pleaded as he turned to Leo and Carl, who were nursing vodka tonics while swaying to the syncopated beats of Adele setting fire to the rain.

Carl had thrown his head back, the contents of his drink gone as he tipsily clapped Leo on the shoulder. "Hey, I didn't mean to kiss you the other night. I was just... fucked up." Jerry's and Mel's eyes had widened, each demanding an explanation as the Adele remix transitioned into a Kelly Clarkson song.

Leo had brought Carl in for a hug, planting a sloppy kiss on his forehead, "It's not a big deal. And by the way, you're a good kisser. Whatever guy you end up with will be very lucky."

Moments such as these had reminded Jerry of what an amazing brother Leo was. He had pushed Jerry in the direction of the bar, toward the empty barstool next to Brandon, their eyes meeting as Kelly's audacious declaration of not being told what's supposed to be right belted over the speakers.

Brandon had pulled Jerry onto the dancefloor, throwing a question in between hip shakes and hand raises, in between Kelly Clarkson catching her breath and Rihanna finding love and Deborah Cox asking *How did you get here,* in between Jerry's smiles back at Mel, Leo, and Carl. Jerry had almost forgotten how to smile. "The essay you sent; why did you do it? Did you really think you could become straight?"

As the dim disco lights disappeared, Jerry moved from the middle of the dance floor, his hips no longer shaking to the syncopated rhythms of remixed pop songs. As he thought about how to answer Brandon's question, his mind flashed back.

• • •

"Welcome to Global Healing from Homosexuality, where change is possible," Becca, the receptionist who had provided Jerry and Percy with initial intake forms, gleefully greeted the duo. Jerry had recalled her rose-colored blouse hanging loosely off her bony frame as she handed him a clear clipboard with a series of questions he had to answer along with directions on how to complete each form. "Answer each question as honestly as you can. The next two forms are releases just stating that you agree to participate in life-changing restorative therapy."

Jerry followed Percy to an unoccupied set of chairs in the corner of the small waiting room. "Once you feel different," Percy assured Jerry as he stared blankly down at the forms in front of him, "we'll tell your mother. She doesn't need to know now."

Jerry nodded absentmindedly in his father's direction as he scanned the waiting room in silence – the dizzying pattern of colorful boxes on the beige carpet clashed with the just-too-bright blue bookshelves. Upon a more careful look, he was able to see some of the titles of the neatly arranged books on the shelves. "Not Born This Way" and "Discovering Your Innate Heterosexuality" immediately jumped out at him, supported by other titles that appeared to provide promises of leading a happy, healthy, heterosexual life. A rush of nausea rushed over Jerry. He thought he might pass out.

• • •

"I think I did it for my dad," Jerry replied, coming back to Brandon and the dance floor and the pulsing pop remixes that all of a sudden seemed far too loud. Brandon had laughed, shook his head, and – without a word – drug Jerry back out to the middle of the dance floor.

Not even an hour later, their clothes lay scattered on the bedroom floor, hastily removed with each kiss and grope and exploration. Brandon sighed as Jerry rested his head onto his chest, the hair on it tickling his face.

"Why did you really go to Global Healing?" Brandon inquired, looking at Jerry with a sincerity that almost demanded an honest reply.

• • •

The question once again sent Jerry back into the waiting room, filling out the ridiculous questionnaire: *How long have you experienced same-sex attractions? How many sexual partners have you had? How do you see yourself overcoming your same-*

sex attractions? Before he could even bring himself to write his name and birthdate at the top of the page, Jerry was interrupted by a bald man with a thin, high-pitched voice, calling his name from an open doorway.

Lester Dawson, Jerry's future therapist whose oversized black polo shirt hung loosely off his large frame, escorted Jerry and Percy down a narrow hallway, the oak colored doors strangely complementing the gold-painted walls. As they walked briskly, Jerry was able to hastily read the names of the other therapists embroidered on the doors: "Calvin Ruben, Gender and Life Coach," "Renee Gabrielson, Psychotherapist."

Lester's office was situated at the end of the hallway, its open door welcoming them into an airy space that pleasantly smelled like a mixture of pine air freshener and expensive cologne. A chestnut shelf crowded with photos of men in tuxedos posing next to women in angelic, white wedding gowns lined the back wall. Even though Jerry wasn't convinced by any of it, he had to admire Lester's commitment to establishing his brand of therapy, despite its untenable foundations. Lester had proudly paraded his own family on his desk, he and his wife, a woman who had a penchant for striped pastel blouses hugged their three children: twin boys and a girl.

"Have a seat," Lester ushered Jerry and Percy to an overstuffed black couch that sat in the middle of the room. Lester wasted no time and got right down to discussing his therapeutic approach with details that Jerry could only describe as nauseating. Lester went on to explain how the therapy was broken down into three main components: eliminating all sexual behavior with members of the same sex, identifying and healing the emotional wounds that caused Jerry to develop same-sex attractions, and reclaiming Jerry's inner masculinity through the help of Calvin Ruben.

"Jerry's never had sex with a man. That first part should be easy," Percy had chuckled, nervously scratching a mosquito bite on his cheek that had started to bleed.

"This also extends to sexual fantasy and masturbation," Lester replied, glancing briefly at Percy before landing his gaze on Jerry.

Jerry's left hand began to twitch as Lester continued his speech, perpetually reiterating the importance of removing people from Jerry's life who affirmed the *gay* identity and surrounding himself with people who believed that change to heterosexuality was possible. Jerry studied his father's disposition, memorizing the frenetic head nods and hypnotizing stare as Lester pointed to photos of his success stories on that chestnut shelf. A glimmer in Percy's eyes had indicated the resurrection of those dreams Jerry had killed once he uttered the phrase, *I'm gay.*

Bullshit was pretty much the only thought Jerry had as he sat in that office and continued to look around. His eyes settled briefly on the prominently framed Master's Degree from Reston University, an online college that Jerry would later find out ran into accreditation issues due to their nonexistent admissions requirements. As Lester droned on, Percy nodded in earnest as Jerry grew increasingly restless. Finally, he stood up and, without so much as a word to his father or Lester, marched out.

Percy shot up out of his chair and followed Jerry down the hall, his venomous hisses stopping Jerry in his tracks: "Get back in there."

"What are you gonna do?" Jerry hissed back, facing his father's hardened features head-on.

"Academic fraud."

Those two words had shackled Jerry to the waiting room, the photo of *Mind. Body. Spirit.* the only discernible object he could identify.

"You walk out that door, I will call the College Board and tell them you took Leo's SATs, and your chances of getting into NYU will vanish."

"Fuck you."

• • •

Jerry rested his head against the rust-colored bedpost in Brandon's room. Brandon's impatience as he awaited Jerry's answer faded once he realized that Jerry's whole body was shaking. Brandon gently reached over and covered Jerry's exposed torso with his obscenely bright purple comforter. The two were silent for a while as Brandon opened the drawer on his nightstand. He unveiled a large maroon binder, the name "Global Healing from Homosexuality Corporation" written across it with a Sharpie. Brandon handed it to Jerry.

"I think Rainbow Warriors will be a good fit for you," Brandon smiled.

Jerry took the binder and opened it. Memories of him kicking stuffed animals across Lester's office flooded his mind, mixed with his screams about Ella's death ringing in his ears and his shrieks about his mother's paralyzing grief sending shivers down his spine. Jerry turned to a section labeled Supporters, which contained an organization chart similar to the ones Jerry saw when he visited OEI. Bishop Earl Wilson's photo was circled with a red pen. Below his photo, connected by a vertical black line, was Mark Perkins.

"Brandon, I don't know." Jerry turned the pages to an article posted on Holy Boldness' website that featured a picture of Mark Perkins and Lester Dawson shaking hands, overly-eager grins plastering their faces below an article title that simply read "Mending the Wounds of the LGBT Community." Jerry instantly thought of Carl and the pain his friend was undoubtedly in as he watched his father's unholy partnership unravel before his eyes. Jerry knew he had to do something.

"You gotta be all in Jerry. What we need is someone who can take these bastards down."

"The gay identity is something you need to rid yourself of," Lester's voice echoed in Jerry's head. Eight months had passed since his last session with Lester; eight months since Jerry threatened to expose his father's secret, an action that had precipitated their estrangement.

"Ok. I can do it," Jerry replied, wondering if Brandon could detect the quiver in his voice.

Brandon smiled as he leaned in to kiss him, the prickly hairs on his chin tickling Jerry's face, "This is obviously painful for you, and I want you to know that I'm here."

Jerry closed the binder and allowed Brandon to hold him, allowed himself to become entranced by the sky blue walls and the Human Rights Campaign posters and the collage of pride parade photos, all of which contained Brandon smiling with a group of friends amidst a crowd of drag queens and bears in leather chaps. His eyes closed as he heard the faint sound of the light being turned off.

10

WHO KNEW?

An emotionally drained Harriet sat in Louisa's dreary living room and looked around. The overtly religious artwork, from the painting of The Last Supper to the dozens of scriptures meticulously written in calligraphy and hung in golden frames, reminded Harriet of why she rarely visited her friend in her home. Today was the first of many planning meetings for the annual Domestic Violence Awareness Gala, an event sponsored by The Ruth and Naomi Project. Harriet wished she had ignored Louisa's phone call on her way to therapy. She had forgotten how depressing Agnes' somber tone could be when she rattled on about this issue's lack of visibility in churches; this was not a meeting she should be attending after the session she had had that day with Dr. Rowan.

"Eve, you made it," Harriet sipped her tea as the pint-sized blond appeared in Louisa's living room wearing a sleeveless salmon-colored blouse. Eve Parsons and Agnes Wilson had attended college together, and although both women seemed to have little in common, they still remained close friends. Their friendship mirrored that of Harriet and Louisa's. Eve was a lukewarm Roman Catholic, while Agnes was a devout Methodist. This event was one of the few things that connected them. As Louisa prepared a cup of coffee for Eve, Agnes shared another tireless anecdote about how women of faith were silent sufferers of domestic abuse.

As Agnes droned on, Harriet's mind wandered to her most recent session with Dr. Rowan. It had begun in the usual fashion – Dr. Rowan had asked Harriet about her week, where she had immediately recalled waking up the morning before in an acute state of panic. Ella had no longer been the focal point of Harriet's dreams. Instead, she had dreamt of rushing to a job interview, frenetically changing into a turquoise blouse while awaiting Amy's arrival. Harriet had remembered clutching her black portfolio to her bosom as she examined her hair in the powder room, remembering the honk of Amy's car, after which she was jolted awake.

"It seems the Wellbutrin is having a positive effect," Dr. Rowan's chimed in. This startled Harriet. How was the absence of her daughter from her dreams a good thing? She spent the next 10 minutes analyzing her guilt while drawing tiny lines in the sandbox on Dr. Rowan's table.

"Harriet, is Jerry available to play the piano for this event?" The women all turned toward Harriet, sipping their coffee from tiny beige cups, oblivious to her exhaustion. Unbeknownst to Harriet, Louisa had already begun discussing entertainment for the evening.

"I'll ask him," she replied absentmindedly, noting to herself that there was quite a lot she'd like to ask her son these days. For one, when had he planned to tell her about dropping out of MIT and moving to New York? And where the heck did he go every day when he left for "work?" Why couldn't he tell her where he was working or how he spent his days? These questions danced around Harriet's mind as Louisa discussed the gala's venue. She and Agnes had booked the BlackRock Center for the Arts, a contemporary arts gallery in Germantown, Maryland. She drifted in and out of attention as Louisa enthusiastically described the original artwork she planned to hang. Harriet's mind churned through Percy's protests at the breakfast table upon Jerry's announcement that he had dropped out of MIT.

"I've known for a while. I was just waiting for you to tell me. When you're ready, can we talk about New York?" Harriet turned to Jerry with a meek smile on her face, unsuccessfully attempting to balance out Percy's anger

"You just can't move to New York without telling your parents, Jerry! What the hell were you thinking?!"

Harriet had remembered that Jerry responded by angrily snatching a slice of Percy's French toast from his plate and walking out the door.

"I don't have to tell you anything. Gotta get to work." Jerry's eyes narrowed in Percy's direction, the tension between them obviously thickening with every passing day. As Harriet had swallowed her Wellbutrin, she looked over at Percy, still perplexed at what point this man with whom she shared her life had become such a stranger. She had to side with Jerry on this. Percy had forfeited the right to know anything about Jerry when he refused to accept who his son was, which included his sexuality.

Harriet felt a light tap on her shoulder. Louisa had taken a seat next to her as Agnes and Eve reviewed the preliminary menu Agnes had drafted, Harriet overhearing Eve's impatient grunts.

"How are you?" Louisa gently touched Harriet's arm, a warm and inviting smile appearing across her face as she adjusted her latest floral patterned dress: yellow dandelions against a forest green background.

"I'm feeling better now," Harriet replied honestly. "I'm taking an antidepressant, and I think it's really helping. I'm starting to feel like myself for the first time in five years."

Louisa's polite nod indicated her uneasiness about a topic she obviously found taboo. In the Perkins' home, Christ was the antidote to depression and anxiety.

"You know, we should all do a fun girls' trip. Just me, you, and Amy. And I really think Agnes could tag along. Wouldn't that be fun?"

Harriet politely nodded as she envisioned Louisa and Agnes gasping in utter horror upon finding out that Amy had tricked them into going to a burlesque show. Harriet immediately texted Amy about Louisa's idea, catching a glimpse of Louisa wincing once she saw who Harriet was texting. As Harriet predicted, her conversation with Louisa idled, drifting into an awkward silence that Agnes thankfully broke when she requested to speak with Louisa in private. Eve joined Harriet, the couch's plastic covering squealing as Eve sighed heavily. The two women stared at each other, their beleaguered glances communicating their irritation over this planning meeting.

"Do you think there's any hard liquor here?" Eve whispered. Harriet shook her head as Eve rolled her eyes. The two women, who were once close, had drifted apart after Ella's death. Eve's daughter, Spencer, had been one of Ella's best friends. The two women had bonded over playdates, throwing back glasses of Chardonnay as their daughters played with dolls, complaining over how much work they brought home. However, those days were distant memories.

"Eve, what's in store for Percy?" Eve sighed as Harriet listened to the hushed tones of Louisa and Agnes in the kitchen, her mind traveling back to her own kitchen as she brought up the preposterousness of Percy's lawsuit.

Just that morning, Percy had communicated with Harriet that he had every intention of continuing with his unlawful termination lawsuit. He said that his lawyer, Landon, thought that he had a chance of winning if he could produce some witnesses that would attest to how Greg had treated him. Harriet was exhausted by all of it and was disgusted that Percy seemed to have more energy to fight for a job that he no longer had than for his relationship with his own son. "Just walk away, Percy," she had told him, "Greg's gonna fight you until you have no money left. And he'll probably win anyway."

Eve's shoulders slumped as the plastic on the sofa creaked against her blouse. She dreaded having to answer her friend's question. "Well," Eve began reluctantly, "a woman claims that Percy sexually harassed her."

Harriet nearly fell over onto the carpet in disbelief. Percy Nelson may be many things, but a misogynist was undoubtedly not one of them, "Eve, come on. Really?"

Eve gently touched Harriet's hand, the cold metal of her bracelet brushing up against Harriet's wrist. "I told Greg about the lawsuit, and on the same day, Heather Carter was in Greg's office. A week later, legal is going over OEI's sexual harassment countersuit."

Harriet and Eve spoke no further on this issue; Harriet absorbed Eve's disillusionment about being a working mother, reveling in the sordid tales of her raucous teenage daughter, her intelligent, yet unfocused son, her useless husband. There were no polite smiles or awkward silences as the two women caught up. As Harriet caught a brief glance of Louisa hugging a disheartened Agnes, she inwardly acknowledged how much she missed her old self. She also acknowledged how unfazed she was by the prospect of Percy's involvement with another woman.

• • •

Faith's disappearing acts had begun way back in April of 2000. Heather had been living in a one-bedroom apartment in Dupont Circle then and had become accustomed to the recognizable knocks on her door of Devin, Faith's then seven-year-old son. The raps were impatient and choppy, indicative of a child in distress. He always appeared the same way on her doorstep – Pokémon cards clenched tightly in one hand, unwashed clothes emanating a faint odor, uncombed hair finishing off the disheveled look. His piercing blue eyes revealed a vulnerability that never failed to sadden Heather deeply. It was usually Devin's brother, Trey, who would announce the reason for their visit, which always came on the tail of their mother riding off into her latest crystal meth abyss.

The boys' visits had become longer as Faith's disappearing acts became more frequent; four days would become one week, then two weeks, then one month. By August 2002, Faith had decided to make their visits permanent, something Heather had expected when she exchanged the queen-sized bed for two twin beds in her room and her ballet videos for an Xbox. She had made the painful, but necessary final exchange: her career with the Alvin Ailey dance company for a receptionist job at a hedge fund.

As Heather reflected on the sacrifices she had made twelve years ago, she took in the majestic view of the Shady Grove Golf Course – the lushness of its grass, the faint murmur of golf carts transporting elite businessmen in khaki pants and white sneakers around the course. These men had once intimidated Heather to the point where she avoided making eye contact with them. As Brendan focused his aim and positioned his golf club at a 45-degree angle, Heather impatiently cleared her throat, clutching her golf club as Brendan swung widely, the golf ball propelling upward and landing in the pond.

"I need a favor."

Brendan's brow furrowed as he scratched his neatly combed blond hair, obviously intent on not letting Heather's request distract him from focusing on his subpar swinging abilities. Greg had apprised Heather in excruciating detail about how golf meetings operated. Business was not to be discussed until both parties had sufficiently participated in a competitive round of golf. *Whatever*, she thought. The urgency of the meeting in question superseded these protocols.

"You're not gonna play a round with me?" Heather groaned as she thought about the looming revelations Alma Velasquez threatened to make. Heather reflected on the young woman whose mercurial state of mind had to be coaxed. Jacquelyn had done the coaxing; she had gingerly held back Alma's hair as she vomited into the toilet, confiding in Jacquelyn about Earl sodomizing her. It was Jacquelyn who had convinced Silas to put a gun to Earl's head and watch him plead for his life; it was she who had given Alma $5,000 in cash as compensation for enduring such an unconscionable act. And because of Alma, Jacquelyn had to erase her identity.

"Brendan, someone's poking a very dangerous beehive, one that involves you." Brendan's golf club lowered as he met Heather's impatient glare. Now she had his attention. He saw his once impenetrable world crumble, envisioning every one of his salacious practices publicized. His face sank; his chapped lips quivered. "Say no more. Greg told me you were discreet."

"We are, and we intend to stay that way. But Alma Velasquez is trying to get her prostitution charge overturned so her DACA status can be renewed."

Brendan shook his head as he took out his phone, landing on a number that he dialed shakily, then introduced himself. "Judge Constance Schuler, this is Brendan Alexander with DOJ."

Heather watched him shrivel into an acquiescent boy as he nervously inquired about Alma's case.

"I see," he squealed. "I can absolutely do that. Thank you, Your Honor. Thank you so much."

He disconnected and smiled widely at Heather, "It's being handled. Alma's DACA status is gonna be renewed. I just have to write her grandson a recommendation letter for Harvard Law."

Heather's phone vibrated before she could respond. A text message from an unrecognizable number appeared on her screen: *Hello. This is Agnes Wilson. I believe you know my husband, Earl Wilson. We need to talk. Please call me when you get the chance.*

Heather hastily fabricated an excuse to leave the golf session early. As she drove to Capitol Boutique, she devised ways to murder Earl and conspicuously dispose of his body. She parked in a vacant spot in front of the brownstone, making a concerted effort not to hit the red Corvette in front of her.

The main sales floor was sprinkled with a few customers interested in buying evening gowns. Padma assisted one woman whose unsightly bat wings precluded her from the majority of the dresses for sale. While Padma beamed her approval as the woman held the black sleeveless gown over her corpulent figure, Heather made her way into her office. She was surprised to find Devin sitting there, hunched over a GRE preparation book with his blond hair hanging over his focused face.

"Devin?" He closed his book as he looked up at Heather and sighed heavily.

"Hand me my laptop." Heather quickly logged in and uncovered the weekly schedule of sessions. Much to her chagrin, Earl was currently in a session with Deanne. One of Heather's indisputable rules was to never interrupt a client's session unless it was an emergency. She paced the floor of her office, shooting furtive glances at Devin as he poured over the exam questions. Red rubber shards of his eraser fell by Heather's feet as she crafted her warning to Earl.

Earl's carelessness had exposed her to Mark Perkins, and Heather's own exposure to this insurmountable risk had warranted a stiff penalty, one that would compensate for the consequences of Earl's wife uncovering her husband's proclivities. As Deanne and Earl walked down the stairs leading to the kitchen, Heather opened her office door and met them at the stairs. The wooden kitchen door slammed shut as she pointed a finger in Earl's direction.

"Deanne, wait in my office, please. Devin will sign you out."

Earl stood before Heather, a euphoric grin plastered across his face, the ridiculous gold cross he wore clinging to his broad neck. That grin faded once she took out her phone and shoved the text message into Earl's face.

He read it, eyes widening. Then silence, followed by a slow and calculated, "Heather, it's not what you think."

Heather stood in front of Earl, his double chin jiggling as she dug her nails into his arm. He winced. "What did you tell Mark?" Heather's nails inched their way into the folds of Earl's soft shoulders.

"I already told you," he began crying as Heather inhaled the smell of sweat mingled with cheap cologne. Earl was lying, each lie emanating from his pores.

"You're best friends. Come on, Earl. You told him something else. Didn't you?" She released her grip as Earl massaged his skin, lifting up his sleeve to a pattern of deep red welts along his upper arm, their shape growing as Earl rubbed his hand over them. Earl fell to his knees, particles of dust from the kitchen floor ascending as he plopped down sobbing.

"I asked Mark to help me if things got out of hand." And there it was, the truth in its entirety. That one question raised Mark's suspicions, and he, in turn, alerted Agnes. "I'm sorry."

Earl's sobs only served to further irritate Heather. She marched onto the main sales floor and snatched a pair of pearl earrings from the display table; Earl's financial penalty glimmered against the fluorescent lights as Padma rearranged shoes that had been scattered across the floor. Heather caught Padma stealing glances at her.

"Finish up. Your client's coming in an hour."

Padma muttered her compliance as Heather opened the kitchen door to find Earl still sitting in his pathetic fetal position. She shoved the earrings in his face.

"What's this?" He slowly stood up and looked at Heather, who proceeded to explain how she had planned to dispel any suspicions of Earl's sexual impropriety. He nodded earnestly as Heather instructed him to retrieve his phone from her office and type his wife a text message that explained how Heather was a freelance jeweler who sold him a pair of earrings as a surprise for Agnes.

"Mention how you didn't have the cash to pay for it upfront." Earl stared blankly as Devin walked into the kitchen. "Why aren't your fingers moving?"

Earl frenetically typed as Devin tapped her on the shoulder. The manufactured sounds of a keyboard tapping increased as Heather listened for the swish sound of the send button.

"Heather, what's going on? I heard someone yelping."

Earl stared at the earrings and gently placed his phone into his pocket. Heather grabbed his elbow as Earl left, his face wincing in pain. "Three grand in cash. Next week."

"What?" Heather's nails dug into Earl's arm, fresh welts undoubtedly forming as she twisted her nails counterclockwise.

"Heather!" Earl gasped as Devin tried to force Heather's nails from Earl's arm to no avail.

"That's the price of your carelessness. Three grand in cash. If it's not here next week, I'm dropping you as a client. Then maybe you can convince your own wife to fuck you in the ass." With that, she released her grip on Earl as he slithered away, the smell of his cheap cologne lingering in the stale air. Heather and Devin stared at each other, the fear and uncertainty that were once in Devin's eyes gone. His disapproval disgusted her; his newfound morality confounded her.

"Heather, did you really have to do that?" Heather was tired of Devin questioning her motives, and at that moment realized she didn't have to tolerate his disapproval anymore.

"Devin, you don't wanna be here. I get it. You're fired."

Wordlessly, Devin walked into Heather's office and gathered his things. She watched as he shoved his GRE preparation book into this black backpack; she silently observed his slumped shoulders, unsure if he was disappointed or relieved. Heather took herself back to the kitchen, back to the one in which she visualized friends dancing in her backyard, drunk off Sangria, oblivious to their middle-class worries. Who were these friends? The only person she talked to was walking out the door with a backpack on his shoulders. She prepared for Devin's deafening silence in the form of unreturned phone calls and declined dinner invitations.

● ● ●

It had been six days since Jerry had hovered over the toilet in the hall bathroom, inhaling the pungent odor of bleach as he shoved his middle finger down his throat, the sound of water coursing through the pipes. His last purge had not been as exhaustive; the entire box of Oreos he binged on was thrown up in a matter of five minutes, the acidic aftertaste not as potent. As he wrote the details he gathered on Global Healing on the whiteboard, his mind traveled back to a disturbing session with Lester. During that session, Lester had implored Jerry to access his anger toward his parents. He remembered that uncomfortable exercise in which he hit a stuffed teddy bear with a baseball bat

"We gotta confront this anger if we're gonna heal from it." Lester's insistent tone unsettled Jerry as the baseball bat he swung made contact with the stuffed animal. As the bear landed against the wall, next to the trophy wedding photos, Jerry screamed every bad thing he could conjure about his father.

"Piece. Of. Shit."

"Louder!" Lester yelled as he stood so close to him that the spit from his words sprinkled Jerry on the forehead.

"You disappeared after Ella died! Your family needed you!"

Jerry had received high praise from Lester for his session that day. Any activity Lester had deemed conducive to change satisfied him, a gleeful smile plastered across his face as his eyebrows arched in sheer astonishment and the vein atop his bald head pulsed excitedly. Jerry had remembered the car ride home with Percy later that afternoon, sitting in purposeful silence as his father endlessly probed him about the sessions. He had also recalled buying a dozen doughnuts from 7-Eleven on that same day, waiting until his parents had fallen asleep before binge eating them in his bed, the powdered sugar falling like snow onto his black comforter. An hour later, he had thrown them up.

"Jerry?" The soft fabric of Mel's white polo shirt lightly brushed against his elbow as he clung to the enlarged photo of Earl Wilson. Her gentle tap brought him back to his present state, the mustard green walls of the war room, the cedar color of the conference room table already littered with case files about Global Healing. As Jerry taped the photo of Earl to the whiteboard and drew an arrow from the picture to Lester's name, his mind transported him back into Lester's pine-scented office, his stoic posture the focus of this particular session.

"You seem closed off. Is there something you wanna talk about?" Jerry had shaken his head, knowing Lester would eventually manipulate the uncomfortable silence to get Jerry talking.

"Earl Wilson!" Jerry snapped out of his painful nostalgia and glared at Earl's unassuming smile in the photo on the whiteboard. His large neck and receding hairline had been decrying the evils of homosexual sex for years, promoting fallacies about the drug-addicted, disease-ridden, despotic gay men who were determined to lure young children into their deviant lifestyle. This same man who preached change through the power of Jesus Christ had been procuring the same sexual acts he repudiated on Christian talk shows.

"A rapist. A man who's leading a double life." Jerry's anger intensified at the mere thought of Earl's hypocrisy. Patrick, Mel's boss, entered the room, hastily apologizing for his tardiness as he took a seat next to Brandon. Brandon's soft hazel eyes locked with Jerry's. Something about Brandon intrigued him. Was it the sly grin? Was it the casual manner in which he inquired about Jerry's state of mind as he poured over case files late at night? Was it the intoxication Jerry felt when Brandon leaned in to kiss him, inhaling the scent of his rustic cologne.

"Do we have proof that Earl is a rapist?" asked Brandon. Mel delicately explained how her client, Alma, had confessed to Earl sodomizing her but then proceeded to explain why she could not testify despite her readiness to come forward with her devastating experience.

Patrick cemented this predicament with his own dire explanation. "Someone very influential does not want Alma to testify. That's why her felony prostitution conviction was overturned." Prepared for this scenario, Jerry proposed a radical course of action. Mel informed him of photos Earl had taken, their discovery imminent. His proposition raised many eyebrows: uncover the images and have them displayed in a public setting, an event in which their authenticity could not be refuted.

"I'm playing at this benefit for domestic violence awareness in a week," Jerry continued. That should be a perfect venue to unveil Earl's proclivities."

Callie, Rainbow Warriors' IT whiz, smiled coyly. Her mind began to spin as her fingers had already started feverishly moving across her laptop's keyboard. During his short time at Rainbow Warriors, Jerry had witnessed Callie's genius over late-night dinners of cheeseburgers and fries. Her exceptional coding uncovered information very few people could access. Today was no exception. As she pounded the return key, her spiky blond hair facing Jerry as she hunched over in concentration, she gleefully squealed and yanked the HDMI cable that projected her laptop's screen onto the whiteboard.

"I won't bore you with all the details, but I've written a code that allows me to automatically download and open any files located on a USB drive or CD. Just need Earl to insert one into his computer." The projected screen began rapidly firing off lines of indecipherable code, the green letters zooming across Earl's photo. Earl had inserted a USB drive into his computer because a screen suddenly appeared with meticulously labeled folders: "Church Finances," "Fellowship," "Memories." Callie opened the folder labeled "Church Finances," which led to bank statements detailing large sums of money withdrawn over a three year period being plastered over the whiteboard. Callie rapidly clicked on another folder, "Fellowship." A series of photos swiftly appeared and revealed Earl's garish figure in an adult diaper, his unruly chest chair and potbelly among two of the many eyesores the images revealed.

Jerry watched as a middle-aged man pleasured himself while being penetrated by a masked hooker wearing a dildo. Lester's fabrications about the unnaturalness of anal sex rang in Jerry's ear; his mind traveled back to that black couch where he had sat in stoic silence.

"How do you think sex with a man feels?" Lester implored.

Caught off guard, Jerry shrugged.

"Well, what gets you off when you watch porn?" Lester's patience had dissipated, the abject silence in which Jerry sat infuriating him. Lester had instructed Jerry to stand, which he did, and close his eyes, which he did. Lester circled around Jerry.

"Two men together. It's hot. Cock sucking. Rimming. Anal. But porn doesn't show you the torn rectum or the fact that you have to purge your large intestine before being penetrated." Lester's viciousness shone through with every word he uttered, which in turn extracted a shame from Jerry for deriving pleasure from two men having sex. Whether or not the phrases Lester had spouted had any veracity behind them, their intentions were achieved.

Snapping himself back to the present moment, Jerry half-listened as Callie discussed her plan to send Agnes an email with a virus in the link. Callie animatedly described how the virus would contain the code that would display Earl's salacious photos when Agnes began her presentation.

"What's your backup plan?" asked Mel.

Callie smirked as she unveiled a tiny, black USB drive. "I'll be there to ensure those photos get displayed. Now how do I score an invite to this event?"

Jerry immediately volunteered to bring Callie as his date. He envisioned Earl's photos against the ivory walls and the aghast expressions on the faces of churchgoers in their stuffy evening wear. He imagined Earl's crippling humiliation, a feeling Jerry knew all too well. As the meeting's culmination drew near, Brandon pulled Jerry to the side and inquired about the inspiration behind Earl being publicly humiliated. His answer was simple: Lester Dawson. Who knew something positive could be reaped from conversion therapy?

11

THE DRAGON THAT NEEDS SLAYING

Carl's depiction of adultery had been that of a married man having a sexual relationship with a woman who wasn't his wife. In church, his father had preached about the twofold sin of adultery more than once, these sermons conjuring up visions of a good-looking man seducing a pretty blond secretary at work while Mark lamented how adultery severely deviated from God's plan for marriage. Even though these visions aroused Carl as he pictured clandestine meetings in hotel rooms with passionate kisses and the hasty removal of clothing, his thoughts always returned to the dire sermon his father preached. Carl's juvenile imaginings of adultery had never included his own recent behavior – until today.

He was barely able to focus on the rehearsal for the gala, his mind perpetually wandering to the night he had driven off the church parking lot to the Penguin, a gay bar in Pentagon City where he would meet Don. The white steeple of the church had quickly vanished in his rearview mirror, becoming out of reach like so many things that were once important to him. *Why had he felt so compelled to be with Don?*

Jerry had begun playing the introduction to "The Heart of Life," Carl's unenthusiastic singing causing him to fall behind the tempo. He stopped singing when he realized Jerry had begun playing the bridge to the song. Carl sat down in one of the dining room chairs and pretended to look over the lyrics he had printed out, the glare of the crystal chandelier reminding him of the Penguin.

The bar had given off a quaintness, yet Carl still had felt the stares directed his way. An elderly man with thinning gray hair had winked at him, his scintillating glances making Carl squirm in his seat. Carl had not been accustomed to being objectified, watching Don chuckle as he tried to avert his eyes from the old man's stares.

"Carl, would it help if I slow down?" Jerry walked over to the dining room table and rested his hands next to Carl's sheet of lyrics. Carl grunted as Jerry brushed away strands of his curly hair to make eye contact with Carl. He knew Jerry had noticed his perfunctory demeanor, but cautiously began playing the song anyway. Carl started singing, his eyes wandering to the sheet of lyrics. As Jerry played the instrumental interlude, Carl briefly traveled back to the dimly lit lounge filled with lustful stares from strangers and Don's gentle massage of his knee.

"You are devastatingly handsome. When you sing at church, every single time you lift up your hands I get so fucking hard that I have to close my eyes and cover my crotch with my Bible."

Carl sang the ending of the song, foregoing his usual vocal embellishments in an effort to return to that evening with Don. He wanted to go back to the waiter who mentally undressed him while announcing the chef specials to him and Don. Carl had discerned that he was the special for the evening, his dark brown hair and piercing green eyes the entrée every gay man wanted to eat. As the night progressed, the conversation had taken a more serious tone. Carl picked at his entrée, roasted duck with garlic mashed potatoes, washing down the meat's dryness with the glass of white wine he ordered, his mind racing with so many questions.

"Do you think change is possible?"

Don had nearly devoured his steak as Carl studied the bemused arch of his eyebrow. Wiping his mouth, he had leaned back in his chair, his eyes locking with Carl's. "I don't know."

Carl transitioned back to Jerry's dining room, surprised to overhear Jerry and Percy arguing. *How long had he been in a trance?* Jerry stood by the basement steps in the kitchen, Carl catching a glimpse of Percy's broad forehead as he positioned himself on the top step.

"I really don't care how hurt you were. You started this, remember?"

"I am your father. I wanted what was best for you."

"Fuck off already!" Jerry slammed the basement door and headed back into the dining room, his face red as he took a seat at the piano. Carl had never seen the two of them argue. He had never heard Jerry curse at his own father. The two of them were silent, Carl deciding to ignore the confrontation and rehearse the rest of the set.

Not knowing what to say, Carl hoped to bring Jerry's attention back to the task at hand. "'The Pieces Don't Fit Anymore' is a good song," he offered.

Jerry nodded and played the introduction as Carl started singing the first verse, its lyrics penetrating Carl to his core, taking him back to late nights in bed wondering how life would be if he came out as gay, to that first sexual encounter with Don, to the dimly lit lounge where he and Don ate. The pieces of his life did not fit into the neat crevices in which they were supposed to. His faith told him that being with a man was gravely immoral, yet he knew this part of him would not go away.

"You've been married to a woman for twelve years, and you don't know?" Carl's indignation had been premature. He had craved answers to questions he could not ask, desired a commitment from a married man, and demanded affirmation from a faith that viewed homosexuality as a choice.

Carl threw the sheet of lyrics onto the table, no longer having the desire to sing. Jerry slowly got up from behind the piano and sat next to Carl. They each fidgeted, Jerry with his hair, and Carl with the crucifix around his neck. The faint hum of the air conditioner as it clicked on was the room's only audible sound.

"I'm dating a married man," Carl finally blurted out.

Jerry's eyes widened as he adjusted his posture and followed a strand of his curly hair that fell to his ears. He chuckled and pointed to the basement door he had slammed moments ago. Jerry's laughs became louder as Carl started laughing. He laughed at the cliché his life was becoming; he laughed at the irony of being in a church that preached conversion to heterosexuality; he laughed to keep from crying.

"My dad blackmailed me into going to conversion therapy," Jerry's laughs had subsided as he leaned forward, picking at that same strand of hair by his ear. The two of them sat at the dining room table, the unencumbered sighs of speaking the truth the only sound between them. Jerry and Carl did not give each other advice, nor did they probe the other for details about their revelations. Instead, they refocused their energy on the rehearsal at hand. The subsequent songs surprisingly applied to Carl's life, their lyrics carrying a potency Carl never knew existed. As he and Jerry finished rehearsing, Carl returned to that evening at the Penguin, the intoxicating memories rushing over him like a tidal wave. And while riding this emotional tidal wave was exhilarating, the crash was unbearable.

"It's complicated, Carl. I don't wanna break up my family. I don't want Nick to have to shuffle between two houses."

Carl felt dizzy from the three glasses of wine he drank. He had put himself in a losing position, one in which someone got hurt. "Then, why are we here?"

Don had gently touched Carl's knee, his fingers dancing along his thigh, inching toward his crotch. "I like you. I like you a lot."

Carl sat back in Jerry's dining room chair, counting the number of crystals on the chandelier, knowing he had to stop seeing Don. The chandelier's glare gave him a headache.

• • •

Mark detested his black suit. If he held his arms out, the suit jacket might fit better. If he took shallow breaths, his pants might not feel so tight. The spiral staircase led to Jerry's keyboard, the fullness of each chord accentuated by Carl's effortless singing. He listened to a song about the painful yet necessary demise of a derelict relationship, the lyrics perpetually reiterating that the pieces don't fit anymore. Mark politely mingled with guests, many of whom were members of New Zion or Holy Boldness. His eyes rested on Percy and Harriet, noticing that the couple looked so miserable at even being in each other's company. He made a mental note to say a prayer for their Holy Union that evening. Mark remembered his raucous college days with Percy, Harriet, and Louisa, filled with spirited debates on current events over games of beer pong and spontaneous road trips to Nashville, Orlando, and Chicago, nursing hangovers while driving on the interstate. As much as Mark missed those days of youthful indiscretion, he loved his new life in Christ. Spontaneous road trips were not as exciting as following the Holy Spirit's guidance.

"Mark! Long time," Percy clapped him on the shoulder as he clumsily grabbed several hors d'oeuvres. The server nearly lost her balance as he snagged another sausage and cheese cracker. *Did Percy realize that other people had to eat?*

"Good to see you. Harriet, long time." The two politely kissed as the three of them stood in interminable silence. Mark's attention was diverted when he spotted Ian, a young man he remembered meeting the first day he visited one of Lester's workshops. Ian's freshly cut hair made him nearly unrecognizable, but Mark would have remembered those eyes anywhere. His blue suit appeared equally uncomfortable as he shook his legs and widened his stance.

• • •

Mark thought back to his drafty office, consoling a despondent Ian who had been unable to make eye contact with him. Ian's distressed state had been magnified by his blue jeans and wrinkled t-shirt, along with his sobs onto Mark's shoulders.

"I got lonely, so I went to this gay club I used to frequent."

Mark and Don had patiently listened as Ian described the palpable loneliness he felt, a pain so acute that it drove Ian to a lifestyle he had forsaken a year ago. Mark had tried to put himself into Ian's shoes, envisioning having desires that were antithetical to God's plan, imagining the subsequent isolation from working to overcome same-sex attractions.

"What happened?" Mark had asked.

Ian sobbed onto Mark's shoulder, "I didn't go in. I just couldn't."

At that moment, the Holy Spirit had implored Mark to implement a ministry for people like Ian. When the Holy Spirit spoke to Mark, his body's physiological response had always been the same – a chill coursing through his body, rushing up his spine.

• • •

Mark greeted Ian as Agnes made her way to the chestnut podium, her composure almost angelic as her pearl earrings glimmered against the fluorescent lights.

"I saw the woman arguing with her husband outside," Ian stood next to Mark as his brow furrowed.

"What were they saying?" Mark made eye contact with Ian as he overheard Louisa's enthusiastic introduction of Agnes. Ian averted his eyes.

"You can tell me," Mark coaxed.

"Something about the pearl earrings covering up his lies."

An Ian relayed this altercation, Mark observed Agnes scanning the anticipating glances. Why had she withheld these reservations from Mark and Louisa? *Why had she fawned over Earl's thoughtfulness if she felt otherwise?*

"Her husband forcefully grabbed her arm," Ian continued.

The room began to close in around Mark. He faced Ian, who in turn nervously scanned the patrons around him. Earl's tenuous behavior was starting to make sense. Resting his hands on Ian's shoulders, Mark diminished his own anxieties, making a concerted effort to quell Ian's anxiety. "Hey, I meant what I said. You belong here," said Mark.

Ian nodded as Agnes shakily began her speech, her PowerPoint presentation revealing statistic after statistic – coupled with compelling anecdotes from real people's lives – about the reality of domestic abuse in the United States.

"In my work, I have seen women beaten beyond recognition by their spouses or partners. One woman had been sent to the emergency room seventeen times over the course of three months. Her husband broke her arm, knocked her unconscious, pushed her out of a moving car with her son in the back seat." There was a pain in Agnes' voice, an implicit cry for help.

Mark had witnessed that same brokenness in Ian, and although he had never experienced their pain, he knew God wanted him to address it.

All of a sudden, pictures of Earl began popping onto the screen. Mark's eyes widened as the resounding shrieks filled the room. With each photo that flashed across the screen, Mark felt like he was getting closer and closer to throwing up. A picture of Earl pleasuring himself while being sodomized by a woman wearing a dildo was followed by one that featured Earl sucking on another woman's breasts. *What kind of sick fetish was this? Who WAS this man that Mark had looked up to as a father figure for years?* Agnes clumsily tried to end her PowerPoint presentation to no avail as Earl quickly grabbed the microphone from his wife's hand.

"These....these photos...are fake." Earl's stammering allowed Mark to connect every suspicious encounter with his friend: the phone call from Heather and Earl's plea for legal assistance if things imploded, the private chat with Lester, Ian's harrowing recount of Agnes and Earl's fight. Agnes snatched the microphone back from her husband and began sobbing.

"I can't. I can't live a lie anymore. My husband has changed." And through these sobs, Mark was able to truly empathize with Agnes. He too had started crying because he had been betrayed. Mark was unsure what was more hurtful: Earl leading a double life or Earl not confiding in him about that life. Ian gently patted him on the arm as Mark covered his face, understanding for maybe the first time in his life the true meaning of a broken spirit.

• • •

The bathroom tiles had a unique cylindrical print resembling that of an Austrian vase. As Jerry clutched the walls of the bathroom stall, mustering up the courage to shove his finger down his throat for the seventh time that night, the unbridled sound of Agnes sobbing pounded his eardrum.

"I feel like a hypocrite every time I talk about domestic abuse because I'm living it. My husband belittled me in every possible way. Nothing I did was ever good enough." Agnes had countered Earl's pitiful attempt to refute the authenticity of the photos, providing shocking revelations of abuse that sent chills down Jerry's spine. Through each heavy sob, she had unknowingly discredited her husband's theories, ones in which LGBT people were inept parents and gay men molested children.

Jerry had not felt victorious, however. Just broken. He couldn't stop his mind from returning to one session in particular with Lester. It was the session in which Lester had addressed Jerry's bulimia head on, his questions ranging from when it started to how often he purged. Jerry had responded with one-word answers, his perfunctory attitude causing Lester's tone to become coarser.

"I'm gonna keep asking you questions for the next 45 minutes," Lester continued impatiently. "So you might as well start answering."

• • •

Moments ago, Jerry had stood on the landing overlooking the men and women of God who stood transfixed by the large image of the strap-on dildo that penetrated the bishop, mortified as Agnes confessed to Earl's recent desire to engage in anal sex.

"Three years ago, he insisted on bringing sodomy into our marriage bed. And I said 'no.' And he hit me. It all makes sense now. It all makes sense," Agnes had collapsed onto the floor, the microphone by the podium amplifying her agonizing wails.

Jerry forcefully shoved his middle finger down his throat, remnants of the platter of cheddar cheese on wheat crackers falling into the toilet, the chunks of food slowly sinking to the bottom. His mind took him briefly back to Lester's office, where Lester's discomforting and haunting presence surrounded him.

"Did kids tease you about your weight?" Lester implored.

Unable to tolerate another question, he had answered tersely, "Yeah. They called me boy with the boobs when I was in third grade." It had been an answer that provided Lester with his flawed correlation between Jerry's bulimia and his same-sex attractions. Jerry had never forgotten Lester's excited disposition as he explained how his bulimia was his mind's way of ridding himself of his same-sex attractions. "That name the kids called you was an assault to your masculinity. Don't you see? You don't want to be attracted to men! You're purging your same-sex attractions."

• • •

Jerry awoke in a hospital bed; the translucent walls and bright fluorescent lights gave him a headache. Percy and Harriet sat on opposite sides of him, their worried expressions puzzling. *Why was he here? Why were Mel and Leo huddled together in a corner? Why did Carl jump when Jerry blinked his eyes? What was happening?*

His father extended his hand toward Jerry's face. As unsettling as it was, he allowed Percy to gently stroke his hair, removing the strands that had obstructed his view. As his vision became clearer, he saw the doctor walk into his room, realizing in an instant the totality of what had happened – his destructive cycle of binging and purging had been discovered.

"Mr. Nelson, you were severely dehydrated."

Jerry was so distracted by Dr. Lanier's colorfully styled afro that he didn't pay attention to the IV line running through his veins. The strong scent of her hair product permeated the space between them as she checked the levels of the IV fluids. Her stern glance traveled from person to person, finally resting on Jerry. As he expected, she asked him how long he had been struggling with bulimia. Jerry answered honestly, revisiting every brief euphoric moment in which he stuffed his face with powdered doughnuts and cheese curls and Oreos, only to descend into a wave of guilt quelled by shoving his finger down his throat.

Harriet embraced Jerry as he struggled to catch his breath, "You're gonna be okay."

"I'm not going anywhere," said his father.

As his parents stroked his hair, Jerry turned to face his father, who was passively nodding as Dr. Lanier explained how Jerry's recent bulimic episodes could be attributed to reliving a traumatic event.

• • •

The doctor's voice faded into the background as Jerry's mind took him back to a particularly dreary Wednesday in November. He had taken a cab to OEI, the suffocating smell of the driver's cigarette smoke permeating his clothes. Heather greeted him in the lobby and led her directly to Percy's office. He couldn't help but notice the overt glances that many of the men in the office gave Heather's chest as she walked by. Yes, her blouse was maroon, shiny, and noticeably tight across her large breasts. *But still,* he thought, *men could be so gross.*

When they entered Percy's office, Jerry couldn't help but conjure up crippling visions of Percy entangled with Heather, probably on the very desk behind which his father now sat. It hadn't been long before this day that Jerry had discovered his father was having an affair, his suspicions confirmed when one rainy afternoon he holed up in his room and used the skills from a semester's worth of programming classes at MIT to access his father's texts and emails. What he discovered was a thread of communication between his father and Heather that graphically depicted a sordid affair. And while he had been utterly disgusted by these depictions, he also knew they held the key to his freedom from conversion therapy.

"Jerry? What are you doing here? I thought I was picking you up from Union Station." Jerry never visited his dad at work, and Percy was obviously a bit unsettled by the unexpected drop in.

"I took a cab, dad. Anyway, I wanted to tell you that I stopped seeing Lester last week."

Not even glancing in his son's direction, Percy picked up his desk phone. Jerry shoved a manila folder in his face. As Percy opened it up, the papers contained within scattered onto his desk. The words from the first one that caught his eye took his breath away: *You should blow me in Greg's chair more often. I came so much. You sucked me dry.* Percy's posture shifted, his face turning to stone as he glanced at another paper, hoping that he was imagining the words spewed across the pages: *Next time let's fuck in the conference room where the board members eat their lunch.*

Jerry couldn't help but smile as he watched his father's sense of righteousness deflate right before his eyes, "Keep reading, dad. That is only the beginning..."

"Jerry, you listen to me."

"No, dad. Today you are going to listen to me. Every time I've told you that I was going to stop seeing Lester, you've threatened to call the College Board to report me for taking Leo's damn SATs. Blackmail I think would be the appropriate term. Well? Now it's my turn. If you ever call the College Board, I'm going to march right into your boss' office and hand over this entire folder to him. Oh, and in case you didn't see them, there's some dick pics you sent to Heather in there too. Then, I'll tell mom."

• • •

"Jerry, I've given you the name of one of my colleagues." Jerry was jolted back to the sterile hospital room by the sound of Dr. Lanier's voice. "He's made a lot of progress in treating eating disorders. Can you call him?" Jerry's gut reaction materialized in the form of a grunt.

"Please Jerry." Mel's pleading tone reverberated in his ear.

As he sat in his bed, his body languishing from the weight of all the secrets he kept, he simply nodded and let out a weak and unconvincing "okay." He felt his eyelids becoming heavy as he drifted off to sleep, dreaming of a lavish press conference in which he discussed the demise of Lester Dawson, his severed bald head rolling down the steps of the Lincoln Memorial. The dream ended with Jerry holding a bloody sword, that dragon finally slain. When Jerry awakened to the darkness of his hospital room and the faint beeping of monitors, he saw his eating disorder in a new light. Lester's theory about his bulimia was grossly inaccurate. He was purging the secrets and shame and suffering he had caused and endured.

• • •

Heather stealthily placed her gun in her lap, the smooth, silky fabric of her black dress forcing her to keep one hand on the gun so that it wouldn't slide onto the floor, as Earl drove them – at her directive – into the parking lot of a deserted warehouse. His phone kept ringing, Heather picking up the gun as Earl reached for his phone.

"It's Mark," his voice quivered as he looked at Heather pleadingly. She didn't care who the hell it was. Snatching his phone from the console, she jammed her ring finger onto the power button, the twelve missed phone calls disappearing as the phone turned black. She then pointed the gun to Earl's head as her mind raced. *How many miles was the nearest toxic waste dump? Did she have access to a chainsaw? Was there a Walmart nearby because she needed industrial-sized black trash bags? Was it in her best interest to just shoot Earl in the head, buy matches and lighter fluid from Walmart, and set fire to his car?*

Earl meekly hovered over the steering wheel, his face wet with tears as Heather loaded a bullet into the chamber of her gun. As she turned off the safety, she realized killing Earl would not actually give her the answers she needed. What she needed was more information on what Earl actually knew. She needed a detailed account of how he had successfully circumvented Heather's checkpoints. After all, flash photography and video recordings were not allowed in any sessions, and Earl had to empty his pockets before seeing Heather's girls. So where had those photos come from?

Heather stared at her reflection in the side mirror, displeased by the frown lines she was unable to conceal with makeup. She had just been trying to go on a date with a man she found attractive. How had that casual evening led her to this situation, where she was strategizing over how she'd dispose of Earl's disgustingly fleshy body once she murdered him. Who was she? It wasn't just the frown lines on her face that she found unrecognizable. Her whole life was becoming something that felt like it belonged to someone else.

She had met Gabriel at an African dance class at the local community center. As she had struggled to find the cadence of the music, her hips arching in unfamiliar positions and her feet stomping to the resounding percussive sounds of the Bongo drum, her eyes rested on the man behind one of the drums. They had talked after the class and had gotten drinks the next night.

"A friend gave me two tickets to this benefit gala. You should come with me."

Heather had not been able to resist Gabriel's brown eyes and gorgeous chocolate skin and easy laugh. As the evening progressed, through fragmented conversations over light piano flourishes and haunting vocals and random indistinct conversations, Heather had felt herself letting go. She had learned that Gabriel's mom recently moved in with him and his teenage daughter, Imani; Gabriel and his ex-wife shared custody of Imani. Heather had told him about Juilliard and the tours with Janet Jackson and Madonna, and for ten minutes, she had not been Heather anymore.

Heather abandoned those wistful moments as she pointed her gun at Earl's temple, firing off her first round of questions. Earl squealed as she asked him how he managed to sneak a camera into his sessions. His response was another squeal; Heather's response was a cock in her gun, the hollow clicking sound resulting in Earl crying.

"I shoved it up...my...anus."

"Where did you store the pictures?" Earl's reluctance to answer Heather tempted her to pull the trigger.

"On a thumb drive."

Heather snickered as she extended her free hand, her eyebrows arching as Earl fidgeted in his pocket for the thumb drive. His fingers shook as he handed it to Heather who examined Earl's pathetic state, the receding hairline, the sweat seeping from his pores, the dirty collar reminding her of those indelible late nights with Percy, the creak of the chestnut conference room table, its cold surface making regular contact with Heather's skull as Percy clumsily penetrated her.

She turned her attention to thoughts of Gabriel at the benefit just a few short hours before, pleased by his tan shirt that accentuated his broad shoulders. Heather had forgotten how sensual a man's touch was as Gabriel caressed her back, stopping to look down at his vibrating phone. His face sunk as he picked it up, and all Heather could hear was the distant sound of a siren on the other end that caused Gabriel's smile to fade as Imani's incoherent phrases indicated a dire emergency, the words *grandma, grilled cheese,* and *fire* the only ones Heather could decipher. Gabriel had kissed Heather goodnight as he profusely apologized for his abrupt departure, leaving Heather at the gala, alone, sipping her glass of champagne.

Earl had begun praying, bargaining with God so that his pathetic life could be spared. Heather had lowered her gun as Earl recited scriptures about not conforming to the ways of the world.

"Any idea who cleverly posted your lovely artwork tonight?"

Earl shook his head several times as Heather again pointed the gun at his head. When Earl continued shaking his head, she lowered the gun. She realized she was too exhausted to even carry out Earl's murder tonight. She had no energy to follow through with her plan, and more importantly, no concrete alibi.

"Just so we're clear Earl, you're no longer a client of mine. Get your jollies off somewhere else."

She slammed Earl's car door as she pulled out her cellphone to call a cab. Concealing her gun in her purse, she watched as Earl drove off the parking lot, his brake lights flashing each time he stopped intermittently. After several minutes, he picked up speed and turned onto the main street, leaving Heather alone.

On the cab ride back to the art gallery, she tried calling Devin several times, only to be directed to his voicemail. As the cab driver made a sharp right turn, he immediately hit the brakes as he nearly crashed into an ambulance parked in front of the gallery. Heather craned her neck to see what was happening, and as she peered over the passenger seat, she saw Percy's corpulent frame embracing his wife as a paramedic forced a young man to remain on the gurney, his curly hair hiding his face. Heather thought back to her tense interaction with Percy.

"Why don't you return my calls?" His hand had reached her waist, Heather brushing it away as if it were a gnat.

"Percy, I can't do this. Not here."

"Who's saying I sexually harassed them? C'mon Heather, you've got to talk to me."

She had shrugged and walked past Percy, feeling suspended in mid-air as the photos of Earl jumped onto the projection; Agnes' damning confessions of Earl's emotional, verbal, and physical abuse had become a threat to Heather's livelihood. She had more pressing concerns than Percy's wounded ego.

Heather felt numb as she handed the cab driver his fare, wanting to scream her frustrations while she ripped off the ridiculous black evening gown. She wanted to find the culprits behind this elaborate orchestration of Earl's demise and strangle them with her bare hands, but even as these thoughts raced through her mind, she knew they were futile.

Heather began to look for the silver lining, a new series of questions dancing in her mind: *How were the photos going to be dispersed? When were they going to be dispersed and to whom?* Heather closed her eyes and rested her head against her seat cushion in an effort to practice active gratitude, a technique that her mother had taught her as a young child that she had long ago abandoned in place of more practical techniques for navigating her world.

She couldn't get her mind to focus on anything positive, except for Gabriel's sensual touch, her mind conjuring up images of the evening that never happened – just the two of them, Gabriel unbuttoning his shirt and placing his fingers up her dress, Heather's hands tracing Gabriel's abs as he hiked up her skirt and forcefully entered her. As Heather orgasmed, a text message appeared on her phone. It was Gabriel, updating her on the emergency that had led to his abrupt departure from the gala. Minor house fire. Damage to the kitchen, but no injuries. His follow up text had asked her if she would like to have dinner next week. Heather replied, *yes*, craving some more time with this intriguing man. She deserved to have a little fun, didn't she, after all she had been through?

• • •

The quality of the image Harriet had captured on her phone was poor. *Who was the woman in the black dress talking to Percy? Why did he reach for her arm as she walked past him? Why wasn't Harriet able to capture a better image?* None of that mattered as she sat across from Amy and Eve in Sally's, their eyes squinting as they enlarged the photo multiple times. Eve's eyes widened as she turned Harriet's phone at a 90-degree angle, covering her mouth in disbelief.

"That's Heather."

"You're sure? I can barely recognize her." Amy's brow furrowed as she studied the picture with Eve. Harriet hoped Amy would bridle her tongue when it came to Percy's alleged infidelity. As a black woman, Amy had often given Harriet unsolicited advice on how black men expected to be treated at home. According to her friend, black men had required unequivocal support and validation from their wives. As she explained it, every time a black man went out into the world he was going to be the subject of denigration and ridicule, so when he was at home, he needed to – deserved even – to be treated like a king. Amy had gone on to explain many times that this unequivocal validation also needed to extend into the bedroom. Amy's conjectures danced around Harriet's mind as a man wearing a tan suit and horn-rimmed glasses appeared at their table. His salt and pepper hair was simply alluring, as were his dimples and meek smile. Harriet hoped she wasn't blushing.

"And here's the man of the hour. How are you, Tim?"

Tim Floyd? Amy's law firm had Tim Floyd on retainer? Harriet had heard about the countless needles in haystacks he was able to find, everything from illegitimate children in Brazil to hidden bank accounts in St. Lucia to secret stashes of paraphilic pornography. If Harriet wanted confirmation that her husband was having an affair, she needed the best. She shook hands with Tim as he took a seat next to Eve. Pleasantries were exchanged as Harriet examined her grainy photo, thinking back to her brief exchange with Percy at the hospital.

• • •

Jerry had drifted off to sleep; Mel, Carl, and Leo had gone home. The familiar stench of isopropyl alcohol had brought back memories of Ella's death; Harriet could recall every conversation, every labored step she walked in those same hallways, every tear she shed.

Percy's impatient groans had unsettled Harriet. "Why is he doing this again? Didn't he get past all of this?"

Harriet had shaken her head ruefully as her mind wandered to the severity of Jerry's bulimia, angrily turning to Percy as he idly watched Wheel of Fortune. "Percy, it is not that simple. You don't just get past an eating disorder! Maybe it's your ignorant attitude that's making Jerry binge and purge to begin with."

"Harriet, don't put this on me. Make Jerry take ownership of his behavior. Or does that only apply to Leo?"

"Great point. Let's all take ownership of our behavior starting with you. Who was that woman you were talking to at the gala?"

Percy had merely shrugged, seemingly unfazed by his wife's frantic questioning.

• • •

Tim inquired about the individuals he had been tasked to follow. Harriet slid her phone across the table as their waitress brought a fresh pot of coffee. Tim studied the photo as he poured himself a cup, slurping loudly as he looked up and smiled feebly.

"Percy Nelson and Heather Carter. Do you think they're having an affair?" Eve pursed her lips and eyed Harriet, who nodded her head. She did not harbor bitterness or jealousy; she did not harbor any of the expected emotions a wife in her position usually harbored. If anything, she felt this overwhelming sense of clarity. In many ways, staying married to Percy was a form of penance for Harriet. The two of them had lost a child, a loss for which they both blamed themselves and each other. Their daughter's death connected them while simultaneously driving them away from each other.

Eve took demure sips of her coffee while expressing her suspicions of Heather as an employee, "I feel like Percy and Heather's affair is a ploy to gain access to OEI's funds. Can you get me information on Greg Hammond?"

Harriet found Eve's claims plausible but worried about the thoroughness of Tim's investigation. Her anxiety was quelled once Tim placed his hand over hers. "I will uncover everything on this woman and your husband. I will also do my best to look into Greg."

"Good, because I'll need it when I file for divorce."

Harriet watched as Amy nodded understandably. In these moments, Harriet was grateful for Amy's friendship. She was grateful for not having to decipher any sighs or endure any well-meaning reflections about the sanctity of marriage like she would have to if she told Louisa. Harriet thought back to the previous night in the waiting room, the chairs with foam protruding from the cushions, the silence between her and Percy. She thought about the nights she spent crying alone in their bedroom; she thought about Percy's blank stares when she talked about those nights, and all of these thoughts indicated a marriage that had ended years ago. The divorce was just a formality.

As she listened to Tim describe his methodology for tracking Percy and Heather's activity, she observed his scraggly facial hair and well-defined jawline. She fantasized about ripping Tim's clothes off in an empty booth and being brought to the brink of orgasm as his tongue explored her clitoris. She fantasized about being fucked in ways that would make her entire body ache for a week. As Harriet tried to focus on Tim's explanation of driving a van with tinted windows and using long-range cameras and procuring closed captioned videos of parking garages and restaurants, she realized sex was one of the things she had given up after Ella died. And she missed it.

12

IT'S NEVER BLACK AND WHITE

Goth night at Towne meant the DJ spinning remixed versions of Fiona Apple songs all night. Carl found them hard to dance to, but desperately needed a respite from Kesha's latest hits. A young man with curly brown hair swayed in the middle of the disco lit dance floor, his tranquil trance reminding him of Kevin, the keyboardist at church. Church was the last thing Carl wanted to think about, and despite his concerted effort to free his mind from the petty gossip and baseless rumors, it was hard to keep his mind from wandering.

The curly-haired man inched closer to Carl, his face illuminated by the disco lights. He smiled perversely while scrutinizing Carl, his dark brown eyes and full lips resting on Carl's torso. The DJ had started playing an Evanescence song as Carl and this young man swayed to the beat. As the song transitioned into an enigmatic instrumental bridge, the curly-haired stranger caressed Carl's back, his nimble fingers traveling up his shirt and exploring Carl's chest.

• • •

Despite the intense arousal Carl felt on that dance floor, his mind just wouldn't stay present. It took him back to one particularly tense rehearsal with the praise and worship team. He had been standing in the empty hallway of Holy Boldness, the choir trading their singing for gossiping. Candace probably had no awareness of how close she was to the microphone as she excitedly speculated about Carl's sexual preference.

"I mean, his excuse wasn't typical of a straight man."

"So he never told you he had a girlfriend?"

"No, Kevin. And I don't think he does. Definitely gay. Right?"

Carl had quietly exited the church after overhearing the grunts and sighs of agreement. This was what people had talked about when he wasn't around?!

• • •

"Hey, wanna go back to my place? It's only a block away," this stranger whose breath smelled of whiskey and cigarettes propositioned Carl with the grab of his crotch.

Carl shook his head, breaking free from this stranger's grasp, "I gotta go." Carl searched for Jerry and Leo amidst a sea of tweaked out twinks and stoned bears and otters with lewd gazes. He contemplated dancing with a blond-haired man on poppers or the bear in leather chaps or simply finding the stranger he just kissed. He wanted to be touched and groped and asked to fuck. He wanted Don, but after last night, he knew that was no longer an option.

Finding serenity in a bathroom stall, Carl locked the doors as the pungent odor of cheap beer and urine permeated the cramped space. He thought back to his sudden appearance on Don's front door. He became aroused thinking about every piece of clothing he removed from Don, his erection growing as he grew delirious with memories of being rimmed in the shower and fucked moments later. Carl started masturbating as that pleasurable moment rushed over him. As Carl ejaculated into the toilet, the random conversations not fazing him, he wondered what Don was doing now, why Don still mattered to him.

"Carl?" Jerry's voice echoed over the distant sounds of house music as Carl zipped up his pants. He opened the stall and washed his hands, catching glances of Jerry smoothing out his black t-shirt. The two walked out of the bathroom and found Leo glued to his phone.

"Can we go home?" Jerry and Leo nodded at Carl, and the three friends quickly exited the club, past tired pick-up lines and pathetic attempts at flirting, past familiar cliques congregating around the bar. The three of them walked in silence as Carl remembered the last conversation he had with Don. They had been in bed holding each other, Carl giggling as Don's beard tickled his face. Carl had told Don that he couldn't keep hiding, but that he couldn't come out either. Don had mumbled that he understood where Carl was coming from, and as Don held him, he knew he had to let Don go. Don was married; he had a son. The circumstances of his life were not likely to change.

"I ended things with my married boyfriend," Carl confessed. Leo deviously grinned as Jerry clapped him on the shoulder. They walked to Jerry's car where Carl began his post-club ritual of changing out of the sweaty short-sleeved button-down shirt Jerry had given him, wiping away the smell of cigarettes and alcohol from his body with the baby wipes Jerry kept in his car and putting on the original t-shirt he had left the house in. Carl thought about how he had refused Don's touch as he said goodbye for the last time. As Jerry drove Carl home, Carl decided to stop singing in the church choir, acknowledging the disconnect with his faith, owning his disbelief in God's greatness.

"I'm proud of you," said Jerry as he merged onto the interstate. Carl nodded as Leo pressed him for salacious details. Carl saw Jerry's eyes narrow in reproach.

"I hooked up with a married woman once. She gave me syphilis." Carl and Jerry both laughed as they pulled up to Carl's house, Carl walking through the door and finding his father in deep concentration, the Bible open, the yellow notepad perched atop his knee. Carl lightly tapped on the wall. Mark looked up and smiled.

"Hey! How was the movie?" Mark rested his notepad on the coffee table as Carl sat down on the couch. He heard his mother talking on the phone upstairs as he read the title of his father's sermon, "For God So Loved The World."

"Good. Dad, I think I need to start focusing on school." Mark nodded his head. "And I know I won't have time for singing in the choir."

His father was not upset, merely concerned. "Okay. You wanna take a year off, and maybe come back?"

At that moment, Carl never wanted to come back. However, he shrugged. "Just wanted to give you a heads up. Goodnight. And I'm sorry about Earl."

Mark got up and hugged Carl. Although Carl was in pain, he knew his father was hurting in ways unimaginable to him. While Mark disapproved of Earl's transgressions, Carl sensed that this issue was more complicated than a man of God who paid for sex. Real life was never black and white, and the Bible did not have all the answers to life's questions. He held on to that sentiment as he hugged his father.

• • •

Mark's sermon needed to be about salvation this week. He knew he needed to preach on the redeeming power of Christ's death on the cross. The public revelation of Earl's sinful sexual deviancies had been mercilessly mocked and ridiculed by the people Earl supposedly marginalized. Staring at the wooden podium in the pulpit, then at his notes on his yellow notepad, he invited the congregation to pray with him. His prayer was short, a simple request to be a vessel of God's will. Mark opened his eyes and instructed the congregation to turn to John 3:16-17 in their Bibles. As he read the passage, he reflected on the downward spiral Earl's career had taken over the past week.

• • •

In Mark's home office, he and Earl had listened as the manager of the Words of God bookstore chain regretfully informed them that they could no longer promote Earl's latest book. Mark had been forced to step into his retired mentality of a corporate lawyer as Thaddeus, the manager, apologized for any inconvenience.

"You signed a distribution contract with Earl last year. I have the document in front of me now, and there is no termination clause." Mark had known of a hidden morality clause in the fine print, aware of that clause's ambiguity and his aptitude for manipulating such terms. Thaddeus had sighed heavily on the other end as Earl sat across from Mark, his contrite demeanor infuriating.

"Mark, there is a video of the man's wife confirming that he paid for sex."

"Thaddeus, Earl's wife reacted out of anger. Those photos might even be doctored." Mark had relinquished any hope of manipulating any contractual clauses to Earl's advantage, knowing such manipulations would not undo the public's distrust of Earl. After he endured similar conversations with the Council of Bishops, the book tour promoter, and booking agents from Christian radio stations, Mark had slammed down the phone receiver and stared at Earl.

"Who's Heather, Earl?"

Earl had sighed heavily at Mark's inquisition as he massaged his forehead. After a long pause, he explained that Heather was the owner of an underground escort service that catered to affluent men. Mark had forced himself to envision the bedrooms Earl described, the sexual acts he paid to have performed on him, and the lurid images of him wearing an adult diaper.

• • •

Mark came back to the present sermon he was preaching. He continued discussing the power of salvation, reminding everyone, but more importantly himself, that all Christians are sinners in need of salvation, "When we get saved and accept Christ as our personal Lord and Savior, we also acknowledge our own imperfection. We will never be perfect. In fact, we will keep sinning. Some of us might even backslide."

Mark gauged the expectant glances on the faces of his congregation; he absorbed their hunger for a word from God, and in that moment of observation, God gave him another sermon. It was one Mark needed to hear.

"If we turn to *man* for affirmation; if we turn to the bishops for guidance on how to live holy, we will be disappointed."

Mark implored his congregation to take heed in the promise of everlasting life through Christ, to not judge a person based on their sins, and to seek guidance from God alone. Mark prayed he would be able to do that as he greeted members at the door on their way out, his mouth becoming dry as he conversed with the deacons and the church ladies wearing large colorful hats and the toddlers still learning to speak. Mark offered words of encouragement to strangers, yet he had been unable to offer Earl any support. Mark's disappointment in Earl still stung.

• • •

Mark had grabbed the edge of his green robe as he tried to ignore his growing stomach ache, "I'm not proud of what I've done, but there are things you don't know about me, Mark." Earl had started crying as he clutched his belly, but Mark was unable to embrace his oldest friend. He had become preoccupied with processing his own betrayal, and the bumpy path toward forgiveness.

"That's why you didn't tell me?" Earl had finally confessed to confiding in Lester about the molestation he endured at the age of eight, sobbing profusely as he talked about being forced to perform oral sex on his uncle and being subjected to images of men engaging in anal sex. Mark had listened with passivity as Earl told him about his struggles with bisexuality.

"Earl, I can't make any promises, but I need you to be honest with me." As Earl had solemnly sworn to be transparent with Mark, something told him to be prepared for the worst. When Mark was alone, he had called Heather. This time, she had answered.

"Heather, this is Mark."

"I've heard about you, Mark. You're Earl's friend."

"Yeah, and I need to speak with you about Earl." Mark had scribbled down an address, Thursday's date, and 1:15 on a post-it note. He had intended to stifle the severity of Earl's situation and was willing to employ the ways of man to achieve that, unable to stand still and let God fight this battle in His time.

13

SAFE SPACE

Dr. Abraham Goldstein wore a black yarmulke, the strands of his curly black hair spilling down his face. Harriet checked her phone as Jerry glanced over at the clock. Percy was late as usual. The clock's ticking appeared to grow louder as Jerry fidgeted. The last therapist's office he had been in was Lester's, and flashbacks of that misery were hard to shake. His palms became sweaty as he and Dr. Goldstein made eye contact, smiling as the door to his office swung open. Percy appeared wearing a too-tight blue suit, wiping sweat from his forehead as he breezed into the office. His mother's scowl turned to uproarious laughter as Percy sat down next to Jerry and clumsily patted his knee.

"Harriet, what's so funny?" asked Dr. Goldstein.

Jerry's mother had typically responded with a certain level of detachment when it came to his father. Today, Jerry sensed that her laughter was intentional. "We're having a session about our son, and his father is unsurprisingly late."

Dr. Goldstein gave a thought-provoking *mmm-hmm* as Jerry watched Percy adjust his posture. Jerry didn't want to be sitting on this orange couch rehashing the bleak realities of his life. He wanted to tell Dr. Goldstein what he wanted to hear and go to work. Dr. Goldstein politely inquired about Jerry's temptation to binge and purge. Jerry looked at his father, who patiently sat upright; he looked at his mother, who gently nodded for Jerry to talk.

"I don't wanna binge and purge." Jerry found it strange that Dr. Goldstein tapped the bridge of his nose before taking notes in his leather-bound notepad. Lester had a similar notebook but always preferred taking notes on loose-leaf paper. He also preferred inundating Jerry with his research on how homosexuality disrupted the natural order. Dr. Goldstein's clear mantle was filled with gold plated plaques that honored his innovative work in psychiatry, substance abuse research, and suicide awareness and prevention. Above these plaques were Dr. Goldstein's three degrees: a Bachelor's from Dartmouth and a Master's in Public Health and Doctor of Medicine from Georgetown. Jerry wondered if these degrees would make trusting Dr. Goldstein easier.

"What triggered you in the first place?"

Jerry sat back on the orange couch and ran his hands along the cloth finish, his eyes locking with his father's. "Stuff," he said.

"Give me an example," Dr. Goldstein offered.

Jerry detected a familiar pattern of verbal tennis, one in which his therapist probed Jerry for information he was unwilling to disclose. Jerry struggled to acknowledge that his unwillingness to open up was due to Lester's knack for attributing his behavior to his same-sex attractions. "My dad and I don't really talk about me being gay. It's like he's ashamed of me."

Percy grunted as Jerry heard a sharp *rip* come from his father's corner of the couch. Jerry saw Percy examining a tear in his suit jacket. "That's not true."

Jerry observed his mother's impatient disposition at his father's quick response, pursing her lips and crossing her arms.

"When Jerry came out, you said you could not accept him being gay."

His wife's demanding tone precipitated Percy's incoherent explanations of his feelings about homosexuality. It was incongruous with what he perceived as an acceptable way of life for a black man; it was a topic discussed with much disdain during his youth; it meant he would never be a grandfather.

As Jerry listened to his father's narcissistic babbles, images of Lester flashed before him. His bald head danced in front of his face, nodding its agreement with Percy's sentiments.

"Jerry, you know I love you, but this isn't something I can just accept."

"Get out," Jerry turned to his father, who remained stiff. Dr. Goldstein cleared his throat as Jerry pointed to the door. "Just go."

Percy got up and left, and as the office door slammed shut, Dr. Goldstein turned to Harriet, who shook her head.

"Harriet, can I talk to Jerry alone for the rest of the session?"

His mother was not insulted by Dr. Goldstein's request. She embraced Jerry as she headed into the waiting room, whispering that she loved him. Jerry sat across from his new therapist as he clicked his pen and crossed his legs. Jerry knew he had to stop pussyfooting, a tear trickling down his face as he recalled his time with Lester. Jerry omitted no details about this tenuous time; he omitted no details about how his father blackmailed him into seeing Lester. His eyes welled up as he talked about the immense burden of keeping his father's affair a secret, unable to recall the last time he had cried as Dr. Goldstein handed him a box of tissues. He dried his eyes as the images clouded by his tears became clearer. The tension in Jerry's body dissipated as he sat back on the orange couch, its material somehow smoother.

"How did it feel?" Dr. Goldstein tapped the edge of his nose with his pen.

"How did what feel?" Jerry suspected he knew the meaning behind Dr. Goldstein's question.

"Being told that your homosexuality was a mistake?"

Lester's voice whispered in his ear. *Change is possible.* Embedded in that phrase was an inherent belief that homosexuality was a problem that needed solving, a conviction that homosexuals were broken individuals, a prejudice his father still harbored. "It hurts, but I know it's not a mistake."

Dr. Goldstein set aside his notepad and leaned in, his long nose pointed directly at Jerry. Jerry's awareness of his sexuality was immaterial to the matter at hand. He had a father who did not accept him, whose prejudices brought out a side Jerry had never seen. "Your father's misguided views are not your fault. His infidelity is not your fault, either. Your therapist was psychologically abusing you, and you had to get out. Sadly, the only way out was to blackmail your father."

Dr. Goldstein did not probe him for details into how Jerry uncovered his father's secret. He did not offer him assurances that he would be cured of his bulimia. He simply provided Jerry a space in which he could talk about his life, about the trauma Lester had inflicted upon him, about the unique struggles of being a black gay man. Jerry concluded that the orange couch and leather-bound notebook and sky blue walls had no hidden agenda. He accepted Dr. Goldstein's offer.

• • •

Mark had not spoken to Lester since the night of the gala, but as he pulled up to a sleek office complex where Global Healing resided, he knew he had to get advice on how to move forward in his ministry to former homosexuals and in his relationship with Earl. Mark got out of his car and walked inside the waiting room. Greeted by a chipper receptionist, Becca, whose salutation included "Change is possible," Mark rested his eyes on the wall of therapists that hung above a row of chairs, the smiles in their photos capturing the jovial ambiance of the waiting room. People came to Global Healing in search of hope, something of which Mark was in desperate need.

• • •

As Mark sat down, he wondered if Heather was right about Earl's inability to be trusted. Resting his elbows against the cold metal armrest, he reflected on Heather's stoic demeanor as they had talked in a damp motel room. She had been impatient as her flat tone informed Mark of the services Earl had requested.

"He came to me in 2011, but a fellow client said he had been shopping around since 2010," Heather had sat across from him as she smoothed out a wrinkle in her peach-colored blouse. "Mostly, he just wanted to be penetrated while wearing an adult diaper. It's a weird request, but it was what he wanted."

Mark remembered Earl's tearful confession in his office as he talked about his struggles with bisexuality, stammering as he inquired about the inclusion of homosexual sex in Heather's services.

She shook her head, "Men are tough to recruit, and most of my clients are only interested in women. If I were you, I'd look out for myself and for the people Earl hurt. I destroyed the photos, but the person who leaked them might continue distributing them."

"He withdrew a grand from his church's checking account for a year," Heather had peered over Mark's shoulder as he viewed bank statements detailing monthly withdrawals of one thousand dollars on the first of each month. Earl had always deposited the money back into the church's account a week later, but that did not negate the fact that he was stealing from his church.

• • •

Mark was jolted back by the sight of Agnes and Earl walking through the doors of the waiting room. The bags under Agnes' eyes were quite prominent as Mark searched her face for any discernible bruises. Mark, Agnes, and Earl walked down the hall and sat down in Lester's office in awkward silence, awaiting Lester's return from the restroom. Mark sighed with relief once Lester walked into the office and gently closed his door, his feeble smile providing a bit of comfort in this tense situation.

"Mark?" Lester handed Agnes a tissue as she cried over Earl's pathetic apologies. *Was Lester planning to apologize for encouraging Earl to keep his struggle a secret?* Lester only seemed interested in preparing a holistic treatment plan for Earl.

"Lester, did you encourage Earl to come forward?" Agnes' sobs drowned out the whirring sound of the air conditioner.

Lester turned to Earl, who shamefully hung his head. "Mark, this is on me. Lester told me to trust you, and I didn't do that."

Mark did not apologize for being presumptuous. Instead, he listened as Lester read from brochures of residential treatment programs for people with sex addiction. Lester strongly recommended Born Again, a Christian based program in Roanoke, Virginia. As his attention drifted to the sleek clear coffee table and the pine-scented odor in Lester's office, Mark thought back to what Heather had told him before she left.

"Don't tell Earl you have these files. Use them to your advantage." Mark had remembered a headline from one of the several anti-Christian, LGBT publications who reported on this story: "Homophobic Bishop Pays For Homosexual Sex." Mark and Earl's ministry to welcome former homosexuals was now sullied. Earl's church had no leader, and the Council of Bishops were already pressuring him to resign.

Mark was left with no choice. He had to continue his ministry without Earl. "Earl, you have to resign and let our two churches merge." Mark saw glimmers of hope and gratitude in Agnes' eyes as he said this.

PART 2

SEPTEMBER 2014

14

WELCOME HOME

Devin's first Christmas with Heather had been blissfully uneventful. Heather had purchased one of those small artificial trees from Walmart, the ones that came pre-decorated with lights. Devin, his brother Trey, and Heather had spent Christmas Eve decorating the tree with glittering bulbs and tiny ornaments of gingerbread men and angels and reindeer. The boys awoke on Christmas morning to the smell of burnt waffles and the sight of Heather with speckles of waffle batter in her frazzled hair. Devin had silently watched as she discarded an entire plate of blackened waffles, her sighs of consternation evolving into deep throttled laughter as Devin and Trey devoured the strawberry Pop-Tarts she eventually served them.

The ding of the toaster startled Devin as he stared blankly at the box of strawberry Pop-Tarts on his kitchen counter. Placing the pastries on a plate, he listened to Mel's off-key singing as she showered. Devin was hesitant about Heather and Mel meeting. For starters, how was he supposed to introduce Heather to Mel? *Mel, this is my foster mom, Heather. Well, technically she's not even that since she never called social services.*

Devin envisioned Mel's quizzical glance as they sat at the dining room table over pizza. He imagined Heather's vexed responses, her rolled eyes and crossed arms coupled with her perfunctory sighs. Who was Devin kidding? Heather had no interest in meeting Mel. She had no interest in doing anything that did not benefit her, and he wished he could stop being nostalgic over childhood memories. Devin prepared a pot of coffee, allowing its alluring aroma to transport him into an empty space devoid of the past. His eyes traveled to an unopened bill from BGE on the edge of his countertop, its slanted angle another ostensible reminder of adulthood.

"You are a saint," Mel greeted him with a kiss, her hair pulled back into a ponytail as she poured herself a cup of coffee. She sat down at the dining room table and devoured one of the Pop-Tarts, Devin chuckling as his eyes darted toward that unopened bill from BGE. It had been over two months since Heather had abruptly fired Devin, and in those two months, he had burned through over half of his savings.

"I need a job." He sipped his coffee while slowly calculating his living expenses. Devin's eyes roamed through his living room and settled on the 64-inch plasma screen television and surround sound speakers. Devin shuddered at the thought of selling them.

"Remember that private investigator I was telling you about?" Mel had begun scrolling through her contacts in her phone as Devin passively nodded. She handed Devin her phone, the name "Tim Floyd" appearing before him. Devin listened as Mel described how Tim needed a hacker who could easily access bank accounts and encrypted files, nodding with forced excitement when she asked him if he wanted his number.

Mel hurriedly placed her plate in the sink and scurried into Devin's bedroom. She grabbed her purse and tan backpack, frenetically preparing to leave for class as she kissed him goodbye on her way out. Devin sat in his empty apartment, thinking about how much of his life he had shoved away. The photos in his living room illuminated his stolen childhood; a picture of him and his brother in green striped soccer jerseys was the only one that survived his father's abrupt abandonment when he was three and his mother's dangerous descent into her crystal meth addiction. As he adjusted his graduation photo, its golden frame surprisingly loose, there was a knock at his door.

Devin looked through his peephole and observed a woman he didn't recognize standing there, nervously twisting her long blond hair.

"Who is it?"

"Devin? Devin, it's me. Faith."

Devin let out a guttural gasp, one Faith heard through the door. His mother was not supposed to be alive. She was a crystal meth addict who could never stay clean. What had changed? Devin opened his door to find a woman whose bloodshot eyes and dirty white nightgown had been replaced with jeans and a long-sleeved white t-shirt and sparkling blue eyes. Faith's once unkempt hair now hung freely to her shoulders and smelled like fresh lilacs. Devin's hands remained at his side, paralyzed by his shock. Faith was at his doorstep, sober.

"What...what are you?"

"I'm home." Her sudden embrace caught Devin by surprise as his stolen childhood flashed before his eyes. Unable to bear the pain of being abandoned again, Devin let go of his mother and slammed the door in her face.

• • •

Heather and Nikki met in the ladies' restroom the morning of Percy's settlement meeting, Heather barely recognizing her without the garish purple highlights in her hair. Speckles of soapy water hurled its way onto Heather's blazer as Nikki copiously scrubbed her hands. Heather sensed she was nervous, an assumption that was confirmed when she noticed Nikki's hand shaking while applying lipstick.

"Heather, I don't think I can do this," Nikki's bony frame teetered as she fastened the top button of her navy blue blazer. Heather placed a hand on her shoulder, exhaling sharply as she struggled to find words of encouragement.

The past month and a half had been spent preparing a methodical counterclaim of Percy's alleged sexual harassment. Greg had tasked Heather with constructing a plausible narrative in which Percy made unwanted sexual advances toward Nikki. In actuality, Percy had made these advances toward Heather, grabbing her buttocks in private and whispering how her erect nipples in her pink blouse made him hard.

Heather had witnessed Nikki's acquiescent disposition devolve into one of profound, unpredictable anxiety, "Why do I have to do this if Percy said those things to you?" Her soft green eyes shone with tears as she grabbed a paper towel to dry her hands.

"We've been over this," Heather gritted her teeth as she and Nikki walked out of the bathroom. A group of software engineers huddled outside of an optics lab, their putrid body odor permeating the air. Heather held her breath as they traversed the back hallway leading to Greg's office.

Before they went in, Heather grabbed Nikki's arm and looked her straight in the eye. "This settlement meeting is happening," she hissed. "Pull. It. Together." Heather had spent hours of her own time convincing Latrice, a software engineer, to write a code that cloned Percy's phone. She had forwarded all of those lascivious text messages to Nikki: *I wanna eat you till you squirt in my face; I'm so hard for you right now; I want you to blow me.* She had revisited every uncomfortable moment with Percy, fixating on the photos of Percy's family or the haphazard stacks of papers on his desk.

Heather's shrink had been correct in her assessments regarding Heather's tendency to dissociate from unpleasant situations.

Nikki wiped away her tears and gave a feeble nod as Greg's door opened. He traded in his checkered suits for a conservative black suit coupled with a red necktie. His eager smile indicated his confidence in OEI's counterclaim.

"Nikki, you look lovely. Heather, a quick word?"

Heather stepped into Greg's office, its self-congratulatory décor seeming especially repugnant at that moment as she noticed that his chestnut shelf displayed three new plaques of excellence along with countless other photos of himself posing with vice presidents of major corporations. Expectantly popping a Lifesaver into his mouth, he expressed his gratitude for Heather's leadership in spearheading the company's sexual harassment countersuit, praising her combative approach and ingenuity. Heather did not have the energy to appear bemused by Greg's compliments. She was simply too tired.

"And if all goes well with this settlement meeting, I'd like to book an appointment with one of your girls. Earl's public debacle made me nervous. You understand?"

Heather fixated on the unfamiliar scent emanating from Greg's potpourri jars. It was citrusy. She tried to detect the other changes in Greg's office: the photo of him posing with a decorated Air Force officer, the sleek black chair behind his desk. Greg continued conversing with Heather, unaware that she wasn't even pretending to listen to him ramble on.

Heather returned to her desk and mindlessly started reading emails, pounding the delete key as she examined the events that led her to this place of loneliness coupled with emotional exhaustion. Heather had pushed Devin away but still missed him. She had foolishly believed that Gabriel was a good man, her assumptions about his integrity debunked when an angry woman hurled insults in their direction at two in the morning on her lawn. Apparently, Gabriel and his ex-wife had never divorced. Heather had thrown him out of her house, tossing his khaki pants and polo shirt down the stairs as he proceeded to explain how complicated his marriage was. For the first time, she felt utterly alone.

Devin's number appeared on her caller ID. She hesitated before answering. As she closed her browser advertising a clearance sale at DSW, she heard Devin's heavy breathing on the other end of the phone.

"Did you know?"

"Know what?"

"Faith's back. She just showed up on my doorstep."

Heather hung up the phone, ran to the ladies' restroom, and locked herself in an empty stall as tears splattered her blazer. Faith was home, and in a rare moment of vulnerability, Heather allowed herself to acknowledge the void her best friend had left. She cried over the years plagued with abject fear about parenting two boys. She cried for those phone calls the two had shared after a breakup or a bad audition. Heather also shed tears of joy for the return of her closest and dearest friend.

• • •

Tim's home office was a space in desperate need of cleaning. Harriet marveled at how the dust particles were entirely suspended in air, wondering if the man had ever so much as dusted his home. Harriet's thoughts quickly shifted to images of his salt and pepper hair, well-defined jawline, and dimples.

Tim unveiled a blue binder labeled "Percy and Heather" as he sat at his desk. Harriet focused on the surveillance footage Tim captured of Percy in the parking lot of a local Chick-fil-A. The black and white image was magnified, the license plate on the BMW matching Percy's.

Tim circled the white Ford Fusion with a red magic marker, "This car is registered to Heather Carter. Once I discovered this, I reached out to local restaurants around the area and requested their CCTV footage. This is what I found."

Tim eagerly turned to another page in his binder, resting on a grainy image of Percy and Heather kissing as they headed inside an upscale French restaurant. Subsequent photos revealed the two of them holding hands as they exited. Tim's brow furrowed as he opened a file on his computer.

"What else did you find?" Harriet peered over Tim's shoulder, stealthily diverting her attention to Tim's dimples as he gritted his teeth. He pointed to Heather's credit report, his deep sighs of consternation indicating something Harriet immediately detected. The credit report only dated back to 2011.

"It appears that Heather Carter did not exist before 2011. No credit cards, no bank accounts, nothing." Tim elucidated the potential nefarious activities Heather was trying to hide, and the possibility of Percy being implicated in such activities.

Harriet's elation over Percy's infidelity faded. It looked like the swift and painless divorce she had dreamed of was going to be anything but. She wasn't sure how many more months of terse exchanges she could endure, how many more holiday dinners filled with caustic conversations over turkey and candied yams she had in her. Harriet brushed a tear away from her cheek as she felt the tiny squeeze of Tim's hand.

"I just wanna move on."

"I know you do. And you are."

There was veracity behind Tim's words that she found comforting. Heather's questionable past did not preclude Harriet from starting a new life or building the home she wanted. The potential lengthiness of her divorce had not changed how she felt about Percy.

"In the meantime, you'll have to suffer through more meetings with me."

Harriet and Tim laughed as his hand gently caressed her arm. Tim mentioned an upcoming interview he had with Devin Ryan, a computer engineering major who could easily hack phone records, as he suggested that this might be the best place to take their investigation next.

15

THE HEART OF THE MATTER

Jerry fidgeted with a strand of loose fabric on his American University hoodie as he watched Dr. Goldstein cross his legs and fasten the buttons of his maroon cardigan. Jerry allowed himself to get comfortable on the orange couch, audaciously taking off his shoes and lying horizontally. Resting his head against the burgundy throw pillow, he stared at the ceiling. Dr. Goldstein had insisted that Jerry not approach therapy with impetuousness, only sharing when he was ready.

"I think I'm in love with my boss, Brandon," Jerry began discussing the serendipitous sequence of events that led him to this realization, its origins a thin manila envelope from NYU. He had been staring at it while working on a proposal to excavate the skeletons from Lester's past.

Thin envelopes from schools had always been indicative of undesirable news, the memories of Jerry reading that brief rejection letter from NYU still fresh in his mind. Brandon had casually strolled by Jerry's cube while irritably smacking his bubble gum. Before Jerry had had time to protest, Brandon had opened the manila envelope.

Waitlisted. There had been a finality to those words Brandon had read. NYU had implicitly rejected Jerry through a short series of palatable platitudes: *While your portfolio was impressive, there were many impressive submissions. We have decided to waitlist you in the interim.* Jerry had felt as if someone had repeatedly sucker-punched him, and despite Brandon's feeble words of encouragement, Jerry had meandered through the rest of his day, glaring at the blank document on his laptop, unable to formulate any plan to excavate scandals from Lester's past.

"That must have been hard for you." Dr. Goldstein clicked his pen as Jerry sat up, the sting of NYU's rejection still fresh. "Did you feel tempted to binge and purge?"

• • •

Jerry nodded as he confessed to having stopped by a local Wawa to stock up on junk food: Snickers, M&Ms, savory bags of party mix. He had intended to binge and purge that night, but a text message from Brandon distracted him. The text's mysterious nature had instructed him to get up, get dressed, and show up to work ASAP in business attire and bring his portfolio along with the article he had written about Earl Wilson. Jerry had acquiesced, arriving to work in a freshly pressed white dress shirt, black slacks, and a red necktie. For good measure, he had even pulled out a new bottle of cologne for the occasion.

Brandon had remained secretive as the two of them drove through the city, the cold blast of the air conditioning in Brandon's Toyota Prius a respite from the unbearable August humidity.

"Welcome to American University." They were greeted by a friendly parking attendant as they drove up to the campus garage. Brandon rolled down his window to exchange pleasantries with a burly security guard he seemed to know.

"Brandon, what's going on?" Jerry implored as Brandon drove past about 100 open parking spots until he found one that apparently suited him way up on the fourth level.

"Dean Oliver Bauer wants to meet you. He heads up the journalism school."

Jerry's heart had started beating rapidly as the two of them swiftly traversed through the empty campus, passing large gray buildings and statues Jerry had never seen. Before he knew it, the two of them had descended upon the School of Journalism, the golden font shimmering against the setting August sun.

Oliver Bauer had met them at the entrance, his tout frame accentuated by the navy blue sweater vest he wore. Jerry had remembered being instructed to call Dean Bauer, Oliver, as the two shook hands. He had recalled the serene sounds of Vivaldi playing in the background as Oliver had thumbed through Jerry's article on Earl Wilson. His thought-provoking *mmm's* had been accompanied by Oliver's healthy gulps of ice water from a blue canteen. He moved onto Jerry's portfolio moments later.

"Quite impressive. There is an authenticity to your writing. I'm surprised NYU put you on their waitlist. We'd be lucky to have a student like you here."

Jerry had smiled, stealing glances at Brandon who had gently squeezed his arm. Jerry had recalled accepting Oliver's offer to be a part of the journalism program, feeling something he hadn't felt in a long time, validation.

"Thank you," Jerry had thrown his arms around Brandon when they got back to his car, inhaling the intoxicating scent of his aftershave as their lips met. They had kissed, and at that moment, Brandon had pulled away.

"We should get back." Brandon had started his car and driven back to the office, the faint sounds of NPR intersecting with Jerry's confounding thoughts.

THE HEART OF THE MATTER

• • •

Jerry sat across from Dr. Goldstein, tracing the crimson letters that spelled American University on his hoodie. Dr. Goldstein politely offered his views regarding the kiss Jerry and Brandon shared, and Brandon's alarming response.

"You're both scared. Why do you think that is?"

"Brandon doesn't know about my eating disorder."

"And Brandon? Why do you think he's afraid?" Dr. Goldstein stopped writing and faced Jerry. Jerry merely shrugged. Dr. Goldstein ended the session by reiterating that Jerry's eating disorder was not a choice and commended him for talking about his feelings instead of suppressing them with food. Jerry was grateful that he did not offer any advice on how Jerry should respond to his feelings for Brandon.

• • •

Mark's ministry for Christians struggling to overcome homosexuality was a disaster. Initially a collaborative effort with Earl's church, New Zion Methodist, Mark and Lester had planned events with the assumption that both churches would make sizable financial contributions to the ministry. Over the past month and a half, Satan had ushered in perpetual tempests, one of which was the newly appointed pastor of New Zion, Frank Saunders.

Mark had laid out a systematic plan to merge his congregation with Earl's, providing written recommendation letters from many members in Earl's congregation. They had been hurt by the revelation of Earl's infidelity and abuse toward his wife and wanted a pastor whose life was not mired by ungodliness. Bishop Emmanuel Crowe had folded his arms across his chest, exposing the faint pattern of armpit sweat as his features had hardened. Several bishops had expressed a desire to give New Zion a fresh start with a pastor who had no personal connection to Earl Wilson or his family. Mark had resorted to supplicating, constructing a narrative in which his ministry flailed and countless Christians struggling to overcome homosexuality were neglected. His supplications had fallen on deaf ears.

Mark and Lester poured over their planned event for pastors, exchanging deep sighs of disappointment as they looked at their original budget.

"Frank Saunders gave me a check for two grand," Mark bitterly reflected on his meeting with Frank, offended by the swift manner in which Earl had been erased from New Zion. Frank had replaced Earl's family photos with his own, Earl's degrees and books and mementos packed away in cardboard boxes. Frank had even replaced Earl's plush white chair with a black cushioned armchair. Mark had to endure these unsightly aesthetic changes along with Frank's pathetic qualms about stirring controversy as a new pastor, which apparently would happen if New Zion collaborated with Mark's ministry.

"I have twenty pastors planning to attend this event, and I just don't think we can lead the workshop on a ten thousand dollar budget."

The two men sat in Lester's living room picking at the fresh tray of vegetables Lester's wife, Tanya, had prepared. She strolled into the living room with a fresh pitcher of lemonade, gingerly placing it on the tray next to the bowl of ranch dip. Seeing her husband's preoccupied disposition, she lovingly placed her hand on his shoulder. Mark averted his eyes as Tanya and Lester kissed, not wanting to disrupt their tender moment. Tanya's floral print blouse and French braided ponytail reminded Mark of a younger version of Louisa, her bright smile and upbeat disposition taking him back to their days as newlyweds, back to their days as newly reborn Christians.

"I just took a special offering last Sunday for this event." Mark and his ushers had counted the money in that offering three times. $526 didn't go a long way. Mark went on to explain to Lester how he felt like he was failing all of the people counting on him and that his anxieties were outweighing his faith in God's providence. He shared with Lester that Ian had been inquiring for a while about when the support groups for ex-gays would begin. Many members had been sending him emails about family members and friends who were determined to leave the homosexual lifestyle but had no resources to support them.

The unpaid invoices weighed heavily on Mark's spirit – $14,000 for food, $2,500 for publicity in three local Christian magazines, $2,000 for publicity on two Christian radio stations, $3,000 for Global Healing's founder, Robert Cannon, to lead the workshops. Mark had to come up with close to seven-thousand dollars in a week or else over two-hundred people would miss an opportunity to witness freedom from homosexuality.

"Are you willing to split the seven grand we owe?" Mark took a giant swig of lemonade as Lester's eyes widened. Mark felt guilty for asking Lester to make such a sizeable financial contribution. Surprisingly, Lester took out his wallet from the side pocket of his sweatpants, unveiling a sleek black Discover credit card.

"This ministry is about healing, and we can't let something as trivial as money get in the way of doing God's work."

Mark's sighs of relief were interrupted by the vibration of his cellphone. A text message from Agnes appeared on his screen. He had busied himself with planning this seminar as a way to avoid the wreckage Earl had left. Agnes' text had dredged up Earl's betrayal, reminding him of their strained relationship. Agnes' text simply stated that she and Earl were separating, something Mark had assumed given her allegations of domestic abuse. However, a subsequent text caught Mark off guard: *Did you know that Frank had officiated several weddings of same-sex couples?* Mark's entire body went numb. *New Zion Methodist was being led by a heretic?* Lester noticed Mark's unsettled posture and gently tapped his shoulder. Mark told Lester he was exhausted, but in reality, he was furious. His stomach churned as he typed a response to Agnes' text: *Call me ASAP.*

• • •

Carl's first weeks of classes had been a welcome distraction from his father's determination to promulgate his message of conversion to heterosexuality. He had thrown himself into his endless reading assignments for Introduction to Sociology; he had suffered through the arduousness of Calculus II, remaining in the library until it closed to finish his homework. He had successfully managed to craft a world in which his sexuality didn't exist, the tiny bunk beds and communal bathrooms and the quaint wooden desk in his dormitory clean slates. Carl had not been involved with a married man in these spaces. The dichotomous realities of being gay and Christian had been silently cast aside and tucked away.

"Carl!" Mel snapped her fingers as he came out of his trance. He was out with Jerry, Mel, and Leo, enjoying live music at a new lounge, Blues Grill. Friday was open mic night, which meant that he would have to suffer through underwhelming poetry and gimmicky renditions of the latest pop hits. However, the acts that did perform pleasantly surprised him; the poetry wasn't that bad, and the singing was anything but gimmicky.

"You and Jerry should perform," suggested Leo as he held up his drink of rum and coke. Vance, the pianist, must have heard Leo's booming voice because he strolled over toward Carl's table, a cigarette between his lips, his left hand adjusting his black top hat. Vance practically grabbed Carl and Jerry onto the stage, fumbling in his pocket for his lighter as he hastily announced his smoke break on the microphone.

"Do you remember the song, 'The Heart of the Matter?'" Jerry adjusted his posture on the stool of the large upright piano as Carl nodded, approaching the microphone and surveying the patrons whose faces were illuminated by the single candlelight in the center of each table. Carl's neatly crafted world where his religion and sexuality were nonexistent was now dismantling. At this moment, he was gay and Christian and lonely. Carl wasn't able to close that part of himself off anymore, and as the song eloquently transitioned into the resounding chorus, the lyrics professing that acute, yet familiar pain of missing a lover while trying to live without them, Carl realized that he still missed Don.

The remainder of Carl's evening was spent in passivity, nodding his head in the appropriate places as Jerry excitedly talked about his journalism classes, smiling politely as Mel explained the disconnect between her civics course and the work she was doing at Justice For All, patting Leo's shoulder as he complained about his latest job as a sales clerk at a uniform store. Carl unlocked his phone's screen and turned to Don's number, drafting a text to the married man he was in love with, asking him if they could meet in a couple of hours. Several vodka tonics later, Carl pressed send.

Carl impatiently wished Jerry would drive faster. Don was picking Carl up from his dorm in ten minutes, and if Carl weren't outside in front of the mulberry tree, Don would drive home. Of course, Carl was unable to proffer this reason for his impatience, merely exhaling sharply as Jerry pulled up to that mulberry tree. Carl waved goodbye to his friends as Don's white Volvo sped down the street moments later.

Carl practically stumbled into Don's car, deliriously dizzy and unaware of how intoxicated he was until the plush interior became distorted figures around him. They drove to a McDonald's and ordered coffee, the diluted drink slightly sobering up Carl. Don asked about classes and Carl's top three choices for a major while an awful top-40 band faintly played in the background.

"I don't know," Carl slurred as Don took a sip from his coffee.

"What are you interested in? Theology?" Don placed his coffee into the cup holder next to Carl, who snorted at Don's suggestion. Theology was the last thing Carl wanted to study. He had been inundated with Bible study since he was a child. Carl merely shrugged, changing the subject and inquiring about Don's life. Was he still in lockstep with Mark on the ex-homosexual ministry? Was he still enmeshed in the beliefs of homosexuality's sinfulness?

"Carl, it's complicated."

"I love you," Carl blurted this declaration as the white interior of Don's Volvo became hazy, the windows mysteriously expanding around him as he swung the passenger door open and vomited directly onto the white line separating parking spaces, the acidic aftertaste lingering in his mouth and mingling with the stale coffee he had been drinking. Don drove Carl back to his dorm, gently rubbing Carl's forehead as he told him things were going to be okay, that everything was going to get better.

Once they pulled up to Carl's dorm, Don quickly got out and helped Carl out of the car, locking his door as he grabbed Carl's waist and guided him down the gravel walkway. The rest of the evening was a blur, except for one thing Don whispered in Carl's ear.

"I love you, too," Don whispered back to Carl. "And I miss you. A lot."

Carl woke up the next morning with a searing hangover, rolled over in bed, and saw an unread text from Don. Carl looked at the timestamp and couldn't help but smile. Even though Carl's memory of the night before was a bit fuzzy, he must have made enough of an impression on Don to not only think about him all the way home but take the time to compose and send a text before walking in the door and crawling into bed next to his wife.

Carl's world now encompassed all of his complex identities. He was a gay man and a Christian and in a complicated relationship with a married man. These identities made him uncomfortable, but at least he was no longer in denial.

16

PEOPLE LIKE US

Heather found Greg's overbearing predilections intolerable in her place of business. He had arrived at Capitol Boutique with a list of additional requests for his session with Deanne: Deanne must wear a transparent red lace teddy; Deanne must address Greg as "Master" or "Daddy;" Deanne must be comfortable with being spanked, slapped, or punched.

Heather's aghast expression as she clutched the index card on which these demands were neatly handwritten surprised Greg. This was not OEI, where his obsequious employees wouldn't bat an eyelash if Greg instructed them to literally kiss his ass. At Capitol Boutique, these unreasonable demands were challenged.

"Greg, I cannot meet these demands at the drop of a hat," she shoved the index card in his face, blotches of ink appearing on Heather's hands as Greg puffed his chest while adjusting his hideous orange bow tie. He resorted to expressing his disappointment in Heather's unwillingness to exceed expectations, a tired passive-aggressive act he had employed when he wanted his subordinates to work over 40 hours a week. The climax of this act occurred when Greg brought up his subordinate's past performances.

"You can't or you won't?" Greg reiterated Heather's impressive leadership skills regarding her work on the countersuit, the door creaking as Deanne meandered into the foyer. Heather appraised Deanne's oversized gray Marymount University sweatshirt and frazzled red hair. Heather instructed her to go upstairs and change her clothes, Greg's disapproving glances toward Deanne's figure making Heather stand her ground.

"We are prepared to meet the demands that you provided to us in advance," Heather motioned for Greg to hand over his phone and empty his pockets, acquiescing once he realized his demands wouldn't be met. Heather instructed Greg to meet Deanne upstairs, placing his phone and wallet in her office and closing the wooden oak door she had installed a month ago. As she locked it, hearing the faint sounds of footsteps ascending, she opened her laptop and emailed Devin about his encounter with Faith.

After Devin had called her with news of Faith's return, Heather had taken the rest of the afternoon off. She had ignored Greg's texts, her cursory glances indicating his elation of the success of OEI's countersuit. Heather had spent that day sobbing in between glasses of wine, envisioning a life she had relinquished years ago. She had resisted the urge to bother Devin with her questions and concerns and raw emotions. Instead, Heather had fallen asleep on her couch, lightheaded and languid as the empty bottle of red wine flashed before her heavy eyelids.

She pressed the send button on her email, startled by the sound of her phone vibrating on her desk. An unrecognized number appeared on the screen.

"Hello?" Heather heard the gnarly sound of static on the other end of the line as she rested her head against the plush black leather headrest of her new chair. The woman's voice on the other end sounded eerily familiar.

"Heather's, it's Annette."

Heather's palms began sweating as Silas' wife, Annette, relayed her husband's sinister ploy to strike a plea deal and reduce his prison sentence. Silas intended to provide the prosecution with substantive evidence of Jacquelyn Metz's whereabouts. "Brendan Alexander can't help you."

"What do you mean, he can't help me?" Heather anxiously tapped her fingers on the wooden surface of her desk. Annette's deliberate avoidance of this question caused Heather to envision Brendan's corpse lying in a shallow grave in a remote section of the woods, a bullet in his forehead, eyes wide open. Heather's breathing became labored as Annette whispered Silas' systematic plan to decimate Heather's tireless efforts to erase her identity as Jacquelyn, the financial and emotional sacrifices Heather had made – among other ways in which she had compromised so much – flashing before her.

"Silas' lawyer convinced a judge to issue search warrants for Dr. Sturgis's office and Uriah's house." The indelible memory of Uriah's hunched frame while meticulously creating the seal on her passport flashed through Heather's mind. "Heather, this was bound to happen," Annette finished, abruptly disconnecting the call.

Heather heard the sound of scurrying footsteps, causing her to compose herself just in time to answer the ritualistic knock on her office door indicating that Deanne's session had ended. Heather opened the door, her sweaty palm slipping onto the golden handle twice.

"Everything good?" Heather's pitch rose two octaves, Greg and Deanne's eyebrows raising confoundedly. As Heather had anticipated, Greg offered unsolicited feedback on how his service could have been better. Heather responded with perfunctory grunts as Greg unveiled a large wad of cash from his wallet. As he handed her the cash, she gave him his phone and wallet. Deanne excused herself and slinked back upstairs into one of the spare bedrooms that Heather had converted into a lounge.

Greg's phone repeatedly vibrated as he scrolled through his missed calls and texts, his demeanor quickly changing from one of superiority to utter mortification as he snatched his tan checkered suit jacket and marched past Heather.

"Brendan's not answering his phone, and his wife said he never came home," he hastily rushed out of the shop, nearly toppling over Heather's newly installed golden shoe rack as he called Brendan's wife.

The door slammed shut as Heather's body went numb. Silas had every intention of getting out of the Richmond Farm Correctional Centre. Annette was right; everything Heather had done would come back to her. She envisioned herself in a three-by-five cell, isolated from the rest of the world for thirty years. Devin was never going to visit her; no one was going to care that she was gone; no one was going to stand by her. Heather collapsed onto the floor, clutching the tan carpet so hard that a few pieces rolled around in her hands. A faint "hello" echoed in her ears as she sobbed loudly.

"Jacks, is that you?" Heather heard the soothing sound of a woman's voice. Jacks. Heather's nickname when she was Jacquelyn. Faith was the only person who called her that. Her irresponsible college days flashed before her, the quaint dormitory with the teal futon where she and Faith drank watermelon flavored wine coolers and derided their overbearing mothers and the Cyndi Lauper albums they blasted at one in the morning after dancing the night away in Brooklyn.

Heather felt a soft hand against her back. A woman whose piercing blue eyes made her instantly recognizable stood beside her, her long blond hair hanging by her side. Faith had actually returned. She had found Heather.

"Jacks, what's wrong?"

Heather violently shook her head as Faith helped her onto the couch. She pointed her finger at the pressed red cardigan she wore; she glared into her best friend's eyes, wondering where the hell she had been for the last twelve years, "No. No! You don't get to do this!"

"I know."

"I thought you were dead," Heather began shaking, tears falling down her face as the totality of all her ignominious deeds hit her, and her reasons for doing them sat before her calmly.

"I'm back now. I'm clean," Faith placed a hand on Heather's shoulder.

Heather dried her eyes, swatting away Faith's comforting hand as she steeled herself. Now that it appeared her best friend was back, she knew that late-night conversations filled with salacious gossip were not going to help her stay out of prison. Heather needed a plan, and she required Faith's help in executing that plan. Heather rushed to find a pen and a notepad, unearthing invoices and receipts and

Greg's laughable note card of handwritten requests in her search.

"Jacks?"

"It's Heather! Stop calling me that!" Heather finally retrieved a red pen and a crumpled piece of notebook paper. She caught Faith's perplexed disposition as she frenetically scrolled through her contacts, landing on Horacio Alvarez, her contact who sold stolen firearms on the black market. Heather scribbled down his name and number and handed the piece of notebook paper to Faith.

"I presume you know how to use a gun," Heather watched as Faith nodded, her apparent bewilderment irritating. "Call this man on a burner phone. Ask to purchase a revolver."

Heather was grateful that Faith did not profess the sanctimonious garbage doled out in Narcotics Anonymous. Faith simply complied as Heather explained her plan to murder Uriah and Dr. Sturgis.

• • •

Devin had developed the unsightly habit of biting his nails when he was anxious, and if there was anything that epitomized an anxiety-producing situation, it was a job interview with Tim Floyd. Tim's red-framed glasses slid down his nose as he scrutinized Devin's resume. Devin self-consciously placed his fingers at his side, hoping that Tim wouldn't notice his nervousness.

"You did some consulting work. Tell me more about that." The job description Tim had just read correlated to Devin's work with Heather. And while he had conceptualized the algorithm for Heather's security system and designed the encrypted platform in which clients submitted their requests for sexual services, putting those accomplishments on a resume was never an option.

"A lot of my friends had startup companies and needed help writing algorithms for managing sales and interfacing with customers. Uh....I did everything from designing firewalls and writing code for a new social networking app." Devin wasn't lying but still felt as if Tim would uncover his unsavory past at any moment.

Tim nodded satisfactorily at Devin's response as he explained a case he was working on, motioning for Devin to examine what he had just pulled up on his computer. Devin brushed off a large piece of lint that had latched onto the front of his black suit. Seeing Tim's love of large flannel shirts and tan cargo pants, Devin felt overdressed.

"I need your help with this," Tim pointed to a file on his computer.

Devin's throat constricted as he saw Heather's name displayed on Tim's screen, tiny particles of dust covering the *1* in her social security number. The photo of Heather, replete with her lip injections and nose reduction and cheek adjustments stared back at Devin. He had remembered fragments of that time period in which Jacquelyn became Heather. He had dismissed the severity of Heather's crimes until he saw the live footage of Silas Greene being arrested for human trafficking, the defeated disposition of the hedge-fund mogul broadcasted on every local news channel.

"We need to find out what she's up to," Tim continued. "What she's done, what her pattern is, who has been helping her."

"I can help with all of that," said Devin as he met Tim's apprehensive glare. Tim smiled, extended his hand, and offered him the job. Devin accepted the challenge to expose Heather without so much as a second thought.

• • •

As Devin accepted the job offer, he couldn't help but relive the bitterness of his recent conversation with Faith. Devin had expected Faith to be apologetic; he had hoped to garner her unequivocal support regarding Heather's amoral business ventures and her inability to listen to reason. These hopes had fallen on deaf ears. No God had bothered to answer his prayers as he was forced to listen to his mother admonish him for his lack of gratitude toward Heather.

"So I'm supposed to just sit back and watch while Heather ruins people's lives?" Devin had regretted listening to the supplications of his doorman, Phil, who had stopped Devin on his way to the gym with a story his mother had spun about her melodramatic desires of reconnecting with her long lost son.

"Heather provided for you when I couldn't. People like us have to do things we're not proud of to survive. Sometimes those things become a part of us," Faith had placed a comforting hand on Devin's as a barista screamed for Carla to get her venti caramel iced coffee. Devin had only been able to muster a disapproving grunt. Faith had emerged from some undisclosed rehab with bountiful compassion for Heather. Devin had changed the subject with inquiries about where she was staying and what she was doing for money.

Faith's response had been succinct, "I've got it covered."

• • •

Devin had devised a plan to tell Mel about his mother's surprising return. He had ordered food from her favorite Indian restaurant: chicken tikka masala over basmati rice with spinach and cottage cheese. He had purchased red wine and whiskey; the whiskey had been stored in a cabinet adjacent to the stove, its location convenient if he needed to take a few swigs before dinner began. Mel had tossed her backpack onto Devin's sofa as her eyes widened to the elegant contraption Devin had laid on the dining room table: red, glowing candles bookending the feast he had lovingly charged to his credit card.

However, despite the conversations he had rehearsed in the bathroom mirror, despite his harsh pep talks to just tell Mel everything, he couldn't. What had been confounding was that he didn't know why.

17

QUEERS DON'T QUIT

The exuberant sounds of a choir singing about the goodness of Jesus penetrated the bathroom walls as Jerry silently mourned his curly locks of hair. He touched his scalp and adjusted the fake beard Brandon had insisted he wear, silently wishing Brandon hadn't also insisted on the olive skin makeup and the fake arm tattoo of a cross. As a female vocalist transitioned into the familiar tune of "Amazing Grace," Jerry's knees buckled as he fully realized the Herculean task in front of him.

In the war room at Rainbow Warriors, Jerry had apprised the group of Lester and Mark's joint venture in training other well-meaning homophobes in the dark art of conversion therapy. Jerry had landed on his PowerPoint slide that depicted the animated dispositions of Mark and Lester, the photos of them interacting with their respective flock juxtaposed in the middle of the audacious advertisement – "Deliverance from Homosexuality." Jerry found the backdrop of blue skies graced by radiant sunlight nauseating. Brandon had leaped up from his seat with an idea that now manifested itself in the form of an itchy black beard taped onto Jerry's face, a bald head, and a fake tattoo of a chestnut-colored cross with a red ribbon swirling around it.

"Jerry should go undercover and establish a relationship with Lester." Brandon's impulsive idea had quickly taken on a life of its own. Within hours, Callie had fabricated a persona for Jerry as a local Christian blogger, Simon Waldorf, who attended Mount Calvary Evangelical Christian Church in College Park, Maryland. Simon was a proud ex-homosexual who had recently married Lucinda Garnett. Callie had inserted herself into Jerry's persona at that point, fabricating an eerily realistic wedding photo of the two of them in Rock Creek Park, which made Jerry wonder if those wedding photos in Lester's office had been similarly fabricated. If he understood anything about conversion therapy at all, it was that it thrived on facades.

Jerry finally composed himself and found a seat in the back of the sanctuary of Holy Boldness. He had only attended this church a few times as a child. Jerry and Leo had spent the night at Carl's house one weekend, Jerry recalling the gentle hum of Louisa's voice at seven in the morning. He had awakened to her lilac scented perfume, gold-colored suit, and the cheery announcement that they needed to get ready for church. In these same red pews in which Jerry had peacefully drifted off to sleep ten years ago, he now vigilantly sat with his notebook and pen ready. Lester approached the wooden podium dressed in a white long-sleeved polo shirt. Jerry surveyed the congregants, many of whom were dressed in jeans and oversized sweatshirts, looking at his blue checkered suit and concluding that his concerted efforts to blend in with well-versed, dogmatic obsessed Christians would always come across as paradoxical.

"Let's pray." Lester had always begun Jerry's sessions with prayer, his thin voice petitioning God to guide his thoughts and actions. He had always prayed that Jerry would find peace. Jerry had taken those fifteen seconds of insufferable invocations of a deity to wonder if Lester had truly believed people could change their sexual orientation. As Jerry bowed his head and listened to Lester's quivering voice as it petitioned God to guide his thoughts and actions, he suspected that Lester didn't really believe that people changed at all.

"Sexual brokenness is something the church has never adequately addressed," Lester began. Jerry's eyes traveled toward the PowerPoint presentation from which Lester had started reading. According to Robert Cannon, the founder of Global Healing from Homosexuality, the religious stigma surrounding homosexuality contributed to the mainstream belief of homosexuality being incurable. Jerry's eyes furtively darted around the sanctuary. *Were other people just as confounded as he was, or was he alone in his confusion?*

"As the body of Christ, we need to welcome those struggling with same-sex attractions. It is up to us to show them that there is hope, that there is freedom, that there is a seat at the table for them." Lester immediately turned to a slide labeled "Before and After." Two photos of Lester appeared on the screen. The first photo was one of Lester in his youth, a cigarette hanging from his mouth as his hands rested on his bony hips. His forlorn demeanor along with his blue streaked blond hair and black tank top made him unrecognizable. The second photo was one Jerry had seen several times in Lester's office, the picture of him with his wife and three kids.

"I'm living proof that with the right set of mentors and with the right mindset, anyone with same-sex attractions can overcome them and live their dreams just like I have."

Jerry was unable to tolerate the thunderous applause, excusing himself as he exited the sanctuary. *How was he supposed to get close to a man that told him the vilest things about being gay? How was Jerry supposed to look past that?* He stood in the church parking lot that had been overcrowded with cars, leaning against a late model Honda Civic with peeling green paint. His hands shook as he dialed Brandon's number.

"Nelson! What's kicking in ex-gay land?"

"Brandon, I can't do this. I just can't," Jerry wished he had worn a sweater as the ferocious wind blew stray leaves in his face. "This isn't gonna work." Jerry listened for Brandon's response as goosebumps appeared on his wrists. At that moment, he wanted Brandon to tell him to leave. Instead, Brandon sighed heavily.

"Jerry, you're the only person who can get to Lester."

"At what cost?"

"What do you mean?" Brandon was unaware of Jerry's triggers. He had no prior knowledge of Jerry's bulimia. Jerry rested his back against the dirty passenger door of the Honda Civic, no longer concerned if his suit jacket became dirty. Jerry swatted away the stray leaves and twigs that blew in his direction as the faint sound of the organ playing in the church sanctuary distracted him. If he was going to get close to Lester, he needed to be transparent about his feelings. He needed to be open about his ongoing treatment for bulimia. In that moment of clarity, Jerry told Brandon everything. He spared no detail about the secret trips to 7-Eleven or his propensity to vomit until his head spun. He mentioned how Earl's expose at the domestic violence gala had fueled his last binge and purge, and how he had awakened in a hospital bed hooked up to an IV drip.

Jerry wandered around the parking lot as the ferocious wind diminished to a calming breeze. He peered inside the cars, scanning the titles of CDs that had been left on the back seats: "Wow Worship 2002," "Wow Gospel 1998," "Hymns of Praise." These albums were as foreign to him as was the belief in Christ's ability to deliver you from anything. Despite the unfamiliarity of conservative Christianity, Jerry felt the shame many closeted gay and lesbian Christians felt. After all, Lester had managed to bring these feelings of guilt front and center in his life.

"Jerry, I had no idea. Just...go. This is too much," Brandon attempted to provide Jerry with some sort of comfort from the other end of the phone.

Jerry's left hand clasped the window of a minivan with copious amounts of bright-colored bumper stickers professing an unconditional love for Christ. This was the world he had to infiltrate, a world in which everyone was welcome except LGBTQ people, a world that perpetuated homophobia, a world in which Lester's influence knew no boundaries.

"If I leave, Lester wins. They all win. And I can't let that happen," Jerry continued.

"Nelson, you've come this far for a reason. Remember this. Queers don't quit."

Jerry chuckled as the gentle breeze intensified again, sending a torrent of branches and leaves in his direction. He sprinted toward the entrance of the church, swinging open the large wooden doors as he watched a thick tree trunk graze a minivan. The foyer of Holy Boldness was now filled with congregants, many of whom chatted animatedly about Lester's testimony as they stood in a long line awaiting food. The smell of barbecue chicken and cornbread permeated the crowded space.

"You okay now?" asked Brandon.

"Yeah, but I gotta go." Jerry disconnected as he stood before a white folding table that displayed pamphlets detailing the day's seminars: "Reclaiming Your Lost Childhood," "A Pastoral Approach to Ministering to Homosexuals." Each booklet had been designed similarly: black and white text against an angelic, sky blue background. It had this subtle, yet subversive message to it – this suggestion that salvation could only be obtained by homosexuals if they were willing to change their deviant behavior.

"Interested in attending a seminar?" A woman whose name tag read "Sandy" extended her magenta-colored fingernails toward the neatly-arranged pamphlets.

"Would you happen to know where Lester is?" Jerry responded, ignoring Sandy's question altogether. He followed her magenta nails in the direction of a crowd of men with whom Lester was engaged in deep conversation. Jerry's body tensed as he politely thanked Sandy and made his way over to the group, listening to the questions the men eagerly asked: "How much do sessions cost?" "What is the success rate?" "What if I can't afford the program?"

"You don't need to see me as a therapist to experience the change I did. You just need mentors who support you," Lester exclaimed as he implored the group of men to attend the seminar about the pastoral approach to ministering to homosexuals, his bald head darting to each man as he explained how that seminar would elucidate effective ways ministers and deacons could counsel men with unwanted same-sex attractions. Jerry saw desperation and blind faith on every single face that huddled around Lester, hanging onto his every word. Some men self-consciously removed their hands from their hips or lowered the pitch of their voices when they spoke. Their beleaguered dispositions disturbed Jerry. Lester exhaled a sigh that Jerry surmised was contentment as the men dispersed and stood in line for food. Jerry steeled himself and approached his bald-headed demon.

"Hi, Mr. Dawson." Jerry extended his hand for Lester to shake.

"Call me Lester. Mr. Dawson makes me sound old." Lester chuckled at his own joke as Jerry joined in, slowly unveiling the photo identification Callie had fabricated: Simon Waldorf, Editor-in-Chief of Spiritual Food. Jerry strongly disapproved of the photo Callie had taken, his fake beard concealing his well-defined jawline. He handed Lester the identification.

"Simon Waldorf. Your testimony was quite remarkable. I'm actually a former homosexual myself." Jerry's heart started beating out of his chest as he pretended to profess his deliverance from homosexuality. Hoping to convince Lester, he took out the crumpled wedding photo Callie had meticulously fabricated of the two of them in Rock Creek Park. Lester's eyebrows raised as a wide grin appeared on his face.

"Praise God. How long have you been married?"

"We just celebrated a year last Wednesday. We're actually expecting our first child." Jerry made a mental note to inform Callie about this additional development in Simon's identity; she would need to use her computer graphic imaging program to manufacture a pregnant photo of herself. Jerry quickly inquired about interviewing Lester for his blog, "Spiritual Food," his spine tingling as Lester handed him his business card.

"See you in two weeks, Simon. The GPS often misses that sharp turn, so call me if you get lost on your way to the office." Jerry's mind flashed to Lester's stoic frame in his sizeable black office chair, replaying Lester's proclamations about how gay men were inherently narcissistic, a trait that precluded them from being competent parents or having meaningful relationships. Jerry thought about the loose floorboard in his room where he had stashed his food. As he thought about hovering over his toilet and inhaling the pungent odor of mint-scented toilet bowl cleaner, his phone vibrated with a text from Brandon – *You've got this!* He stared at it for what seemed like an eternity, amazed by how much Brandon cared about him.

• • •

Mark had finally found a few moments of quiet reflection amid his chaotic day. He savored the cornbread and barbecue chicken, licking his fingers copiously as the crimson barbecue sauce trickled down his fingers and onto his hands. Mark's day had begun at 5 a.m. when he shuffled into the bathroom, the soft golden night light illuminating the crusty sleepers in his eyes and the bags that hung below them. Mark had muttered his prayer as he brushed his teeth and washed his face, asking God for both the energy and enthusiasm of which he was in short supply.

A gentle tap on his ajar office door startled Mark as he jolted up, embarrassed. His desk was scattered with napkins smeared with grease and barbecue sauce; his hands were sticky, and he had crumbs on the corners of his mouth. This was not how a pastor was supposed to look.

"Give me a minute," Mark tidied up as his door slowly swung open.

Don stood in the doorway wearing a light gray suit and forlorn glance. "Sorry for missing the opening session. Uh...Liz is pregnant."

Mark watched as Don sat down in the plush brown chair across from Mark's desk, visibly unexcited by the news he was sharing.

"Should I be congratulating you?" Mark asked with trepidation, watching as Don waved his hand dismissively.

"Yes. Of course. I'm feeling a bit overwhelmed is all." Don's attempt to placate Mark's concern was unusual. Mark had never remembered a time in which Don had openly expressed feelings of being overwhelmed. However, Mark was well aware of the implicit demands of ministry, and that Don was juggling these demands along with being a full-time professor at Washington Bible College. These responsibilities that came with visiting distressed church members and counseling wayward youth steeped in sin did not lessen because you worked a full-time job and had a family. And yet Mark still sensed there was something else at the root of Don's overwhelm.

"This new ministry can be my sole responsibility. If you could preach more Sundays, that'll be very helpful," Mark implored as he examined Don's reserved posture, feeble smile, and perfunctory nod. *What if Don or someone close to him was struggling to overcome a sin too taboo to say aloud?* Mark tried not to project his distrust with Earl onto Don as these questions danced around in his mind like unfettered praise dancers at Holy Boldness' praise festival. "You know you can tell me anything. Right?"

Don acknowledged Mark's offer to listen to any of his present or future troubles, assuring Mark that he was just tired and needed rest. The two of them headed into Lester's seminar on the pastoral response to homosexuality. Lester had already connected his laptop to the white projector screen, his aptly titled presentation – "A Pastoral Response to Homosexuality" – flashing before the screen. Sitting on one of the burgundy folding chairs in the tiny overflow room, Mark ruminated on his role in Earl's silent suffering. He saw Earl's face and recognized Earl's wounds as Lester accurately identified the shortcomings of many clergymen regarding the issues of homosexuality and transgenderism.

"Pastors are human, which means they're imperfect. They're not without sin, and it's this fact that causes them to poorly minister to people with same-sex attractions." Lester presented the dichotomous spaces in which homosexuality and transgenderism resided in Christianity. Pastors were either too quick to condemn or celebrate these issues, and Lester surmised that the pastors who celebrated same-sex marriages did so because they had been lured by secular psychologists and militant LGBT rights activists.

"Many pastors who take these extreme positions condemning homosexuality are internally struggling with sins many church members view as unforgivable. And unfortunately, the pastors who condemn homosexuality are readily exposed for their hypocrisy by the same militant LBGT activists." Lester flipped to another slide that showed several dozen LGBT-affirming organizations, many of which espoused Christian principles in their names – Dignity, Reconciling Works, Evangelicals Concerned. The bright, pastel-colored logos of these purported Christian organizations glared at Mark as he thought back to his last conversation with Earl. His hand traversed the circular cloth patterns on the chair as Lester's voice faded into the background.

Earl had reached out to Mark the previous Saturday afternoon. Mark had finally carved out time to visit Carl on campus, and they met at a local diner for cheeseburgers and Cajun French fries. During lunch, Mark ignored multiple phone calls that came through, instead choosing to focus on Carl, whose bloodshot eyes and pale skin alarmed him. *Was Carl forfeiting sleep to study?* Were classes that grueling?

"You're not stressing yourself out. Are you?"

Carl shook his head as Mark's phone rang again. Earl's number flashed across his screen as he dipped two fries into a tiny saucer of ketchup. Mark silenced his phone.

"I'm thinking of majoring in philosophy," Carl offered, explaining how his interest in the subject was piqued while writing an English paper on William Faulkner's novel, "As I Lay Dying." Mark's attention shifted toward the eight missed calls and five missed texts flashing across his screen. Excusing himself, Mark hastily stepped into the corner by the restroom to return Earl's call, dismayed when he realized the motivation behind Earl's frantic attempts to reach him. Agnes had informed Earl that she wanted a divorce and that she was no longer interested in either reconciliation or a more temporary separation. Mark responded with bitter indifference when Earl requested that Mark represent him as his lawyer in the divorce. He abruptly disconnected as an impatient patron glared in his direction. Mark failed to realize he was standing in front of the men's restroom, just noticing the garish sounds of the hand dryer whirring in the background. Mark returned to the table as Carl scrolled through Facebook on his phone, absentmindedly shoving fries into his mouth. Mark forced himself to pay attention as Carl continued discussing his sudden interest in philosophy.

Mark was jolted back to the present to find Lester continuing to drone on, having now moved to a presentation of statistical evidence that illuminated the disparities of religious institutions in matters of homosexuality and transgenderism. Mark took a cursory glance at the data displayed on Lester's slide – an overwhelming majority of church leaders acknowledged that homosexuals were being unfairly attacked in the church, but agreed that homosexuality was still sinful and harmful to society.

"People with same-sex attractions will slip up. They will fall and make mistakes," Lester lectured before turning to another slide that showed a study he had completed in grad school – *Fifty percent of males who were being treated for same-sex attractions experienced a relapse into deviant sexual behavior during treatment.*

"As a church, we must practice the true meaning of forgiveness and unconditional love," Lester's voice broke as he shared revelations about his own journey out of homosexuality. He candidly spoke of how he would abstain from sexual fantasies and masturbation for months, and then be triggered by a memory of his past abuse. That memory caused him to masturbate to gay pornography for hours. Mark watched as Lester brushed away a tear that trickled down his cheek.

"Despite my relapses, I had a committed mentor, Robert Cannon, who understood my pain. And I'm free because he forgave me and loved me unconditionally. As church leaders, you must do that. It can literally be the difference between life and death." Lester concluded his presentation to a round of deafening applause that burned Mark's ears. A searing pain shot through his entire body, originating in his sternum before migrating to his stomach and extremities.

During the break, he called Earl and listened to his cries of profound sorrow as he watched congregants crowd around Lester to speak with him.

"I'm sorry I was so terse the other day."

"It's my fault for putting you in this position," Earl cried. "I'm sorry I failed you, Mark."

"I forgive you. Can you forgive me?" Mark's eyes shone with tears as he darted down the hallway toward his office, closing the door behind him.

"Of course," said Earl. The two spoke about Earl's remorse, and how he didn't want his marriage to end. For the first time, Mark listened without prejudice or disappointment regarding Earl's shortcomings. He saw Earl as a man of God who had made a mistake and wanted another chance to prove his devotion to God and his flock. After all, bishops were not infallible.

"Agnes wants to trust you, Earl, but you have to show her you're worthy of her trust. She needs to believe that you're still the same Christian man she married. The world needs to believe that. Otherwise, snakes like Frank Saunders will take over." Mark professed his disdain over the council's decision to appoint a bishop who had a sordid history of affirming same-sex marriages. Earl offered his advice: take down Frank the same way the militant homosexual activists took him down. Their conversation ended with Earl imploring Mark not to disregard the burgeoning culture war being fought in the Methodist church. Mark thought about the relentless spirit of the homosexual activists determined to normalize their lifestyle before God, and as he thought about the unending ramifications of a bishop who celebrated homosexuality, he scrolled through the contacts in his phone, landing on Heather's number. He needed her help to eviscerate Frank Saunders and his progressive agenda. Mark had a suspicion that she could assist with fabricating the financial records showing Earl's misappropriation of New Zion's finances. He began a text to solicit Heather's help as a text from Carl came through. Beneath the text was a photo of Carl staring at a desk full of his notes and an open philosophy textbook. Mark replied with a smiley face emoticon, ransacking his brain for the specific reasons Carl wanted to study philosophy in the first place. He finished typing his text to Heather and pressed send.

• • •

Extramarital affairs had proven to be tedious. Carl had arrived at this sobering conclusion while peering at the stray sock he had left on the bedroom floor. He had crawled underneath the bed after hearing Don's front door slam shut, his heart rate skyrocketing when he heard Liz calling out for Don and Nick running through the house yelling, "Daddy I scored a goal today at soccer practice." This had not been a part of the plan. Carl and Don had agreed to meet Thursday evening because Liz was supposed to take Nick out for ice cream after practice. The two had not planned on Liz and Nick coming home an hour early.

"Cookie?" Carl snapped out of his daze as he stared at a circular raspberry contraption placed before him on a paper plate. He reminded himself that he was not at his married boyfriend's house, but at a PFLAG meeting in Arlington, Virginia. Carl had stumbled upon a flyer on the red canvas board in the student union building, its wrinkled edges eclipsing an advertisement for an open mic night in two weeks – *Be who you are in a safe, affirming space.* Carl had taken down the address of St. Christopher's United Church of Christ, unsure about what to expect as he parked his car and surveyed the quaint red brick church.

"Thank you," Carl smiled up at the woman as he glanced at her name tag. "Emily Davis, mom" was written in bright red marker. She wasn't the only parent in the audience. Carl scanned the room and counted over ten parents present, their eyes glued to a corpulent bald-headed man wearing the traditional black shirt and white collar most priests wore. His name was Father Jiffy, and his traditional garments were accentuated by rainbow-colored pendants affixed to his shirt. Carl was not expecting a dissection of the clobber passages that condemned homosexuality in the Bible. He just wanted to sit in a circle and listen to people talk about their coming out experiences.

"Leviticus' condemnation is not about consensual sex between two people of the same gender. It's about male prostitution being carried out in temples or in a woman's bed." Jiffy proceeded to explain that eating shellfish and having sexual relations with a woman who was menstruating were also forbidden in Leviticus. Jiffy returned to his jovial disposition as he expounded the reasons why committed same-sex relationships were pleasing in God's eyes, offering reasons such as God calling everyone to be true unto themselves.

● ● ●

As Jiffy soberly acknowledged the continued injustices many gays and lesbians suffered at the hands of church leaders, Carl couldn't stop thinking about scurrying underneath Don's bed, holding his breath as he counted dust bunnies. Liz had paced the floor before plopping down on the bed, causing it to creak loudly and the dust bunnies to scatter.

"Are you sure?" Don's incredulous tone at Liz's pregnancy announcement shook Carl to his core.

"I took a pregnancy test at work, and it came back positive. Yes, I'm sure."

Carl had listened to Don and Liz argue over the pregnancy's inconvenience. Don had expressed concerns over Liz's relentless quest to make partner at her law firm and the strain it had caused in their marriage. Don had a propensity to walk on eggshells when faced with a difficult situation, often dancing around the issue at hand to placate the other person. Listening to this situation unfold had been revelatory for Carl; should he suppress his own attractions to men, he too could wind up one day married with a son and having an affair with a man half his age.

"We have Nick. I've got the church."

"Do you want me to go to Planned Parenthood and flush it out?" Liz had started crying softly, her sobs increasing as Don sat down on the bed, Carl enduring more creaks and dust bunny tornadoes.

"Liz, don't be ridiculous. We'll figure this out." Don had inched closer toward Liz as Carl closed his eyes and prayed to be released from this Norman Rockwell prison.

Jiffy went around the room and asked each person to share something interesting about themselves. When all eyes landed on Carl, he briefly thought about sharing his confounding and ignominious relationship with the group. He decided to save this part of his life for a future meeting, resigning instead to share his life as a former worship leader. As he examined the raised eyebrows from the group of eclectic teenagers, surveying the pink striped highlights and colorful sweatshirts professing queerness, Don's voice rang in his ear.

• • •

"I miss your singing in church." Don and Carl had just finished having sex in the shower, Carl inhaling the calming scent of Don's body wash that emanated from the bathroom. Carl had explained how he wasn't in a position to lead anyone into worship but admitted that he, too, missed singing. Don began talking about his childhood as Carl's head rested on his shoulder. He listened to Don describe family vacations where his dad would sing off-key to every Beatles song, his mom erupting in laughter as he missed every note. Carl tried to imagine a young Don covering his ears as he and his sister rode in the back seat, excited to get to Disney World. Don had fond memories of camping trips and barbecues and Sunday evenings cheering for the New England Patriots.

"I think my dad secretly wanted me to go into politics. Run for office. He seemed disappointed when I decided to get a Ph.D. in theology." The two had lost the opportunity to discuss this further once the front door opened.

• • •

A girl named Jenna mentioned her love of Siamese cats and a boy named Liam talked about his interest in chemical engineering, the latter of which was met with several eye rolls and groans. The meeting continued in this fashion for several minutes before ending with announcements regarding upcoming events and guest speakers. Carl helped himself to more cookies as a young man, Daniel, walked over to make himself a hot chocolate.

"Jiffy's gonna ask you to sing the next time you come. He never forgets." Carl chuckled as he watched Daniel sip his hot chocolate. The two chatted for a while about their favorite movies and books. As Daniel told Carl about his recent obsession with Molly Ringwald films, Carl instantly became drawn to his smooth bronze skin and piercing green eyes. Jiffy finally came over to the table and gently tapped Daniel's shoulder.

"Someone has a paper to finish for AP Euro." Daniel groaned as he and Carl said their goodbyes. Carl exhaled sharply as his eye caught a painting of Jesus with his arms outstretched, donning a white robe against the multicolored stained glass window. A warm feeling came over Carl that felt oddly like safety.

18

GUNPOWDER AND LEAD

Heather was astonished by her friend's attention to detail as Faith calmly walked Heather through the last 24 hours and the meticulous way in which she had followed through on all of Heather's orders. Heather sipped her wine while Faith described her encounter with Hector Alvarez, her body convulsing as she remembered the grimy apartment's pungent odor and the roaches darting out of empty pizza containers scattered on the living room floor.

"Did he count the cash?" Heather's first purchase from Horacio had been the revolver she kept in a safe underneath her bed, and he had counted the cash three times before showing Heather his vast collection of firearms.

Faith nodded and proceeded to show Heather photos of Uriah and Dr. Sturgis from the burner phone, bullet holes in their foreheads, their eyes wide open. "I texted them the meeting spot you suggested, and they showed up."

Heather had instructed Faith to text Uriah and Dr. Sturgis an address near a deserted park in Leesylvania County, a meeting spot both men had routinely used when acquiring cocaine. Heather's inside knowledge had once again paid off.

"The park was deserted like you said," Faith shuddered as she told Heather how both men had resorted to useless supplications once they saw the gun pointed at them, her calm composure dissipating. Heather gently placed her hand over Faith's and reassured her that this was something that needed to be done.

• • •

Heather thought back to her meeting with Mark, a meeting that provided her with much-needed clarity regarding her actions of self-preservation. The two had met at a Super 8 motel in College Park. They had sat on twin beds facing each other in the dark, musty room. Heather had been surprised by his text soliciting her assistance but agreed to meet. As Mark had outlined his novice scheme to frame a newly-appointed bishop for fraud, Heather had mulled over her own scheme.

"The quickest way to doctor bank records is to have someone hack into Frank's account and transfer funds from the church into his personal account. It establishes a pattern of malfeasance," Heather offered. She watched as Mark diligently analyzed her advice, deciding to inquire about ways in which she could establish a concrete alibi during Uriah's and Dr. Sturgis' murders. Heather had conveniently omitted the aforementioned fact.

"In my experience, a person seeks out someone they trust. This person needs to have a good reputation. No prior convictions or felonies. No scandals attached to their name." Mark had cautioned Heather about leaving a paper trail or digital record. The two had gleaned useful information from one another, and had found a commonality in their respective fields: self-preservation was something that transcended occupation and religion.

• • •

"Who did Horacio tell you to rent a car from?"

"Some guy named Bubba from Greenbelt," Faith noted, reassuring Heather that everything was executed according to plan. She explained how she wore gloves to avoid the possibility of leaving fingerprints behind, dragged the bodies into the river, and drove off the parking lot.

Heather rested her head on one of the cushions on her white couch, Faith walking over to sit beside Heather. She flinched as Faith gently patted her knee.

"Devin still won't talk to me," Heather offered up feebly before turning on the television and beginning to idly flip through channels. She landed on one of those dance competition shows and became fixated on a young woman performing a complicated lyrical dance routine. Heather followed her limber figure, amazed by how the girl's movements perfectly aligned with the rhythm of the song. For a second, she pictured herself wearing that same black leotard and performing the exact same routine on stage.

"Give him time, Heather," Faith replied and then got up and headed into the kitchen. Heather muted the TV and listened to the sound of ice falling into a glass in the kitchen. She eventually changed the channel to a morose documentary about endangered pandas, placing the remote on the coffee table as her phone rang. It was Greg, who was probably calling her about the previous evening. Heeding Mark's advice, Heather had solicited Greg's assistance in preparing a slideshow of OEI's latest products. They had worked through the night of those two murders, Heather dropping subtle hints that she could not be home alone.

"Greg, I'm having dinner," Heather didn't even offer up so much as a "hello" when she answered the call. She could hear the faint sounds of a violin playing in the background along with Greg's interminable sighs that irritated her to no end. Faith returned with a glass of ice water, her eyebrows raised perplexedly. Greg politely asked Heather why she had needed his help last night, assuring her that her presentation skills always epitomized professionalism.

"I was lonely," Heather blurted out. "Is that so surprising?" Heather heard a chuckle on the other end of the phone.

"Not at all," Greg replied. "You should join us for happy hour sometimes. We never properly celebrated your win with our countersuit against Percy." Greg droned on for an additional ten minutes about how fun drunk karaoke was. Heather was relieved once he disconnected. Faith sipped her ice water and stared at the muted documentary.

"You are lonely, Heather. I'm glad you acknowledged it to *someone*." Faith placed her glass onto the coffee table as Heather grabbed her glass of wine, gulping the rest down. Heather shrugged, uninterested in exploring her inner feelings. "What were Devin and Trey like as teenagers?" Faith continued, abruptly changing the subject.

Faith's question caught Heather off guard. She never enjoyed excavating her past life; it was unpleasant to revisit those years of utter helplessness and perpetual anxiety. Against her better judgment, Heather told Faith everything, sparing no detail about Devin's pipe dream of becoming a professional soccer player or Trey's ambitions of becoming a professional musician. She and Faith laughed when Heather told stories of her haphazard construction of a diorama depicting Mayan civilization. For once, Heather no longer felt encumbered by the past. After she and Faith talked for hours, Heather glanced at her phone while putting on her nightgown. Latrice had sent her a text message an hour ago, informing Heather that all digital records of Dr. Sturgis and Uriah had been erased. When Heather finally drifted off to sleep, she dreamed of confronting Silas in prison, gleefully gloating on the other end of the glass about how she thwarted his ploy to destroy her.

• • •

Devin's hand shook as he walked into Justice For All, unsure if he should spill his guts to Mel at her place of work. This was simply another excuse for avoiding the truth, and Devin was tired of adding excuses to his list. The office space reminded him of a tech startup, makeshift workstations with lowly laptops perched on folding tables. Mel and her boss, Patrick, were discussing a new case in his office, Patrick writing on his whiteboard a name Devin had seen before – Deanne Blake. His insides churned, and his heart raced.

Last week, Devin had finally proffered his personal connection with Heather to

Tim. He had expected Tim to be angry with him for not disclosing this information during the interview. Instead, Tim had eagerly listened as Devin unearthed every detail about Heather's past, honing in on her true identity as Jacquelyn Metz. Devin had then provided Tim with every single contact Heather utilized to change her identity and fabricate documents.

"I believe my mother is also helping Heather. I'm not sure how, though," Devin had offered up as he watched Tim search for his mother's name in the database, amazed by the several aliases that appeared on Tim's screen – Alicia Headley, Vanessa Phillips, Denise Kemp, all of which had active arrest warrants for petty crimes.

Tim had shaken his head ruefully as he read the crimes associated with each alias, "Shoplifting, solicitation, indecent exposure. I gather your mother was quite busy."

Devin had chuckled at Tim's grim observation, envisioning his mother debasing herself for a high. He had so many questions he wanted to ask but didn't. As if reading his mind, Tim landed on a page that provided the answer to Devin's first question of how she had been able to get clean.

"It looks like your mom was in a residential rehab facility run by St. Mary's Catholic Church in Philadelphia," Tim had reported as his cursor rested on "Faith Ainsley," the dates of January 2012 to May 2014 next to the address of the church. Devin had gotten his answer, although he knew there was more to the story than this simple explanation of his mother's journey to sobriety.

● ● ●

"Devin?" Mel appeared outside Patrick's office, her bemused demeanor reminding Devin that he never informed her he was dropping by. Devin steeled himself and cleared his throat, no longer content on hiding behind the complicated nature of his upbringing or the shame he felt when thinking about his mother.

"I need to tell you something, Mel."

She motioned for Devin to sit. He danced around the issue for several minutes, biting his nails as he finally arrived at the truth. Mel grew silent. Devin reached for her hand, but she pulled it away.

"All this time you were lying to me?!"

Devin's apologies fell on deaf ears as Mel quietly asked him to leave. Not wanting to make a scene, Devin complied, walking across the street to Sally's as the colorful sign of Rainbow Warriors stared back at him. He was not surprised by Mel's reaction; he was relieved that she maintained her composure, although he imagined that she was fuming inside.

Devin ordered a cup of coffee and nursed it while scrolling through the contacts on his phone. His mind kept honing in on Deanne's name written on the whiteboard. *Why was she in need of legal representation? What did Heather do?* Devin shakily dialed her number, each passing ring making him more restless. When she finally answered, he was relieved to hear her voice.

"Devin?"

"Hey, Deanne. Is everything okay?" Devin listened as Deanne's breathing became labored. Was she running away from someone?

"I had to get to a quiet spot. Something happened to me." Deanne spoke about a private encounter with one of Heather's clients in his home. Devin knew that such meetings were forbidden, a clause explicitly delineated in Deanne's contract. If Heather were to find out, Deanne could be fired. Deanne's harrowing account of passing out on Greg's bed after drinking a glass of ginger ale sent shivers down Devin's spine. He knew what had transpired, and he knew that Deanne would have an uphill battle when it came to proving she had been raped.

"You don't have to do this," Devin remembered the wide-eyed girl whose innocence had been vanquished by Heather. Devin wanted to help her reclaim that, but he knew it would be near impossible to do so.

"Listen, I gotta get to class." She disconnected as Devin sat in Sally's nursing his diluted coffee, the cream and sugar lingering on his taste buds. The bitter truth of his life spread before him, its ugliness punching him in the gut over and over again. He did terrible things, and no matter how hard he tried to atone for them, people still ended up getting hurt.

• • •

What were Harriet's best qualities? What lessons did she learn from her last position? These were questions Harriet had rehearsed in the bathroom mirror while brushing her teeth, making concerted efforts to remove filler words such as "uh" and "um" from her responses. Kathleen MacGregor, the principal of Montgomery Learning Academy, patiently waited for Harriet to answer, her large hoop earrings dangling each time she smiled.

"My best quality is my tenacity," Harriet watched as Kathleen wrote down her answer on the back of her resume.

• • •

Tim had casually mentioned to Harriet how tough she was during one of their meetings. This was the same meeting during which he had uncovered Percy's financial records over the past year and a half, highlighting credit card purchases that were suspicious in nature: a sapphire necklace, pearl earrings, suede Manolo Blahnik high-heels. Harriet had watched in amazement as Tim turned to the photos in which Heather wore the items Percy had purchased. Harriet had listened while Tim introduced Heather's previous identity into the case, Jacquelyn Metz, a woman who had been charged as a co-conspirator in operating an illegal prostitution business and trafficking a person for purposes of sexual servitude. These revelations had not shaken Harriet to her core. One recurring credit card charge that wasn't highlighted had disturbed Harriet. The $150 monthly fees had been allocated to an organization known as Global Healing.

"Do you know anything about Global Healing?" Harriet's finger had rested on the charges as Tim searched the organization on his computer. Harriet's face had turned a bright shade of crimson once she discovered that Percy had been paying a therapist to change Jerry's sexual orientation.

"I can't believe he would do this," she had screamed and cried and cursed Percy's name, vowing to do everything from castrating him with a steak knife to strangling him with her bare hands. Tim had calmed her down, encouraging her to breathe deeply and not do anything that could land her in jail. At that moment, he had reminded her that she survived worse and that this would not kill her.

• • •

"Why do you say that's your best quality?" Kathleen rested her elbows on top of her sleek black desk, her purple acrylic nails lightly tapping its surface. Harriet had practiced a professional response, one that highlighted her ability to work under pressure and improve standardized test scores. But that response did not seem to portray the woman she was now, the woman who had lost a child, the woman who had spent five years meandering through life in a listless disillusionment.

"For five years, I mourned the loss of my daughter. I quit my job. I barely spent time with friends." Harriet's transparency did not deter Kathleen, who sat attentively while Harriet chronicled her uphill battle out of depression and hopelessness, a struggle that culminated in her desire to return to the career she had once cherished. Once Harriet finished, she nervously picked at a stain on the cuff of her tan suit jacket.

"I can't even imagine how devastated you were," Kathleen studied Harriet's resume, her purple fingernails moving horizontally across each accomplishment Harriet had listed. Kathleen asked Harriet her original follow up question of what lessons she had learned from her last position, which prompted Harriet to discuss her affinity for solving problems holistically and delegating responsibilities in a fast-paced environment. Kathleen fervently transcribed Harriet's responses.

Harriet was pleasantly surprised by Kathleen's readiness to reveal personal details about her own life, wearing the same sunny disposition as she discussed her impending divorce.

"I'm so sorry," said Harriet after Kathleen confided in Harriet that her estranged husband had sex with a waitress while on a business trip in Oklahoma. Kathleen waved her hand dismissively, her large golden bracelets bouncing around her wrists.

"Honey, I'm not sorry at all. I was relieved because I no longer had to pretend to love dick. FYI, I'm a lesbian. I came out once my husband told me he shagged the blond bimbo who served him waffles at Waffle House." The two women laughed at the irony of celebrating the dissolution of a marriage. Harriet, in turn, revealed Percy's torrid affair with his secretary who happened to be a white-collar criminal. She promised to disclose every salacious detail over martinis. After the two finished talking about their deadbeat husbands, Kathleen leaned over, smiling widely.

"I'm gonna do something I rarely do. You're hired, Harriet. We need someone who can relate to parents on a personal level. I know you can do that."

Harriet wanted to do laps around Kathleen's office; she wanted to jump over the mahogany table in the corner and collapse onto the red bean bag chairs. Harriet Thompson-Nelson, Assistant Principal.

The two women shook hands, Kathleen informing Harriet that she should expect to receive her employment contract within the next two days. Harriet performed a modest victory dance once she got into the parking lot, swaying her hips while unlocking her car door. She was back in the workforce. Harriet activated her Bluetooth and called Amy as she pulled off the parking lot.

"What's up, mama?" Amy's chipper tone made Harriet laugh as she pulled off the parking lot, stopping at a red light. Rolling her windows down, she loudly proclaimed her new position as Assistant Principal at Montgomery Learning Academy to the driver in a red Tesla.

"I'm back, girl!"

"We've gotta celebrate," Amy mentioned seeing Chelsea Handler, the feisty blond comedian infamous for her raucous sense of humor, and excitedly rattled off plans for a girls' night out.

"Doesn't Chelsea Handler have an entire segment about riding a well-endowed rapper in her hotel room?" Harriet pictured Louisa's aghast facial expressions when Chelsea unapologetically joked about her casual sexual encounters with men around the world and her two abortions. Amy replied that Louisa needed to act like an adult who's seen a dick other than Mark's. Harriet drove onto the main highway, delving the damning details about her recent discovery. Amy's chipper tone turned venomous once she heard the words "conversion therapy."

"Do you need me to get my shotgun? My grandpa taught me how to use one now."

Harriet chuckled as she merged into the far right lane, glancing at a vanity plate that read "GODROX." She impatiently honked her horn as the gold Pontiac meandered in the right lane, almost hitting the "GODROX" plate. Harriet swore loudly as she swerved into the middle lane, honking her horn at the elderly man whose thinning white hair and hunched frame peered over the steering wheel. Harriet rebuffed Amy's offer to blow Percy's head off with her shotgun, although she did revel in the image of Percy's broad forehead gushing with blood.

"I just need to get out of this marriage." As Harriet exited off the ramp to her house, she listened as Amy laid out a method by which Harriet's assets can be protected – Harriet would have to angrily confront Percy about the conversion therapy and request that they separate. While Harriet processed her anger, Amy would draft a separation agreement with ambiguous legal clauses that would protect Harriet's assets, subsequently leaving Percy with nothing. Harriet wholeheartedly agreed to this plan. Tough women did not tolerate men manipulating them. She and Amy relished at the thought of Percy being exiled into a one-bedroom apartment, surviving on Ramen noodles.

"You'll get through this. You've got Tim," Amy's devious tone indicated her knowledge of Harriet's insatiable desire to pounce her private investigator. Amy disconnected as Harriet turned onto her street, passing the neatly manicured lawns and wilting hydrangeas, excited about preparing her wardrobe for work.

19

LIES UPON LIES

Lester's office was a lot smaller than Jerry had remembered. In the year since he had set foot in this God-forsaken atmosphere, Lester had rearranged his furniture, the white couch now situated on the other side of the room and the black mantle of trophy wedding photos next to the couch. Jerry sat across from Lester as the lumps in the couch cushion pinched Jerry's buttocks like sharp cactus thorns. Lester employed his usual self-assuredness, sitting upright in his beige chair with a smug look plastered across his face.

The strategy had been straightforward; Jerry was to interview Lester, his questions beginning with his, or rather Simon's, personal story of redemption from the despotic gay lifestyle. Jerry had recommended this avenue of attack, believing Lester would be more forthcoming about his purported deliverance and therapeutic approaches if "Simon" opened up right away in this manner. Once the interview ended, Jerry would present Lester with a token of gratitude, a plant with a camera embedded in its stem.

When Jerry had protested to the video surveillance idea, citing the criminality of conducting such surveillance, Callie had countered with the argument of the illegality of a licensed psychotherapist promising a non-existent cure for homosexuality. She had blown a large bubble of her watermelon flavored bubblegum, popping it in Jerry's face as she shoved the plant into his hands. She also let him know that Global Healing kept no records on their internal servers, so he'd need to be on the lookout for a file cabinet somewhere in the office where this information might be stored.

Jerry turned to a blank page in his red spiral-bound notebook, opened the audio record app on his phone, and scribbled the date and time of the interview on top of the page. He quickly pressed the record button on his phone as an enthusiastic grin appeared on Lester's face. The two briefly made eye contact as Jerry unveiled a folded piece of paper on which the interview questions were typed.

"Your story of change moved me to tears. I saw myself in your journey," Jerry recited Simon's fabricated journey out of the gay lifestyle, painting a vivid picture of wild sexual escapades with strangers in bathhouses and cramped stalls in the bathrooms of gay clubs, recreational cocaine use, and a litany of failed relationships. Lester hung onto every single falsehood Jerry spoke. Tears brimmed in his eyes as Jerry's tall tale ended with a drug-induced orgy in which Simon had engaged in unprotected sex at a stranger's loft in Brooklyn, a harrowing experience that had resulted in Simon contracting syphilis.

"God had spared your life, and you knew if you continued living that way, you'd die," Lester's voice cracked as Jerry steeled himself to ask his first two questions.

"What were the specific steps you took to heal? How did you ultimately achieve heterosexuality?"

Lester patted his abdomen and toyed with the shiny gold watch on his wrist. Lester emotionally recounted a rainy Friday night in April of 2004 when he had gone to a gay club, high on poppers and drunk on tequila. Jerry became enmeshed in Lester's tale, imagining a younger version of the man in front of him waiting alone in the back alley for a stranger to take him home for sex. He imagined the horror Lester had described when a group of thugs dressed in low-hanging jeans, gold chains, and baseball caps ambushed him, kicking him to the point of unconsciousness while screaming "faggot." Lester had awakened in a hospital bed with Robert Cannon sitting beside him, holding his hand, gently explaining why his left arm was in a cast and why his scalp was dressed in a blood-soaked bandage.

"Robert allowed God to use him to save my life. He gave me a place to live, and slowly, started to share with me his own journey out of homosexuality," Lester explained the arduous task of severing ties with his "gay" identity – Robert had been adamant about removing all temptations of gay sex from his life.

Jerry wrote these responses in his notebook as Lester continued explaining how he specifically healed from the past wounds that had caused his homosexuality. "Robert made me revisit the painful memory of my molestation; he wanted me to feel the confusion and shame that I had felt at fourteen. He made me confront the man who had abused me. It was hard work, and there were days where I wanted to quit."

Lester admitted to backsliding several times, giving in to his same-sex attractions by watching hours of porn and masturbating. However, as he and Robert continued their work and as he identified the root causes for his same-sex attractions, the need to act on his attractions diminished. According to Lester, his same-sex attractions had arisen out of a need to bond with other men in a non-sexual way.

"When did you start experiencing opposite-sex attractions?" Lester grew silent at Jerry's question, his pointer finger grazing his lips as if looking for an acceptable answer. Jerry wondered why Lester hesitated to answer the question.

• • •

Jerry's memories of his sessions with Lester came to the forefront once again. This time, Jerry had sat with his arms folded, impatiently waiting for his session to end so that he could go on a food binge. He had placed a bag of powdered doughnuts underneath the loose floorboard in his room before seeing Lester.

"So when exactly will I be straight?" Jerry had remembered the flippant manner in which he asked that question, and Lester's puzzling response.

"On average, people start feeling different within two to five years. Every person's journey is different."

Aside from that terse exchange, nothing peculiar had happened in that meeting. Lester had postulated that the death of Jerry's sister precipitated an unhealthy dynamic between his parents that caused Jerry to detach from his distant father and cling to his grief-stricken mother. Jerry had listened with his usual passivity.

• • •

In Lester's office, Jerry placed his phone in the pathway of Lester's mouth, trying to decipher Lester's ambiguous response to Jerry's question. Apparently, there was no quantifiable timeframe an individual experienced opposite-sex attractions. "Change" was defined by the patient.

"The biggest thing I tell my patients is that same-sex attractions aren't biological. They're symptoms of the emotional deficiencies I discussed earlier. And once those deficiencies are addressed, the sky's the limit."

Jerry ended his interview, grabbing the shiny silver gift bag housing the plant with the video camera and handing it to Lester. Lester's eyes widened, impressed by this token of gratitude.

"Just my way of saying thanks for taking the time to talk with me," Jerry smiled.

The last step in the plan had been simple: Jerry was to purposely leave his devotional book in Lester's office, and return during Lester's lunch break to retrieve it; the video camera would provide the pertinent details such as the exact location of those patient files. Jerry suspected they were hiding in that gray file cabinet.

The waiting room of Global Healing had the familiar atmosphere of unhinged desperation, the nervous leg bounces and frenetic head jerks of mothers and fathers who wanted a straight child still commonplace. Jerry wondered how long it would take for these parents to realize that their hard-earned money was being wasted on a cure that never existed. Maybe the point of conversion therapy was to offer a credible façade of heterosexuality. Jerry intended to get to the bottom of this, as well as any other hypocrisies behind the practice.

As he reached his car, Jerry was surprised to find that he didn't feel the desire to binge and purge. His thoughts wandered to Brandon with his curly hair and scraggly beard. Jerry pictured his soft hands cradling Jerry's face before he came in for a kiss. Jerry decided to tell Brandon how he felt as the engine in his Volvo station wagon revved and he drove off the parking lot of Global Healing.

• • •

Mark's case against Frank Saunders had amounted to falsified church records in which Earl's withdrawals over the past three years had been forged to give the appearance of beginning in August, the month Frank took over as pastor at New Zion. He had watched as a brash African American woman, Latrice, wrote lines of code to hack into the financial records of New Zion, holding up her bony pointer finger to silence Mark when he asked a question.

Mark looked around at the quaint studio apartment Latrice occupied, bemused by the modest life of a woman who earned six figures as a software engineer. He had cautiously taken a seat on the black leather couch, avoiding the tear in the middle cushion. While she had meticulously organized files containing Frank's sordid secrets and proclivities, Mark had scanned the contents of Latrice's modest entertainment center, a collection of classic novels by James Baldwin, Shakespeare, and Chinua Achebe. Mark had grown uneasy by the absence of family photos or any personal memorabilia as she tersely instructed Mark to review the files she had unearthed on Frank, practically shoving a file of photos in Mark's lap. Mark had surveyed the grainy photos, each showing Frank's receding hairline as he hovered over a tiny bag of white powder.

"Read these," Latrice had handed Mark a thick file replete with detailed credit card statements from a facility called Clean Living. The charges had occurred weekly from October 2012 to January 2013. Latrice's perpetual frown had morphed into a sinister grin.

"Rehab for cocaine addiction. With these files and doctored financial records, you should have no problem destroying that tree-hugging pastor you despise."

It was Heather who had suggested Mark contact Latrice for assistance, assuring him that her work was impeccable and that she operated with the utmost discretion. Mark had acquiesced to Heather's suggestion out of the urgent need to remove Frank from ministry. Since taking over pastoral duties at New Zion, Frank had slowly eroded the traditional framework that Earl had worked tirelessly to build. The emails Agnes had shown him were disturbing, to say the least. Frank had implemented a "Tolerance Coalition" whose main goal was to educate church members about different faiths and lifestyles. Mark had nearly choked on his oatmeal raisin cookie when Agnes showed him these emails from concerned church members.

• • •

Mark's emergency board meeting to vote on a unanimous decision to remove Frank Saunders had quickly devolved into an informal rant about how overpaid musicians were. Mark tapped his pen on the chestnut conference room table as Deacon Hubert Adams droned on about the need to reduce the salaries of the musicians, his wrinkly neck quivering as he audaciously declared that all musicians should be volunteers. This was not the first time he suggested this.

"The musicians are being paid two hundred dollars per Sunday. It's quite excessive if you ask me." The other board members groaned as Hubert's wrinkly neck bounced up and down, his scratchy voice grating on Mark's ears. Why Hubert felt the need to belabor the irrelevant issue of musician salaries during every leadership meeting was beyond Mark. The pressing matter at hand was decimating Frank Saunders' underhanded efforts to undermine Biblical teachings with secular ideals. That was the reason why they were all enduring the smell of mothballs and stale bread.

"Let's shift our focus to Frank Saunders," Mark offered as he instructed the board members to examine the copies of the petition he had placed at each seat. As part of his broader effort to encourage Agnes and Earl to reconcile, Mark had orchestrated an informal lunch at his home, complete with cold cut turkey subs, sweet tea, homemade potato salad, and Louisa's world-class dark chocolate chip cookies. The exchange had softened Agnes' rather stoic disposition, her shoulders relaxing once Earl had discussed his concerns for the members of New Zion who felt hoodwinked by the Council's appointment of a liberal, gay-affirming, bishop. Agnes had even managed to emit a light chuckle when Earl had facetiously predicted that Frank Saunders would eventually officiate marriages between a man and a dog; Frank's perverted predilections knew no limits, according to Earl.

Members of the board scrutinized the petition to have Frank Saunders removed from ministry, their eyes widening as they turned the pages detailing the Tolerance Coalition's true intentions.

"What foolishness has the devil dragged in?" Sandy's disapproval pleased Mark as she dramatically waved her hands, her garish gold bracelets jingling with each hand wave. He fielded questions from many board members, the common theme being the strategic methods Mark would employ to remove Frank from ministry.

Mark assuaged the board members' concerns with responses centered on God providing a solution to Frank's heretical vision for Christianity. He omitted the details about the private meeting with the Council of Bishops he intended to call regarding Frank's misappropriation of church finances for the sole purpose of acquiring cocaine; he left out Frank's ignominious history of cocaine addiction, and how he planned to exploit that history.

"Let's take a vote. All in favor of removing Frank from his current post?"

Everyone around the chestnut conference room table proudly raised their hands. Mark was so ecstatic that he entertained ideas on how to ensure a smooth transition when Holy Boldness and New Zion merged. Sandy conjured up grandiose plans for expanded hospitality ministries and elaborate revivals replete with a large gospel choir and even larger offerings.

The excitement of the board carried Mark as he finally found a few moments of solitude in his office, resting his head against the cushion of his black desk chair and closing his eyes. Between the healing seminars and late nights compiling the files containing Frank's excavated skeletons, Mark had little time for quiet reflection or conversation with God. He started asking God why He would allow someone so misguided as Frank to preach His word. Mark sincerely wanted to know how heretics infiltrated the church. While he awaited that answer, his phone rang. Louisa's name appeared across his phone. He quickly answered it.

"Hey! Great news on the Frank issue." He quickly apprised Louisa of the board's unanimous vote to remove Frank from his position at New Zion, her effusive praises to God quelling the tinge of guilt he felt from his plans to expose Frank's history of substance abuse.

"God is always faithful. Follow Him and all will work out. I just wanted to tell you that you should avoid I-95. There were two bodies recovered at Leesylvania State Park in Virginia."

"What?!" Mark immediately opened his laptop and scanned the headlines detailing the development of the two homicides: Dr. Kerr Sturgis and Uriah Rolle had been reported missing two weeks ago. A jogger had noticed a black scarf floating in the river. Uriah's body had surfaced moments later.

"Just be careful, honey."

Mark sat back in his chair, murmuring a prayer for the two victims and their families. He also asked God's forgiveness for exploiting Frank's disease.

• • •

Callie's unbridled excitement upon the newly installed surveillance camera in Lester's office was quite nauseating. Jerry thought her squeals and sporadic leaps out of her seat were unwarranted. The team congregated in the conference room, viewing the enlarged live video feed of Lester with a patient named Ian. Lester's posture was starkly casual – he had hugged Ian when he arrived at his session and had opened the session with prayer. Callie increased the volume on her computer as Lester inquired about Ian's progress with restoring the strained relationship with his father and brother.

"It's a struggle," Ian said timidly.

"Why?" Lester's casual tone quickly became challenging, one that Lester had used on Jerry when he felt a lack of effort on Jerry's part.

Jerry, Brandon, and Callie studied the pair's interactions, quietly observing a predictable pattern in which Lester placed undue blame onto Ian for his perceived shortcomings; Ian would speak openly about the challenges of bonding with his father and brother, explaining how impatient the two would get when trying to show Ian how to play basketball or throw a football; Lester would callously counter Ian's efforts with absurd accusations. Jerry's body tensed as the interaction progressed.

"They probably sense that you don't wanna be there. That you don't really wanna bond with them."

An awkward silence descended upon the conference room. Lester's head cocked to the side as Jerry felt Brandon's hand graze his, their eyes meeting for a brief moment, their uneasiness apparent. Ian mumbled that his father and brother wanted to know if he liked girls, revealing that they had been asking him for two months now. Lester's response was anything but conciliatory. He adjusted his maroon tie while firmly telling Ian that this therapy would not eradicate his same-sex attractions.

"Ian, you have to understand that your same-sex attractions are not about some primal urges you're born with. They're about all the hurt and pain and lack of affection you've experienced." Lester's brash tone reverberated throughout his office as Ian began sobbing. Through these muffled sobs, he expressed his desire to discontinue sessions immediately.

Lester's response to Ian's request to end sessions was to reiterate the emotional wounds he had encountered throughout his life: the father who was never home because he was always working; the middle school boys who mercilessly ridiculed him because he "threw like a girl;" his three failed relationships with men. Ian ran his hands through his brown hair, shrugging his shoulders as Lester encouraged him to stay and work through these issues.

Jerry felt a tap on his shoulder, turning around and finding Brandon pointing toward his office. As he caught a glimpse of his reflection in an opaque frame with the Rainbow Warriors' logo, he saw his tearstained face beneath the portion of the rainbow-colored image.

Brandon sighed heavily as he handed Jerry a tissue. Jerry dabbed at his eyes as the sound of paper rattling caught his attention. Brandon had popped a piece of chocolate into his mouth, smacking his lips.

"You did good, Nelson."

Jerry thought back to the awkward car rides home with Percy, the questions always the same: *What did you discuss? Are you still attracted to men? Do you like women?* Those car rides had ingrained a harsh reality for Jerry, one in which he and his father would never understand one another. This reality seemed to be universal among gay men and their fathers.

Brandon got up from behind his desk and kneeled down next to Jerry, grabbing his hand, "What's going on Jerry?"

Jerry stared into Brandon's eyes, resisting the urge to run his fingers along those soft lips, fighting the temptation to kiss him. He told Brandon about those awkward car rides in which Percy had asked him if he liked girls. He spilled his guts about practically rushing to 7-Eleven to buy junk food and shoving dozens of cookies and doughnuts down his throat until his stomach hurt, only to throw it all up minutes later. Jerry told Brandon everything, including his feelings for him. "I'm in love with you, and if you don't feel the same way, just tell me because I can't keep living a life full of secrets and lies."

Brandon drew Jerry in for a kiss, their lips locking for what felt like an eternity. Callie impatiently barged into Brandon's office, rolling her eyes as Brandon grudgingly pulled away from Jerry.

"Knew that was gonna happen. I'm texting my roommate Edwin now. He owes me fifty bucks," Callie told Jerry and Brandon that Lester had called Robert Cannon, concerned that Ian might harm himself. She informed the two of them that Robert had mentioned a name, Roger Clementine, over the phone, and that Lester had nearly collapsed at the sound of that name.

Jerry walked back into the conference room, wondering where Lester's expose would take him. *Was he going to see reflections of himself through each of Lester's patients? Was he going to catch glimpses of his own dysfunctional family? Would he see mirrored images of his own disapproving father?* Callie pointed to the black file cabinet behind Lester's desk, the residence of all of Lester's patient files.

Jerry's mind replayed the last words his father had said to him that morning: "Jerry, I was only trying to help you. One day, you'll see the wisdom in what I did and thank me."

Without a word, Jerry had slammed his dirty dishes in the sink, gathered his books, and walked out. On second thought, he glanced back at his father and replied, "Percy, one day you'll die. And if God is kind, that day will be soon."

Jolted back to the present, Jerry started strategizing with Brandon and Callie on ways in which they could track down Roger Clementine. He wondered how much damage Lester had done to Roger. He also wondered if he'd have the courage to confront the wounds Lester had mercilessly exposed in his own life. Brandon winked in Jerry's direction, and Jerry was grateful that he didn't have to venture into Lester's world alone.

• • •

Deanne nervously fidgeted with her Marymount hoodie as she sat in Tim's office, her eyes darting to the bookshelf with its vast collection of classic and contemporary novels. Over the past two weeks, Devin had managed to convince Deanne to open up about being raped. He had convinced her that Heather was a sociopath who had willfully lied to Deanne about her job and had conditioned Deanne into a mindset that painted Heather as a friendly facilitator. Devin had painstakingly presented the grave reality of Deanne's profession: an escort who, if caught, would be charged with felony prostitution. Devin had met her in the student union building on the campus of Marymount, watching her casually sip a chocolate milkshake as she reluctantly listened to Devin's speech about how Heather only did things that benefited her. Two milkshakes and a bear claw later, Deanne had absorbed Devin's message. It had coursed through her veins in the most volatile of ways, reducing her once stoic frame to a puddle of tears. Devin had held her while her tear-soaked red hair brushed up against his shoulder.

In Tim's office, Devin scanned the contents of Tim's report, scrutinizing a photo of Heather and Uriah sharing a cup of coffee at a local café near Uriah's apartment. Heather's blond hair had been French braided, her concerned demeanor registering on each discernable frown line.

"Did you get the surveillance of Faith on the night of Uriah and Dr. Kerr Sturgis' murder?" Devin's suspicion regarding Faith's culpability behind these murders had been swift once he saw the news about Uriah's and Dr. Kerr Sturgis' bodies being recovered from the stream at Leesylvania State Park.

• • •

He had received confirmation of Faith's culpability during an emotionally stifling dinner at Heather's house. The dinner had been Faith's idea. Much to Devin's dismay, Faith had remained unwavering in her support of Heather and had insisted that Devin join the two of them for dinner to set their differences aside. Devin had grown tired of being stuck in the middle and agreed to dinner against his better judgment.

Devin had numbed his discomfort with four glasses of wine, its intoxicating effects traveling to his head quicker than usual; hearing Faith and Heather's animated conversations about his quirks made him lose his appetite. Heather and Faith had chatted as if Devin weren't there, only acknowledging him when they needed him to pass the takeout containers of chow mein and greasy egg rolls. Heather's jovial demeanor had caused a tightness in Devin's stomach, the constriction in his abdomen increasing with each raucous story from college.

Devin had remained distracted throughout dinner, feeling more than a little unsettled by the fact that Mel had not returned any of his recent calls. He really did love Mel. He was enamored by her passion for affecting positive change in the world. He adored her infectious laugh and the way she tugged on a strand of her curly hair when she was nervous. He was aware, however, that he was going to have to work hard to earn back her trust.

At some point, Devin had passed out on Heather's couch. He woke up to the sound of Heather's voice and – upon realizing the topic of conversation – kept his eyes closed so that neither she nor Faith would know he was awake and listening.

"You wore gloves when you dumped the bodies, Faith, and even if you didn't, the water washed away all the DNA evidence."

Heather's words had confirmed a suspicion Devin had had since pulling up the news story showing the forensic technicians recovering the bodies from Leesylvania State Park – that Heather had orchestrated the two murders of Uriah and Dr. Sturgis and had employed Faith to execute her plan.

• • •

Tim enlarged the virtual map of the park, his calloused thumb pressing against the far end of the computer screen which showed the Powell's Creek Nature Trail. Devin knew he was grasping at straws, biting his nails as Tim reiterated the trail's absence of surveillance cameras, a convenience that worked in Heather's favor. Once again, Devin was a step behind. Out of the corner of his eye, he saw Deanne fidgeting with her sweatshirt, twirling her hair, and murmuring her desire to go home.

"Look!" Devin clapped his hand around Tim's shoulder, taking control of his mouse and zooming in on a grainy image of Faith driving outside one of the park's entrances. The security cameras had thankfully managed to capture his mother driving away from the murder scene, the faded license plate of the 2002 Toyota Camry reading C67095. Tim's brow furrowed, countering Devin's unhinged enthusiasm with cautious realism. He quickly opened the Department of Motor Vehicle Database and entered the license plate number. The car showed an expired registration, its owner, Doris Tomlin, deceased since 2010. Tim substantiated his cautious realism with harsh truths about the evidence. The area where the murders had occurred was not monitored by surveillance cameras, and the bodies' submersion in the Potomac River had left no trace of physical evidence.

"The best I can do is talk to my contact at the Prince William County police department. I can ask him to look into this car's expired registration and see if he can possibly get a search warrant," Tim proceeded with the slim possibility of being able to tie that car and Faith to the murder.

His reproachful disposition softened as he turned to Deanne, gingerly taking her hand in his. Deanne had bravely recounted her harrowing evening at Greg Hammond's house, her eyes brimming with tears as her head rocked back and forth. She was still in some denial about what had happened. She had kept muttering how she had broken Heather's cardinal rule regarding contacting clients outside of work. Devin chimed in and quickly assured Deanne that none of what happened to her was her fault. Greg had initiated contact with Deanne, calling her from a blocked number at one in the morning; he had enticed her with two grand in cash for a private evening in a penthouse suite outside Alexandria; he had slipped a muscle relaxer into her ginger ale, and had done unconscionable things to her while unconscious.

"I can't do this," Deanne tugged at a loose fabric on her hoodie as Tim handed her a tiny black circular chip that closely resembled a horsefly. Her head shook violently as Tim instructed her to place the black chip inside the lapel of the jacket she would wear when meeting her clients.

"Deanne, this is the only way you can stop Heather," Devin said as he went on to remind her that Greg would not pay for his crimes unless he was exposed as the impetus behind Deanne's acquiescence.

Deanne softly whispered "okay," and even though she sounded unconvincing, Devin still felt her thin whisper to be a silver lining from the universe, a supernatural sign that he was redeemable, that he could maybe right all of his wrongs. He walked to his car and called Mel, rambling incoherently about how he needed her and missed her and wanted her to forgive him. He relayed all of his regrets into Mel's voicemail, pouring his wishes for a different life with a present mother and a healthy upbringing into each pained sentence. The automated voice on the other end abruptly cut him off after two minutes. He started his car once the call was disconnected, listening to the latest array of top 40 hits as he drove to his apartment. Devin changed the station as a gravely baritone singer sang about getting lost in rock and roll and drifting away, landing on an upbeat country song about being stuck like glue. Devin eventually turned the radio off as he stopped at a red light, desperate for a miracle, desperate for something that would stop Heather and Faith from ruining more lives. When he pulled up to the parking garage in his apartment, the first thing he did was check his phone. Mel didn't call back or text. So much for a miracle.

20

THE LORD WORKS IN MYSTERIOUS WAYS

Carl's reluctance to set foot in a church had transformed into a full-blown phobia. He had been subjected to recurring dreams in which Don stood before the pulpit in a white robe, its color morphing into a crimson red as Carl was yanked onto that same pulpit. The congregation had pointed their fingers at Carl, yelling "sodomite" and "faggot" as his father forced his arms and legs into an orange jumpsuit with the words "Adulterous Sodomite" plastered on the back. Mark had then opened his Bible to the book of Leviticus, reciting how abominable it was for a man to lie with another man. His father had then pointed to him and Don, the gold cross he wore around his black robe swinging as he professed each sin they committed, the congregation nodding in agreement as armed police officers appeared and escorted Carl and Don out of the church while the congregants continued their condemnations.

Carl always woke up in a cold sweat right at the moment in which he was being carried away by the police, his t-shirt and pillowcase soaked with sweat, the mildew smell and distorted silhouettes of lamps and books jolting him back to reality. Although St. Michael's was a church that affirmed LGBT people and performed same-sex marriages, Carl still felt paralyzed by his irrational fears of bursting into flames once he set foot into a church. He listlessly examined the black slacks and white shirt situated on his bed, neatly ironed and hanging over the right edge. These clothes had been his traditional attire to Holy Boldness, yet as he ran his hand along the cotton fabric of his white shirt, it felt rough, its smoothness vanquished and replaced with a coarse material that Carl never felt before.

A gentle knock at his door startled him, the familiar voices of Jerry, Leo, and

Mel begging Carl to let them in. He opened it to find his friends standing in dress slacks and sweaters, thankful that they weren't attending a service at Holy Boldness. Jerry's burgundy sweater and Mel's form-fitting, cream-colored blouse were sure to have been met with slanted eyes and reproachful glares. Leo's gray sweatpants and sweatshirt caught Carl by surprise as Leo hastily explained how he didn't get a chance to do laundry.

"I can't go to church. Any church," Carl rapidly recounted the moral quagmire he had gotten himself into with Don, omitting Don's name as he described the abject horror of nearly getting caught with his married lover, ducking underneath the bed as Liz arrived home to announce her second pregnancy. He plopped onto his bed, wondering how Jesus felt about his actions. *Did he forgive Carl? Did he understand the complexities of adult relationships?* Carl's image of Jesus was always that of an authoritarian parent. He knew Jesus loved him, but he did not accept sin. Jesus implored his followers to live virtuous lives, not make excuses for their unsavory behavior.

Mel sat down on the bed next to Carl, taking his hand as their eyes met. He noticed her eyes were red and swollen. *Had Mel been crying?*

"A week ago, I found out my boyfriend has been a longtime accessory to an underground sex trafficking ring, and I'm still in love with him. Life is complicated. Everyone here knows that," Mel confessed.

Jerry grabbed her hand and squeezed it as she went on to share her agonizing days of uncertainty around her relationship. Carl's eyes darted back and forth from his friends to his clothes, as he realized that his irrational fears were never going to dissipate unless he got dressed and showed up to church. Jerry and Leo listened as Carl described his dream, complete with descriptions of the armed police officers and orange jumpsuit.

His friends countered Carl's hesitance with a humorous anecdote: Earl Wilson had not been escorted out of the church by armed police officers while acquiring sex from prostitutes. And if Earl were still able to walk into a church, well, then Carl would be just fine. Carl smiled at his friends as he shooed them out of his room so he could get dressed for church.

The white shirt and black slacks felt uncomfortable against his skin, and Carl spent the entire car ride squirming and adjusting his posture, unable to get comfortable. Mel politely asked if Carl was okay as Jerry pulled into the parking lot of St. Michael's church, the sound of gravel greeting them as Jerry's car jolted into a parking spot. According to Daniel, St. Michael's had been one of several churches in America to embrace a burgeoning liberal theological practice known as Independent Catholicism. Carl had tuned out a large portion of Daniel's explanation of the vast distinctions between this brand of Catholicism and Roman Catholicism, only remembering the important ones: Independent Catholicism affirmed LGBT people, celebrated same-sex marriages, and allowed women to be priests.

Carl, Jerry, Leo, and Mel were greeted by high ivory ceilings with a majestic stained glass painting of "The Last Supper" at the altar. Carl observed the intricate stained glass paintings depicting the Stations of the Cross along the side windows, his attention quickly diverting toward the front of the church as a long haired man with a full beard strummed jazz chords on his acoustic guitar. Carl found himself entranced by the organic feel of the music, its subdued aura the antithesis of Holy Boldness' music ministry. A young woman with pink highlights in her blond hair and outrageous facial piercings effortlessly sang about how strength, courage, and wisdom had been inside of her all along. Carl sat down in one of the back pews as a little girl wearing a purple dress came up and hugged him.

"Taylor loves meeting new people. I'm Bethany. This is my wife Suzette." The two women wore matching University of Virginia sweatshirts as they hugged Carl and his friends. He forgot how comforting a hug could be, especially in church. Bethany and Suzette did not critique his appearance with eye slants or grunts. They simply welcomed him.

"And stay for coffee and doughnuts after mass," Suzette chimed in. She politely told Carl and his friends about the fellowship hour that occurred downstairs after each service. Carl remembered his father briefly offering refreshments after church, discontinuing it once he realized that Dunkin Donuts had drained their budget by nearly fifty percent one month.

Father Jiffy approached the pulpit, his corpulent frame accentuated by the white robe he wore. Today, he proudly donned a rainbow sash and wooden cross necklace. The pews in St. Michael's were oddly warm, Carl's hands tracing the smooth wooden finish of the bench as Father Jiffy began his sermon with a personal anecdote. One Saturday evening, Jiffy had poked his head into Towne and had taken in the disco lights and trance-like movements of the diverse inhabitants on the dance floor. Carl remembered that dance floor well, and memories flooded back to the night he had made out with a stranger with the whiskey breath.

"I approached a young man dancing alone, and politely asked him if he was interested in coming to church. His response saddened me. He told me he was 'done with all that God stuff,'" Jiffy paused, his big green eyes scanning the congregants, bringing his large index finger to his lips. He boldly implored his congregation not to turn away from God. He acknowledged the painful reality of the lingering homophobia in many Christian churches but countered this reality with an optimism centered on Christ's two main commandments: loving God with all your heart and loving your neighbor as yourself.

Carl had never heard Christianity explained with this level of simplicity before, and he was enamored. He was not used to love and compassion being preferred over strict dogmatic adherence to the apostle Paul's teachings regarding sexual purity, and it wasn't until Father Jiffy preached that he realized how far removed he had been from these two cornerstones of Christ's teachings. Carl found Jiffy's sermon surprisingly comforting, and he didn't miss at all the laborious analysis of a cluster of scriptures God had placed on Mark's heart at four in the morning. For once, Carl didn't feel constrained by his faith.

The fellowship hall was filled with the aroma of fresh coffee and doughnuts. The young woman who had been singing earlier in the service approached Carl with Daniel in tow. Today, Daniel looked incredibly cute in his red hoodie, Carl stealing glances to watch Daniel whip strands of his dark hair away from his face.

"Daniel tells me you sing. I'm Lani by the way."

Carl's eyes were glued to the seven earrings along the cartilages of both outer ears. Carl introduced himself as the two shook hands, Lani politely inquiring about the church he used to attend and how he had found out about St. Michael's. Carl sat down on one of the metal folding chairs, recounting the afternoon he stumbled across a flyer for PFLAG on Georgetown's campus one day in the student union. Lani chuckled as she shoved a powdered doughnut into her mouth, licking her lips as she confessed to absentmindedly sticking the flyer onto the bulletin board and forgetting to post additional flyers around campus.

Lani was a sophomore art major who shared an apartment off-campus with her 15-year-old brother John. She had recently been awarded guardianship over him, a victory she celebrated with St. Michael's. Carl was in awe of Lani's resilience in the face of unimaginable adversity, struggling to imagine having his life turned upside down because his mother aided and abetted a murder orchestrated by her drug-dealing boyfriend. *How was Lani able to make it through each day with the memory of her mother being carried away in handcuffs in the middle of the night? How did Lani cope with the finality of her mother's 20-year prison sentence?*

"St. Michael's really supported me during all of it." Lani relayed how Father Jiffy had fostered John while Lani worked to get full custody of him; she pointed over to Suzette and Bethany, telling Carl about the countless home-cooked casseroles they personally delivered to Lani's apartment when she had worked a double shift at the diner and was too tired to eat, let alone cook. Emily's husband, who was an attorney, had taken on Lani's case pro bono. Carl felt tiny goosebumps forming on his arms, in awe of the strength a community of faith could provide. As Lani went on, Carl didn't hear one mention of exploratory committees or board meetings that analyzed how members were going to help someone in need. Carl had always found these church politics useless, and the absence of them was refreshing.

Lani and Carl exchanged numbers, Carl finally catching Daniel alone by the table of doughnuts and coffee. He casually made his way to the table and poured coffee into a paper cup, stealing glances at Daniel as he mixed powdered non-dairy creamer into his drink. Carl smiled as he noticed Daniel's plate piled high with tiny glazed doughnut bites.

"Careful, might go into a sugar coma," Carl slowly approached Daniel as he chuckled, wiping a crumb away from the corner of his mouth.

"It's totally worth it," Daniel laughed as he shoved an entire donut bite into his mouth, loudly smacking his lips. Carl thought about how he would muster up the courage to ask out this man – who was obviously a step up from Don. He didn't have a wife and kids, he wasn't closeted in the least bit. Carl fidgeted with his cup of coffee and was about to walk away when he looked across the room to see Jerry giving him an encouraging, if a bit conspicuous, nod.

"Ummmm... Daniel, would you like to maybe catch a movie or go bowling sometime? Do you like bowling? Or maybe roller skating."

"It's a date. But you have to sing. Promise?"

"Promise." The two exchanged numbers as Carl's pulse raced. He was experiencing butterflies without shame or guilt. Carl never imagined scoring a first date with a guy he met at church. The Lord truly worked in mysterious ways.

• • •

The Wounded Souls ministry had flourished thanks to the successful merger of Holy Boldness and New Zion. Mark and Louisa had both personally met with the new members, many of whom were former homosexuals or family members of homosexuals. As Mark pulled up a metal folding chair in the fellowship hall where the Wounded Souls ministry had begun their weekly meeting, he relinquished the lingering guilt behind threatening to expose Frank's drug-addicted past once he heard the powerful testimonies from members who had renounced homosexuality in the name of committing fully to a heterosexual lifestyle.

Mark had dropped by New Zion on a Thursday morning, armed with his manila envelopes containing Frank's convoluted past. Frank had been on the phone chatting animatedly with Bishop McGrath, a fellow heretical clergyman who had joined forces with Frank to form the Tolerance Coalition. As Mark had suspected, this organization was a satanic smokescreen for glorifying homosexuality. Frank had let suspect phrases such as, "transgender visibility," and "scriptural debates" slip as he puffed out his chest, the gray collared shirt expanding with each laugh.

"I haven't felt welcome in a church for years," Donnell began, looking around the fellowship hall of Holy Boldness/New Zion nervously. Donnell had been one of the first members to offer up his experience, one that illuminated a tenuous relationship with the church that was commonplace with ex-homosexuals.

Mark observed the relaxed disposition of Donnell, who was a friend of Ian's. Donnell was working hard to restore his broken relationship with his father, a man who had abandoned him and his mother at the tender age of four. Donnell was consequently raised by his mother, grandmother, and aunt, and had no male role models growing up. Mark's spirit broke as Donnell relived days spent cooking and gossiping with these women, all while silently longing for a man to guide him through life. Mark's heart broke for the gay men and lesbians who believed they were born homosexual.

"What was the lifestyle like?" Hubert asked this question with a sincerity Mark had never before heard. Since the inception of the Wounded Souls ministry, Mark had struggled to train church members on how to effectively reach Christians struggling to overcome homosexuality. Many members were reluctant to support people who were transparent about these struggles. Sandy said that once a person had committed to renouncing homosexuality, no discussion was needed. In her mind, the word of God was the only support any person struggling to overcome sin required.

"Lonely. Scary at times, because I would meet guys online. I tried to find a community of gay men who would support me, but all they seemed to want was sex," Donnell's voice broke as he chronicled his brief affiliation with an LGBT affirming non-denominational church, quickly realizing that many of the gay and lesbian members were swingers.

"By the fifth month, I had discovered that many of the gay couples secretly hooked up with one another. One couple had asked me to do a threesome," Donnell explained. Mark became disgusted by this blatant disrespect of Christianity, silently applauding Donnell's bold decision to leave that church.

• • •

As Mark listened to Donnell, he reflected on how he had tried to explain this reality to Frank, but Frank had no intention of opening his mind. The two men had gotten caught in a loop of theological arguments and suffocating silences, and neither side was willing to compromise. When Mark had grown weary of reasoning with Frank, he uncovered the first file in the manila envelope: the photo of Frank purchasing cocaine. The photo had effortlessly slid in front of Frank, whose eyes widened as he undoubtedly traveled back to the dark alleys where he procured that white powder.

"How did you get these?" That had been Frank's first question as the color in his face faded. Mark had responded with New Zion's fabricated financial statements that tied transactions from the church's expense account to Frank's personal checking account. Frank had begun sobbing.

Frank had begun pleading for Mark to understand that he would never steal church funds to purchase drugs; Mark had endured fifteen minutes of incoherent explanations as to why the financial statements were not true. If Mark had not paid Latrice to doctor them, he seriously would have suspected Frank was stealing church funds to buy drugs.

"I've been sober for over a year. I have a wife and two kids. Please, Mark," Frank had pleaded.

"Okay. I won't show these to the bishops on one condition," Mark began, and then went on to demand that Frank resign as a pastor. Frank listened, but emphatically refused to meet Mark's demands, which included not only resignation but also very specific instructions on the type of sermon he should preach before announcing his resignation.

When Frank had proclaimed that New Zion needed his guidance, Mark had unveiled the signed petition and emails to have Frank removed.

"New Zion wants you gone. They want a pastor, not a dirty liberal, baby-killing, sodomite-loving heretic whose main goal is to shove sexual deviancy down their throats!" The conversation had ended with Frank quietly asking Mark to leave. Four days later, the bishops had called Mark, begging him to merge New Zion and Holy Boldness.

• • •

After Mark closed the session with prayer, he scanned the crowd for Donnell, finding him picking at a cube of cheese on his plate. He politely made small talk with other members but seemed preoccupied when alone. Mark surmised that it had something to do with Ian.

When the Wounded Souls ministry had its final budget approved, Mark had called Ian to relay this good news. Much to his consternation, Ian hadn't answered and never returned his call. Mark had texted Ian and received no response.

As Donnell rolled the cube of cheese around his plate, Mark approached him. "Haven't seen your friend Ian. Everything okay?"

Donnell sighed heavily as he bit into his cheese cube, reluctantly informing Mark that Ian had decided to terminate sessions with Lester. When Donnell had pressed Ian for the reasons why he decided to stop seeing his therapist, Ian had abruptly changed the subject, rambling about changing his major and possibly taking a semester off from college. As he thanked Donnell for sharing, gently clapping him on the shoulder, Mark hurried to his office, closing the door and calling Lester on his cell phone. As Mark was dialing Lester, an unrecognizable number appeared on the screen, and he answered it.

"Hello?" Mark sat down at his desk, as the sound of heavy breathing greeted him over the line. A woman's voice shakily asked if he was Mark Perkins. The color in Mark's face quickly faded as he glanced at his reflection on his desktop screen. The woman introduced herself as Gertrude Davies, the mother of Ian Davies. Gertrude's sobs eventually came through the other end of the phone. Mark knew Ian was in trouble.

"Ian tried to commit suicide. He...he...he swallowed an entire bottle of his Adderall."

Mark quickly fetched a pen and paper as he wrote down the name of the hospital Ian had been taken to, violently jumping out of his chair and swinging open his office door. He dashed down the hallway and out the main entrance of the church, with Gertrude still on the line as he unlocked his car and sped to the hospital.

"Gertrude, what happened?" Mark wove through the heavy traffic, listening as Gertrude explained Ian's frustrations over still having same-sex attractions. Mark dangerously changed lanes as he honked his horn at a truck driving several miles below the speed limit, nearly making contact with the Sam's Club logo as Gertrude told Mark she had to go. The line disconnected as Mark exhaled sharply once he saw the exit for Holy Cross Hospital. Questions and worries danced in his mind, their uncertainties forcing him to wonder what had caused Ian to quit working with Lester. What had made Ian abandon his desire to change?

The odious smell of rubber and isopropyl alcohol greeted Mark as he rushed toward the front desk of the emergency room. A nurse impatiently held up her finger while rummaging through a patient file as Mark inquired about Ian Davies. He scanned the woman's neatly pressed pink scrubs, the name "Margie" written in cursive on the upper left-hand corner. Around him, doctors hurried down a wide hallway as a code blue announcement blared on the speakers.

Margie finally looked up from her file, the impatience in her voice replaced by a softness Mark found assuaging, "Are you family?"

"I'm the family pastor." Mark wasn't lying. Ian was technically a member of Holy Boldness on paper. Margie pointed to the wide hallway, Mark following as he heard the familiar sounds of Gertrude crying.

"He's stable now. That's the good thing," a doctor in dark blue scrubs said calmly as he placed his hand on Gertrude's shoulder. Her left hand shook uncontrollably as her right hand stroked her son's hair. Mark observed the young man who now lay unconscious in a hospital bed, his brown hair nearly covering his eyes. Upon noticing Mark's presence beside her, Gertrude threw her arms around his neck, explaining the disastrous two weeks that had culminated in this fateful event.

She relayed how Ian had been exploding into fits of rage since he abruptly ended sessions with Lester, blaming her and his father for encouraging him to pursue therapy with a quack. Gertrude's concerns had caused her to call Lester, who relayed an alarming message regarding the outcome of his therapy: Ian would deal with same-sex attractions for life, but would now be equipped with the tools to overcome them.

"I asked him if was change possible, and he said it was up to Ian to define what change would be for him. Mark, Robert Cannon's reading materials told us that Ian would be attracted to women once he completed the program."

Mark held Gertrude, listening to her sobs as a man's voice greeted them. Ian's father and brother arrived, their eyes red and their cheeks flushed. Gertrude updated the two men with the news that Ian's heart had stopped briefly, but the doctors were able to stabilize him.

Mark stepped away from the family to call Lester, unsure now what he even believed about conversion therapy. *Did Lester beguile all of his prospective patients with a nonexistent cure? Did Mark buy into this cure? Was Lester lying all along?*

"Mark, I was just about to call you," Lester's cheerful tone infuriated Mark as he went over and sat down in a gray leather chair in the waiting room.

"Lester, what happened with Ian?" Mark inquired, deciding to omit the details regarding Ian's suicide attempt as he awaited Lester's response. He prayed that Lester's side of the story would be believable and that Gertrude had just misunderstood Lester. Lester told Mark that Ian did not want to commit to doing the hard work of restoring his broken relationship with his father and brother. According to Lester, Ian terminated his sessions against Lester's advice.

"His mom thought that Ian would like girls right away, and I think there was a lot of frustration on her end," Lester's went on.

Mark found Lester's evasiveness suspicious, and his suspicions were cemented once Lester hurried him off the phone by what seemed to be a hastily fabricated excuse of needing to deal with a patient in crisis. Mark hung up the phone, nervously opened his email on his phone, and began typing an email to Robert Cannon. Amid this tragedy, Mark saw how God was working. Ian's suicide attempt had alerted Mark to the very plausible possibility of Lester behaving in an unethical manner. For Lester to espouse that change to heterosexuality was possible, and then proffer a contradictory picture of that change, one that was antithetical to Robert Cannon's research and mission, troubled Mark. Maybe God used this horrific event to open Mark's eyes and alert Robert Cannon to the serpent in his garden. Mark read Robert's studies, read the books, and believed that Lester was hiding something.

21

TURNING TABLES

Tim slept soundly next to Harriet, his gray chest hair protruding from the green wool blanket covering his naked body. She still found it difficult to fathom that she was in Tim's bedroom, lying in his bed. She couldn't believe that she had actually acted on the impulses and fantasies that danced in her mind daily. Being with Tim felt amazing. She was surprised at how completely alive she felt when she was with him, how comfortable in her sexuality she was with a man who was not her husband. The sad thing was that she hadn't ever remembered feeling this way with Percy. *Was it sacrilege to compare her orgasm to baptism,* she wondered, *the waves of endorphins coursing through her body akin to the act of being dunked into holy water?*

Harriet had confronted Percy about the credit card charges pertaining to Global Healing earlier that day. She had allowed her feelings of confusion, rage, and betrayal to fester for weeks, as she struggled to focus on the curriculum she had been developing for students with special needs. Kathleen had walked in on her one afternoon while Harriet had been reviewing her proposal draft, unaware that her hand had been shaking as she wrote notes in the document's margins. When Kathleen had asked Harriet what was wrong, she had broken her pencil while trying to formulate a calm response to her unbridled rage.

"You left one of your old credit card statements on the dining room table," Harriet had rehearsed the lie she had uttered for days, ensuring that it was believable enough to not alert Percy to the fact that she had been investigating every detail of his extramarital affair with Heather. Percy had shrugged while hastily pouring himself a bowl of cereal. He had managed to gain twenty pounds in the last two months, the undershirt he wore exposing the pouches of fat around his waist and accentuating his expanding gut.

"So, what?" Percy had begun pouring skim milk into his cereal, Harriet growing more disgusted as large chunks of corn flakes fell onto his shirt as he chewed loudly.

"Global Healing from Homosexuality Corporation."

Percy's face had turned to stone, his once perfunctory disposition gone, replaced with a defensiveness that immediately indicated his culpability. Harriet had stood with her hands on her hips, too riled up for coffee as she slammed her fist onto the kitchen table and motioned for Percy to have a seat.

"How dare you," she had hissed. "How dare you fill our son with beliefs that he is damaged! That he is not beautiful and perfect just as he is! How dare you!"

Percy had proffered an apology that had underscored his hurt upon realizing Jerry was gay. He had provided Harriet with the common justification for encouraging Jerry to explore conversion therapy: Life as a black man in America was hard, and being gay would only make Jerry's life harder.

"I'm his dad. I want him to have a better life than I had."

Harriet had laughed at Percy, her belly springing forth a guttural sound that surprised her. For years, Percy had quietly resented Harriet for her white privilege, secretly looking down upon her while reaping the benefits of that privilege: his tuition for graduate school, the house in which they resided, a private school for Jerry, Leo, and Ella, countless vacations with five-star accommodations. Harriet had grown tired of being dismissed as a privileged white woman who had no understanding of the burdens of existing as a minority in America. Percy's decision to force Jerry into conversion therapy had epitomized that dismissal most unforgivably.

"So your solution is to have Jerry morph into you? Maybe he'll be so lucky and find a rich, understanding, white girl he can sponge off of!"

"Harriet, I... I realize it was a mistake."

"You know what? I'm starting to think that *we* were a mistake. A big one. You need to leave. I want you out of my house by the time I come home."

Harriet had driven by her house after work, satisfied that Percy's car was no longer in the driveway. She had accelerated her speed down the cul de sac, reveling in her assertiveness, basking in the dominion she now had over her life. Tim had detected all of that when he opened his door to find Harriet standing there hungry for his touch. She had kissed him on the mouth, allowing him to fulfill every single one of her carnal desires; she had encouraged Tim to fuck her with a ferocity that would make her scream. And he had done just that.

Tim woke up to find Harriet sitting up in bed, staring at her silhouette that reflected in the moonlight. She thought of the messy divorce ahead of her; she knew Percy was going to fight her, and that she needed to inoculate her assets from Percy's malicious attempts to seize them. Tim gently kissed the nape of Harriet's neck, purring softly into her ear while rubbing her shoulders softly.

"What's on your mind?"

"Percy's gonna fight me, and it's gonna get ugly. I know you're focusing on my case, but is there any way Percy was connected to Heather's illegal escort service?"

Tim exhaled sharply as he provided Harriet with his conjectures about Percy's involvement, underscoring his plausible theory that Percy had been a pawn in Heather's nefarious dealings. "But a pawn can easily take the fall for something," Tim promised Harriet that he would connect with Eve and request unfettered access to OEI's financial records, particularly the ones that Devin had fabricated for Heather. Harriet drifted off to sleep as Tim assured her of the possibilities in which Percy could be scapegoated. Her dreams were reflective of a life she now knew was possible: a job that kept her busy, two kids who were far from perfect, but who realized their full potential, a man who didn't resent her for being rich or successful or sad because her daughter had died.

She awakened to the sound of pots and pans shuffling in the kitchen, her nose greeted by the aroma of freshly brewed coffee. As Harriet stretched in Tim's king-size bed, briefly closing her eyes as the sun's rays showered the room with light, she opened her eyes to find Tim placing a tray of scrambled eggs and toast in front of her, greeting her with a kiss. Harriet pinched herself on her wrists to make sure she wasn't dreaming.

• • •

Heather's aversion to risk had intensified after Uriah and Dr. Sturgis' bodies had been discovered. Silas Greene had always reiterated the importance of remaining two steps ahead of your enemies, and in Heather's line of work, making enemies was commonplace. Heather had to mitigate these risks, and Latrice's microchip that downloaded data from cell phones was the perfect tool to ensure her employees were not suffering from that deadly condition known as "loose lips."

Heather plugged Padma's phone into her computer, growing impatient as the text messages slowly loaded on the computer screen. The mundanity of the messages bored Heather – friends scheduling study sessions for Calculus III or Padma's mom reminding her to apply for summer internships before the end of the fall semester. After rummaging through emails and finding nothing suspect, Heather placed Padma's phone back into her purse and checked her watch to ensure Padma's session did not go over the allotted time.

Deanne was scheduled to arrive in fifteen minutes, and Heather anxiously awaited the sound of the creaking in the front door. Over the past few weeks, Heather had detected an unpleasantness in Deanne that she had never witnessed before. In addition to catching her sobbing in one of the changing rooms, Heather had noticed that Deanne had started to neglect her appearance, showing up without makeup and with her hair unbrushed. Heather needed to speak to Deanne about her unprofessional behavior and its potentially detrimental effect on the business if it continued.

A gentle rap on Heather's office door caught her off guard. She looked up to see Padma quickly grabbing her purse and, without so much as a word, turning and walking down the hall toward the main sales floor. Heather got up and followed her, gently tugging on her shoulder as she caught up to her. As if anticipating a slap or punch from Heather, Padma turned around and covered her face.

"Ms. Heather, what did I do?" Padma's thick accent was grating to Heather's ears, but she disregarded that to get to her point, politely inquiring about Deanne's emotional state. Heather even pretended to have a close friend who was a therapist, and who would welcome taking Deanne as a patient.

"You can trust me. I'm just concerned about her," Heather offered. Although her concern was sorely misplaced, Heather hoped Padma wouldn't detect the difference.

Padma shrugged, said she knew nothing, and hastily reminded Heather that she had an exam to study for. Heather motioned for Padma to leave and wished her luck on her exam. Moments later, the familiar creak in the front door alerted Heather to Deanne's presence. Deanne turned off her phone and stashed it in her purse, Heather's eyes fixating on its garish floral print. *Who had told her that that purse was fashionable?*

"I'll go get ready," Deanne muttered quickly.

Heather noticed that Deanne's appearance was somewhat acceptable today, her long red hair pulled back into a neat ponytail. The blush on her face was conservatively applied, the light eyeshadow an appropriate touch. Heather listened for Deanne's ascending footsteps before rummaging through her purse and retrieving her phone. As she heard the upstairs bedroom door close, Heather began to unravel Deanne's digital life.

As Latrice's program started collecting Deanne's texts and emails, Heather focused in on a series of texts that indicated Deanne's dissatisfaction with her job, one of which read "Never accept a job posted on a fashion blog." The text had been sent to one of Deanne's friends from school. Heather deemed the texts innocuous and moved on to emails. What she found here made her a bit unsettled. A string of emails from a man named Patrick Hartley confirmed Deanne's appointment with him and an intern named Mel. Heather conducted a Google search on Patrick Hartley, her eyes resting on a photo of a man with salt and pepper hair smiling in a teal suit. The text above his smiling face read "Tired of overworked public defenders? Unable to afford a costly private attorney? Justice For All is the place for you!" Heather's hands shook as she weighed the implications of Deanne's meeting with a man dedicated to fighting for underrepresented individuals. Deanne classified as one, her parents unable to afford college tuition and straddled with debt. *Why had Deanne reached out to Patrick?* Heather wondered, a bit unsettled. *Why did she need legal assistance?*

Heather found her answer in a series of texts between Deanne and Devin of all people. Heather's unease quickly turned to rage. Devin was coaxing Deanne into working with Patrick to destroy her life.

"She's going to pay," one text from Devin to Deanne read. *Devin was always so confident,* Heather thought, *perpetually smug about his superior morals and his compassionate attitude for those who were suffering.* The subsequent text messages were revelatory, their nature implicating Greg Hammond as a purported rapist.

"No one's gonna believe me," Deanne had responded to a string of Devin's texts that had encouraged Deanne to meet with a man named Tim Floyd. Once again, Heather employed Google to assist her in finding out who Tim was. Her search ended up being futile, the only Tim Floyd that appeared being an elderly man who had retired from a tenured position at Virginia Commonwealth University. Clearly, a former English literature professor was not the man to whom Devin was referring. So then who the hell was Tim?

Heather decided to place Deanne's phone back into her purse, numb to the possibility that Greg had raped Deanne, the severity of the situation not sinking in until after Deanne had collected her belongings from Heather's office.

The drive back to OEI was plagued by a deafening silence, the hum of Heather's engine ringing in her ears as she pulled into the parking garage. She luckily found a parking spot near the entrance, and silently thanked a deity in whom she didn't even believe for facilitating conditions conducive for a hasty meeting with Greg.

Greg had taken an insufferable liking to working late at the office, often sending emails and texts at 10:00 in the evening and encouraging his subordinates to do the same, oblivious to the fact that many of them had families and other responsibilities outside of work. For Heather, Greg's preference for pouring over contracts and sales goals until midnight served her well. She knew that if she cornered Greg while he was working, there would be a slim chance of him bullshitting her, which was the last thing that Heather needed right now.

Heather made her way past the empty cubicles, the hum of the refrigerator in the breakroom greeting her as she walked to Greg's office. His door was open as he hummed to the music playing in his office. Hall & Oates were singing about a rich girl depending on her father's wealth, Greg attempting to hit the high notes in the song's bridge. Peering up from a large binder on his desk, Greg smiled at Heather as his glasses slid down his nose. The numbness that had briefly coursed through her body moments ago faded, replaced by a primal urge to topple every single plaque in Greg's office. He had willfully broken Heather's rules regarding establishing contact with her employees outside of her establishment. He had contacted Deanne and had given that girl a reason to believe she had been raped.

"Surprised to see you here. What can I do for you?" Greg turned the music off and folded his hands on his desk, a wide grin appearing across his smug face.

Heather had to take a deep breath to compose herself. "Did you meet with

Deanne outside of my establishment?" she asked, her tone doing nothing to conceal her disgust.

Greg's smile quickly faded once he realized the severity of the situation, watching as Heather plopped into one of his plush green office chairs without ever taking her eyes off of him.

"Once. I met with her once," Greg admitted as he went on to explain that he had contacted Deanne through a burner phone and invited her to come see his penthouse suite. He admitted to offering her a thousand dollars for three hours of her time. Heather sensed Greg wasn't telling her the whole story. From the texts she had read between Deanne and Devin, Heather suspected that Deanne had been given a substance and that a non-consensual sexual relationship had ensued.

Knowing this, she couldn't help but grow even increasingly enraged as Greg offered a disingenuous apology.

"Let me rephrase my question, Greg. Did you give Deanne any substance that would have allowed you to have your way with her?"

The silence between Greg and Heather was deafening, Greg finally breaking it with a damning confession. Yes, he had given Deanne a muscle relaxer and had engaged in sexual intercourse with her while she lay unconscious. Heather grabbed hold of the cloth finish on Greg's chair, wishing she could unleash her unbridled rage onto him right at that moment. He merely stood there, seemingly unfazed by the implications his actions posed. Heather informed Greg that Deanne had sought legal counsel, and had every intention of exposing Heather's crimes, which were inadvertently Greg's.

"How much money do you think it'll take to keep her quiet?" Greg reached into the pocket of his suit jacket and grabbed his wallet, his obliviousness making Heather impatient. Deanne was not after money. She was after justice.

"No amount of money will make this right, Greg. And since we can't make it right, we need to make this problem disappear."

Heather began envisioning the many ways in which Deanne's body could be dismembered. She began conjuring up methods of killing her quickly and painlessly – poisoning her with a lethal combination of stimulants and benzodiazepines, smothering her with a pillow, offering her pudding prepared with a deadly dose of household cleaning products. Greg placed his hands over his face, fully comprehending the criminality behind his actions.

"Brendan's not here to save us," Greg stared at the photo of the two men smiling behind the golf course, remarking at the grim possibilities of him being found alive. Greg's voice lowered as he offered up a contact that made issues of a similar nature permanently disappear. Heather inquired about the methods this contact employed to dispose of the bodies, her head nodding impressively as Greg mentioned multi-limb dismemberment that made it virtually impossible to positively identify a victim.

Heather agreed to allow Greg to reach out to his contact, reiterating that he needed to take full ownership of this egregious act. Greg placed his hands over his face and sighed heavily, chuckling quietly as Heather turned her attention toward Devin's betrayal. His idealism had fueled a situation in which Heather and Faith could face serious prison time. His strong desire to acquire the moral high ground had forced Heather into a mindset of self-preservation at any cost. It had been a mindset she disliked, but one to which she had grown accustomed.

• • •

The timeline of Lester's checkered past and career had been meticulously tracked on the whiteboard, its contents accompanied by photos during each career milestone. Jerry kept that image of Lester's life splayed out on the whiteboard front and center in his mind as Brandon drove up Interstate 295 toward Baltimore, his reckless driving in full display as he rapidly changed lanes and impatiently honked his horn at drivers adhering to the 55 miles per hour speed limit. Jerry wondered if they would get pulled over by a cop or rear-end another car. While Jerry loved many things about Brandon, he found his impulsivity scary.

By this point, Jerry had mastered his ex-homosexual persona of Simon Waldorf, succumbing to an obsequious disposition when he had met Lester at his office. Phase two of Lester's destruction had been enacted, and Jerry had to retrieve those pertinent patient files locked away in that black cabinet in Lester's office.

"Simon, what brings you here?" Jerry had caught Lester as he was preparing to leave for lunch, his usual cheerful manner replaced by one of extreme preoccupation. Jerry had mentioned how the article had sparked a lot of dialogue at his church, underscoring how inspirational Lester's change had been and how it was bringing people out of a deadly lifestyle. He had also unveiled a doctored photo of Callie holding a fake ultrasound photo, a picture that had caused Lester to give effusive praise to the Lord.

"Sorry to stop by unannounced, but I think I left my devotional book here."

Lester had mustered a smile, hastily welcoming Jerry to have a look around while he went to lunch. Jerry had received the text from Callie indicating her successful disabling of Global Healing's security cameras as Lester quietly closed the door behind him. Jerry had begun searching for the key to the cabinet, trying to remember where he had seen Lester stash it. His mind raced with images of Lester shaking clients' hands and taking their intake forms. He had remembered seeing Lester overturning a wedding photo to retrieve the key, the photo's location on the middle shelf. Jerry's hand shook as he began flipping photos over, relieved when the fifth photo revealed the silver key. He quickly chuckled at the gullible smiles plastered on an overweight man and his morbidly obese bride. Up close, the absurdity of these facades had been overwhelmingly obvious.

•••

"Move your ass!" Brandon forcefully honked his horn as a woman with obscene blue highlights in her hair merged into Brandon's lane, her bumper almost making contact with Brandon's Prius as he was forced to slam on the brakes to avoid hitting her. Several minutes and a slew of obscenities later, the traffic thankfully dispersed and the woman with the obscene blue highlights exited the interstate around Ft. Meade.

"Guys, convince me why tracking down Roger Clementine is a good idea again."

Brandon groaned as he reiterated the crucial information Roger possessed, information that cemented Lester's unsavory therapeutic practices. Jerry felt uneasy about reaching out to Roger, the contents in his file indicative of gross misconduct on Lester's part.

•••

Jerry had taken photos of the ten patient records Lester had in the cabinet, the intake form similar to the one he had completed a year ago. Lester had asked about past homosexual and heterosexual experiences; he had asked each patient to envision their lives as heterosexuals. Jerry had made a concerted effort to capture Ian's and Roger's files, the two young men who had voiced concern over Lester's therapy and his inability to quantify change. Jerry's heart had raced as he landed on Ian's file, remembering the conversation Lester had had with Robert once news of Ian's suicide attempt had surfaced.

"You've got a knack for deviating from my program," Robert had admonished Lester for his failure to adhere to the therapeutic practices Robert had spent a decade implementing. Lester had countered Robert's scoldings with painful realism regarding homosexual desires, namely that the desires never dissipated and were never replaced with opposite-sex attractions. This conversation had remained at the forefront of Jerry's mind as he took photos of Ian's file and approached Roger's record, appraising an anomalous piece of evidence – a letter alluding to an inappropriate relationship between Roger and Lester. Jerry had taken a photo of the letter along with the other pieces of information in Roger's file. The session notes had indicated a history of self-harm and suicidal ideation, along with tendencies to dissociate from stressful events.

"Nelson, if anyone can reach Roger, it's you. You've been where he is." Jerry thought back to the previous night in Brandon's bed and his head resting comfortably against Brandon's chest. They had spoken about the pasts that had shackled them to victim mentalities, and how their expose of Lester was forcing them to confront the futility of such a mindset.

"I didn't go to conversion therapy, but my parents didn't exactly throw me a coming-out party either," Brandon offered.

Jerry had never heard Brandon talk about his coming out experience, as Brandon had always dismissed it as a boring story with a predictable ending. Jerry had perched his head onto the cold wooden bedpost, trying to get comfortable as his head made contact with the smooth, hard surface. He had listened to Brandon talk about awkward dinners with his parents, the topic of conversation filled with misconceptions about what it meant to be gay. He had described a particular occasion in which his mother had instructed him to carry condoms in his pocket whenever he went out. Brandon had felt insulted by the implication that – just because he was gay – it, therefore, followed that he would engage in casual sex when he went to the movies or to the grocery store.

"Eric told me to approach my parents with compassion."

"Who is Eric?" Jerry asked, suspecting that Eric was a former love, possibly the first love. There had been a tinge of sadness and regret in Brandon's voice when he mentioned Eric's name.

"Someone too good for this world. He's not with us anymore."

Jerry had tried to quell his anxieties about who Eric was, instead focusing on Brandon's message of using his weakest, most vulnerable moments to reach Roger. Jerry had not been able to do that. Instead, he had focused on the newly enigmatic presence of a dead boyfriend Brandon had never mentioned. The two had agreed to be boyfriends, and Jerry had shared the most unpleasant parts of himself – watching his sister die, blackmailing his father. He had thought Brandon would do the same.

"Anyway, Roger needs you. He needs your kindness and patience to open up."

Brandon's Prius pulled into the Residence Hall dormitories, the brown and white exterior appearing faded as the sun began to set behind it. Callie had created a fictitious Facebook profile for Jerry, one in which he was a freshman piano performance major at the Peabody Institute. Roger had accepted Jerry's friend request and had even initiated a casual conversation through Facebook's private messages feature. The two had found a common interest in classical music, Jerry digging through his memory of days and nights spent practicing "Moonlight Sonata" and "Clair de Lune." Jerry had fabricated a plausible excuse for not living on campus: commuting from his parents' house in Towson was cheaper, and as the two spent more nights talking about the unique demands of music majors, Roger had asked Jerry if they could meet for coffee at a nearby Starbucks a block from Residence Hall. Jerry's knees buckled as he scanned the crowd for a freckled redhead with sharp, bony elbows. The hodgepodge of hoodies and backpacks congregated underneath the giant oak tree made finding Roger challenging.

"Any words of wisdom as I tell Roger he's been catfished by a former patient of Lester?" Callie mumbled some variation of "knock 'em dead."

Brandon brought Jerry in for a kiss, his hands resting squarely on Jerry's shoulders, "Best of luck. And in the words of the illustrious Ru Paul, don't fuck it up."

Jerry chuckled as he walked onto the sprawling lawn in front of the brown and white structure, his eyes scanning the crowd for Roger. The front door opened shortly, and a skinny kid with red hair and discernable freckles descended onto the lawn, moving closer to Jerry and to the realization that every message the two had exchanged was a ploy.

"Jeremiah Thompson?" Callie had used Jerry's real name, and his mother's maiden name when creating his profile, Jerry almost not responding as Roger animatedly waved his hand and jogged to where Jerry was standing.

"Hi, Roger."

The two shook hands as Roger gestured for them to walk the short block to Starbucks. Images of that whiteboard with Lester's sordid history splayed across it flashed in front of Jerry: 1998 to 2002 - Lester's identification as a gay man immersed in the D.C./Baltimore club scene; June 22, 2002 - Lester's hospitalization after being attacked outside of Leon's, a local Baltimore gay club, an event that had been the impetus behind Lester's decision to denounce homosexuality; August 2002 to May 2005 - Lester's matriculation through a Master's program in Counseling from Reston University while undergoing conversion therapy under the direction of Robert Cannon; June 2006 - Lester's acceptance of a position at Global Healing Corporation as a psychotherapist; April 2012 - Roger Clementine's complaint alleging gross misconduct by Lester. As they approached Starbucks, these facts were inescapable. The lively chatter of college students pouring over textbooks and sipping lattes did not nullify the fact that Jerry had lured Roger under false pretenses to convince him to speak about his time in conversion therapy.

Roger ordered a green tea Frappuccino with whipped cream while Jerry ordered a hot chocolate; caffeine was the last thing he needed at this moment. Roger and Jerry sat next to a group of girls studying chemistry, the formulas for balancing chemical equations briefly catching Jerry's attention as he sipped his hot chocolate, forcing himself to get into the character of a freshman piano performance major.

"My practicing schedule is crazy. I'm up at five. I do two hours of pure scales and "Hanon" exercises, then I focus on my performance piece for the week. What about you?"

Roger's mouth was pouted as he slurped his drink, swallowing what appeared to be eight ounces of his Frappuccino in one gulp before answering Jerry, "I do a lot of vocal exercises in the morning, anything to expand my range and improve my pitch. My performance pieces are quite rangy."

The idle conversation continued for around 20 minutes, Jerry and Roger swiping stories about the jitters behind their first performances. Roger somehow steered the conversation to performing in church, and the freedom he experienced when he simply let go. Jerry took that as a sign from the universe to explore this facet of Roger's life. The church was clearly something he still cherished, and Jerry surmised it was the primary motivating factor behind seeing Lester.

"What church do you go to?" Jerry watched as Roger's demeanor shifted, a forlorn expression manifesting itself onto Roger's face as he surprisingly changed the subject back to school. Jerry apologized if he had touched a sensitive topic, Roger waving his hand dismissively through each "sorry" Jerry had offered. Jerry decided not to push Roger to share insight into his ostensibly fraught relationship with his church; instead, he would allow Roger to lead the conversation now and ambush him later once he seemed more at ease.

"My church isn't the most accepting place for someone like me," Rogers's nostrils enlarged as if he was steadying himself for a fight.

Jerry nodded as Roger spoke candidly about the church he grew up in, recalling memories of attending Sunday school with his mom and singing in the choir. Jerry tried to picture himself in the foreign atmosphere Roger was describing: the white steeple with a large golden cross atop it, the booming voice of Pastor Belmont as he proclaimed the evils of homosexuality. How Roger remained in a space so intolerant and judgmental was beyond Jerry's comprehension.

"May I ask what happened when you came out?"

That question startled Roger, his dismay now devolving into one of abject mortification. He sipped the remainder of his green Frappuccino and hunched over.

"Never mind. It's none of my business. I'm sorry I asked," Jerry recovered.

Roger shook his head as he went into the crucial details leading up to his time with Lester, the gay pornography his father had found on his computer, and his mother's tearful supplications that her son wasn't gay. Those supplications had prompted his father to find a conversion therapist who had success with helping clients rid themselves of homosexual desires.

"I understood myself a lot better, but then things started getting weird."

"Between you and your therapist?" Jerry took Rogers's reluctant nod as confirmation that a relationship had taken place between the two men, one that was sexual in nature. Jerry saw his opportunity to disclose his true identity. However, he waited until Roger explained the weird turn of events in his and Lester's relationship.

"We spent time outside the sessions. We'd go to the movies and concerts. It felt good." Roger started biting his upper lip, quickly shaking his head as if he had said too much. Jerry studied the freckled-face guy in front of him, the fear apparent on his face. Jerry had to come clean now, and drop this act of being a casual friend who just wanted to hang out with Roger.

"Roger, I was a patient of Lester's last year. I'm not a student at Peabody."

The color on Rogers's face faded as his expression contorted.

"What?" was all Roger was able to utter.

"I'm Jeremiah Nelson, and I'm a field reporter for Rainbow Warriors. We've been following Lester's career, and we could really use your help."

Roger began shaking as his head started jerking violently, bangs of red hair swinging horizontally as Jerry caught glimmers of tears in Roger's eyes. Jerry thought back to that electrifying night on the dance floor at Towne, to the abject terror of being confronted with an experience he had tried to forget. Roger was in a state of shock, and Jerry needed to safely guide him through this state. As Roger started convulsing, the group of girls studying chemistry looked up, their concern apparent yet also somehow judgmental. Jerry rushed over to Roger's side, planting his hand on his shaking shoulder. He felt phrases such as "Lester can't hurt you anymore" and "You're safe" seemed empty and meaningless at this moment, so he chose silence instead. The indelibility of conversion therapy was something that could not be washed away with superficial words of encouragement. Jerry needed to reach Roger on a personal level.

"You lied to me," Roger's voice cracked as he tried to hold back his tears.

"Would you have met with me if you knew who I really was?"

Roger shook his head as a tear fell down his face. Whatever Lester had done to Roger warranted more than a letter alleging misconduct. Jerry revealed the crucial part of his identity, the part he too had banished into the deep recesses of his brain. Jerry hoped the commonality of their experience would help Roger see that he wasn't alone in this fight.

"He told me he loved me," Roger sputtered through labored sobs.

Jerry gently guided Roger out of his seat, away from the prying stares and stolen glances of college students who would never understand the acute journey of self-acceptance that was common in the LGBT community. Jerry slowly ushered Roger into the crisp autumn air, a light breeze tickling his face as Roger continued to sob. When they reached the empty oak tree facing the Starbucks, Roger's sobs subsided, his eyes red and swollen as he wiped away tears with the sleeve of his hoodie.

"What was your relationship with Lester like? What did he do to you?" Jerry inquired, his mind swarming with visions of a vulnerable Roger being forced to strip naked in front of a mirror while shouting all of the names he was called as a boy. What Roger told him next was much worse than any perverse scenario Jerry could have conjured. Lester had slowly groomed Roger into having a sexual relationship with him, gaining his trust by offering to hang out as friends. The movies and baseball games had made Roger feel secure in his masculinity. He had cultivated a non-sexual friendship with a man who intimately knew his struggle; he thought nothing of Lester's occasional knee rubs or arm squeezes.

"I could never tell anyone, especially my parents or Robert. Lester said our friendship was frowned upon. Those were his exact words."

Jerry listened as Roger described the chilling moment when Lester had kissed him. Roger's eyes welled up as he took Jerry back to that cold December night two years ago. Roger and Lester had seen a Christmas concert at a local church, arriving separately and parking their cars on opposite sides of the parking lot to avoid any suspicion. They had met at the red double doors leading into the sanctuary, never making direct eye contact.

"We sat in my car and talked for a while after the concert. He told me that he still liked men and still thought about being with a man. Then he looked at me," Roger went on to describe a clumsy kiss and Lester's feigning of an unhinged fear that he had done something immoral. Little did Roger know at the time, the kiss had only been the beginning of what would become a very complex sexual relationship.

"I'm so sorry," was all Jerry could muster. He knew that nothing he said could ease the pain of reliving the trauma of sexual abuse.

"The baseball games ended with us kissing in his car, and eventually, I'd give him a blowjob," Roger confessed that the two would eventually go on long hikes, each hike culminating with a sexual act on a remote portion of the hiking trail. On their last hike, Lester had insisted on having anal sex with Roger in the backseat of his car. Lester had promised to be gentle but quickly became aggressive despite Roger's protests. During the act, Lester had whispered he loved Roger into his ear. Each subsequent encounter had ended with Lester quietly professing his love in that same manner. Jerry surmised that Roger never told anyone the details behind his relationship with Lester. If Roger had, Lester surely would have been in prison by now.

"You can come forward, Roger. You can get the justice you deserve. We can help you."

Roger scoffed at Jerry's offer, the vulnerability he showed Jerry vanquishing as he got up from the grass and brushed off his jeans, "No. You can't help me. I shouldn't have told you all that. This was a mistake."

Roger ran off into the direction of his dormitory, his red hair bouncing up and down as his shadow quickly faded into the dusk sky. Jerry let out a guttural scream, one that cemented every feeling of frustration and rage he harbored toward Lester and the people who supported him. He hoped Roger would realize that remaining silent served no one, that burying the negative effects of conversion therapy only fueled the fire of the therapists who espoused a fictitious conversion to heterosexuality. Staying silent perpetuated the abuse, so Jerry screamed alone, hoping the entire campus heard how royally pissed he was.

• • •

Carl's first date with Daniel started off in the worst possible way. Carl had stopped at a gas station on his way to pick up Daniel for a karaoke night at St. Michael's when he spotted Don leaving with a bag of junk food: chocolate doughnuts, bear claws, Skittles. The two former lovers briefly exchanged glances as Carl's knees buckled while the clicking sound of the gas pump reverberated in his ear. Pleasantries were exchanged – Don had missed seeing Carl in church, something that didn't surprise him. Don's casual disposition did not surprise Carl either. He wordlessly placed the pump back onto the latch when Don gently grabbed Carl's hand.

"Come on, Carl. It's me," Don pleaded.

Carl jerked Don's hand away as he grabbed his receipt and opened his car door.

Carl picked up Daniel, unable to shake his encounter with Don. He hoped Daniel didn't pick up on Carl's mood as the two rode in silence to the church. Karaoke night at St. Michael's was something akin to a holy day of obligation. The first Friday of every evening was spent gathered around the large cubic television belting out the most horrendous pop songs ever written. Liam's impression of Katy Perry, coupled with his near tone-deaf singing, did not make "Teenage Dream" tolerable. Daniel sat next to Carl, clutching his waist as he laughed uncontrollably at Liam's singing.

Emily clapped loudly as her son bowed in a fashion suitable for a diva, "You were so good, honey! I think Broadway could be in your future."

Carl and Daniel both snickered as the smell of pizza turned everyone's attention toward the door leading to the staircase. Lani and Jiffy arrived, each carrying four boxes of pizza. Carl and Daniel quickly relieved Jiffy and Lani of their towering stacks of pies.

"John can use some help carrying the sodas from the car," Jiffy huffed and puffed as he massaged his achy joints in a nearby folding chair.

Once Carl and Daniel finished lining up the pizza on the large table, they scurried outside to grab cases of ginger ale and Pepsi from Jiffy's car. A loud grunt from inside Jiffy's car startled Carl, and in a matter of seconds, John appeared from the backseat with a satisfied grin on his face. He took a lighter out of the pocket in his navy blue windbreaker and revealed the object of his desire, a blunt.

"Don't think we've met. I'm John," John said as he extended his dirt ridden hand in Carl's direction.

Carl shook it as he examined the blunt between the 15-year-old's lips, tempted to ask him for a hit even though he knew he shouldn't. When he and Leo had gotten high in the past, Carl was always trying to escape the internal turmoil within himself. Today, he didn't want to do that despite encountering the manifestation of that turmoil in a gas station parking lot two hours ago. John lit his blunt, offering Daniel and Carl a hit before gesturing to the cases of ginger ale and Pepsi in the trunk of the car. Daniel opened the trunk as John inhaled deeply, a puff of gray smoke emanating from his lips as he exhaled. The stench of marijuana faded as Carl and Daniel each lugged two cases of soda into the church.

"Does he always get high?" Carl asked.

"Once in a while. I've gotten high with him a couple of times."

Daniel's confession oddly made Carl feel as if he could share his recent encounter with his married ex-boyfriend without fear of condemnation. Daniel seemed to understand the complexities of adulthood. The two of them decided to carry one case of soda at a time, gingerly walking down the stairs to the fellowship hall. The animated chatter and loud smacks indicated that the pizza was quickly being consumed. Daniel and Carl set the cases of soda onto the end of the table and headed back upstairs to grab the other two cases, surprised when they saw John marching down the stairs with both cases balanced underneath his arms.

"I got these," he smirked at Daniel and Carl as they turned back around and headed downstairs.

"You okay?" Daniel stopped and studied Carl, his sleek black hair hanging over his forehead.

"No, I have to tell you something," Carl confessed, no longer stifled by the irrational fear of bursting into flames in a church. He revealed the tense interaction with Don at the gas station and the frustration he felt toward himself for even being in such a toxic relationship with a married, closeted man to begin with. Daniel wrapped his arms around Carl as he sobbed for the first time. He mourned the loss of Don, a loss that was inevitable in hindsight. Daniel released Carl from his embrace and placed a kiss on his lips, a warm sensation coursing through Carl at that moment.

"You don't have to hide anymore," Daniel wiped a stray tear from Carl's face as they both headed into the fellowship hall. They ate and laughed and resumed their karaoke session. All eyes were on Carl.

"I wanna hear Carl sing!" Lani chanted for Carl to approach the large television and grab the microphone. Since he had technically promised Daniel that he would sing on their first date, he knew that protesting now would be futile. Carl got up and decided to grace the audience with a song, realizing that he didn't have an image to uphold once he started singing, an immensely freeing realization.

Carl thumbed through the list of songs as Lani excitedly blurted out recommendations. He wasn't sure he could pull off Journey's "Open Arms" or Rascal Flatts' "God Bless the Broken Road." He scrolled back to the top of the list, landing on a familiar Adele song, "Turning Tables." The lyrics eloquently described that unpleasant conversation with Don, lamenting Carl's fortitude to walk away and forge his own path.

As the opening piano sequence cued Carl to sing, he transported himself back to that terse exchange with his former tortured lover, recalling every bitter detail: the bags under Don's eyes, the questions whose answers were painfully obvious, the harshness in Carl's voice as he slammed his car door shut.

"You never returned my calls. Are you okay?"

Carl had scoffed and gotten into his car, Don following him as he turned on the engine. He had had enough, rolling his windows down and narrowing his eyes. "I'm amazing. Your wife almost catches us in bed. No big deal."

"I'm sorry."

"I don't care. I'm done," Carl's voice had lowered as a large pickup truck pulled behind his car. "I'm done with smiling in your wife's face and coming on yours. I'm done with being your dirty little secret. I am done."

Carl felt the veracity behind each lyric he sang, aware that he had no choice but to let Don go, acutely aware that he had been brave, had saved himself. He looked around the room and found everyone silently watching him, their awestruck gazes catching him off guard. When he finished, everyone applauded loudly, a response Carl welcomed with bows. This was his life now, and it was not mired in conditional love or unrealistic standards of living. It celebrated authenticity, and he had never felt happier.

PART 3

JANUARY - MARCH 2015

22

THERE'S A STORM OUT ON THE OCEAN

Harriet's decision to serve Percy with the separation agreement after the New Year had backfired. He had planned on visiting some college friends in Pittsburgh over the Christmas holiday; she had planned on telling Jerry and Leo about her true intentions behind asking Percy to leave, as well as about her new boyfriend, Tim. Her strategic plan had all been in vain once her nosy mother-in-law, Krystal, appeared on her doorstep with a pineapple-glazed ham wrapped in aluminum foil.

"My mother-in-law is in my dining room as we speak," Harriet had stood in the kitchen with Tim beside her as Jerry and Leo scurried inside, dazed and confused as to how they were supposed to behave. Krystal had been the last person Harriet planned on seeing during her divorce. Yet, she had inconveniently shown up to her house, expecting to see her happily married son. In hushed tones, a consensus had been reached about how to proceed with the dinner: Leo would call Percy and inform him of his mother's presence at Harriet's house and firmly request his attendance at dinner; Jerry would call Mel and ask if she and her parents could casually drop by and pretend that Tim was their guest, all while Harriet stealthily hid Tim in the basement until Mel's arrival.

"My mother is on her way, and I am not keen on seeing her. We'll be over in a jiffy," Amy's excited tone had quelled the anxiety bubbling in Harriet's stomach as she swatted Jerry's hand away from the opaque ceramic bowl of candied yams. He had been sneaking spoonfuls of the dish as they strategized how to pull the wool over Krystal's eyes. Harriet had been aware that this scenario would run the risk of being seen as implausible.

Harriet's plan of attack was being enacted with the precision of a well-trained militia going into combat. Unbeknownst to Percy, whose smug appearance mirrored that of his self-righteous attorney, Tobias Walther, Harriet's secret weapons were about to be unleashed. First, there were those damning photos of Percy and Heather kissing. There were also credit card receipts of the gifts he had purchased for Heather, the invoice Tim had acquired from Eve clearly depicting Percy's signature authorizing twenty-two grand from Mid-IR Solutions. And as Amy opened the binders with their multicolored dividers neatly partitioning the evidence, Harriet's eyes rested on that black divider, its lethality making Harriet utterly delirious with satisfaction.

Tim had connected the dots to Percy's involvement in Heather's underground sex trafficking ring, the link beginning with that signed invoice from Mid-IR Solutions. Devin had confessed to creating that shell company for Heather, tracing that twenty-two grand transfer to an offshore account in Barbados that had automatically sent a money order to a local deli in Adams Morgan whose owner contacted Heather upon its arrival. This evidence was coupled with Deanne's recording during a session with a client, one in which she clearly identified Heather Carter as the organizer and sole executor of an underground sex trafficking ring. Although unable to definitively tie Heather to the illegal money transfer, Devin's readiness to approach the authorities with this information had made proving Heather's guilt and Percy's plausible complicity feasible. Harriet had wept with joy as she collated this information and placed it behind the black divider.

• • •

A few weeks later, Harriet sat across from Percy in what was supposed to be a divorce mediation session. Percy's lawyer Tobias began with a polite inquiry about the amended terms of the separation agreement he had faxed. Harriet exhaled deep sighs of consternation as she reflected on how she had spitefully thrown the separation agreement in Percy's face after enduring a barrage of criticism from Krystal that ranged from her mediocre cooking to her inept parenting. Percy had sat in silence as his mother gave Harriet advice on how to ensure her ham would never be undercooked, haughtily pointing her finger to a supposedly undercooked section.

"We reject all of those proposed amendments."

Amy motioned for Harriet to unleash the firing squad, beginning with the photos of Percy and Heather kissing and holding hands. Tobias and Percy both looked in abject horror at the skeletons of Percy's infidelity being paraded across the table. These skeletons made Harriet wish she hadn't ignored her mother's stern warnings and reproachful speeches about marrying for love. Each invoice and photo made Harriet want to slap her idealistic 22-year-old self who had fallen madly in love with the smart and charming Physics major determined to get a PhD.

"How did she find out? You told me you were discreet."

Tobias' reproachful whispers to his client enraged Harriet. She found out because she was no longer a spineless woman mired in grief; she found out because Percy had been anything but discreet. Deciding to deliver that final blow, she turned to that invoice Percy had signed, removing the large stack of documents substantiating Percy's involvement in an underground sex trafficking ring. Harriet venomously slid it across the table, watching as it landed directly in front of Percy.

"We have a mountain of evidence that proves Heather Carter is a sex trafficker, and that your client knowingly assisted in the illegal transfer of OEI funds to aid in the financing of an underground sex trafficking ring," Amy was incensed as she subsequently announced her plans to inform the authorities of this information.

"That's not true. Harriet, come on!" Percy's pleading tone did not move Harriet one bit. She grabbed the original separation agreement, turning to the page requiring Percy's signature and sliding it across the table.

"Sign. The. Fucking. Agreement." That proclamation released Harriet from a decade's worth of frustration in her marriage. It released Harriet from Krystal's expectations on how black men needed to be reared. It released Harriet from Percy's blame over not getting over her daughter's death fast enough. It freed her from a marriage she had stayed in for the sole purpose of mourning the death of her child.

Percy signed the agreement, confounded by his wife's newfound strength, resigning any resolve to fight Harriet. No words were exchanged as Percy and Tobias left. Harriet and Amy squealed as they heard the door slam in the distance.

Amy's assistant, Debbie, gently rapped on Amy's office door as Harriet looked up restaurants that served bottomless margaritas at noon. Tim appeared behind Debbie's towering beehive hairdo, a look that invoked the style of receptionists circa 1965 when coupled with her large hoop earrings and teal blouse.

"You need to see this," Tim's fingers enticingly held a black thumb drive in his hand as he closed the conference room door, kissing Harriet on the lips as it slammed shut, wagging his finger as Amy "tsked" her approval of this affair.

Tim instructed Amy and Harriet to examine a recent file labeled "Percy's Recent Whereabouts," Amy inserting the flash drive and opening the folder on her computer. More salacious pictures of Percy were displayed, this time kissing a young redheaded woman whose face was recognizable to Harriet – Deanne Blake. Harriet stared at the images of the two of them leaving Percy's apartment, Percy's smitten expression evident as he buried his broad forehead into Deanne's neck. This revelation was complicated by Harriet's newfound knowledge of Deanne's employment as an escort under Heather's guidance. According to Amy, Mel and her boss, Patrick, were working on a deal to ensure Deanne immunity once she delivered that audio recording confirming Heather's nefarious business dealings. Once again, Percy was embroiled in the middle of everything.

"Tim, I have a bad feeling about this," Harriet began, her fears confirmed once

Tim's phone rang. Harriet sat there in silence as she listened to Tim's attempt to placate Devin's illogical worries about Deanne's lack of communication over the past 24 hours.

"Devin, what do you mean she's missing?" Tim listened as Devin explained Deanne's week-long absence from class, unreturned phone calls, and her failure to show up for a meeting with Mel and Patrick. At that moment, Harriet knew these harmless photos of Percy and Deanne kissing were more than just proof of Percy's infidelity. These photos were evidence in Deanne's disappearance, a definitive implication of Percy as a suspect. The time stamp on the pictures disturbed Harriet – 12/25/2014, 11:58 P.M. Percy had seen Deanne hours after he had left Harriet's dinner. She scrutinized each subsequent time stamp, the dates ranging from the end of November to the second week in January.

"When was the last time someone saw her?" Once Tim uttered the words "three days ago," a sickening sensation started coursing through Harriet. Something terrible was about to happen, and this premonition permeated the office as Amy recommended a criminal defense attorney that could help Percy. Harriet immediately knew that Heather was responsible for Deanne's disappearance, and that she had begun crafting a narrative in which Percy was the perpetrator. Harriet's stomach clenched at the prospect of the father of her children behind bars, serving time for a crime she was sure he didn't commit.

• • •

Devin's frenetic response to Deanne's sudden disappearance had led him down the dark recesses of his mind, the somber scenarios in which Deanne's body ended up being extracted from a river or swamp by a forensic technician, her red hair mangled, her neck purple from the bruises of strangulation. Heather had been at the center of each scenario, her menacing smirk dancing in front of him, mocking his determination to be a good person, laughing at his quest to do the right thing.

Deanne's college roommate, Racquel, was clueless as to the last time she had seen Deanne, more concerned with liking posts on her Instagram feed than trying to remember the last time she and Deanne spoke. She flipped her blond locks and giggled while typing a message into her phone. Devin fought the urge to snatch the girl's phone and smash it against the linoleum floor. His patience wearing thin, he kindly repeated his question about why Deanne had returned to her dorm after two in the morning.

"Oh, right. She was like out with some guy she just met. Said she saw him nursing one of those round, glazy things at that bakery down the street?" Devin surmised that the round, glazy things to which Racquel was referring were doughnuts. He also guessed that Deanne was with Percy, a relationship she had not disclosed to anyone.

"Is she like in trouble or something? She hasn't been to class for like two days."

Devin began scanning the contents of Deanne's desk: a notebook, a red textbook on the history of contemporary fashion in America, a syllabus for English 102. Notably absent, was her laptop. He went through the sparse contents of her desk in the desperate hope of finding a lifeline to Deanne's world. As he flipped through impressive sketches of evening gowns and pantsuits, Devin knew he would not find contact information for Deanne's parents.

Devin's heart began racing as he swiftly exited the halls of the dormitories, rushing past students engaged in a social media fantasy, oblivious to the serpent that had struck once again as they lounged in the common room and showed off self-indulgent selfies. He sprinted toward the parking lot where his car was parked, determined to trace Deanne's whereabouts via her cellphone. On his drive home, he methodically mapped out all of Deanne's digital fingerprints, including her Facebook and Instagram accounts and email. He resolved to find out where Deanne was, no matter what.

The elevator's ring grated on Devin's ears, the loud creak as it opened up to the fourth floor startling him. For 45 minutes, the only sounds he had entertained were his incoherent ramblings regarding the various nefarious methods he could employ to hack into Deanne's phone and social media accounts. As he walked down the hallway toward his apartment, a familiar figure stood by his door, her curly brown locks whipping around to face him as she pointed at her phone impatiently. Mel was standing before him, their shared desperation to find Deanne leading them to embrace. At that moment, the complicated nature of their relationship didn't matter. Whether or not Mel trusted Devin or whether or not they got back together was immaterial to the matter at hand.

"I've been trying to call you for the past hour. Deanne never showed up," Mel's urgent tone echoed throughout Devin's messy apartment, past the pile of dirty underwear leading to his bedroom and unwashed dishes in the sink. He briefly permitted his mind to go back to the days where he and Mel would wash the dishes together, playfully flinging soapy water at each other over the kitchen sink.

"I just left Deanne's dorm. Her roommate was useless except for confirming that she was with Percy."

Mel groaned as she opened cupboards in search of alcohol. Devin pointed to a cabinet by the refrigerator, and Mel opened it and grabbed a bottle of vodka. Tim had apprised Mel on Deanne's burgeoning romance with Percy, and judging by the four ounces of vodka she generously poured into one of Devin's mugs, she was quite displeased. A loud thud startled Devin as he saw Mel unscrewing the top to his orange juice, pouring juice into her vodka-filled cup. She winced as she took a swig, burping loudly. Devin chuckled. Mel chuckled shortly afterward.

"She told me she had started seeing someone two months ago. Someone older.

Someone who knew Heather. I knew it was Percy when she started describing his chunky face and love handles," Mel took another swig of her drink, laughing as she leaned on the countertop. Through muffled laughter, Mel relayed her conversation with Tim during the Christmas holiday regarding her suspicions about Deanne's secret relationship with Percy. Her curly hair swayed as she drank and burped and laughed about the dire situation in which they found themselves.

"I hope Heather didn't make her suffer. Knowing her, she probably got my mom to kill her. She's done it before."

Mel's eyes widened as Devin provided her with the sordid history between Faith and Heather, their inexplicable sisterly bond that superseded basic morality. As he delved into his dysfunctional childhood, Faith's addiction, and subsequent abandonment, Devin realized that this was the first time they were having an honest conversation about his past.

Mel stood at the counter, listening to Devin describe a side of Heather that had become foreign to him over the past three years. He pointed to his bedroom, countering Mel's disapproving eye slant with the explanation of needing to retrieve his laptop. As her posture relaxed, Devin wondered how likely it was that Deanne was alive. *How did Heather discover that Deanne and Devin had been communicating?* Devin racked his brain with the preventive measures he had taken to ensure Heather could not access Deanne's calls, texts, and emails – the firewalls on Deanne's phone that blocked emails from suspicious sources, the self-destruct software that activated when her phone was connected to an unrecognizable PC. Yet as he snatched his laptop from his unmade bed, he had a feeling that Heather had cleverly circumvented his digital inoculations.

Devin opened his laptop and ran his self-destruct program, his eyes widening as each line of code he had meticulously poured over produced perpetual error messages. At that moment, his foreboding had been confirmed.

"Heather found a way past my programs and my firewalls. Shit!" Slamming the laptop shut, Devin cursed his painstaking efforts to thwart Heather's diabolical actions. He also cursed himself for not doing the obvious, which was destroying Deanne's phone and forcing her to use burner phones. Mel walked over toward Devin and wrapped her arms around him. She didn't tell him to calm down or fill his ear with cliched phrases. She just held him.

Once Devin collected himself, he called Tim and informed him of Deanne's disappearance. He made a concerted effort to remain calm, but his anxiety overpowered these efforts, his speech becoming incoherent as he envisioned locks of Deanne's red hair covering her face as her body was exhumed from an unmarked grave. Tim's promises of calling in favors with police chiefs fell on deaf ears, Devin expecting the police to reach multiple dead ends similar to the ones they reached with the murders of Uriah and Dr. Sturgis.

Tim's requests for Devin to remain calm infuriated him to no avail. Devin hung up, concurrently running his programs to hack into Deanne's email, social media sites, and phone. Devin scrutinized each line of code, searching for that digital needle in a haystack that would unveil the culprit Heather had employed to do her dirty work. Devin's self-destruct program revealed the culprit's IP address. As he multitasked, opening a third program that would identify the person behind the IP address, he felt strands of hair tickling his face as his program pulled up the identity behind the IP address. A retired farmer from Idaho was the unlikely culprit. Whoever circumvented Devin's program had been smart enough to ensure they were untraceable.

"Take a break."

Devin looked up from his multitude of browsers and lines of code to find a plate of strawberry Pop-Tarts in front of him, their sweet aroma and white frosting calling him to devour the pastries like he used to do as a child. With each bite, he traveled back to the days in which Heather's simplistic approach to Faith's abandonment of her two children had sufficed, back to Friday nights eating take-out from the barbecue chicken restaurant on Rhode Island Avenue and watching "20/20" with Heather. He needed to be reminded of the innocence his life once possessed, and that he had the choice to reclaim that innocence.

"Heather used to live by these," Devin mused as he pointed to the small pieces of pastries that he hadn't been able to stuff inside his mouth, sharing memories of Heather he had nearly forgotten, remembering the clumsy, apologetic woman who was trying to figure out parenthood despite all odds. Mel's eyes widened at the stories Devin told her, unable to envision the version of Heather he described. Devin was barely able to envision that person himself.

One of his programs displayed the results of Deanne's social media account activity, confirming his fears – the last activity on either her Instagram or Facebook account was five days ago.

"Were you able to track her phone?" Mel asked as she glanced over Devin's shoulder.

Devin pulled up the other program that had been concurrently pulling data from Deanne's phone. The black screen was devoid of code, an indication that the data had been erased.

"Shit," Mel muttered. Devin had no way of finding out where Deanne was. *What did she do before she went missing? Who did she see? Why did she see them?*

In a frenetic attempt to glean any discernible information from Deanne's digital life, Devin ran a traceability program on Deanne's social media accounts, hoping it would display the IP address of where she had last logged in. What he found disturbed him and Mel. Deanne had last logged into her Facebook account from Percy's apartment, a coincidence that would serve as the perfect circumstantial evidence against Percy, and would invariably rule out Heather as a suspect. Devin covered his face with his hands, tears falling onto the counter as he felt a warm kiss on his lips, a gentle touch across his face, a whisper in his ear that told him that he was a good, kind, brave man. Mel's voice proved to be the perfect remedy for his guilty conscience, the antidote to the poisonous world he couldn't seem to escape.

• • •

Heather was steadfast in her convictions regarding the need to establish rigorous checks and balances in every aspect of her business. With her profit margin at 58 percent, she had decided to hire Latrice as a full-time security analyst, running background checks on all of her clients, hacking into the social media accounts of all her employees – albeit one at the moment, and apprising Heather of any suspicious activity she noticed on such accounts.

Deanne's departure had been the impetus behind Heather's newfound convictions, the frustration and inconvenience of dealing with an insolent employee manifesting itself in losses Heather would never recoup. There had been the diligent monitoring of Deanne's calls and texts, and thanks to Latrice's program to overwrite Devin's self-destruct code, Heather had been able to track Deanne's activity. She had gleefully squealed upon realizing that Deanne had begun a relationship with Percy Nelson, grateful for being in the comfort of her own bed when those racy text messages between the two lovers appeared on her laptop. Heather had decided to schedule Deanne's abduction after one of her dates with Heather's former lover. Greg's hitman Tank, a slim man with a bald head and a grotesque amount of arm tattoos, had not acquiesced to Heather's request.

"What part of me operating independently did you not understand?" Tank's perturbed response to Heather's request had made her more insistent as she watched the man chain-smoke inside her recently detailed car, utilizing her car's ashtray as a trail of gray smoke escaped from his pursed lips. Heather had shot Greg reproachful looks as she held her breath and reiterated the reasoning behind her request through gritted teeth.

"Do you really think the police are gonna ignore the murder of a white, suburban, college girl? We need a scapegoat, and Percy is that scapegoat," Heather had nearly choked on her words as Greg calmly elucidated the feasibility of Heather's plan.

Tank had surprisingly agreed to this course of action, grunting his approval to the schedule Heather had created. On Thursday, Tank was to follow Deanne in his unmarked sedan, posing as an Uber driver, a guise the bald-headed man had employed in past hit jobs. Deanne had frequently used the Uber app, electing to pay the ten-dollar price of riding back to her dormitory after visiting Percy over getting a ride from him. Tank had planned to drive Deanne to a remote park off the interstate, inject her with a poison that would paralyze her entire body, strangle her, and dump her lifeless body at the local toxic waste facility. However, that plan had gone awry.

A knock at the front door startled Heather, her concentration waning as she sipped a dirty martini while reviewing the application of a young woman named Elena. She heard Faith's footsteps pattering down the stairs as the knocks became more urgent, a deep voice identifying himself as law enforcement.

"Ms. Carter, we have some questions we'd like to ask you," the deep baritone voice propelled Heather off her couch, the impatient tone inciting a frenetic attempt to leave no trace of her business plan in plain sight. The sound of Faith opening the door and greeting the detective occurred just as Heather slid the binders underneath her couch.

"Hi, Detective. May I offer you a drink?" Heather tried to conceal the nervousness in her voice as she chastised herself for not taking another swig of her martini.

• • •

Detective Barnett's heavy footsteps and burly appearance caught Heather off guard as she thought back to how that seamless plan of murdering Deanne had dismantled. According to Tank, Deanne had remained vigilant during the entire car ride, pointing out discrepancies in the route such as the unfamiliar back roads and sharp left turns she never encountered on past rides with Uber. Tank had claimed she squirmed a lot and started screaming once she realized the true destination of her trip. Deanne had fought the bald-headed hitman, scratching him on his cheek and lower lip and elbowing him in the ribs as she screamed into the dark alleyway for help that would never arrive. Tank's elbow had accidentally grazed the unlock button during his scuffle with Deanne, allowing her to open the car door, hurl herself out of it, and sprint down the gravely alleyway screeching at the top of her lungs.

"So your solution was to put a bullet in her head? This was not part of my plan," Heather had snarled as she viewed the photo Tank had handed her of Deanne's body, wisps of red hair covering her eyes, a pool of blood around her head. Tank had unsurprisingly begun smoking a cigarette in Heather's car as she took conservative sips of air, turning to a perfunctory Greg in her backseat who seemed unfazed by the increased chances of Deanne's screams garnering the attention of a random person passing by or the potential concerned citizen calling the police to report gunshots being fired. Tank had explained how he dismembered Deanne's body: he used a chainsaw to sever the head from the rest of it; he chopped off her hands as his DNA was most likely underneath her fingernails when she scratched him; he buried her corpse in a remote wooded area near Percy's apartment, tossing the bloodied rag used to wipe away the pool of blood into a green communal dumpster a block away from the apartment.

• • •

The detective's voice jolted Heather back to the present: "Ms. Carter, a missing persons report has been filed on Deanne Alexis Blake. She was an employee of yours. Is that correct?" Detective Barnett plopped his large frame onto Heather's couch, sprawling his legs in a relaxed fashion.

"Yes, but she actually quit a while back, detective. I have her letter here somewhere," Heather muttered as she scurried into the dining room to grab the fabricated handwritten letter from her table. Employing her gift for imitation, Heather had studied Deanne's handwriting, astutely observing the tiny curls in her *y*'s and her propensity toward dotting her *i*'s with open dots. She handed the detective the handwritten letter, the edges of the torn notebook paper giving it the appearance of having been shoved into a backpack or purse, as evidenced by the smudges of purple lip gloss in the middle of the page. Heather had found a half-empty bottle of it in Deanne's bag, gingerly placing an uneven swipe of it across the paper. Detective Barnett's eyes narrowed as he read the letter. Faith reappeared in the living room, politely offering the detective a drink as he fired off more questions: "Did she ever give any indication of being unsatisfied with her job? Did you notice any changes in her demeanor? When exactly did she quit?"

"Maybe a glass of water," Detective Barnett replied impatiently as Heather stood in front of him, making a concerted effort to appear nonchalant. She answered the detective's questions with platitudes that indicated her unawareness of Deanne's state of mind. Heather was busy. It was reasonable to assume that she didn't have the time to study Deanne's body language or notice any discernible changes in her behavior. After all, she had a business to run, one in which clients inundated her with countless questions and concerns.

"I'm sorry I wasn't much help," Heather smiled in the detective's direction as he took a giant swig from the glass of water Faith had placed on the coffee table. As drops fell from his square jaw onto Heather's sofa, he took out a brown leather wallet and handed Heather his business card. The title "Detective Geoff Barnett" was written in staunch black Arial font. Heather wanted to ask the detective a multitude of questions such as if he had reached out to Deanne's parents and if they have reason to suspect foul play. But she knew that appearing too eager to assist in the investigation would only implicate her.

Heather thought back to that meeting with Greg and Tank, huddled in her car in an abandoned parking lot near the Fair Oaks Mall. They had performed the customary exchange of the proof of death for the final cash payment, Tank meticulously counting the one thousand dollars in cash Greg had handed him.

Tank looked up from the stack of cash briefly. "Someone should anonymously call in the bloody rag in the dumpster. It'll make it easier to tie Percy Nelson to the murder. Sucks to be him. That's for sure," he offered.

Heather made a mental note to purchase another burner phone and make the phone call. Better yet, she decided to make Greg do it to avoid any culpability on her part. Surely Detective Barnett, in all his astuteness, would make the connection between the anonymous phone call and the visit he paid to the victim's former boss and her chipper friend.

"Well, if you think of anything, give me a call. Have a good evening, ladies," Detective Barnett shook both of their hands and saw himself out, his thick black trench coat trailing behind him as he closed the door. Heather listened for the start of his engine, catching a glimpse of his bright headlights as his black Ford Fusion pulled out of her driveway. Heather steadied herself, steeling her nerves and qualms about her uncertain future. There was no need to concern herself with these issues. The matter at hand was finding Deanne's replacement.

Faith meandered through Heather's dining room, observing the artwork Heather had purchased over the years, the sculpture of a lion catching her interest. Heather peered over her file on Elena Valdez, a young woman from Colombia who had been granted asylum from the recent Colombian conflict that had claimed nearly five hundred lives. Latrice's extensive file on the young woman provided Heather with insight into the kind of employee she would be. The mother of three who fled her violent country and physically-abusive husband clearly had no intent to return to her war-torn village, or to the man who repeatedly put a knife to her throat while raping her. This was a woman Heather could control. If Heather made that clear upfront, she would not have to arrange for her execution in a dark alley. The logistics of tasks like that were quite cumbersome.

"Heather, when did you buy this?" Faith saw Heather's furrowed brow and sly grin as she turned the page of Elena's file. Gently, Faith tapped Heather's knee.

"I don't know Faith. Maybe a year ago." Heather saw the preoccupied expression on Faith's face, surmising that it had something to do with their recent visit. Heather sat across from her friend, and although she appreciated Faith's concern, she needed Faith to realize that this situation would never happen again.

"Faith, what happened tonight won't ever happen again. Okay? Devin's pitiful crusade against my immoral ways is over. He has no case against me or you, and once he realizes that, he'll move the fuck on," Heather placed her file on Elena onto the coffee table and took a sip of her martini, allowing the gin to warmly course through her body.

Faith's response was succinct. "I'm sorry," she offered.

Heather reluctantly explained the sculpture of the lion to Faith, "The lion represents power. I never wanna feel powerless again."

Whatever came next, whatever challenges Heather would face, she silently vowed to never again be vulnerable. She had spent so much of her life at the mercy of others – allowing Silas to dictate her success, blindly trusting Greg to follow her rules, blindly trusting her employees not to betray her. Heather was done with this blind faith, its naivete costly and disheartening. She was also done with harboring resentment toward the past, and decided to relinquish Faith of any lingering guilt she still carried with those three powerful words, "I forgive you."

23

NO LONGER SILENT

Jerry's sessions with Dr. Goldstein were challenging. Dr. Goldstein's approach had become interactive, and Jerry would sometimes have to spend an entire hour dissecting a conversation he had with Brandon or his reaction to a professor's choice of words during a lecture. Last week, they had delved into Jerry's discomfort regarding his journalism professor's tireless crusade for objectivity. Dr. Caryn Stevens had openly expressed her disdain for the popular polemical style many journalists employed, claiming that opinions and emotions often overshadowed the facts of a story and, in turn, compromised the credibility of a journalist.

"Opinions and personal experiences are the reasons why people change their minds on critical social issues," Jerry had animatedly explained his point, his arms waving passionately as he offered countless examples of the veracity behind his statement: interracial marriage, declassifying homosexuality as a mental disorder, marriage equality. Dr. Goldstein had inquired about why personal experience mattered to him so much, why it was at the forefront of his mind that day, and what his commitment to telling those personal stories said about his character. Jerry had left the session with a throbbing headache.

Today, the clock against the back wall in Dr. Goldstein's office ticked loudly, each second inching closer to a question Jerry would undoubtedly dread. Earlier in the session, Jerry had expressed his frustration behind Roger's unwillingness to discuss his experience as one of Lester's patients with a community that could help him. He had, of course, omitted the fact that he had acquired this knowledge through illegal means.

Dr. Goldstein's garish purple cardigan distracted Jerry from the echo of his therapist's voice in his ear: *"Why can't you just come forward with your experience? If everyone's personal experience should be heard, wouldn't yours be just as compelling?"* Unbeknownst to his therapist, Jerry had suggested coming forward to Brandon, who had not been supportive of the idea.

"My experience isn't moving enough," Jerry said through labored breaths.

Dr. Goldstein clicked his pen, rapidly scribbling on his notepad as Jerry reflected on what Brandon had said. Juxtaposed with his professor's denouncements of emotionally charged opinionated journalism, he felt stuck. He did not know how to move forward.

"Why does it matter if your story's not sensational enough?" Dr. Goldstein's challenging method reared its head once again. It mattered to Jerry because his boyfriend had diminished his experience. And if he dismissed this profoundly painful period in Jerry's life, what else would he diminish?

• • •

"Nelson, unless that sick fuck fondled you from behind, your story's pretty typical. It's been heard before," Brandon barely looked up from the files in front of him to glance in Jerry's direction.

The entire team at Rainbow Warriors had laboriously scrutinized every one of Lester's patient files, arriving at the same bitter conclusions they had three hours earlier: Ian and Roger were the only patients who had stories that would garner public interest into the fraudulent nature of conversion therapy. Brandon had been chugging Red Bull energy drinks the entire day, impatiently flipping through the patient files Callie had printed out. Every one of Lester's patients had been textbook cases of pious Christian men not wanting to own the reality of their homosexual orientation. Each case had contained summaries of various journal entries, as journaling was a mandate Lester had imposed on every single patient whenever they engaged in sexual fantasy or masturbated. One patient, Elliott, had gone into disturbing detail about his lecherous desire to be penetrated by his boss over the board room table, describing the man's brawny biceps and sinewy shoulders thrusting against Elliott's body as he came onto the oak colored table. Elliott's journal entries had also contained scriptures about how to find joy in suffering. Another patient, Ira, had recently recounted three hours of watching pornography while home alone, admitting the intense feelings of guilt after having an intense orgasm. Ira had attributed his relapse to being lonely.

"These patients are still soaking up Lester's bullshit. Do we want to read another file?" Brandon had angrily pushed the stack of notes away as Jerry and Callie collectively groaned.

Jerry had nothing to say, too exhausted to argue with Brandon. Although he had omitted the lurid situations and lascivious acts, he informed Brandon and Callie of the inappropriate nature of Roger and Lester's relationship, cautioning them against trying to persuade Roger to come forward. However, Jerry and the rest of Rainbow Warriors had grown frustrated by the absence of patients willing to denounce Lester's brand of quackery.

Jerry had expressed his disapproval with Brandon once Callie left the office, pushing Brandon's hands away from his waist as he caught whiffs of the blueberry-flavored Red Bull his boyfriend had chugged. Jerry had languished in his failed attempts to reach out to Roger, Roger reiterating his unwillingness to talk about the sexual abuse he encountered at the hands of Lester. Reaching out to Ian also had proven tedious, Jerry foregoing any planned decoys when messaging him on Facebook. After weeks of unreturned messages, Ian had succinctly denied Jerry's requests for him to talk about his time with Lester.

• • •

"I want to let Roger and Ian know that I support them no matter what," Jerry exhaled sharply as a grin appeared across Dr. Goldstein's face.

Destroying Lester's career was not supposed to come at the expense of two people's well-being. It was not worth it if innocent lives were ruined further. Jerry's session ended with Dr. Goldstein's advice to love himself and honor the progress he made thus far. The latter was harder when he felt powerless to stop a tyrannical therapist who knowingly hoodwinked vulnerable people.

Standing in the hallway of Dr. Goldstein's office, Jerry typed a text message to Roger, the message cementing his support of Rogers's decision to not discuss the sexual abuse he endured. He offered Roger a list of therapists who could help him. As he pressed the send button, the swish sound echoing throughout the narrow hallway, he received a phone call from a number he didn't recognize.

"Hello?" As Jerry listened to heavy breathing on the other end of the line, he darted into the restroom to ask who was calling.

"It's Ian. Can we meet?" Ian's thin voice, its tiny tremor, made Jerry's throat clench. Ian rattled on about a restaurant he had sought refuge in around Adams Morgan, Jerry reciting it to himself as he hurried out of the restroom and headed toward the parking lot. As he started his car, he typed a text message to Brandon, the frenetic motion of his fingers emanating all the anxieties about this meeting. Jerry decided to tell his story regardless of whether or not it was relevant. Ian and Roger needed to see that someone would stand up to Lester. Why not, Jerry?

• • •

When souls were on the line and when salvation was predicated on his ability to provide these lost souls with tangible evidence of change, Mark found himself resorting to pitiful platitudes and supplications, all of which asked God to put Satan in his place.

Robert Cannon's home was a modest one, the high ceilings and Victorian architecture evocative of Louisa's early paintings from graduate school. Mark sat on the beige couch, hearing the clinking sound of spoons mixing sugar into cups of tea. He checked his watch as Robert's wife, Nia, brought out a tray of black tea and lemon cookies. She gingerly set the plate in front of Mark, her corpulent frame accentuated by the form-fitting Duke sweatshirt she wore. Mark sensed Nia's discontent as she grunted an acknowledgment of Mark's gratitude without so much as a smile, but he couldn't help but wonder if she was just irritated that her husband was late or if there was something more to her beleaguered disposition. *Maybe it was the result of weathering the countless storms of angry militant homosexuals,* Mark surmised. *Perhaps Robert's professing an unpopular message day after day had taken its toll on his wife and children.*

The first thing Mark had noticed upon entering Robert's house was the family photos that filled the walls of the entry hall. In one, Nia proudly stood by her husband's side, one arm around Robert, the other arm around her youngest son, Caleb. Robert's oldest son, Wayne, proudly stood on the other side of his father, their same cheekbones and wide grins a subtle declaration that homosexuality no longer resided in this home. Mark had read Robert's book "Not Born This Way," his own skepticism diminishing as he read Robert's detailed account of his unfulfilled life as a gay man, the dead-end relationships based on superficial qualities such as body fat and phallus size, the disconnect between his lifestyle and his relationship with God, the bleak reality that life as a gay man precluded him from having children. The book substantiated the perils of the gay lifestyle with psychological studies conducted by secular therapists, quelling any doubts Mark had about Robert's authoritative voice on this subject. Mark had sought out Latrice's technical stealth to find any scandals or unsavory behaviors attached to Robert's name. Latrice's digging had uncovered no such scandals, no secret boyfriend in Atlanta or New York, no record of marital discord. Robert had dedicated his life to developing a program to convert people to heterosexuality, and Lester had systematically destroyed it.

"Robert is on his way. He will be bringing Global Healing's attorney," Nia offered up with the first trace of a smile Mark had seen since he arrived. Not a minute later, Robert appeared in the doorway, his long trench coat peppered with snowflakes on its shoulder pads. Behind him, a woman who had a penchant for dark eyeshadow appeared, her blond hair pulled back into a tight bun.

"Mark, this is Lucy Hill, our lawyer. Thought you two should meet."

The two shook hands as pleasantries were exchanged. Lucy was a graduate of William and Mary law school and had recently left a lucrative position at a prestigious law firm to support Christian businesses and organizations whose mission aligned with conservative family values.

Nia brought out an additional tray of lemon cookies as Robert immediately began discussing the matter at hand, namely Lester's insubordination. Ian's suicide attempt, coupled with Lester's erroneous declaration that same-sex attractions will never go away, had created a slippery slope on which Ian's family had some ground to sue Global Healing. Mark was not thinking about the legal implications of Lester's behavior, even though he maybe should have been. He was more concerned with Lester's grave decision to falsely inform his patients that homosexual desires never dissipated, a decision that would lead many men to disavow their faith altogether.

"Mark, we've reached out to all of Lester's current patients and asked if Lester told them similar things about their same sex attractions. Through this inquiry, our suspicions were confirmed – yes, Lester told all of them some variation of what he told Ian."

When Mark had previously questioned Lester as to why he had told Ian that his same-sex attractions would never go away, Lester had adamantly denied ever telling Ian this at all. He had, however, said he believed that Ian's frustrations were a result of his unwillingness to do the hard work required to reclaim his masculinity. Unwilling to risk giving church members a therapist who willfully deviated from Robert Cannon's well-respected program, Mark had decided to seek advice from Robert himself. After weeks of phone calls, Mark had requested a face-to-face meeting with Robert to assess the damage Lester had done. Judging from Lucy's presence, the damage was severe.

"Lester thinks he's qualified to create his own program. He's found my approach unrealistic," Robert began.

Mark exhaled sharply and took a bite out of a lemon cookie, its bitterness settling on his tongue as he listened to Robert's painstaking chronology of the course of treatment he had created, citing his personal experience and the scientific evidence that supported the actual conversion to heterosexuality. Mark sensed that Robert had more troubling information about Lester's duplicitous practices, and as Robert went on, these suspicions were quickly confirmed.

"Mark, I've suspended Lester without pay. Upon reviewing some of his recent patient reports, I found something troubling about Earl Wilson," Robert continued.

Mark watched as Lucy unearthed notes from her maroon briefcase, her handwriting discernible across Lester's notes.

Lucy got right to the point, briskly reading sections of Lester's notes that revealed a recent disturbing encounter: "Mr. Wilson believes he might have forced himself onto his own wife, Agnes, last night. Mr. Wilson claims to have choked her, pinned her down, and sodomized her. The patient has already admitted to raping a sex worker named Alma Velasquez in 2011 and expressed that he wanted to engage in BDSM with his wife, who objected. He says how remorseful he is, but believes he might do it again."

Lucy cleared her throat as Mark's body went numb. Earl had raped a woman in his chaotic quest for hedonism. Mark knew that Lester had omitted crucial information about Earl's disorder. Earl had willfully omitted this sin because he knew that if he were to confess, he would face criminal charges. Mark didn't allow himself to feel anything, his mind only focusing on the bitterness of the lemon cookies he mindlessly shoved into his mouth.

"Did you know about this?" Lucy now directed her attention to Mark, explaining that any potential public outcry would not be in Mark's favor and would adversely affect his ministry. Mark shook his head. He had to completely sever ties with Earl. His ministry needed to be a credible one, one free from ignominious indiscretions. In order to preach a message the world scorned, the messenger needed to surround himself with people who truly embodied that message. Mark had no time for impostors, and he surmised that Robert didn't either.

Clasping his bony hands together, Robert plainly stated that he would confront Lester about Earl's purported rape, insisting that Lester inform the authorities about this development.

"My recommendation is to terminate Lester immediately," Lucy's blunt tone was punctuated by the ferocious sounds of her chewing a lemon cookie.

Robert's head tilted to the side as he sipped his tea. Mark was still chewing his cookie, the monumental task of severing ties from a man he viewed as a father, brother, and confidant still not fully registering. He wished God had given him a warning or a sign that two imposters were among him. He wished he had not encouraged Agnes to reconcile with her husband.

"Let me handle Lester's termination. In the meantime, Mark, you have my full support with your ministry. I can do workshops, seminars, everything Lester was doing," Robert offered.

Mark surveyed Robert's lanky frame, the way he smoothed his wisps of gray hair and furrowed his brow indicative of another looming issue.

"Robert, I trust you, but I need to know if there's anything else I should worry about," Mark went on.

Robert and Lucy exchanged hesitant glances, their silence confirmation that Lester's damage extended farther than concealing a rape and falsely proclaiming that same-sex attractions never dissipated.

"Roger Clementine," Nia's strained voice reverberated throughout the living room, her fatigue evident. She approached the three of them, her stern disposition indicating the threat Roger Clementine posed. "A complaint was filed against Lester over two years ago alleging misconduct."

Lucy chimed in to explain how baseless the complaint had been as she uncovered the letter written by Grace Clementine, Roger's mother. Mark scanned its contents, agreeing with Lucy's assessment, yet realizing its lethality given the circumstances. Mark exhaled sharply, strategically planning his course of action. He instructed

Lucy to investigate the complaint. He wanted to acquire the meaning behind the phrases such as "crossing the lines of the patient-therapist relationship." Did a sexual relationship occur between Lester and Roger? Did Roger plan to come forward with the unsavory details? Mark steeled himself for these possibilities; he needed to fortify his ministry from the devil's evil desires to vanquish the will of God.

•••

Ian's hesitancy about discussing his time with Lester was evident; he would stop midstream and scratch his head, his brown hair swinging across his face as he did so. Jerry found Ian quite self-conscious about everything he said. *Did he genuinely believe that Lester had lied to him?*

"You were a former patient, right?" Ian's voice quivered as he asked that question. Jerry briefly recounted his time under Lester's guidance, Ian nodding along nervously.

"I didn't make it to the part where he told me I'd always be homosexual," Jerry shared. At the sound of this, Ian clammed up. It undoubtedly brought up the painful realization that he would never feel attraction to women. "Did he tell you that you'd eventually like girls? That's what he told me," Ian continued, the bitterness in his voice piercing through Jerry like a dagger, the tinges of disappointment and anger evident. Ian had placed his faith in a program that didn't work, a program that preyed on vulnerable people whose fear of eternal damnation superseded reality.

Jerry took a deep breath before encouraging Ian, "Tell the world. We can do this together. You and me. You can save someone from the heartache you experienced. You can save someone from this abuse."

Ian sat against the plush multi-colored chairs, breathing heavily and slowly nodding. The two discussed logistics for the next half hour over falafel, Jerry taking notes about Ian's childhood that included a torrent of bullying in school for being artistic and effeminate, and parents who were relentless in their quest to make their son masculine. Jerry was about to devour the last falafel on his plate when his phone rang. Brandon's name appeared across the screen.

"Nelson, we need you. Breaking development!" Brandon rattled on about the story taking the conservative Christian community by storm. Concerned about Ian's state of mind, he told Brandon he would call him back and asked if Ian wanted company on the train ride home. He waved his hand dismissively, assuring Jerry that he would be fine riding the train alone.

"I have this really good audiobook that'll keep me company. I'm gonna be fine. Promise," Ian politely told Jerry to get back to work and thanked him for gently encouraging him to come forward. Jerry hoped that he wouldn't have a change of heart.

The train ride back to Rainbow Warriors was filled with a lively phone call in which Brandon excitedly recounted Earl Wilson's walk of shame into police custody. Over the past hour, someone had informed the authorities of a rape Earl Wilson had committed against his wife, and it had already hit news outlets. The train came to a screeching halt as the conductor announced Jerry's stop over the speaker. Jerry quickly gathered his things and made the three-block trek to Rainbow Warriors' office as Brandon continued to talk about how this story could work in their favor. Jerry listened patiently for his boyfriend to stop talking, deciding to incorporate his and Ian's story into the one that was unfolding before the world. Their stories were interconnected, the common threads of deception and hypocrisy evident.

Jerry was sure of this as he entered the conference room where everyone had congregated. Excited chatter erupted as Brandon pointed to a skinny man with wisps of gray hair pacing the floor of Lester's office. He spoke to a woman named Lucy, confirming that Lester had notified the authorities regarding Earl's rape of his wife. Jerry cleared his throat to announce his arrival.

"Jerry, cancel what you're doing for the rest of the day. Skip whatever class you have. We have a story to report!" Brandon planted a deep kiss on his lips as Jerry gladly acquiesced to skipping the snooze fest that was World History 101. Callie's mind was moving at its usual frenetic pace, strategically crafting the story behind the "leaked" police files she would acquire. Jerry had to proffer the news he had, the interview he just secured with Ian and his vision of publishing both his and Ian's story of abuse by Lester's hands.

"Ian's gonna talk. He's... gonna come forward. And so am I," Jerry announced loudly.

All the chatter in the room ceased. Whatever plans were being formulated stopped as everyone turned to stare at Jerry. Brandon smiled and nodded his approval. Lester was about to be decimated by the very people he claimed to help. He was no longer going to be portrayed as the powerless victim who simply wanted to help others live their lives according to biblical teachings. He was going to be portrayed as the ruthless predator who preyed upon vulnerable young men, men who were terrified to identify as gay.

For the next several hours, pizza was ordered, and copious amounts of caffeine were consumed as Jerry wrote the first part of his ongoing investigation into Lester Dawson, focusing on his willful disregard for public safety by allowing a professed rapist with sex addiction to walk the streets. His correlated Lester's inaction to the generous financial support Earl provided to the conversion therapy crusade. Jerry's mind raced, his adrenaline and anger propelling him more than the Red Bulls he chugged. Catching a Christian con-artist who sexually abused a client and inflicted emotional pain on countless others was a once in a lifetime opportunity. Nothing else mattered to him at this moment.

• • •

"I'm gay. I've always known, and I know God loves me just as I am," Carl sat in his driveway, rehearsing aloud what he was going to say to his parents once he walked through his front door. He turned off the radio, tired of hearing the insufferable whining of the latest collection of auto-tuned one-hit wonders. His heart thumped; his pulse raced.

Between the Skype conversations with his grandfather and his poignant discussions with Father Jiffy, Carl had found the courage to investigate those clobber passages in the Bible that condemned homosexuality. Big Jim had said that the Apostle Paul was at best tolerant of the institution of traditional marriage, advocating for lifelong chastity.

"All those straight Bible thumpers never mention that, do they?" Big Jim had poured himself a glass of whiskey while continuing his rant about the hypocrisy of Christianity and all other religions. Carl had wished he could easily disavow himself of the sermons he heard and the worship songs he sang and the sense of community he once felt when he entered a church. In many ways, St. Michael's had provided Carl with a vastly different perspective of church, and Father Jiffy had welcomed him with open arms. He had enjoyed dinners with Jiffy and Daniel, debating ways in which small non-traditional churches can reach out to marginalized communities. The dinner last night had ended with Jiffy discussing his fraught journey back to the church, one that had begun with his unceremonious expulsion from the Roman Catholic priesthood. Carl had been on the verge of tears as Jiffy told him and Daniel about the priest who outed Jiffy to his bishop.

"I was betrayed. Telling a fellow priest I had homosexual desires was hard, and to have him tell the bishop was hurtful, to say the least," Jiffy had choked back tears as he started clearing the table, deliberately sliding the apple pie away from his runny nose. He had spent 25 years rudderless without a church home, spiritually parched for a community of faith that affirmed his identity as a gay man.

• • •

Carl forced himself out of his recollections and headed inside his parents' house, slowly walking up the steep driveway as light snow flurries blanketed the grass. He was about to profess his identity as a gay man, no longer resigning to living in the shadows of secrecy and shame, no longer satisfied with coexisting in his contrived dichotomous universe. As Carl turned the key inside the lock, he overheard a familiar wail, a guttural proclamation of sorrow and despair. He also overheard his mother's gentle words of comfort and her humble prayers beseeching God's everlasting peace countering these sorrowful wails.

"God's gonna bring you through this. He always does," Louisa murmured.

Carl walked into the living room to find Agnes crying in Louisa's arms, noticing the bruises immediately around Agnes' neck and wrists as she sputtered the words "rapist" and "sociopath" more than once.

Louisa looked up from her comforting her despondent friend and gently explained what had transpired over the past hour. Earl Wilson had been arrested and charged with sexual assault. In Louisa's words, the media had descended upon Earl like vultures, gleefully ready to denounce the teachings of a man publicly struggling with fleshly desires. Raping your wife and procuring sexual services with church funds encompassed more sins than just adultery and fornication. Judging from Agnes' bruises, Earl had become a person who was unable to control his sexual desires.

"Sexual deviancy is hard to overcome, but you have to be strong now. You have to leave him and let him get the help he deserves," Louisa assured Agnes that she and Mark would stand by her during Earl's trial, and would assist her in caring for her two sons.

"Where's Dad?" Carl suspected that his father was taking the news just as hard, if not harder than Agnes. To find out your best friend and mentor, a man whose counsel you sought during those formative years in Christ, was a rapist on top of being an adulterer, was a painful reality to accept. Louisa replied with a long, interminable sigh, finally revealing that Mark was holed up in his office at church praying for guidance.

As Carl clearly recognized that today was not going to be his big coming-out moment, he thought back to the night he had spent with Daniel, strands of his black hair tickling Carl's beard as Carl gently ran his hands down Daniel's shoulder, the smoothness of his skin comforting. They had made love, slowly and tenderly, not rushing to avoid being caught by someone's wife or kid, but honoring the moment. Daniel had chuckled to himself afterward.

"When I came out, my dad said that I'd die of AIDS. My mom said she loved me but didn't love my lifestyle," Daniel shared.

Carl had never known the exact words Daniel's parents said to him when he came out; his heart broke as he heard Daniel discuss these unpleasant memories. "Do you ever regret running away?" Carl asked.

The two had never discussed Daniel's home life before Jiffy. Had Daniel missed the holiday dinners and family reunions? Had he secretly longed to be with his parents? Had he silently hoped for their approval? His response had been a firm head shake. Daniel had gladly traded Thanksgiving dinners over football with Thanksgiving dinners at Jiffy's, the two of them dropping by Jiffy's sister's house for a quick visit, or going to the movies on Black Friday. These had been the moments he craved during his teenage years but never received. Daniel had accepted that his parents would never have the mindset needed to seek out an authentic relationship with him.

•••

Carl came back to the present to see his mother once again hunched over Agnes' fragile body, holding her bony hands and praying for God's comforting presence to engulf Agnes during this tumultuous time. He exited the living room, that strange amalgam of guilt and relief coursing through his body. He wasn't going to come out today. That much was clear. And as Carl made his way down his steep driveway, a foreboding came over him, one that stayed with him during his entire drive back to campus. Carl's parents were never going to accept him as a gay man. They were never going to come around or approve of his "lifestyle." He needed a fallback plan, one which ensured his financial independence. The sheer thought of that terrified Carl.

24

DIRTY LAUNDRY

Amy's brother-in-law, Dennis O'Malley, was the best criminal defense attorney around, and Harriet was in desperate need of the best. The media attention surrounding Deanne's disappearance had already thrust Percy into the spotlight, with photos of Deanne and Percy leaving a coffee house and kissing plastered across the television screen during the evening news. Percy's apartment had turned into a campground for news reporters.

Dennis brashly barked at his lowly clerk to provide him with a new headset for his desk phone, Harriet flinching as he angrily slammed his current headset onto his opaque desk. Apparently, one of his high-profile clients had created a charity for the sole purpose of hiding his earnings from his advertising firm.

Dennis chortled as his client inquired about how much prison time he was facing because of his fraudulent behavior, "You don't wanna know. Just write a damn check for St. Jude's Hospital or some other charity that *actually* helps kids with cancer."

The line beeped as Dennis abruptly disconnected the first call, Harriet immediately deciphering Percy's labored breathing on the other end of the phone.

"Talk," Dennis barked. Percy's stammering only infuriated Dennis, who bluntly asked Percy if he wanted to spend life in prison for first-degree murder.

"Of course not. I didn't do this," Percy's gruff tone forced Dennis to sit down. Harriet immediately explained the circumstances in which Percy found himself, sparing no detail about Heather's diabolical plan to frame Percy for Deanne's abduction and possible murder. Dennis sighed loudly as he inquired about the evidence they collected that proved Heather had a motive to hurt Deanne.

"The recording," Harriet blurted out. "And the financial records Eve's company won't turn over." Harriet bitterly reflected on the phone conversation with Eve, where her old friend told Harriet in no uncertain terms that any investigation into Heather was above her pay grade, regardless of the strong evidence of wrongdoing.

Dennis was unphased, "I will subpoena the legal department if OEI doesn't turn over their financial records. This recording that identifies Heather as a sex trafficker cannot be used in court as I'm assuming it was obtained illegally." Harriet and Percy collectively groaned, Harriet turning to Dennis and asking him what she could do to help in the meantime.

"For starters, you and your P.I. can find out who Heather has been using to do her dirty work, especially this potential murder," Dennis instructed. He went on to assure Harriet that the key to exonerating Percy was to get ahead of Heather's moves. Harriet nodded, although deep down she suspected that the evidence had already been planted to implicate Percy for the crime.

• • •

Harriet had decided to inform her children of the real reason she and Percy were divorcing over pizza and hot wings from Dominos and had even fetched a six-pack of beer for the occasion that Percy had left in the den. Jerry and Leo had devoured the pizza, each reaching for beer as Harriet told them the bitter truth about their father, and the predicament in which he found himself. She had spared no detail, discussing everything from Percy's long-standing affair with his secretary, Heather, to the insidious implications about his involvement in Heather's underground sex trafficking ring. Leo had nearly choked on his pizza when Harriet relayed the news about Percy's involvement with his casual girlfriend, Deanne. Harriet had also applied her philosophy of full-disclosure to herself, admitting that she and Tim were more than friends. Jerry and Leo had seemed unfazed by her love life, their troubled dispositions focused on their father.

"I knew about the affair. I blackmailed dad to get out of going to conversion therapy," Jerry had confessed as he had searched Harriet's face for reproach or condemnation. Harriet had assured her son that she wasn't angry, that she had found out about his stint in conversion therapy at the start of her investigation into Percy's infidelity. Leo's face had turned pale once Harriet divulged the unpleasant details surrounding Deanne's occupation and disappearance. At that moment, Harriet had firmly cemented Percy's innocence behind Deanne's disappearance.

"You can be mad at your father for having an affair, but we can't let that get in the way of helping him. Despite his faults, he loves you both."

• • •

Devin had never sought advice from his advisor on personal matters. However, he needed to employ as many resources as possible to find out what happened to Deanne. Dr. Stanley's office was similar to that of Tim's, filled with stacks of papers and binders, many of which had been haphazardly strewn across the floor in several semicircles. Devin composed himself, deciding to ease into his request with a legitimate academic inquiry into the revisions he had on his thesis. Clearing his throat to get Dr. Stanley's attention, he reached into his backpack and retrieved the wrinkled copy of his revised thesis. Dr. Stanley looked up from his lesson plans, adjusting his spectacle like brown glasses.

"Mr. Ryan, what can I help you with?" Dr. Stanley's brow furrowed as he set aside his red marker, its wrath commonplace on theses and personal statements.

"My thesis. Have you had a chance to read over my revisions?" Devin asked, watching as Dr. Stanley scoured his crowded desk for Devin's thesis. Devin quickly handed his impatient professor the wrinkled hard copy he had printed. Dr. Stanley scrutinized the crumpled piece of paper, loudly smacking his lips as he licked his finger to turn pages.

"I'll have to look at my notes and get back to you next week. I'm buried in proposal work at the moment."

An awkward silence ensued between the two men, Devin deciding to abandon any small talk and get to the point. Devin reached into his backpack and dug out his laptop, formulating the innocuous scenario he intended to present to Dr. Stanley; he would surely omit the gruesome assumption about Deanne being a murder victim. Devin's voice shook as he opened his laptop to the failed security program he had written for Deanne's phone, slowly explaining the program he had created to track persons of interest for his boss. Dr. Stanley hunched beside Devin as his pitch steadily rose once he scrolled down to the seemingly infinite error messages, explaining how someone had overridden his firewalls and simultaneously erased data he had collected.

"The person who circumvented your self-destruct function was quite sophisticated. I must say this code is impressive. Any idea who did this? They have to be a former intelligence analyst for the C.I.A. to be able to penetrate these firewalls."

"How do I fix this?" Devin stared at Dr. Stanley, hoping his professor had some sage advice to dispense.

Dr. Stanley regretfully informed Devin that there was no chance for him to recover any data from this phone. Sensing his student's despondency, Dr. Stanley dialed a phone number from his desk phone, winking at Devin as he greeted Dr. Clayton, a professor in the cybersecurity department. He mouthed for Devin to write down the phone number he was tracking.

"Dr. Clayton, do you still have that contact over at the F.B.I.?" Dr. Stanley gave Devin a thumbs up as he recited the number to Dr. Clayton. Dr. Stanley hung up the phone and exhaled sharply, his astute comment eerily reassuring Devin.

"You're doing the right thing, Devin. But please be careful," Dr. Stanley encouraged as he gently clapped him on the back. "Dr. Clayton will email you the data from the phone number within a couple of hours."

• • •

Deanne's phone records had aligned with her last known social media activity, a satellite one block away from Percy's apartment detecting Deanne's number. Dr. Clayton's F.B.I. contact had been able to extract the apps Deanne used on her phone; Uber unsurprisingly had been accessed moments after Deanne left Percy's apartment. Deanne's digital journey had culminated in a dark alley off the main road of I-66, an ostensible foreboding that a murder had occurred on this isolated street with no cameras or lights. Devin had solicited Jerry, Leo, and Mel's support as he drove to this location, all of them trying to remain apprised of the quandary they had found themselves in.

"So aside from being my dad's mistress and a sex trafficker, Heather was your foster mother?!" Jerry scratched his head as Devin pulled into a gravel filled parking lot of an abandoned brick building, a faded logo of a tire shop barely discernible as Devin parked his car and killed the engine.

"It's complicated, but yes. You're up to speed."

"And Deanne was gonna come forward about everything Heather did," Leo stated with a mortified expression on his face. "Anything else I'm missing?"

"Deanne was raped by your dad's former boss," Mel said through labored breaths.

"That's fucked up," was all Leo managed to say.

As they all got out of the car, Mel gently patted Leo's shoulder and affirmed the veracity of his statement.

"Knowing Heather, she'll try to pin Deanne's murder on your dad," said Devin as he guided his friends through a forest with no leaves on the trees, the ferocious, freezing winds whipping them so hard that the tiny branches broke off and fell to the ground. Devin tried to imagine how scared Deanne must have been during those last breaths, realizing she would never go home and knowing her life was about to end. Devin scrutinized the phone records in his hand, his finger resting on a text message that Deanne had sent Devin. The message had failed to send due to service being lost.

"Guys, look at this," Devin directed everyone's attention to the wrinkled pages of Deanne's cell phone activity, pointing to the contents of that failed text message – "I'm in the car with C.J., my Uber driver. Something's not right. Just FYI, he has a large tattoo of a python up his right arm."

Silence. Everyone stared at Devin in horror as he finished reading Deanne's ominous text, Devin's voice quivering as he quickly called Tim while dashing back to his car. With certitude, he left a voicemail instructing Tim to pull whatever strings he could to find an Uber driver by the name of C.J. with a python tattoo on his right arm.

Everyone piled back into the car, soberly reflecting on the reality of Deanne's death. There were no more optimistic scenarios, no more bright sides to look on or silver linings to consider. Deanne was gone, and Heather was responsible. For Devin, he was determined to bring Heather down by any means necessary.

"We all have to stick together if we're gonna destroy Heather. Deanne deserves justice, and so do the countless lives she's ruined," Devin stated with resolve as he started his car. He felt a gentle touch on his hand, his eyes meeting Mel's concerned gaze. He kissed her hand and hit the gas.

• • •

Elena Valdez had arrived to Heather's orientation 15 minutes early, wearing a cheap red blouse and a ghastly black blazer with unsightly golden embroidery along the shoulder pads. It was as if a distasteful fashion magazine ad from 1982 had appeared in front of Heather.

Heather reviewed the rules and regulations of Capitol Boutique, emphasizing the company's commitment to exceptional customer service at all costs. Patrons were paying five hundred dollars an hour to have their most sinister sexual desires fulfilled, and Elena was expected to fulfill those desires cheerfully.

"Do you object to any of these guidelines?" Heather watched as the young mother earnestly shook her head. She continued, "Do you object to any particular sexual act like anal sex?"

Elena became quiet once Heather asked this question, slowly shaking her head in a fashion that conveyed her uncertainty. Once Heather informed Elena that such acts increased her commission, Elena perked up. Money had a way of making the most repulsive behaviors palatable. Excited that Elena had acquiesced to Heather's directives, Heather politely pointed out that Elena should look to local grocery store magazines such as "Woman's World" for helpful contemporary fashion tips.

"I'll do that, Ms. Heather. Thank you for the advice."

The two parted, Heather thankful for the brief respite she had between her next client's visit. She closed her office door, and turned on her CD player, pressing the play button to "The Nutcracker Soundtrack" she had uncovered in a box of her old college items. Heather imagined her younger self spinning in the air to the "Dance of The Sugar Plum Fairies," perfectly landing as the dance's dramatic conclusion yielded thunderous applause from the audience. These wistful daydreams were interrupted by the garish sound of her phone's ringtone, an unknown caller appearing across her screen. Cautiously answering the phone, Heather heard a familiar rasp on the other end of the line.

"We've got a problem," Mark began, abandoning all pleasantries as he informed Heather of two mutual liabilities to their enterprises: Earl Wilson and Lester Dawson. Heather snatched the nearest envelope on her desk and began scribbling down an address on the back of it as she thanked Mark for the information and quickly hung up the call. She dialed Latrice and was thankful that her IT analyst answered on the first ring. Latrice agreed to come in early to supervise Padma's session with a hedge fund owner who enjoyed being choked. Heather dashed out of the store, yanking the "Closed for Lunch" sign from the corner of the front door, and sticking it to one of the window sills before nervously fumbling and cursing as she looked for the right key to lock the door. Heather's profane rant continued she sped down I-95, honking her horn at drivers adhering to the speed limit while praying that there were no speed traps between D.C. and the Waffle House where she and Mark were meeting.

When Heather hastily pulled into the parking lot of the Waffle House, she found Mark in his car with his head bowed, Christian rock music beseeching the Holy Spirit's guidance blasting from his car. *Did Mark think that the Holy Spirit would overflow this meeting with a peace that passes all understanding?* Heather took a deep breath as she allowed Mark the time to pray or fast or do whatever religious people did in times of great distress. She entered the empty Waffle House and ordered a cup of coffee, groaning as the suffocating sounds of LeAnn Rimes questioning how she would survive without her lover blared through the scratchy speakers.

Mark joined her after a few minutes, exhaling sharply as he sat down across from Heather, his beleaguered disposition evident as he massaged the dark circles underneath his eyes.

"Earl's been arrested for sexual assault," Mark began as he delved into the disastrous turn of events that had culminated in the defrocked bishop being escorted away in handcuffs, apprising Heather of how Earl's therapist, Lester Dawson, had notified the police that Earl had raped his wife. Lester's session notes had indicated Earl had admitted to raping Heather's old client, Alma Velasquez.

"Fuck," said Heather under her breath.

Mark winced at Heather's use of profanity as Heather focused on the dominoes that were falling around her, including the backroom deals Earl would undoubtedly make to avoid jail time. Mark knew the repercussions Earl's actions would have on his career, the godless liberal media branding him a hypocritical misogynist by association. His eyes narrowed as he leaned in, struggling to articulate the only rational remedy to the precarious situation that lay before them.

"Am I wrong to assume that you know how to make problems permanently go away?" Mark's color faded from his face as he asked this question, swallowing a huge lump in his throat. He nearly snatched the pitcher of water the waitress brought over and poured himself a large glass, quenching his dry mouth and washing down the bitter taste that came with discussing murder.

Heather took demure sips of her coffee as she watched the spectacle before her. Slowly, she explained how the demise of Earl and Lester needed to appear believable to the public.

"Explain again why Lester is a problem," Heather set her coffee mug down and glared at Mark.

Mark gave a perturbed sigh before explaining Lester's alleged inappropriate relationship with a former client, a relationship that had sexual implications. Heather sat back, formulating a plausible chain of events that would result in both Earl and Lester's deaths. She spoke with an authority she had grown accustomed to employing, discussing how the wives needed to be complicit in this scheme. Heather recommended that Lester's wife should pull the trigger. Mark shook his head fervently as this suggestion, objecting to Heather's plan to have Lester's wife steal her husband's phone, text Earl to meet him at their house, and shoot Earl and Lester. Mark did not see the brilliance behind Heather's plan; he did not understand how easy it would be to have Lester's wife plant a gun on Earl to make it look as if Earl attacked her and Lester; he failed to comprehend the plausibility behind Earl shooting and killing the man who reported his rape to the police.

"Tanya's not a murderer. She'd never go for this."

Heather scoffed at Mark's unwillingness to acquiesce to her plan, getting up from the table and heading to her car. She had no time to ease a man through his turbulent moral dilemmas. A business awaited her. Mark had to figure out his inner conflicts on his own. Mark followed her out to the parking lot.

She turned to face him, "Well, neither are you. But here you are asking me for help. Call me when you're finished praying over this decision." Without another word, Heather got into her car and headed back to Capitol Boutique, certain that Mark would wake up, take his head out of the Bible, and do the sensible thing.

• • •

Jerry paced the floor of Rainbow Warriors as he awaited Ian's arrival. The clock kept ticking annoyingly as it inched closer to 2:00 pm, the moment in which Jerry would press the record button on his phone and begin the exposing interview of Ian. He removed the enlarged real-time footage of Lester's office projected onto the wall, not wanting Ian to know the real reason behind how they contacted him.

"I think I'm ready," Ian appeared in the doorway, sporting a blue sweater and khaki pants along with a feeble smile and bangs that reminded Jerry of a One Direction poster he had seen in Target a year ago. A woman with a penchant for cross-shaped jewelry stood behind Ian, her apprehension evident. She was undoubtedly Ian's mother, Gertrude.

"Let's shut this crazy voodoo therapist down," Brandon began, his enthusiasm obviously unsettling Ian and Gertrude, who both exchanged uncertain glances with each other as Jerry's boyfriend practically pranced to the front of the conference room and unveiled the visual timeline he, Jerry, and Callie had labored over for several weeks. The timeline had encapsulated Lester's life before his so-called conversion to heterosexuality and after he had embarked on his career as a conversion therapist. Ian and Gertrude gaped at the detailed history of Lester's quest to change homosexuals. Their eyes rested on the final milestone, the one in which Lester's session notes about the defrocked bishop, Earl Wilson, had been displayed. Gertrude covered her mouth when she read the portion of the notes that explicitly described Earl raping his wife. Her eyes darted toward the bottom of the poster to Earl's photo and the red arrow connecting the two men, the word "benefactor" written in all capital letters.

"This timeline is pretty self-explanatory. This interview will discredit him for good," Brandon shared, going on to explain the interview process as he handed Ian and Gertrude release forms that elucidated their rights. Jerry reiterated that Ian had the right to stop the interview at any time if he felt uncomfortable. Jerry also reminded Ian that he would be answering the same questions in tandem with Ian.

"You are not alone," Jerry reached over and squeezed Ian's hand. Ian read over the release form, quickly signing it and signaling Jerry to begin the interview. Pushing the record button on his phone, Jerry asked Ian the first question: "What drew you to conversion therapy?"

Ian steadied himself, brushing a strand of hair out of his face as he talked about his upbringing in an Evangelical Christian home, the tight-knit community of well-meaning people who believed homosexuality was sinful. Ian had begun having sexual feelings toward other boys from the time he was eight. He had heard the sermons condemning the gay lifestyle and had told his parents he wanted to be straight and please God. The other impetus behind seeking out conversion therapy was Ian's three failed relationships with guys he had met in college. Unbeknownst to his parents, Ian had joined his college's gay/straight alliance club, and had started dating guys he met through the club. Ian admitted that these short-lived relationships were toxic, his last boyfriend cheating on him at a college party with a mutual friend.

When Jerry had to proffer his reasons for seeking out conversion therapy, he thought back to the advice Brandon had given him the night before. The two had sat in Brandon's bed, Jerry gazing at the ceiling as he mulled over an acceptable reason for being drawn to conversion therapy. He had not thought it wise to reveal that Percy had blackmailed him into seeing Lester. Jerry had known that admitting to committing academic fraud would jeopardize his matriculation at American University.

"What were your biggest fears about being gay?" Brandon had asked as he brushed a strand of hair away from Jerry's face, patiently awaiting his response.

"Being alone. Not finding someone who would love me."

Jerry elucidated these rational fears to Ian, digging through his mind to include his father's selfish desires for him to marry a woman and have biological children. Jerry watched Ian's features relax; he observed Gertrude's lip quiver, her veiny hand holding her son's as Jerry continued to the next two questions: "Did Lester explicitly promise a change to heterosexuality? Was there a definitive timeline for realizing any sort of change?"

Ian's voice broke as he recalled those earlier therapy sessions, confirming Jerry's suspicions that Lester had promised Ian a change that would never come. The timeline for realizing a change was questionable at best, Ian confessing that Lester had provided a timeframe of six months to five years for realizing change.

Jerry's response to these questions had been similar to Ian's: "Lester told me I could be straight during our first session, but he said that everyone was different when it came to change. We never got that far."

Jerry continued his line of questioning, the nature of the subsequent questions fairly innocuous: "What activities did you participate in to reclaim your masculinity? How hard was it to eliminate sexual behavior?"

Ian laughed at his failed attempts to master throwing a football or shooting a basketball. The elimination of sexual behavior had been easy since Ian was a virgin and only watched gay porn sporadically.

"I only fooled around with my ex-boyfriends... kissing and jerking each other off," Ian admitted. "I always told them I wasn't ready to go all the way."

Jerry nodded as Ian chuckled humorlessly at his reluctance to have sex in his past relationships, knowing that Lester had attributed Ian's reluctance to engage in gay sex to a hidden deisre to be validated and loved by males in a non-sexual way.

"What did Lester say about your past relationships with men?" Jerry asked.

"He said I didn't feel like a man. That in those moments of brief sexual pleasure, I was secretly craving the intimacy women craved," Ian's regret was palpable, as if he had blamed himself for believing Lester's fallacies about same-sex attractions.

Staying true to the format of the interview, Jerry told Ian he had not tried to reclaim his masculinity in any arbitrary manner, instinctively knowing that mastering a sport would not make him attracted to women. Jerry laughed as he identified the commonality in his and Ian's journey – they were both virgins at the time they had started conversion therapy and hadn't frequented gay bars or bathhouses looking for sex.

"I still masturbated every other day. I just couldn't replace that urge with exercising or meditating," Jerry confessed as Ian laughed at Jerry's candid admission of indulging in the carnal pleasure that Lester had viewed as problematic.

Relieved that Ian had relaxed, Jerry continued to the more serious questions: "How did you come to realize a change wasn't possible? How did you react once you found that out?" The gravitas behind those questions made Jerry's body tense, a sharp pain piercing his abdomen as Ian and Gertrude's eyes shone with tears. Through labored breaths, Ian spoke about the day Lester had callously told him this therapy would not make his same-sex attractions go away. He bitterly recounted Lester's condescending proclamations about the purpose of his kind of therapy: accepting that same-sex attractions are not biological, but symptomatic of a childhood fraught with an overidentification of femininity and a longing for validation of masculinity.

"I wanted to die when Lester told me that. I tried... I attempted suicide a week after that session." Ian had ingested an entire bottle of his ADD medication, Adderall. His mom had found him unconscious on his bedroom floor. It had been the scariest day of his life.

"I blamed myself for encouraging him to pursue this therapy," Gertrude sniffled as she dabbed her tear-stained eyes with a tissue, acknowledging her complicity in Ian's failed journey to be straight. Gertrude took ownership of the religiously oppressive environment in which she and her husband had raised Ian and his brother.

Jerry discussed how he had always suspected Lester's therapy was futile and had coped with his father's disappointment by binging and purging, an issue he was still working to understand. Jerry thought back to those tense car rides with his father, Percy probing him for details about the painstaking hour he had spent with Lester accessing his anger or healing his inner child. Each car ride had triggered a walk to 7-Eleven, Jerry hunched over his toilet two hours later regurgitating Oreos or powdered doughnuts.

A heaviness hung in the air after these last questions, Jerry relieved that they had made it through the interview with some semblance of sanity. Trying his luck at two more questions, Jerry inquired about Ian's current situation. Was he in a better place with his parents? Did he find a church that affirmed his identity?

Ian smiled as he squeezed his mom's hand. Life after Ian's suicide attempt was not easy, but he and his parents agreed that being gay was not the death sentence they had once thought. Ian's dad was reading books about how dads can better support their gay sons; Ian's brother helped him create a profile for a gay dating site; Ian's mom found a progressive United Church of Christ faith community that explicitly welcomed LGBT people and their families. Jerry smiled as he talked about his current family situation post-conversion therapy. Leo and Harriet had not known about his stint in conversion therapy and were upset with Percy once they had found out. When Jerry tried to articulate his precarious relationship with his father, he choked up, his head spinning with those venomous exchanges that had been commonplace.

"My dad and I are a work in progress," Jerry shared. "Most days are rough, but we're not gonna give up on each other." Jerry pressed the stop button on his phone's recording app and exhaled a sigh of relief. Ian and Gertrude thanked Jerry for going through this process with Ian, both assuring him that his willingness to share his story propelled Ian to share his.

An hour after Ian and Gertrude had left and Jerry had begun drafting his article, an email appeared across his laptop. The sender was Roger Clementine, and several audio files had been attached to the email, a succinct message in the body of the email – *Hope these help. I'm taking them to the police after you publish your story.* Clicking on the audio files, Jerry heard Lester's voice, a crackling sound in the background as Roger explicitly asked what the purpose of their sexual relationship was. Lester responded with a sickening assurance that their bond was special, that the sexual behavior they had engaged in transcended societal expectations of heterosexuality.

"Brandon! Callie!" Jerry's voice went hoarse as the two of them dashed into the conference room, peering over Jerry's shoulder as he replayed the audio file. Their gleeful squeals intensified as Jerry played the subsequent audio files, each one detailing Lester's despicable justification for having sex with Roger, every file explicitly describing the covert manner in which Lester had conducted his sexual activity with Roger.

"We got him! We got him! Let's air this bastard's dirty laundry." Jerry frenetically typed the draft of his article, excited for the simultaneous blows he was about to deliver to Lester's career and life.

25

STILL WITH YOU

Carl remembered the last time he was in a hospital, the translucent walls in Jerry's room providing an eerie sense of impending doom for anyone who set foot inside. Daniel clung to him for dear life, fighting to keep his composure as Dr. Cooper offered the unacceptable excuse of having done everything he could to save Jiffy. Carl watched as Dr. Cooper's shiny bald head and bronze skin glistened with sweat, his eyes weary, his voice hoarse. The 12-hour surgery had clearly taken its toll on the hospital's most experienced cardiothoracic surgeon.

The prior evening had been a busy one for Carl. He had quickly left his English literature class and sped to St. Michael's for a PFLAG meeting, Father Jiffy giving a special presentation on coming out to family members who had hostile views toward LGBT people. Halfway through his talk, he had complained of shortness of breath, clutching his chest as he toppled over. Carl, Daniel, and John had caught him just as he was about to fall face-first onto the linoleum floor. He had suffered a massive heart attack due to arterial blockage and had been rushed into surgery to remove the blockage. Now Carl was being told that Jiffy had not made it through surgery. This was surreal. Jiffy had survived the AIDS epidemic, excommunication from the Roman Catholic Church, the death of his partner of 20 years, onslaughts of homophobic slurs, and blatant discrimination. He was not supposed to die on the operating table. His heart was not supposed to give out.

"What...what do you mean he didn't make it?" Daniel lost his composure, shaking violently as tears fell rapidly from his eyes.

"There was too much damage to his heart. Too much blood had been lost," the doctor explained.

Carl's entire body went cold; his throat became constricted, his limbs numb. He had forgotten that several of the PFLAG members were in the waiting room with him and Daniel, sobbing and yelling and cursing at the world for taking Jiffy away too soon. Their primal wails reverberated throughout the waiting room, as Carl held Daniel as he cried on his shoulder.

Carl skipped class the following day, staring at the faded yellow paint in the living room, watching vapid housewives throwing drinks at each other in expensive gowns and crying over insulting tweets and Instagram posts. By the evening, Jiffy's sister, Francine, had arrived, carrying bags of McDonald's in both of her hands. Carl got up and took the bags, inhaling the stale scent of processed meat and greasy fries. If Jiffy were here, he would have chastised his sister for putting that poison in her body. Francine was the opposite of Jiffy, a briskness emanating from her even amid sudden loss. Jiffy hadn't been deceased for 24 hours, and Francine was already discussing funeral arrangements. She plopped down onto the couch while discussing the nieces and nephews who wanted to speak at the funeral, grunting in annoyance as the doorbell rang. Daniel's tearstained face turned to the hallway leading to the front door, and with a heaviness only grief could conjure, he answered the door. Mel, Jerry, and Leo came inside, Lani and John following them.

"Carl?" Leo tapped Carl's shoulder as he turned and faced his best friend, too weary to speak, too tired to nod or grunt. Francine rambled on about how the pianist at St. Michael's conveniently caught the flu three days ago and wouldn't be well enough to play. Carl saw Jerry's hand raise, timidly offering to play for Jiffy's funeral. Francine beamed at Jerry's offer and continued smiling when he informed her that Harriet had insisted on having the reception at her house.

"My mom will take care of the food. She just needs to know if there are any dietary restrictions," Jerry offered.

Jerry's voice echoed in Carl's ear as that unpredictable wave of grief overtook him. He stood, feeling as if someone had repeatedly punched him in the gut. "He was fine two days ago. He was fine. He was...he's not supposed to be dead," Carl muttered before he collapsed onto the carpet, allowing himself to feel every emotion he had been too numb to feel, permitting himself to be angry, sad, shocked, and confused.

Carl had more questions for Jiffy. He needed more time with this renegade priest who had audaciously professed that Christianity had room at the table for LGBT people. *How was Carl supposed to find his way? Who was supposed to guide him now?* He asked these questions to himself through loud sobs, tasting his tears, falling into Daniel's arms, feeling his friends squeezing his shoulder and holding his hand, hearing that he wasn't alone in this.

The funeral was a majestic sendoff fit for a king. Carl had decided to sing with the small choir at St. Michael's, doing his best to keep his composure as each song and personal story reminded him that Jiffy was gone. The oak casket covered with white lilies was going to be lowered into the ground in a few hours, death's finality displayed in the center of the church, dressed up with flowers and hopes of life after death.

"Carl, you ready?" Jerry whispered to him from across the piano, Carl's signal that it was time for him to sing. Two days before the funeral, Carl had spoken to Harriet about the numbness of loss, asking her questions he had wanted to ask Jiffy, but would never get the chance to. This conversation had led to an obscure song Harriet had stumbled upon days after Ella's funeral.

"Listen to it. I think it'll help you feel a piece of Jiffy forever."

Carl had listened to the melancholic piano melody, becoming absorbed in the lyrics that assured Carl that Jiffy's love was all around him. "Still With You," that obscure song Harriet had stumbled upon years ago, had encapsulated a message Jiffy would have proclaimed to anyone who would listen.

Carl stood before the packed congregation, listening to that lethargic piano introduction, singing those profound lyrics, not caring if his voice broke or if his pitch was accurate. In those four minutes, Carl felt Jiffy's presence strongly. It didn't minimize the pain of losing him, but it assured Carl that Jiffy's spirit would live on through the countless nieces and nephews he helped, through Daniel, through the PFLAG kids he inspired, through Carl, who now knew that God loved him just as he was. Carl collapsed onto the floor, unable to sing the last line, unable to stifle his grief. His sobs echoed throughout the entire church.

• • •

Devin received a call from Tim during Jiffy's funeral, his body going numb once Tim apprised Devin of the news he knew was coming. Deanne's remains had been recovered from a wooded area near Percy's apartment, her fingers amputated, a single bullet found in the back of her head. As congregants filed out of the church, Devin grabbed Mel's hand and stared into her eyes. At that moment, she ascertained that Deanne had been found, her lip quivering as tears shone in her eyes.

"At the reception, all of us need to figure out how to get to Heather. She's gonna frame Percy," Devin began. He knew that his friends were grieving the loss of Jiffy, but Heather's timeline did not sympathize with their loss. Her methodology was cold and callous. The more Devin realized this, the less nostalgic he became. Those simplistic days of his childhood were never going to be reclaimed. Faith was never going to be the mother he needed. These were harsh truths that had been cemented with the certain news of Deanne's murder.

Harriet's house buzzed with Jiffy's seemingly endless family members as Devin, Jerry, Leo, and Mel gathered in the corner of the den to discuss the path forward in exposing Heather. Jerry mentioned how Earl's arrest could potentially work in their favor if Earl struck a plea deal.

"That could take months. We have to act now," Devin's hands began to shake as he presented his idea to his friends, thankful that Percy's liquor cabinet was only a few feet away.

Devin shared that he had hacked into Heather's security system, conducting surveillance on her every move and identifying the areas in her house where she kept the evidence of her crimes: the safe in the bedroom containing the notebook of phone numbers for her mercenaries and unfathomable amounts of cash, the loose floorboard in her office that housed another safe with her encrypted laptop. Convincing his friends to break into Heather's house was an insurmountable request, one that came with criminal repercussions if caught by someone other than Heather or Faith. Devin was fully aware that those two women would not hesitate to end their lives if they caught them.

"I can disable Heather's security system for an hour. That'll give us time to photograph all the evidence we need to put her behind bars once and for all," Devin continued, noticing his friends' apprehension as Jerry, Mel, and Leo exchanged uncertain glances. They were emotionally drained and were most likely still processing the fact that Deanne was dead.

"Guys, Deanne's dead. Jiffy's dead," Leo chimed in. "People we love and care about are dropping like flies. I say we do it."

Devin was shocked by Leo's certitude but appreciated his faith in Devin's plan. Jerry and Mel acquiesced after talking out the multiple scenarios in which Devin's plan failed, agreeing that getting justice for Deanne trumped whatever crime they'd be charged with. Jerry and Mel reiterated that Devin needed to establish a clear timeline for them to break into Heather's house and had to validate that timeline before any action was taken.

Devin stayed in Percy's den, mulling over his last shot at bringing Heather to justice. If someone in her employ talked, if they sensed that they could be prosecuted for their crimes, Heather stood no chance. Pouring himself a glass of whiskey, Devin recalled a meeting with Deanne in her dorm. She had been hesitant about coming forward; she had rightfully doubted the arc of justice and had questioned whether she deserved it.

"No one forced me to be a hooker. I chose this," Deanne's words rang in Devin's ears as he thought back to those words Carl had sung at Jiffy's funeral: "Dream in peace, when you wake, you will know I'm still with you." Devin knew he had to persevere for Deanne.

26

NO TURNING BACK

Harriet had forgotten how draining funerals were. When Ella died, Harriet had been too numb to process her emotions at the funeral, too shocked to weep and cry out for her baby; those screams would come months later in the solitude of her bedroom.

"Thank you, Harriet, for doing this. It means a lot," Carl offered as he appeared in the kitchen carrying a half-eaten tray of deviled eggs.

Once he set the silver tray on the countertop, Harriet grabbed him, hugging the tortured young man who was just beginning to find his way. Moments like this made Harriet wish she was closer with Louisa, the barrier of her incessant need to represent Christ vanquished by her undying love for Carl.

"Jiffy helped you a lot. I can tell," Harriet had surmised Carl was dating Jiffy's foster son, Daniel, when she saw them holding hands throughout the service. She knew Carl's coming out was complicated by the fact that Mark was steadfast in ministering to the ex-homosexual community. At that moment, Harriet blatantly told Carl he could live under her roof if he felt unaccepted by his parents.

"I mean it. The basement has a pullout sofa. Stay here as long as you want."

Carl whispered a "thank you" as a notification appeared across Harriet's phone. An article Jerry had written flashed across her screen: "Ex-Gay Therapist Exposed - Change Was Never Possible." Within a few moments, she heard Jerry's footsteps scurrying down the stairs, watching as her son jumped for joy at the news that his article was being published. Leo rushed into the kitchen and hugged his brother, and Carl and Harriet joined in the embrace.

"You did it, Jerry!" Harried cried as tears filled her eyes.

Not a minute later, Tim burst through the front door. Managing a feeble smile, he kissed Harriet on the lips and broke the news of Deanne's body being found. Harriet's stomach churned. Carl's face turned pale.

Tim didn't waste time with pleasantries: "Did these guys tell you about their plan, Harriet?" Tim then glared at Jerry and Leo reproachfully, Harriet following suit as she demanded to know what her sons were planning.

"Devin told you?" Jerry asked him.

Tim scoffed at Jerry's question, his reply encompassing Devin's elaborate plan to disable Heather's security camera, break into her house, hack into her encrypted computer to download her files, and photograph the notebook of the information containing her on-call mercenaries. Harriet's head began spinning as she listened to this dangerous plan.

"Devin asked for my help. Harriet, your kids won't do this without your blessing," Tim continued.

"No. Absolutely not," Harriet responded emphatically.

Jerry and Leo protested with grandiose arguments about bringing Heather to justice and providing closure to Deanne's family. Harriet stood her ground, shaking her head as she placed the deviled eggs into a clear container, the snap of its top aligning with Harriet's click of the tongue. Harriet had just gotten her life back, found her footing, and revived a career she was passionate about, and she was not about to approve of her children risking their lives to prove their father's mistress murdered their high-school classmate.

After several protests and arguments, Harriet was able to wind down with Tim, the two enjoying a glass of red wine while swaying to Nat King Cole. Since the advent of their relationship, they had never had a moment of peaceful bliss, one that wasn't spent strategizing ways to punish Percy. Harriet clung to Tim as he whispered those three words she hadn't heard in years: "I love you." The room froze in time as Tim professed his love, his salt and pepper hair tickling her face, the sweetness of the wine detectable on his breath. Before Harriet had time to respond, the phone rang, its harsh sound grating against her ears.

"Hello?" Harriet heard Percy's voice on the other end, incoherently formulating sentences as the sound of sirens drowned out his frantic voice.

"Why are... why... the police?" Percy whimpered.

Harriet heard the pounding on Percy's door, heard the police officer declare that a warrant had been issued for his arrest, heard that same officer read Percy his Miranda rights as he explicitly told Percy he was being charged with the murder of Deanne Blake. The call disconnected. Harriet slowly turned to Tim, whose face had turned pale.

"Heather wasted no time," she grimaced.

Swallowing a massive lump in her throat, Harriet collapsed onto her sofa, the room spinning as Nat King Cole's smooth baritone voice echoed in her ear. Tim walked toward the couch and sat down next to Harriet, embracing her as she stared at the photograph of her, Percy, and their three children at Disney World, the wide-eyed smiles a distant memory of a life that no longer existed.

"I'm in. Let's take that bitch down and put her sex-trafficking ass behind bars where it belongs," Harriet proffered a caveat to Tim's plan: she was coming with them. Tim brought her in for a kiss.

"I love you too." Harriet rested her head against Tim's chest and closed her eyes. Despite her growing overwhelm, she found the daunting task ahead of her somewhat bearable with Tim by her side.

• • •

Heather browsed a news site she had never seen before, Rainbow Warriors. A salacious, salient story about an ex-gay therapist leading a duplicitous double life had piqued Heather's interest. Lester Dawson, one of the burgeoning shining stars in conversion therapy, had apparently carried out a sexual relationship with an underage client two years ago, and had recently admitted to another client that achieving heterosexuality was not possible. Heather's eyes widened as she listened to the audio files of Lester's thin but authoritative voice justifying his ignominious deeds with Roger Clementine. She was amazed by how clever the writer was in weaving his own personal experience with conversion therapy into the article, ransacking her brain to figure out why the writer's name, Jerry Nelson, sounded so familiar.

The front door chimed. She scrolled through the rest of the article as she walked toward the door and opened it to find the tail of Greg's trench coat proceeding his petite frame as he clapped demurely and bowed down before her. Greg was utterly impressed by Heather's continuous displays of ingenuity, the latest scheme to frame Percy for Deanne's murder the epitome of diabolical.

"Having Latrice disable the security cameras in Percy's apartment so that Tank could break in and plant Deanne's bloody scarf under his couch cushion was fucking brilliant," Greg praised.

Heather smiled in relief that one problem had been solved, and as she watched Greg prepare for his appointment with Elena, Heather had a suspicion that the other problem of the defrocked butt-sex loving bishop was about to be solved.

A "blocked" number appeared across Heather's phone, Mark's voice barely a whisper as he uttered those fateful words she knew he would eventually utter: "Do it." Heather calmly took down Tanya's number, disconnected the call with Mark, and retrieved a newly-purchased burner phone from her purse. When Tanya answered, Heather began the conversation with firm directions to read an article on Rainbow Warriors' website. The woman surprisingly complied and started wailing in horror on the other end of the phone.

"Who are you?" Tanya's voice was muffled by her sobs, a normal reaction for a wife who had just discovered that her husband had been indulging in his pedophilic predilections. Heather responded with instructions for how she could make Lester's death appear accidental. She instructed Tanya to call Lester and falsely profess her belief in his innocence, encouraging her to reiterate the liberal media's insidious agenda to normalize the gay lifestyle at all costs. Heather asked for Tanya's address, surprised when the woman handed it over.

"A package will arrive in thirty minutes. It will contain a 22-caliber handgun and a burner phone. Hide it from Lester. Do you understand?"

Tanya muttered a feeble "yes" as Heather provided Tanya with her final instructions. Tanya was to call Earl on the burner phone, have him come to their house to discuss a peaceful path forward, and shoot Lester with the gun once Earl walked through the door.

"I can't." Tanya cried her pathetic tears, lamenting biblical mandates for not killing.

Heather vanquished those arguments in minutes: "The prosecution will come for you if Lester's arrested. If he's dead, I can make sure that doesn't happen. Do you own a gun?"

Heather closed her door as Tanya uttered another feeble "yes," Heather proceeding with the final two instructions for Tanya to execute. She was to call the police and inform them that Earl Wilson came into her home and shot her husband. Tanya was to then shoot Earl with her own gun in the act of self-defense.

"There are some logistics you should keep in mind," Heather went on, explaining how the trajectory of the bullet into Lester's skull could easily contradict Tanya's story of Earl shooting Lester. Therefore, Tanya needed to stand behind Earl and kill her husband from that angle. Shooting Earl would be simple. All Tanya had to do was stand in front of Earl and pull the trigger on her personal firearm.

Heather suffered through similar moral quandaries Mark had experienced, but was pleased when the poor woman finally acquiesced to Heather's plan. The two hung up, and Heather did joyous plies around her office. Her excellent mood prompted her to call Faith and convince her to go dancing at a salsa club in Dupont Circle. Heather wanted to bask in these rare, uninhibited, blissful moments. Faith echoed Heather's joy, the two making plans to go out that night and dance to their bright futures.

• • •

Mark tried to focus on the next phase of Wounded Souls, a phase he and Robert Cannon had both agreed was essential to the recovery of men and women with unwanted same-sex attractions. Ian's denouncement of change had felt like a shot to the heart coupled with a stab to the abdomen. Mark had experienced many of those lately, from Earl's proclivities for sexual assault to Lester's secret sexual relationship with an underage client. Despite these profoundly painful setbacks, Mark believed God's will was still going to prevail.

Robert had brazenly shared his vision of a one-month residential program for ex-homosexuals, the location of Camp Wabana idyllic for outdoor, rough-and-tumble activities for men and indoor, domestic activities for women. Mark had immediately supported this idea and had even pushed to implement it as soon as possible. Robert had joyfully confirmed that eight participants had expressed interest in this program.

A gentle knock on Mark's office door pulled him out of his trance, the faint creaking sound bringing him back to the present situation. Louisa appeared at the door, looking despondent, her eyes red and swollen.

"Honey, what's wrong?" Louisa unlocked her phone and turned to a breaking news story, a newscaster standing behind a house encased in yellow caution tape. The woman flatly discussed the deadly situation that had just unfolded. Earl Wilson had shown up at Lester Dawson's home, shot and killed him, and had in turn been shot and killed by Tanya Dawson, who had called the police from her basement once she heard shots being fired upstairs.

"They're dead. Oh, my goodness. Earl would never do this," Louisa sobbed onto Mark's shoulder as an email notification appeared across Louisa's phone. Carl had sent his parents an email, professing his identity as a gay man. Mark went from the frying pan to the fire in that instant.

"Honey, we have a bigger problem." Mark pointed to the email that Carl had sent, Louisa scanning its content and sobbing uncontrollably. In that moment of rawness, in those seconds of utter vulnerability, God told Mark what had to be done. Carl wasn't a hopeless case. He wasn't going to become Ian, and Robert's residential program was going to put Carl back on the path to righteousness.

"Louisa, this is a blessing. Okay? Carl's admission of his homosexuality hurts now, but we can fix this."

Mark rushed over to his desk and retrieved the booklet of Robert's one-month residential program. He convinced his terrified wife that God was in control, that this program would change Carl, that Robert was not Lester. Louisa and Mark composed themselves, dried their tears, and formulated a plan in which they would covertly take Carl to Camp Wabana before any further damage could be done.

• • •

Jerry did not expect a celebratory occasion when he arrived at Rainbow Warriors, nor was he in the mood to celebrate. Percy had been arrested the night before, and Jerry had been in a hazy fog of anger, guilt, and relief ever since. Callie and Brandon popped open a bottle of champagne in the conference room as a newscaster announced a fatal shootout between Lester Dawson and Earl Wilson.

"Lester the molester is dead!" Brandon gleefully poured champagne into a styrofoam cup and toasted with Callie.

Jerry stared at them in utter disgust. Justice was not served because two men were dead. If anything, attaining justice for Roger and Ian would now be more difficult since these men were killed. Furthermore, celebrating a murder was never acceptable.

"That should totally be our new headline," Callie burped as she chugged her cup of champagne.

"We're really doing this? We're rejoicing in the loss of two lives?" Jerry stared at Brandon and Callie, both of whom responded with indifferent shrugs and giggles. He grabbed his backpack and headed out the door, Brandon quickly grabbing his arm and bringing him in for a kiss. Jerry pushed him away.

"Nelson, come on. These are two rapists. The world is happy that they're dead. You should be too," Brandon pleaded.

Jerry just stared at him. Brandon was unrecognizable to him at that moment. Jerry no longer saw the boyfriend who had moved heaven and earth to get him into American University. *Where did that kind, generous man go? And who was this stranger standing in his place?*

"My dad was arrested yesterday for a murder he didn't commit. He's done a lot of shitty things, but he didn't deserve to be framed by his ex-mistress who's a sex trafficker!" Jerry practically screamed.

"Nelson, I... I didn't know," Brandon stammered for comforting words. The words didn't come, but Jerry wasn't sure if he would believe them even if they had.

"Well, I don't know if I can be around someone who celebrates someone being gunned down," Jerry replied, ignoring Brandon's calls for him to come back as he turned and marched out of the conference room. He ignored his instinct to hear Brandon out, to forgive him for his misplaced sense of justice.

Moments later, Devin called Jerry and informed him that they were executing the plan tonight. Heather was going out dancing with Faith and would stay out until the early morning hours. Jerry steeled himself for the monumental task that lay ahead.

27

MAN DOWN

Devin had never felt the taste of victory so strongly as he did that night. Jerry, Mel, Leo, and he were actually about to follow through with his plan to take Heather down. They were about to gain the upper-hand on an adversary who had always managed to outsmart her opponents.

Tim and Harriet had parked in an unmarked white van down Heather's street, allowing the four of them to enter Heather's house through the back door. Once inside, Jerry was to unlock Heather's safe in her bedroom and photograph the pages in her notebook. Devin had been able to discern the combination thanks to Heather's overly-cautious decision to install security cameras in every room in her house. Mel and Leo were going to assist Devin in copying the content of the burner phones onto Devin's tablet. Devin was tasked with the Herculean effort of decrypting Heather's laptop.

Once inside, everyone split up, scurrying to their assigned locations donning their leather gloves. Devin turned the combination on Heather's safe in her office, gazing at the silver contraption holding Heather's proof of her precious misdeeds. Devin heard the click of Jerry's camera as he checked the time to see how long he had before Heather's alarm would be reactivated. 48 minutes. He had 48 minutes to decrypt Heather's laptop. Devin prayed for the very first time in his life.

• • •

Harriet did a double-take of a photo of Faith as a woman resembling her drove up the street. When Tim confirmed it was indeed Faith, Harriet quickly called Jerry, Leo, and Mel.

"Fuck! Why are these calls going to voicemail?" Harriet tried again and again. Tim instructed her to stay in the car as he got out and ran toward Heather's house. A sickening sensation overtook Harriet, one that told her that someone was going to be hurt. She questioned if she had made the right decision. Her mind transported her back to the Falls Church Correctional Facility, watching Percy being escorted in shackles to the visiting lounge, already sporting bruises on his face and a black eye.

"Got a little roughed up."

Harriet had reached out to touch Percy's face, feeling his pain as he winced when she examined his black eye. Harriet had promised Percy that she would do everything in her power to get him out. Regardless of their marriage's impending dissolution, he was the father of her children, and he had not deserved to be framed for murder.

"Listen to me, Percy. You were a terrible husband and a lousy father. You can change the latter," Harriet offered.

For the first time in as long as she could remember, Percy had shown remorse for his actions. He had grabbed Harriet's hand and muttered a feeble, "thank you."

Tim sprinted down the street, a horrific expression on his face as he ran toward the van. Harriet got out of the van as his labored breathing indicated something terrible had gone wrong.

"Get plastic bags and a chainsaw from the back," Tim ordered.

Harriet narrowed her eyes and demanded to know what had happened. *Were her children okay? Was Mel okay? Was Devin okay?* As if reading her mind, Tim assured her that everyone important was safe. Faith, on the other hand, was not.

"Oh, my God."

"Listen to me," said Tim firmly. "Your children need you to be strong. I know you can do that."

Harriet followed Tim through the wooded area leading to Heather's house, a gentle breeze gaining momentum as she caught glimpses of a trail of blood leading into the kitchen. *What in the hell had happened?!*

• • •

Devin's neck ached, his head spinning as his mother's venomous glare came to the forefront of his mind. He stared at the trail of blood seeping from his mother's bludgeoned skull. Jerry stood over Faith's lifeless body, his hand holding the bloodied, bedazzled ruby cane Heather had kept as a souvenir. Hushed chatter ensued around Devin as his code activated the decryption of Heather's laptop and its subsequent extraction of her files onto Devin's flash drive.

"Honey, it's not your fault. It's not your fault. Okay? It's gonna be fine," Harriet purred in her son's direction.

Devin watched as Harriet embraced Jerry, his arms relaxing as that bloodied cane fell beside Faith. Devin checked his watch. They had twelve minutes before Heather's alarm was activated.

In the course of 36 minutes, Faith had arrived home and descended upon Jerry, the gun she had apparently kept on her drawn and pointed at Jerry's temple. Mel and Leo had stealthily made their way downstairs as Faith opened the front door, hiding in the broom closet as they heard those fateful words Faith had uttered – "Drop it, or I'll shoot."

Devin had acted quickly, grabbing the cane from the corner of Heather's office and purposely making noise to distract Faith. With her gun drawn, she had crept into the hallway and into the crosshairs of Devin's trap, his arm arched as he struck his mother across the face. He had grabbed the laptop and sprinted down the stairs once Faith had collapsed onto the floor, Jerry behind him. Out of the corner of his eye, he had caught Jerry firmly grasping the cane, a decision that would prove life-changing only moments later.

Devin's mother had grabbed hold of his ankles as he ran into the living room, the laptop falling onto the carpet as Faith yanked her son and dragged him into the foyer, her hands finding his neck, her grip tightening. The objects around Devin had become blurry and indecipherable; his eyes had started to close.

"Mom, please," Devin pleaded as a loud thud had forced Faith to relinquish her grasp. In a matter of seconds, Jerry had begun repeatedly swinging the cane into Faith's skull, bludgeoning her to death, saving Devin's life.

"Devin, we need a hand," Tim implored steadily.

Devin quickly nodded and handed a shell-shocked Mel Heather's laptop, ordering her to put it away. Leo began spraying the floor with bleach, blood-soaked paper towels in his hands as the trail of his mother's blood diminished. Jerry, Tim, and Devin grabbed Faith's lifeless body and carried it out the back door, into the wooded area behind Heather's house.

Mel and Leo came running out of the house wearing mortified expressions. In Mel's hand, was Faith's phone. She had six missed calls and four text messages from Heather, all of which inquired about Faith's whereabouts and whether or not she located her driver's license.

"What do we do?" The phone vibrated in Mel's hand, Heather's number appearing on the screen.

"Text her back," Tim's command had a sobering effect on the current situation.

None of them could have anticipated the sequence of events as they had transpired. Devin had not foreseen standing over his mother's dead body, her bludgeoned skull now posing a potentially deadly risk. If Heather were to discover the fate of her best friend, she would decimate all of them one by one. Of this, Devin was sure.

"Jerry, thank you," Devin offered as he looked at Jerry's horrified face in the moonlight, obviously nowhere near ready to accept that what had happened wasn't his fault. "You saved my life. Please remember that."

They had six minutes before Heather's alarm was reactivated. Devin searched his pockets for his flash drive and exhaled sighs of relief once he saw Mel holding it in her hand. Devin ran to Heather's backdoor, dashing upstairs to make sure all of Heather's precious files and notebooks had been placed into their respective safes. With two minutes left, Devin rushed outside, locked the backdoor, put the spare key underneath the flower pot on the deck, and ran to the woods to begin the arduous task of dismembering his mother's dead body.

• • •

Heather danced the night away, losing herself in the hypnotic beats of Mark Anthony, Celia Cruz, and Gloria Estefan. She indulged in far too many tequila shots, her body becoming lighter with each one. Heather hoped Faith would make it back in time to join her but found contentment in dancing alone.

A burly man caught her eye, his face familiar as he casually swayed to Gloria Estefan's number one hit, "Conga." Inching closer, Heather recognized him as the detective who had stopped by to question her about Deanne's disappearance.

"You're an amazing dancer," he yelled over the music.

Heather felt the man's large hands caressing her lower back, enticed by the way her hips moved in perfect concert with the music. The two danced for the rest of the night, Heather's lips eventually meeting his, her hands migrating to his chest as they swayed to the music.

Geoff's hands continued to explore Heather's body as he led her to his apartment a block away. They enjoyed each other sexually for the entire night. The next morning, Heather awakened to find Geoff staring at her.

"I'm sorry if I scared you by coming to your house that night," Geoff brushed a strand of her hair away from her face as she sat up in bed, eyeing the wisps of chest hair around his nipples, hungry for another orgasm.

"You were doing your job. It's so sad that she's gone. I really liked her," Heather feigned grief at Deanne's murder.

Heather's remorse was apparently plausible because Geoff kissed her shoulder, moving his hands over her erect nipples as he kissed her abdomen. Before Heather knew it, Geoff was hungrily eating her out in a way no man had ever done. They spent the rest of the morning fucking in every corner of Geoff's apartment, Geoff bringing Heather to the point of orgasm multiple times. In those beautiful moments after she climaxed, Heather silently chastised herself for not texting Faith back. She knew her best friend would understand that she had needs and would appreciate the fact that she now had an inside connection to Deanne's murder, something that would preclude her from getting caught. Heather was finally able to revel in her power, discovering freedom she never knew existed.

• • •

Carl was not supposed to be at a campsite for men and women with unwanted same-sex attractions. He needed to get out of here. He had to escape these sad, sympathetic stares from counselors who claimed to know his struggle. Homosexuality wasn't a struggle. And it wasn't something from which Carl or anyone else needed to be delivered.

"Group starts in ten minutes. Meeting will be in the dining hall. Do not be late," one of the counselors announced to the men and women milling about the fellowship hall.

Carl observed the desperate dozen people whose beleaguered dispositions indicated a hard life of unfulfillment. *Was this supposed to motivate Carl to be something he couldn't be? Were their testimonies of escaping the clutches of the supposed gruesomeness gay life entailed meant to scare him?*

The day after he had emailed his parents, Mark had called Carl to tell him he loved him and that he would always be his son. Their conversation had ended with the two of them deciding to go on a drive to talk, and as Mark had driven down unfamiliar highways and had passed frost-covered farmland, Carl panicked. His father had quelled his anxieties with the promise of making everything better; he had assured Carl that nothing terrible was going to happen. Once Mark had pulled into the entrance of Camp Wabana, Carl knew these assurances were farthest from the truth.

Mark had sighed regretfully as he explained the one month program Carl was entering into, promising his son that God was giving him a gift with this program. Carl had watched as his father opened the trunk and gave him a suitcase filled with clothes that had already been packed and plans that had already been made.

The counselor, whose name Carl had already forgotten, had confiscated his phone and wallet. Carl had to utilize the office phone to make phone calls home and had been warned that all calls would be monitored.

"Let's go. One minute before group."

Carl sat in a poorly formed semi-circle, as the counselor stood in the middle, his lanky frame and freckled face the nucleus of this group of people who desperately needed to be straight.

"My name is Shawn, and I'll be one of three counselors you'll work with over the next thirty days. This program is a blessing, a labor of love crafted by Robert Cannon. Please don't waste this time. Do the work, and I promise you, you'll reap the benefits."

Carl focused on anything but the sound of Shawn's voice, his eyes traveling around the semi-circle, meeting the gazes of men and women beaten down by a world and a god who told them they were damaged.

"Carl, why are you here?" Shawn's gaze landed on Carl, those gazes shifting onto him.

He shrugged, a gesture Shawn viewed as heretical.

Shawn pressed him, "You don't know, or you don't care?"

When Carl didn't respond, Shawn instructed Carl to go into the office and wait for him to arrive. An hour later, Shawn came inside the office, sitting down on the off-white vinyl chair, inching it closer to Carl.

"I've met guys like you," Shawn said with a sneer.

"Really?" Carl shot back. He prayed that God would send him Jiffy's courage at this moment; he prayed that God would show him the way out of this dystopian nightmare that promised conversion to heterosexuality.

"This is your first day. By day five, you'll break down that armor of those repulsive "born perfect" messages you've told yourself. You're on clean-up duty for the rest of the day," Shawn pointed Carl to a mop and a bucket resting in the corner of the fellowship hall.

For the rest of the day, Carl mopped floors and washed windows as his peers talked about their sexual brokenness, attributing their homosexuality to the failed relationships and drug addiction and inability to maintain employment. Shawn directed sinister glances toward Carl after each activity.

Carl's limbs ached as he plopped down onto his bed that night. His roommate, a young man named Donnell, engaged him in conversation.

"Parents forced you here, huh?" Donnell moved over to Carl's bed as Carl wordlessly stood up. "It's not the worst thing in the world."

"Enlighten me. What is worse than this?" Carl inched closer to his new roommate, the young man gently placing an arm on his shoulder.

"Ending up alone. Bouncing from relationship to relationship. Being scared to death as you take another HIV test. Take your pick."

Carl sneered as he walked into the bathroom, making a concerted effort to remain unfazed by Donnell's certitude. For the first time that day, Carl felt his insecurities about life as a gay man profoundly. He hoped and prayed Jiffy's courage would envelop him like a shield over the next month. It was his only way of getting out of this prison alive.

EPILOGUE

THE LONG AND WINDING ROAD

In the past two weeks, Harriet had done her best to put on a brave face. As it turns out, courage wasn't easy once you dismembered a dead body and tossed the remains into a swamp. Harriet was sobbing nightly, drowning her fears into her pillow, hoping that her son would find the strength to absolve himself from the guilt he carried around.

Her monthly book club had been a welcome distraction to the angst that permeated her house, Harriet surprised that she had actually finished "The Handmaid's Tale" in time for the discussion. As the women passionately discussed the parallels between the events in the novel and the current culture war of religious liberties being wielded as a weapon to subjugate LGBT people, Louisa took a phone call from Mark, Harriet and Amy growing concerned.

"Have you heard from Carl?" Amy whispered her question while scooping hummus onto her pita chip.

Harriet shook her head, her concern intensifying as her ears detected troubling words in Louisa's conversation. "The program" and "Carl will thank us later" were not things Harriet found comforting. *Where was Carl? What did Mark and Louisa do?*

"I'm so sorry. Mark wanted to know how long to heat up the leftover meatloaf," Louisa offered to her friends. Louisa stared at Harriet, who mouthed the words "straight camp" to Amy.

"Where's Carl, Louisa?" Harriet stared at her friend, who appeared bemused by Harriet's question and offended by the harsh tone in which she asked it.

"He's on a service trip for school," Louisa's cheeks turned red as Harriet stood up, and requested Amy's presence in the kitchen.

Harriet and Amy discussed in hushed whispers what Harriet had overheard, Amy concurring with Harriet's suspicions that Carl had been shipped off to a conversion therapy in-patient program. Harriet and Amy got to work on trying to figure out where Carl was, each delving creative and possibly illegal means to get Louisa to tell the truth. As they hurried back into the living room, Louisa was gone, the sound of her car pulling out of the driveway infuriating Harriet to no avail.

"I'm going home. Jerry can find out where Carl is before it's too late," Harriet announced before walking out of Amy's living room. She sped down the side streets to her house and rushed inside to find Leo in the kitchen, warming up pizza in the microwave. "Where's your brother?"

"Still upstairs. What's wrong, Mom?"

Harriet replied that Carl needed their help. Leo scurried behind her as she opened Jerry's bedroom door. Jerry sat in an upright position staring at the walls, his face pale, his eyes weary from two weeks of sleepless nights. Harriet sat down on Jerry's bed and grabbed her son's hand. As a mother, Harriet realized her job sometimes involved giving her children harsh truths. And the harsh reality was usually the very thing they needed to make a change.

"Jerry, Carl was taken to a residential conversion therapy program."

"What?" Jerry's eyes widened as he collapsed onto his bed.

Harriet grabbed him and forced him upright, "You can fix this Jerry. It's time to move forward!"

Harriet went on to lament facts Jerry didn't need to hear again for the umpteenth time: Faith's death was not his fault. If he hadn't done what he did, Devin would be dead. Harriet left her son and headed into her bedroom, a smile of satisfaction appearing in the mirror as she heard the sound of the shower running in the hall bathroom. Jerry was going to be okay. They were all going to be okay.

• • •

"Louisa, calm down," Mark tried to comfort his wife to no avail.

She rambled on about Harriet and Amy catching her in a lie, blaming herself for showing up at her book club amid all her personal turmoil. Mark watched Louisa pace the floors of their bedroom, her calm demeanor now restless and unhinged.

"Did we do the right thing? We should have just put him in outpatient therapy," Louisa broke down crying as Mark rushed to console her. He reminded his wife that the worldly influences Carl had absorbed would pull him back into the mentality that celebrated homosexuality. Mark encouraged his wife with her own words, ones that strengthened Mark as Carl still refused to speak to his parents after two weeks.

"He will thank us in the end. This is just a rough patch. And your friends can't do anything."

"Jerry outed Lester Dawson. He's become a militant gay activist. Don't underestimate him," Louisa's implored.

Her warnings prompted Mark to make a call to Camp Wabana, breathing sighs of relief as Shawn answered. As Mark described Jerry and Leo's appearance and the lethal gay agenda they brought with them, Shawn assured Mark that the police would be notified if Jerry or Leo Nelson set foot onto their property. Mark sat on the bed as Louisa dried her eyes, praying for God to comfort him and his wife during this time, praising God for sending a program that would put Carl back on the righteous path. Mark knew he had a lot to answer for if Carl was to reclaim his stolen heterosexuality. Mark prayed for God's guidance on how to repair their damaged relationship. After all, it was the first of many steps for deliverance from homosexuality.

• • •

Jerry knocked on Brandon's door, becoming increasingly impatient with each knock. The two had not spoken since Jerry stormed out of Rainbow Warriors two weeks prior. Brandon had called Jerry the following day and had sent a series of angry and impatient text messages that accused Jerry of being childish and insolent. After a week, the calls had stopped.

"Nelson?" Brandon opened the door to find his estranged boyfriend standing there. Jerry walked inside, noting how neat Brandon's apartment was. There wasn't a single item out of place. A loud, harsh ring came from the iPad on the counter, Jerry walking over to find a notification from Grindr displayed on the screen. "Bottomtwink93" was on his way to Brandon's apartment. Jerry did not even acknowledge this message.

"Uh... are you okay? I... that guy isn't a... we're not a thing," Brandon stammered.

"Brandon, it's fine. I didn't call you back. You assumed we were on a break."

"Are we?" Brandon turned over his iPad and grabbed Jerry's hands, kissing them as their foreheads touched affectionately.

"I don't know," Jerry sighed as he sat down on the couch and relayed the news that Carl had been shipped to a residential conversion therapy program. Carl's parents were never going to accept their son as a gay man and were doing everything in their power to erase that part of him.

"Okay," Brandon said. "Let's get ready to take down some more bigots. You up for this?"

Brandon's question echoed in Jerry's ear as the recurring image of Faith's mangled skull flashed before Jerry; these images wouldn't magically disappear, the sound of the chainsaw grinding through her clavicle would not dissipate. This act of taking a life, no matter what the circumstances, would haunt Jerry for the rest of his life.

"I killed someone," Jerry gasped for air as he uttered the words.

Brandon turned around and grabbed Jerry as he collapsed forward. He sobbed into Brandon's arms, catching a glimpse of that man who had shown Jerry he was worthy of love. A gentle rap came from Brandon's front door, the two ignoring the impatient complaints of "Bottomtwink93."

Once the footsteps descended down the hall, Brandon placed a hand on Jerry's tear-stained cheeks, "Whatever happened wasn't your fault. I know you, Jeremiah Nelson, and you are not a murderer. You are a kind, funny, complicated, and insanely smart man. But most of all, you're strong."

Jerry nodded as Brandon embraced him again, doing his best to believe all of the things Brandon said he was. Jerry had to be strong now – for Carl, for Percy, for himself. The war was far from over, the first battle being the one Jerry had to fight within. As Jerry fell asleep in Brandon's arms, he prepared himself for that long battle, his pervasive shame and fear his most lethal enemies.

GRATITUDE

First, and foremost, I'd like to thank God for giving me the vision to write this story, and for providing me with the strength to finish this book. My faith in You has surely grown as I've agonized over whether or not I was worthy enough to write this story. Thank you God for showing me that I have always been worthy in my darkest moments.

Thank you to my amazing, fearless, astute, and hard-working editor, Dr. Marina Gillmore, CEO and President of Full Circle Press. I could not have done this without your guidance and support. Thank you for believing in me, and for believing in the message I needed to convey with this book. I have grown so much as a writer and a person because of you, and I am honored to call you my friend.

Thank you to my amazing team at Full-Circle Press: Laura, my graphic designer, and Sibyl, my project manager. Laura, you took my idea for a cover and transformed it into a brilliant, evocative work of art. Thank you for all of your hard work. Sibyl, your texts and email reminders kept me on track. Thank you for working around my crazy schedule to ensure I had a meeting with Marina. Your effortless ability to multitask amazes me.

Thank you to my faith community, the Catholic Apostolic Church in North America (CACINA), for welcoming me into your loving, inclusive community, and for encouraging me to share my gifts and live my truth. Special thanks to Father Al Risdorfer (Our Lady UnDoer of Knots), Mother Monica Kennedy (St. Charles of Brazil), and Father Peter Smith (Holy Trinity) for your words of support and encouragement. They've helped me through my hardest days. To my church family:

Joe W., Ruth, Joe B., Nora, Jay, Patti C., Tim, Damien, Patti E., Charlie, Sharon, Stacey, Jeanie, Mike, and John, thank you for always being there for me. Ed, I miss you every day. I know you're watching over me.

To my friends, and original beta-readers: Melanie, Alani, Randy, and Tony, thank you for always lending your ear as I read iteration after iteration of this book. I am grateful and honored to call you my friends.

To my friend, Richard Yeagley, thank you for coming into my life at the right time. You're doing amazing things with your platform. Keep spreading love and light into the world.

To my parents, who sacrificed so much to give me a great life, thank you for your all your many sacrifices. There's not enough room to list them all. I love you both.

And finally, Jerry, my love, thank you for loving me unconditionally. You are, and always will be, my reason to smile.

ABOUT THE AUTHOR

Jared Dixon holds a Master's Degree from the University of Maryland, Baltimore County. *Corrupted: The Truth Shall Be The Nail in Your Coffin* is his first novel. An accomplished pianist, he is active in the music ministry at St. Charles of Brazil. He resides in Baltimore County and enjoys doing yoga in his spare time.

ABOUT FULL CIRCLE PRESS

Full Circle Press is a socially-conscious, purpose-driven independent publishing house with a deep commitment to contributing to the greater good through helping to write, edit, publish, and market books that matter. We believe in changing the world one story at a time, and we envision a world where quality books and literacy resources are available to all. We are educators at heart and are passionate about teaching what we know, sharing resources when and where we can, and empowering others to do and be better. Visit www.fullcirclepress.org to learn more about our products, programs, and services.